MISSING PERSONS

"BUILDS SUSPENSE FROM THE FIRST CHAPTER
AND NEVER RELEASES THE READER
FROM ITS FEARFUL GRIP."
ALA Booklist

"AN ELABORATE CAT-AND-MOUSE GAME . . .
A VERY SCARY PEEK INTO INSANITY."
Chicago Sun-Times

"A REAL PAGE-TURNER!"
Tulsa World

"LEAVES THE READER FEARFUL OF PICKING UP
THE NEXT DAY'S NEWSPAPER."
Best Sellers

MISSING PERSONS

C. TERRY CLINE, JR.

FAWCETT CREST • NEW YORK

A Fawcett Crest Book
Published by Ballantine Books
Copyright © 1981 by C. Terry Cline, Jr.

Library of Congress Catalog Card Number: 80-70215

ISBN 0-449-20015-9

This edition published by arrangement with Arbor House

Manufactured in the United States of America

First Ballantine Books Edition: February 1983

I saw myself
Reflected in her eyes
And it was the image
Of a man whose life
Was about to begin . . .

To my wife: Judith Richards

Chapter One

ON a corner, books in her arms, laughing with friends, she stood out. They always did. Like creatures apart. There were similarities—superficial physical characteristics; hair parted down the middle and combed evenly to the sides, shoulder length or longer. Wide mouth, a quick smile that had a practiced effect. The beauty queen. Pretty.

But it was not her appearance that drew him. There were many attractive women who passed unnoticed. It was an ambiance, a demeanor. A certain toss of the head, a tilt of the chin. A way of walking. Better-than-thou, that's how he thought of it. Look-but-don't-touch.

As artificial and manufactured as plastic, their smiles, the sound of their laughter, the way they stood with heels touching, backs straight—practiced, deliberate.

From across the street he watched, eyes shaded by polarized lenses, afternoon heat rising in shimmering waves from baked cobblestone paving. He chewed gum with methodical, slow masticating movements, mouth dry despite it.

His innards twisted, irritated by her although he had never seen the girl before. He didn't have to know her. He knew her type well enough.

Beyond the girl and her friends, like a dusty mirage, the red brick school house grew somber and more deserted. Inside the fenced perimeter, younger students played in pools of purple shade beneath water oaks. Swing chains squealing, seesaws levitating, a staccato of youthful cries, adolescent girls taunted by mischievous boys. A yellow Bluebird bus lurched out of a parking lot and turned away south, double rear tires churning silt in ocher plumes.

The girl made moves to disengage—and that's what it was. A pulling free; pressing matters awaited, time enough in camaraderie. As if in ballet, she side-stepped, heels always coming back together, designed to accentuate posture and announce, "Look at me. Pretty!"

1

Yes. Well.

He sucked the gum, trying to wet his mouth, but the Chiclet adhered to his teeth. His belly drew taut, abdominal muscles quivering. Fingers straight, splayed, he wiped them on the steering wheel of his Volkswagen "beetle." He watched her, but all the while with peripheral vision he watched all who might be watching him.

A final gesture, one hand extended toward a friend palm down, her books clasped to bosom by her other arm. Then with a half turn, a toss of her hair, she walked away as if aware of all eyes following.

He waited until she turned a far corner, then started his car. Pulling away from the curb, he reached behind himself on the floorboard, touching the cold steel of a tire iron. One end was wrapped with adhesive tape for a better grip. He drove past the street where she walked, glancing casually in her direction. Then he circled the block and met her at the next corner.

"Hi!"

She started to cross and he called again, "Say, I'm lost, can you help me?"

The critical moment. Had she kept walking, he'd have driven away. She hesitated.

He got out, the motor running. He saw himself as if through her eyes—right arm in a sling, a friendly, genuine smile, brown wavy hair, tennis shoes, wearing shorts.

"Hurt my arm when I slipped trying to make a return," he said. "Do you play tennis?"

"Sometimes." Wary, aloof.

"Great game." He grinned. "But a backhand is best performed with feet well beneath the body. My name's Bob."

A quick nod.

"I was born here." He winced as he adjusted the "hurt" arm with his other hand. "I've been away ten years. Things have changed, haven't they?"

A tentative smile, but still alert.

"I was looking for the house where we used to live. Green shutters, slate roof, two-story house. Do you know it?"

"I don't think so."

"Next door neighbors were named Ziebart." A name he'd seen on a furniture store downtown. "Do you know them?"

"Randy Ziebart?"

2

"Could be. On the other side lived my cousin and his family—do you know the Murphys?"

"Murphy." She gazed past him. "You mean the Murphys who own a Texaco station on Main Street?"

"Now that you mention it, I believe they did say something about that."

"They live across town from here."

"*Now,* you mean. They used to live right around here. I went to Lake City elementary school with my cousin." He put a foot on the bumper of the idling VW, smiling. "Those were great times. We lived on Pine Tree Boulevard—"

"That's about six blocks from here."

"Oh, yeah?"

"Straight ahead," she advised.

"Can't miss it, right?"

"Right," she said.

"I once got lost on a dead-end street. It was one-way."

She laughed, stance easing. He avoided prolonged eye contact, allowing her time to assess him—handsome, winsome, with a hurt arm.

"You must be packing in the studies." He indicated her books.

"Trying to rack up the credits."

"You're a senior?"

"No. Eighth grade."

"You look older. That's a compliment."

Her face flushed.

"Straight ahead, you say?"

"Right. About six blocks."

"Give you a lift?"

"I'm not going far."

"Don't mind at all," he volunteered. "I'm going that way."

"Well—"

"Hop in," he opened the door. "Forgive the clutter."

She saw remnants of fast-food containers, a tennis racket in the rear seat, some tools on the floor. "I don't have far to go," she hedged.

"Hey look," he teased, "I'm harmless! Be a good Samaritan and show me the way."

She got in. The seat slipped beneath her, loose on its track. He rounded the car, got in beside her. "That seat is broken," he said.

3

"I'm only going a couple of blocks——"

"So you know the Ziebarts?" He shifted into low gear awkwardly, obviously pained by the effort.

"I know Randy."

"How are they doing?"

"I think Randy's fine."

"Buckle up, honey, that seat scares me."

She did so, the seat slipping with each acceleration. "I want to look them up," he said. "I had a lot of good times with the Ziebarts. And you know Randy?"

"He's a classmate."

He had to reach across himself to shift gears, his right arm useless, each time grimacing.

"Boy, I bet I never use a backswing again."

"I go right at the next corner," she directed.

"Do you suppose you could show me the way to Pine Tree Boulevard, first?"

"No, I really have to go on home."

"Sure," he smiled at her. "I understand. Say, can you just hand me that map under your seat—right under your feet?"

She bent forward to see, shifting books on her lap. Suddenly, he yanked his arm from the sling and seized her by the nape of her neck, shoving her down; he jammed the brake and the seat shot forward, her head under the dashboard, her waist cinched by the seat belt. Holding her, he stepped on the gas.

She grappled for his hand, his fingers intertwined in her hair, but he pushed her head down harder, growling, "Stay put or you'll get hurt."

She tried to turn and he shoved her violently, her breath expelled by the pressure of books against her abdomen, held by the seat belt. She scratched at his hand and he shook her, warning, "Be still, or else!"

The town wasn't large. The residential area quickly passed and still he held her.

"You're hurting me," she cried.

"Put your hands behind you."

The cutting belt, her lungs aching, sides hurting—she complied. He snapped handcuffs on her wrist, demanded she bring the other hand nearer.

"No!"

He slammed on brakes and momentum threw her into

4

the dashboard. He was on her with both hands, dragging her other arm up, cuffing it, also.

Only now did he release her, saying, "Keep your head down, or I'll knock it off. I don't want to have to hurt you."

"Stupid!" she shrieked, damning herself. "Dumb!"

The vehicle swung wildly, bumped, knocking her head again. All the while, his right hand rode her back, prepared to restrain or harm as need be.

He stopped, cut the motor and allowed her to sit up.

"Don't hurt me," she said.

He lit a cigarette, inhaled, staring through the smudged windshield. They were under pine trees, surrounded by underbrush, adjacent to a plowed field with a stubble of cornstalks jutting from the soil.

"Please don't hurt me."

Not so haughty now, arms locked behind, her facade torn away—not so godalmighty now.

"Are you going to hurt me?"

He looked at the glowing tip of his cigarette, flicked ashes, drew again.

"Are you?" she asked.

It was his eyes which terrified her most. A moment ago dancing, cerulean blue, filled with warmth and friendliness. She remembered something she'd read in literature class— something about the eyes being windows to the soul—now distant, utterly cold and without compassion. He smoked, peering through pine trees down a rutted sandy lane overgrown with weeds.

"Please don't hurt me." *Rape* she meant. There had been a class—home economics—she struggled to remember the advice offered, all the girls giggling nervously as the teacher mechanically listed the threat, alternatives, proper responses. *Rule One:* don't take up with strangers. *Rule Two:* stay out of their cars. *Rule Three*—

He flicked away the cigarette, spit gum out his window. Turning, he looked not at her face but at her neck and chest.

"Please—"

"If you don't cooperate, I'll kill you."

"Oh, no, please—"

He unbuttoned her blouse, slowly, as if savoring the moves.

"Oh, please—"

5

Unexpectedly, he bit her.

"Help!" she screamed.

He slammed her against the door, a hand over her nose and mouth. She tried to bite back but missed; he was expecting it. Wrenching aside, she screamed, "Help me! Help!"

Incongruously, a flip remark made by a pimply-faced student came to her mind, "Relax and enjoy it . . ."

"Help me!" He smashed her face with a fist, the taste of blood rose on her tongue.

He hauled her out onto the ground, threw her down and pulled off her clothing.

It hurt, even when she tried to ease it by cooperating, it hurt. It would be over soon. Be over soon. Be over soon—

He finished with her, turned her onto her belly and for a grateful instant she thought he was going to remove the pinching handcuffs.

He left her there and she heard him raking among the tools on his floorboard.

Instinctively, she whimpered, "I won't tell. I promise."

What was he doing?

"I don't know you," she reasoned.

His feet beside her.

"Let me go home now," she begged. Her mouth was gritty, sand between her teeth.

She tried to twist and face him, and he pinned her bare shoulder with a hand. The hand made a soothing stroke and she dared hope—

Then he swung down hard with the tire iron, aiming at the base of her skull. She quivered. Again, harder—a spastic twitch, skull crushing. Again, with all his might . . .

Chapter Two

DR. Joanne Fleming sat at her desk and opened a file folder marked MISSING PERSON. She studied the form pinned inside. Nothing was as impersonal as a police report.

... caucasian ... female ... age fourteen ...

Last seen by other students outside Lake City Junior High School. A ten block walk home. She never arrived. A description of clothing, books. Joanne noted the date. Four weeks ago. As usual in such cases, it had taken the police this long to become convinced the girl was not a likely runaway. Now, an investigation had begun with a cold trail, fuzzy memories and an ominous sense of tragedy. Attached were depositions from frantic parents, teachers, classmates, a minister.

"Dr. Fleming?" Beatrice Malbis stood in the office door, a clipboard in hand, not one but several No. 2 Eberhard pencils jabbed into her bun of black hair. "Youse want your calls now?"

The student-secretary was a study in paradox: ebony eyes, first-generation American of Greek parents. Bea was southern born and reared, but with a definite Brooklyn accent. It was in New York that her parents had learned English. As a result, this beautiful descendant of Hellas jolted her Florida listeners by saying, "Youse-all."

Bea licked the tip of a forefinger and flipped notes. "Let me see," she said. "Marcie called."

"My daughter can wait." Then on second thought, "Did she say what she wanted?"

"Something about a date and disco."

"If she calls back, 'No.'"

Joanne ignored a disapproving glance. Bea said, "Ken called."

"Mr. Blackburn," Joanne amended.

"Something about a date and disco."

7

"Not funny, Bea."

Bea laughed anyway, teeth made all the whiter by her smooth olive complexion. "Youse ought to remember what it was like to be young, Dr. Fleming."

"Thirty-six isn't old."

Bea riffled papers, chuckling. "Women's Club speech is the twenty-eighth. They want a photo of you for their bulletin."

"No."

"The District Attorney says don't forget the hearing with Judge Alcorn. They said youse know which case."

"Pull together all data on the Swain case. Have it ready for presentation."

"Right."

"Anything else?"

"Marcie needs to know if she can stay out until eleven."

"When?"

"Tonight when she goes to the disco."

"I said, no. She can't go."

"Youse didn't ask with who?"

"It doesn't matter with *who*. She wants to go to that place right off campus where the college crowd goes. She can't go."

"So she's got to sneak."

"She'd better not."

Bea shrugged one shoulder and turned to leave.

"Bea—" Joanne held her temples with the fingertips of both hands. "I know you intercede for Marcie with good intentions. But if you could concentrate your energies on the duties of this office and not my child—"

"Sure," Bea said amiably.

"Marcie is going through a critical stage."

"Typical," Bea suggested.

"All critical stages are typical. Nonetheless, critical."

"Her date is a nice high school student her age."

"Who, Charlie? He has a forged identification card that says he's twenty-four."

"He isn't old enough to shave!"

"No," Joanne agreed, "but he assumes if his lie is exaggerated enough, nobody would dare suggest he's only sixteen."

Bea persisted, "I only know youse can't make a kid be what she isn't. Youse can make her lie and cheat and sneak, but she's going to do what she wants to do."

8

"Which means incorrigibles are beyond help?"

"Criminology aside, yes."

"Fortunately, society does not operate on that premise altogether."

"So crime ascends," Bea recounted, "criminals run loose and everybody suffers. Lock the suckers up! Throw away the keys."

"Bea, I hope you never get in trouble with the law."

With the door closed, her secretary gone, Joanne suffered niggling doubts. She dialed home.

"Hi, mom," Marcie's first words.

"How'd you know it was me?"

"Nobody calls me but you and Ken. I don't have any friends."

"Marcie, don't be maudlin."

"They've all been driven away by chastity and purity, an image created as I decline one date after another. They fear my puritanical mother—"

"Marcie, Marcie."

"I have a tattoo outlined on my forehead. Paint by numbers, anything but scarlet."

"The day will come—"

"Listen, mom," Marcie cupped the receiver, voice intense, "Charlie Mason is so square he's a cube. A solid cube. Yes, he wants to take me to Sherrods. Yes, he wants to be hip. That's what he says, 'hip.' He learned it in a sixties novel. So to *be* hip he's taking me to Sherrods. Not an orgy, because Charlie Mason wouldn't be found dead at a team sport. He doesn't drink, he doesn't smoke pot or Chesterfields. He doesn't even dance."

"You cannot go, Marcie."

"He drives a TR-7, mom. Split seats. Gear shift between. Any luggage has to go outside on a rack."

"No, Marcie."

"Mom, you couldn't be immoral in that car if you tried! He wears a chastity belt. His mother has this thing about communicable diseases—"

"Not this time, darling."

"Mom!" A rush of air exhaled into the phone. "How about the Subway, then?"

Every parental instinct rebelled, but Joanne paused, considering.

"I'll be in by eleven," Marcie promised.

"You'll be in by nine."

"Oh, mom—garl"

"What?"

"It's a fish."

"Marcie, the Subway is permissible, Sherrods is not. In by nine promptly, or you're grounded."

Another exhalation in Joanne's ear. "All right," Marcie yielded, "in by ten."

"*Nine*, Marcie."

"It isn't even dark by nine o'clock, mom!"

As soon as Joanne hung up, the intercom buzzed and Beatrice purred, "Good for youse, Dr. Fleming."

"Bea, you were listening?"

"No, ma'am. I knew you'd call. I knew you'd compromise and knowing nothing more I said, Good for youse."

"Beatrice—"

"Mr. Blackburn is here," Bea announced.

Ken entered, grinning. He still wore the uniform of a Leon County deputy sheriff.

"I assume you know about Marcie," Joanne suggested.

"Yep. Subway's okay, Sherrods isn't. Marcie one, mother one—it's a draw. That's fair."

"Collusion," Joanne complained.

Ken reached across her desk and took the file folder Joanne had been reading. "Another one," he said.

She watched his eyes dart back and forth over the report. Ken was a man destined to his profession by fate. A former Marine with two tours of duty in Vietnam, he was like a character plucked from a movie about Rome at its zenith. His eyes deeply set, "hooded" by a prominent skull and accentuated by bushy brows, he could be a centurion misplaced in the twentieth century.

"This one bothers me," Joanne said. "I'm not sure why. Now and then out of a hundred missing persons reports, something touches a nerve."

"Meaning she isn't just a runaway?"

"That's right."

"You can't assume a crime has been committed without more proof than this."

"I know that."

He tossed the folder on her desk.

"Parents seldom admit their daughters are runaways," Joanne noted. "It would be a confession of their own failure. But there've been several cases in a three-state area that have a disturbing similarity."

"In what way?"

"To tell the truth, I'm not sure yet." Joanne withdrew several folders from a lower desk drawer. "They range in age from twelve to thirty-one. From tall to short, stout to petite. But look at the photos, Ken."

She spread several before him.

"The way they comb their hair," he said. "Down the middle, most of them. But this one didn't. Nor this one."

"Don't they all strike you as similar in appearance, though?"

He examined the photographs again. "They're all pretty."

"Their eyes. Their lips. Wide, full mouths. They *are* pretty."

"Pretty girls can be runaways too."

"Four of these girls were described as 'winning contestants' in beauty pageants."

"So?"

"Several were last seen at or near schools. From junior high through college level. Two girls at Winter Park attended Rollins College, didn't know one another, and both disappeared within the same week."

"Coincidence, maybe."

"Maybe." She reassembled the materials.

"How about Mexican food and margueritas at El Chico's tonight?"

"I suppose so." She was immersed in the Lake City report again.

"I'm working the eleven to seven shift tomorrow night," Ken said. "So tonight's my night for margueritas."

He clasped beefy hands, waiting. Finally, "Pick you up about seven, then?"

"Um-hm."

"I could come a little earlier. Six, maybe."

"Six is fine," she said, absently. "Tell Bea to make a note."

He leaned over and tapped her desk for attention. "Do me a favor. Don't get depressed about those girls. Let's have some smiles and happy thoughts tonight."

Joanne nodded. But when he left, she grimly returned to the folder, a knot in her abdomen.

The story was all too familiar. In Florida alone, in the

past five years, over a hundred women were reported missing who had never been heard from again. Runaways, usually, studiously avoiding contact with families. Some would return. But many—how many?—would never be located.

Oregon, California, Washington and Utah had been through a rash of similar disappearances. Thirty-seven cases with no witnesses, no clues, nearly all disappeared from areas in and around colleges. Suddenly, it had stopped. As if an abductor had departed, and now—here. Joanne closed the folder and turned her chair to look out the office window.

The girl in Lake City could have been grabbed by a transient who had detoured from busy Interstate Highway 75 going north to Atlanta, or south to Miami. If it were a spur-of-the-moment crime by a passing abductor, it would be almost impossible to solve. If there was a victim, if a body was found, the remains would be turned over to pathologists, often unable to answer the prime question: was this murder? Rape? Robbery?

"Dr. Fleming?"

"Yes, Bea?"

"Time to go home."

"Go ahead, Bea."

"Don't forget Ken. Six o'clock."

"Six? I thought he said seven."

"He said youse would say that. Six o'clock, your house."

"Right. Good night."

Bea extinguished lights in the receptionist's area, locked the office door behind herself. Joanne stared across campus. Beyond Bellamy Hall, the Florida State University "Seminole warrior" was painted on a three-tier diving platform above a swimming pool. In the afternoon sun, nearly nude bodies lay in tanned splendor. Uninhibited, carefree, tonight many of those girls would be drinking beer, experimenting with the process of maturation and confronted with adult decisions. In the act of growing, emotionally. There was no way to protect them from themselves, she thought. Perhaps, in fact, she *was* too strict with Marcie.

A tickle of apprehension traced her spine. She looked past the pool to a distant parking lot adjoining the campus. Young men loitered there. Could one among them be *him*—watching, waiting, planning? Did he plan? If she

12

knew that, she could do a better psychological profile. Or did he respond to a glandular urge and strike the first available victim? The urge—was it chemical, organic? Sane or not?

She stood, stretching, flexing her shoulders to ease tired muscles. If only there were bodies. One could not guess at the mind which committed a crime, without clues to suggest the progression of events.

She put the missing person files into a briefcase. She would study these over the weekend, try to answer her own question: what was different about these girls? More specifically, what was the *same?*

She turned off her office lights and groped past Bea's desk, emerging into the hall. This was the lull between day and night classes. The sound of her footsteps rebounded from tiled floor to acoustical ceiling, echoing down a long corridor. Somewhere afar, laughter.

When Ralph decided to divorce her, *the sonofabitch,* Joanne had wallowed without purpose for nearly a year. She was a psychologist. She saw her own quandary, the sure approach of neurasthenia, apathy. She had to do something. So she returned to college, got her master's and doctorate in criminology. The diplomas hung in her office, symbols of accomplishment to the world but to her milestones toward sanity regained. Finally, when she reached a point where Ralph's mellifluous voice on the telephone did not induce instant rage, she had become emancipated. She joined the FSU staff, gained tenure, earned respect for her work. In the world of academic pursuits, it was "publish or perish." She'd done that. Of her two books, *The Modality of Sex Crime* had been particularly well received. Published by Tulane Press, it had sold over a hundred thousand copies.

She took an elevator down to ground level and stepped from air conditioned comfort into a humid, hot North Florida afternoon. She walked the concrete path toward her parking space, head high, alert. Ken had accused her of "professional paranoia," a result of the cases she studied and courses she taught. There was truth in that accusation. She had her car keys ready, scanned the lot before she opened her car door, quickly locked herself in, and even now behind the steering wheel she checked rearview and side mirrors for any suspicious person—always aware.

Waiting for a traffic light on Tennessee Street, she

couldn't help but wonder how alert the missing girls had been. Surely, pretty young girls were naturally suspicious! By age fourteen, most had been conditioned to beware male advances. Surely. Then, how had they been taken? By force? Forcible abduction draws attention, creates witnesses. There were no witnesses.

She pulled into traffic, the sweetish aroma of exhaust wafting through an open window. It was a twenty-minute drive home during rush hour.

A car loaded with boisterous youngsters roared past, weaving from lane to lane. Automatically, Joanne studied the occupants, half expecting to see Marcie among them, their radio blaring, laughter punctuated by girlish squeals.

"You're too skeptical, Jo," Ken often chided.

"That's an odd thing for a deputy sheriff to say."

"Hey, listen, a healthy amount of suspicion is common sense. It can keep you alive. But too much can be dangerous."

"You never have sneaky hunches?"

"When I have a sneaky hunch, I start trying to figure out *why* I have it. There's usually some evidential reason. A car with a license plate that's too muddy, the driver going precisely five miles slower than the speed limit, two guys slumped down in a front seat—I have a hunch and pull them over. But it was a combination of evidential clues which caused my hunch. You have no basis for suspecting Marcie of anything. If you did, I'd shut up."

"Uh-huh," Joanne had responded curtly. "Marcie overdressed, caught in a minor fib or two, a friend inadvertently mentions they had a good time dancing when Marcie said they'd been to a movie. That's evidential, too. Marcie lied."

"Okay," Ken reasoned, "so she lied. It's a part of being a kid her age."

"That Great Psychologist in the Sky." It was a comment he had once used against her.

Easygoing, good-natured Ken Blackburn—he had extended two palms calloused from lifting weights, a gesture of resignation. "I call it like it lays, Jo."

Which he did, actually. She realized that. She also saw herself clearly enough. *Admit it.* She was jealous. Jealous! Marcie taunted, wheedled, needled her mother, then flew to her bedroom in tearful defeat, only to bare her soul to Ken when he went to see about her. Ken, the man who'd never had children, a cop, and Marcie hinted she'd tried marijuana, "popping pills," drinking beer—

Joanne forced herself to ease her grip on the wheel. Deep breathing; stop clamping your jaws, Joanne.

Pay attention!

A car passed so close Joanne could've sworn she heard a ping of bumper to chrome. Angrily, she pulled out of traffic onto a side street—a longer way home, but less competition for roadway.

When she reached the house, Ken's car was there. Out of an open bedroom window came *basso profundo* throbs from Marcie's stereo. Over it all, Marcie yelling into a telephone, her voice rising above the din of her own making.

Ken sat in the living room, size thirteen-D shoes discarded on either side of an ottoman. The TV blared news, man and child trying to outdo one another in decibels. Seeing Joanne, Ken lifted a can of beer, winked, and returned to the program.

Passing Marcie's bedroom Joanne leaned in and instantly Marcie covered the telephone receiver with a hand and shouted in artificial glee, "Hi, mom!"

Joanne moved her lips without sound. Marcie ignored the ploy, answering, "Sure, go ahead, I've had my shower already."

Determined not to mention the cacophony, Joanne went straight to her bathroom and shut the door.

"Oh, Charlie," Marcie shrieked into the phone, "that sucks!"

Joanne sagged against a lavatory, staring at her image in the mirror.

"Sucks, Charlie," Marcie cried. "Sucks, you hear me?"

To her reflection, Joanne murmured, "Welcome to planned parenthood."

More critically, she examined herself. Eyes she described as "round brown." Her best feature. Hair to match, like the fuzz of a mouse's underbelly, but on Joanne it always looked as if she'd endured an afternoon shower. Like Marcie, Joanne's hair tended to bleach blond in sunlight. Unlike Marcie, Joanne's became unruly, brassy, ends split. She avoided the sun. It produced enormous freckles. When she opened the refrigerator door and the fifteen watt bulb came on, she had to worry about third degree

15

flash burns. She was not a "sun person" like Marcie. Joanne *looked* thirty-six.

Undressing, more objectively, she examined her trim five feet six inches of well proportioned torso. Good legs. But if she flicked flesh with a forefinger, a tremble traversed her like a jiggle in gelatin. *Women age from the top down,* Benjamin Franklin had quipped.

From the bottom up, she looked pretty good.

In the shower, hot water laving away tensions, the rush of water drowning outside noise, Joanne's thoughts returned to the folio she had received from the Lake City Police.

Where might that child be at this moment? And to what end?

Joanne washed her hair, the full force of the shower making her feel refreshed.

The rapist—had there been a rape?—where was he? Rape or not, chances were the missing girl lay dead somewhere. Murder was a definite possibility.

It occurred to her that the disappearances were all about equal distances from Tallahassee—north, south, east and west. She pondered, eyes closed, rinsing her scalp—wouldn't it be something if the perpetrator were here in Tallahassee?

She opened her eyes wide, the shower pouring a sheet of water over her face.

Of course.

Yes.

Not one of those missing girls had disappeared from here.

She swallowed, mouth acid. She shut off the shower and stood dripping, listening. The music had stopped.

Marcie had gone.

Chapter Three

"THIS hearing is an informal one," Judge Alcorn said. He unbuttoned his shirt and loosened his tie as if to reinforce the statement. He looked from Sheriff Rogers to the District Attorney, then to Joanne. "Go ahead with your report, Dr. Fleming."

Hired by the court to prepare a pre-sentence psychological profile, Joanne found herself in the disturbing position of defending a rapist. By legal definition, the man was criminal, by a vote of his peers he was guilty.

"George Swain, age twenty-nine, black male," Joanne synopsized. "His formal education is to grade four. He is a functional illiterate, works odd jobs for minimum wage, mostly gardening and yard work. His intelligence is below normal—"

"How far below?" Judge Alcorn interrupted.

"Eighty-five, just above 'trainable.' "

"Go ahead, please."

The District Attorney, Phillip Dupree, drummed his high forehead with short, pink, pointed fingertips, waiting his turn to speak.

"Swain is not a man who constitutes a threat to society, in my opinion," Joanne said. Dupree grunted derisively. "Swain is a large man who, in the grips of sexual excitement, physically accosted his victims using the sheer weight of his body. There was no weapon. No verbal threats were made. He simply overpowered the two women involved."

Dupree and Sheriff Rogers exchanged glances.

"Does Swain know right from wrong?" Judge Alcorn questioned.

"Yes, he does."

"Is he capable of controlling his emotions, or not?" the D.A. asked.

"Under most circumstances, yes."

"So he's only dangerous part-time." Dupree widened colorless eyes.

"There are mitigating circumstances, Judge Alcorn," Joanne insisted.

"Let's hear it then," Alcorn suggested, peevishly.

"In one of the rapes," Joanne said, "and I use 'rape' advisedly—"

"Now damn it," Dupree snapped, "Swain stands convicted. Let's not debate his culpability. He's guilty as hell."

"This isn't a courtroom," Judge Alcorn advised. "Go ahead, Dr. Fleming."

"One of the two women has been in court before, with claims of rape," Joanne noted. "She has been a 'victim' no less than five times, according to my interview with her."

"Oh, really now!" Dupree stood abruptly. "Judge Alcorn, this is ridiculous."

"Phillip," Alcorn ordered, "let the lady finish. Then you can rant and rave."

"Swain physically overpowered both victims," Joanne continued. "But in each incident, the women had put themselves into compromising positions—out with him alone, drinking. The rapes did not involve kidnapping. Swain had enticed these women to secluded areas, had been buying drinks, and when they did not readily comply, he bullied them. One is always suspect of rape victims who have cried rape before. Statistically, the same women seem to get raped again and again, which raises some very disturbing questions."

Judge Alcorn nodded, eyes half closed.

"Obviously," Joanne explained, "Swain cannot continue to overpower women to achieve sexual favor. But what the man needs is therapy, not prison. In his stratum of society, many cases like this are never reported. In Swain's case, he was unlucky enough to accost these two particular women. In a psychological profile I did of one of his victims—"

"I object," the D.A. cried. "Now, by God, judge, I do object. The *victim* was not convicted, Swain was."

"I have to agree, Dr. Fleming," Judge Alcorn said.

"Suffice to say then," Joanne added, "they asked for it. Swain is confused and surprised that he stands accused of rape, when he knows many other men who have had

18

sexual relations with these women—and yet the women did not accuse those men of rape."

The judge adjusted his bulk in his chair, sighed. "Okay, Phillip, play district attorney."

Phillip Dupree stood, as if to fully use his vocal cords he had to be perpendicular to the floor. "Al," he addressed Judge Alcorn, "we've got to stop this nonsense of letting these felons go. We're under tremendous pressure from a skeptical public. The police officer on the beat is convinced that it isn't worth the effort to prepare a case. Really now, we need to make an example of this guy. It's more than Swain's guilt. He stands convicted. He should be punished. Sheriff Rogers and I were careful to prepare this case in a secure, airtight way. From Miranda to final deposition we walked this case through court."

"That's why you got a conviction," Joanne interjected.

"The sonofabitch is guilty, Fleming," Dupree snarled. "Since he's guilty, he should go to prison."

"What you and Sheriff Rogers are doing," Joanne said, "is trying to find a safe and sure example—hey, folks, look what we did during this election year. Caught us a rapist."

Dupree's cherubic cheeks flushed. "It galls me to get a criminal convicted in the courtroom, then have to go into chambers and seek conviction all over again."

"Why make an example of Swain?" Joanne said, hotly. "If you convict this man, then you should lock up half the males at FSU on charges with as much credence."

"Nobody has accused the males at FSU of rape," Dupree retorted.

"If they did," Joanne said, "you'd wheedle the victim into dropping charges, Phillip. But because Swain is indigent, black—"

"I'm no racist!" Dupree exploded.

"Then be sensible." Joanne was standing now, too. "Swain needs counseling, not confinement. Find yourself a more suitable scapegoat."

"Hold it, hold it." Judge Alcorn rapped the table with his knuckles. "My job is to see justice done. If you two will present your arguments less passionately, with more facts than emotion, we'll all be in a better position to do what we must."

In the end, she argued, chided, berated—to no avail. It was not rehabilitation these men sought, but public vengeance. She left the judge's chambers feeling frustrated and angry. As many times as she had participated in this aspect of the judicial process, it never became easier. She had seen moderately well-to-do convicted men receive a legal slap on the wrist and probation for crimes which had a portent for violence. Men of lesser means, usually the ones most liable to be accused of crimes, received everything that law would allow a judge to impose.

In silence, Joanne rode the elevator with Sheriff Rogers and District Attorney Dupree. As the doors opened on the ground floor, Dupree said, "You did a good job on that Swain thing, Joanne."

"So did you, Phillip."

"Look," he cooed, "if you want to keep your equilibrium in this business, operate under the credo 'some you win, some you lose.' This one you lost."

When the elevator door opened, Sheriff Royce Rogers —his detractors called him "Cowboy," and his wife "Trigger"—walked down the hall, boot heels clicking on terra cotta tile. Phillip Dupree fell back, touching Joanne's arm to slow her.

"I'm having a beer and barbecue bash at my place on the lake, Jo—next Saturday. Can you make it?"

She forced a more cheerful note. "I'll look forward to it. My escort included, I assume."

"Sure," Dupree grinned, "I like Ken Blackburn."

They halted on the steps of the Lewis State Bank building, watching Sheriff Rogers stride toward the Capitol complex a couple of blocks away.

"Rogers didn't say a word," Joanne observed.

"He didn't even have to be there."

"Then why did he come out on Saturday morning to attend?"

Dupree stared after the sheriff with pale eyes enfolded by flesh. "Running scared, maybe," he said softly. "Sheriff Rogers faces reelection for the first time."

"He has reason to worry, does he?"

"No, he doesn't." Dupree mopped his rosy face with a handkerchief. "But even an unopposed politician worries that a demon will descend on him. I ought to know, this will be my third reelection bid. Judge Alcorn's tenth."

As they started to part company, Phillip Dupree turned. "Joanne? Listen. It gives me no pleasure to railroad a man like Swain. For what it's worth, I admire you for standing up for the man."

"Phillip, do you sleep well?"

The D.A. raised blond eyebrows, forehead wrinkling. "There are two kinds of justice, Jo. What you teach from the textbooks; and what really is. This today is what really is. See you next Saturday. We'll begin about four. Come any time after that."

Ken sat in an easy chair, rubber thongs hanging on otherwise bare feet, wearing a baseball cap which said "FSU SEMINOLES."

"How'd it go?"

"Justice was not done," Joanne said.

"Too bad."

"Yes, too bad," she said, sharply. "It costs the taxpayer close to twenty-five thousand a year to keep a man in prison. If they'd devote that sum to re-education and counseling—"

He grabbed her wrist and pulled her into his lap. "I'm going to suck your earlobe," he warned.

"Where's Marcie?"

"Gone to Panacea."

"Panacea!"

"Blame me, not her," Ken restrained Joanne. "She asked me and I said okay."

"Of course she asked *you*. She knew perfectly well I'd tell her she couldn't go."

"Which proves she isn't stupid," Ken grinned.

"With Charlie Mason, I assume."

"Right. I saw his car, Jo. Little bitty thing. If they do anything in that vehicle, they'd have done it in a telephone booth anyway."

"Ken, I swear—you know how Marcie uses her father to usurp me. Must you join in that, too?"

"She'll be home by eleven, Jo and—"

"Eleven tonight? She'd better be home by—"

"Eleven," he said, firmly. "Now stop huffing and enjoy the nibbles."

When she refused to relax, he let his head fall back and stared at the ceiling.

"I'm sorry, Ken. I'm still upset about the hearing this morning."

He allowed her to sit up.

21

"Would you like a beer or something?" she asked.

"Can't. I'm going on the late shift tonight."

"Iced tea, then?"

"Guess I'll head to the house for a nap."

"You can take a nap here."

He looked at her, expressionless.

"Give me awhile to unwind," Joanne placated. "Who knows what will transpire?"

"If you don't, nobody does."

"The Phantom knows," she said, huskily.

He stared at the ceiling again, head resting on the back of his chair. Joanne removed the baseball cap, brushed from his forehead a thick shock of hair which instantly returned to place.

"We're down to three men on the eleven-to-seven shift," Ken said. "We're supposed to have fourteen and we have three. You know what my district is? North Leon County. How can we cover seven hundred square miles with three men?"

"No new applicants?"

"They come, learn law enforcement, complete classes at the academy, stay a year and quit. You can't get anybody to work these ungodly hours for ten thousand a year. If I were married, had kids—I couldn't make it."

A moment later he added, "It won't be much longer, I guess."

"Before what?"

"I quit."

Joanne backed off to arm's length. "You quit? What will you do?"

"I didn't take this job for a lifetime career," he reminded.

"What will you do?"

"I've got another quarter before I get my degree. I've been thinking about security work for some large company. White collar crime, computer theft, industrial spying and sabotage. They need good investigators."

"Where would you find such a job?"

"There've been ads in the trade papers lately."

"Where?" Joanne persisted.

"Des Moines, Chicago, here and there."

"You wouldn't be mentioning this if you hadn't already made inquiries."

"Yeah."

"So it's fairly certain."

"They seem interested in me. The lowest offer is thirty-five thousand to start. Good medical and retirement plans."

"I see." Joanne forced a smile. She bent forward and kissed him.

"Want to have some fun?" he asked.

"Here?"

"I think I can make it to the bedroom."

"Okay."

She gave him a hand, pulling him up from the chair, then he seized her in burly hirsute arms. They weren't going to make it to the bedroom.

She thought of the unlocked doors.

"They're locked," he said, kissing her neck.

"Not the garage door."

"Nobody comes through the garage door."

"Marcie does."

He eased her to the floor. "Marcie is in Panacea until eleven."

"That girl."

"Good girl," Ken said. Joanne wasn't sure whether he meant Marcie, or herself.

Joanne sat in the kitchen, one leg beneath her, clad in a bathrobe. An overhead swag lamp bathed the Formica table in yellow light. Before her were spread the sixteen files of missing girls, their photos aligned in a four-by-four square.

"You're worrying about those?" Ken kissed her in passing. He smelled of cologne.

"I guess I am."

"How about breakfast with me in the morning?" He paused at the back door.

"Sounds good."

His thick eyebrows lifted, lowered. "Thanks, sweetie. For everything."

She rotated a shoulder. "Anytime, big boy."

She heard the lock snap, the door rattle as Ken tested it from outside. A moment later, his car motor rumbled and he departed.

The refrigerator droned, fighting humidity and heat. Outside open windows, insects thumped the screens, seeking light. With Ken gone, she pulled from her lap the legal-size pad which she had deliberately concealed from him.

It was a list of facts: age, height, weight, hair styles, time of day of disappearances, days of week, distances from Tallahassee. She had learned the system from her father, and papa had taught her the joys of investigative thinking.

"Everything you can think of, Joanne," papa would urge. "Make a cross-index and you'll see how things change. You'll see the similar, or dissimilar."

Papa had made it such a game. She had spent hours in his study, following the process until papa would grin and pull her to his side. "Ah," he'd whisper, the end in sight, "now I see this culprit—do you see him, Joanne?"

"I think I do, papa."

"Can you feel his heartbeat?"

"Not yet."

"Keep working on it," papa would chuckle. "When you feel his heartbeat, his thoughts are your thoughts and you can do no wrong."

Papa's system sometimes made the trivial glaringly important. And, sitting alone like this, she could feel him at her shoulder, smiling, nodding approval.

There were no clearly defined coincidences or remarkable differences, so far. Yet, she could not shake this vague uneasiness. She got up, poured coffee from a percolator and returned to stare at the photos.

Once, in court, an attorney had demanded, "Since you feel qualified to say my client suffers abnormal sexual desires, Dr. Fleming, perhaps you'll tell the jury what *normal* is?"

It was a good ploy. What is moral to one is sinful to another. Joanne had skirted the issue by turning it slightly.

"Normal sexual desire," she said, "is directed at someone of the opposite sex, of comparable age to the one who feels the desire. Some psychologists would argue that normal love and intercourse would be that which is necessary for fertilization of the female."

"Otherwise," the attorney had demanded, "you would call the act a sexual deviation?"

"That is a loose term," Joanne had countered. "If the act is unbiological, it is a deviation. As, for example, sex with an animal, sex between an adult and a child, or acts of copulation between members of the same sex."

24

All that she had said was true. As far as it went. But by whose definitions? Some societies termed any person under age eighteen a child; others said twelve, nine, whatever. What of consenting homosexual adults in the privacy of their own dwelling? What of masturbation? Fellatio, cunnilingus?

It was easier to define the legal parameters. Alas, she was seldom asked for that clarification. Hers was the task of unraveling the minds of those who deviated dangerously, thereby posing a threat to society.

Of all aberrations, rape-murder was the most horrendous of crimes against persons. Assault and a human life extinguished. Rape was an affront to dignity. But murder!

With these sixteen women there was something—something which stirred a subconscious warning. It was a hunch which Ken would call "sorely lacking in evidential proof."

Absently, she glanced at the clock. Fifteen more minutes until eleven. Marcie certainly would not arrive one microsecond sooner than her self-appointed deadline.

Sipping coffee, Joanne noted the random facts on her pad. Fourteen of the sixteen had disappeared on Friday night, or Saturday. This would suggest the abductor had a regular job, perhaps.

The singular most striking coincidence was the proximity to institutions of learning. Students. Yet of the sixteen, three were not near schools. One had been last seen in a shopping center. Another had gone to a drugstore, left her automobile motor running and door open—and so it was found, battery dead, gasoline consumed, the woman gone. Then there was the girl who'd gone out to "meet a friend," in Jacksonville, Florida—and never returned.

Sigmund Freud believed that sexual deviations were wrought from a traumatic experience during an early stage of development. Some researchers believed sex crimes were the result of primordial "biological residue." One criminal was more "animal" than another.

But this—sixteen girls, maybe more—this was something else again. If she was correct, if indeed these were the result of a single perpetrator, this was a crime by the most dangerous of all predators. This man would prowl a territory as surely as a carnivorous beast. He used his victims to relieve a tormented psyche, venting a hatred and bitterness so acute that he was merciless at that instant.

25

In such a man, hate was the emotional currency of his actions, whereas with a normal person it is love. To a psychologist, this kind of killer was a "sadist-murderer." The sadist injured parts of a woman other men wished to caress. Within the sadist bubbles the lava of supreme anxiety. Until, finally, in a violent eruption, the act of sexual assault and murder was a form of relief.

The psychological irony was, the sadist-murderer did to others that which he subconsciously feared might be done to him. But when the sadist was also a psychopath, a condition of pure terror resulted. The murderer had nothing to inhibit antisocial behavior. In committing heinous crimes and unbelievable cruelty, he was an animal without conscience. Yet legally, and from a psychiatric point of view, such a man was adjudged to be sane.

Goosebumps prickled Joanne's shoulders. She shuffled together papers, placing them in order, pertinent materials relating to each girl.

The goosebumps suddenly raced across her back, down her arms, neck hair rising. What was it? A bump—something—no! Silence. Insects no longer thumped the screens.

Ken had locked the door. She knew that.

But she walked into the dark alcove anyway, clutching her robe at the breast. She pushed the portal, testing.

It opened.

"Hi!"

Joanne vaulted backward, screaming.

"Mom?"

"Marcie—girl—I—"

"I'm sorry, mom. I thought you heard me and came to open the door."

Trembling, Joanne clasped her hands to still the quaver of fingers.

"Ah," Marcie indicated the clock. "Eleven, right on the dot."

Chapter Four

JOANNE bumped her desk going to the drapes in her office, which she closed. She dropped a notebook, and retrieving it, dislodged books from shelves spanning one wall. With concentration, she returned to her desk and collapsed, arms hanging. "Dr. Fleming," Bea was fond of saying, "takes morning coffee intravenously."

Blearily, Joanne contemplated her secretary's alabaster incisors. Bea placed a cup on the desk, commanding gently, "Drink."

Eyes closed, Joanne sipped, wincing when the telephone rang. She heard Bea answer in the reception area, "I'm sorry, Dr. Fleming will be indisposed for another twelve minutes and forty seconds."

When the girl returned, Joanne demanded, hoarsely, "Who?"

"Youse don't want to know."

"Ralph," Joanne deduced. "He always did that. When we were married, Ralph hit the floor talking. What'd he want?"

"He'll call back."

Joanne stared.

"Drink."

"He should've married a disc jockey," Joanne cracked. "Wants to discuss life and death decisions at the break of dawn. We really weren't very well suited for one another."

She opened a folder containing clippings from weekend editions of newspapers. Police reports. She scanned articles, turning pages, laying them aside.

In tabulating the incidence of criminality, newspapers had become a primary source. Crimes reported to police were a more accurate indicator than the F.B.I. *Uniform Crime Reports.* The farther a criminal proceeded through a judicial procedure, the more distorted the final figures.

Only a fraction of those charged ever came to trial; even fewer were convicted, fewer still actually went to prison. By then, the original crime was often altered by plea bargaining and lesser charges accepted for the sake of expediency.

It was a story in the Jacksonville *Times-Union* which brought Joanne upright.

"The nude body of a Jacksonville woman was found by hunters in a swampy area near the Georgia state line Saturday night. Identified as Donna Hightower, she was reported to have been abducted while attending adult night classes at a local high school."

The details following made Joanne's heart leap. "Panty hose around her neck . . . death by strangulation . . . blows to the skull . . ."

"Bea," Joanne said, "call Bud Diehl with homicide, Jacksonville police."

She read the story again, a flutter in her stomach. Call it intuition. A tremor which, long ago, she'd learned never to ignore. Elation blended with foreboding. The body could be a physical affirmation that she was on to something substantive.

"Dr. Fleming," Bea on the intercom, "Marcie is calling."

Joanne subdued irritation, lifted the receiver, "Yes, Marcie, what is it?"

"Did daddy call you?"

"I haven't spoken with him yet."

"He didn't call?" Marcie persisted.

"Yes, he did. I was busy." She heard background noise, the shouts of students in a hallway changing classes.

"Are you going to talk to him?" Marcie's tone was accusatory.

"Yes, Marcie."

"Listen to what he has to say, will you, mom? Keep an open mind and listen all the way through."

"I'll try."

"Don't shut him off, all right?"

"I'll struggle to be mature."

"See! That's what I mean. Don't be sarcastic, mom. Listen to his reasoning."

"I will try, Marcie. I have another call. Anything else?"

"Hey, mom, I really have to go. Talk to you later." The phone went dead. Joanne pushed a button, transferring to a second line.

28

"What's going on, Jo?" Bud Diehl's low voice conjured an image of his walrus mustache, sleepy yellow-flecked eyes.

"I'm calling about the Hightower case, Bud."

"What can I do for you?"

"You remember my inquiries some time back about a girl who disappeared over there—I've got her name here someplace."

"Ramirez," Bud said. "I remember."

"Do these two cases have a similar flavor to you, Bud?"

Long pause.

"That's funny," Diehl said, softly.

"What?"

"It will be in the papers this evening. We found the skeletal remains of two other bodies out there. You don't suppose—"

"I *do* suppose, Bud." Joanne couldn't conceal excitement. "Did you find enough for an ID?"

"I don't know. A couple of pieces of jewelry, some bones which the coroner believes to be fragments from two skulls."

"Bud, can you share any details that weren't in the *Times-Union* article?"

"Let me get the preliminary, Jo. Hold the phone."

The long distance line hummed as Joanne waited impatiently. When Diehl returned, he cleared his throat, rustled papers.

"When you call," he said, "I have mixed feelings. It's always good to hear your voice, but I sure by-God don't need a psycho on my hands."

"Let's hope this one isn't."

"Here we go." Diehl cleared his throat again. "The bones were widely scattered by animals, Jo. They're doing a fine-tooth search out there today. So far, a complete lower mandible. Ah, this is good—capped teeth, so that means there's a dental record somewhere."

"Yes," Joanne conceded, "that's good."

"Temporal, parietal, one ulna." Diehl read a list of bones retrieved. "Spinal, three segments of—say, Jo, what makes you think these might be connected in some way?"

"A hunch."

"Yeah. One earring, pierced type, fourteen-karat gold. A piece of jewelry they think is from a bracelet. That's about it on the two unknowns."

29

"How about the Hightower body?"

"She'd been dead about forty-eight hours. She and her husband had just eaten dinner, so the stomach contents are a pretty fair indication of time of death, which is estimated at two to five hours following ingestion. You want to hear the coroner's report on this?"

"Yes, please." She turned aside, calling, "Beal Pick up the phone, please. Okay, Bud, go ahead."

"Donna Hightower, caucasian, age twenty-three married, five-five, one-twenty, hair brown, eyes brown; husband, John A. Hightower; reported missing after leaving class to get a book from her automobile which was parked fifty feet from the school entrance where the couple attended adult night classes in accounting. According to the husband, he watched her until she reached the car. Five minutes later when she hadn't returned, he went looking and found the car door ajar, the book still on the rear seat, and his wife gone. This was verified by other witnesses. They immediately called the police. She was listed as 'possible MP' until the body was found Saturday night by two men hunting coons in a swampy area north of Jacksonville near the state line."

"The coroner's report?"

The detective's voice assumed the clinical, detached tone which his profession demanded if one was to remain stable in the face of madness. "She'd been dead about forty-eight hours when found," Diehl synopsized. "Dark blue panty hose wrapped tightly around the neck . . . strangulation indicated, the pathologist is working on that now. Blunt trauma involved; blows to the base of the skull . . . type weapon not determined . . ."

Joanne waited, heard papers rustling.

"Blows to the back of the head," Diehl enunciated each word like a student reading from a primer, "one fine, deep cut on the ear which may have been caused by a sharp instrument. A broken tooth, consistent with the head injuries. Analysis of stomach contents—do you need that?"

"No."

"Time of death, Friday, May eleventh, between seven and midnight. Acid phosphatase test on the vagina, positive."

"Did the husband report intercourse had taken place?"

"I haven't talked to him yet, Jo. It says here, marital relations none. Let me holler at the fellow who wrote this."

30

He cupped the phone and Joanne asked Bea, "Are you getting it all, Bea?"

"Yes ma'am."

"Jo," Diehl on the phone again, "the wife was Catholic and they were on the rhythm system. No intercourse. So that would suggest rape."

"Right."

Diehl returned to the report, "Samples of head and pubic hairs taken, blood and organs reserved for toxicology tests. It is believed the woman was killed elsewhere and dumped at the site where found. That's about it, Jo."

"Thanks, Bud."

"Hey!" he yelled. "Don't hang up on me."

"I'm not—what is it?"

"I remember that course you taught at the University in Gainesville two summers ago. I know well and good you aren't passing the time of day out of curiosity. So give— what's behind this?"

"I'm really not sure."

"Speculate then—turn about and all that."

"Bea," Joanne suggested, "you may hang up now."

With her telephone cradled, Bea could be heard muttering in the other office. Joanne closed her door and returned to the call.

"You know how you get a hunch now and then?" she said.

"Yeah."

"There've been sixteen female MPs in a three-state area. I'm hoping one or more of these skeletal remains will match up."

"Oh, damn," he groaned. "You think it is a psycho."

"I'll let you know when I do."

"Can you send me the files on those sixteen, Jo?"

"I will. Listen, Bud. I'd like to work with you on this."

"I need all the help I can get. Damn it, damn it. Excuse me, Jo. The air conditioner went out on us. It's hot as a pawnshop pistol, we're all jittery about racial tensions since the riots in Miami—and I don't need a psycho running around attacking women."

"Perhaps this isn't that at all," Joanne said.

"I didn't want to say this with Bea on the line," Diehl said. "There were human bite marks. The breast and buttocks."

"Bite marks. Well. That implies what we know it implies, doesn't it?"

Diehl sighed. "Psycho," he concluded.

Later, sitting in contemplation, Joanne looked at notes she had been scribbling. The numerals one through six, each bracketed by parentheses. Six characteristics of a type of criminal classified as "sadistic-murderer."

(1) The murderer strikes at regular intervals.

(2) The body has puncture wounds, cuts, sometimes biting wounds, and the murderer may suck the blood or even eat the flesh of his victim.

(3) Sexual excitement would occur during commission of the assault and murder.

(4) The killer occasionally revisits the scene of the crime.

(5) Between murderous assaults, the criminal exhibits normal behavior, follows usual routine.

(6) He is sane.

If either or both of the skeletons were similar victims, Joanne had four of the six factors she needed to form a profile of the killer. If she assumed he followed normal, mundane activities between murders, she could sketch his personality with some accuracy.

That left only a last question: was he, despite the other five characteristics—sane?

If so, Bud Diehl faced the most elusive of all criminals. Because, Joanne knew, such a monster was usually of above average intelligence, and utterly cold-blooded.

"Dr. Fleming," Bea on the intercom again, "Mr. Fleming is on line one."

"Hello, Ralph."

"Jo, this is Ralph."

I said hello Ralph. "What may I do for you, Ralph?"

"We need to talk about Marcie, Jo."

"What about Marcie?"

"She's almost grown, Jo."

"You noticed that."

"She needs more latitude, Jo. She's nearly adult."

"What is she trying to get from you now, Ralph?"

"Why do you always presume she's wrapping me around her little finger?"

"Because she so often wraps you around her little finger."

"I'm capable of coming to a few conclusions quite by

32

myself, Jo. I'm simply trying to give you the benefit of my observations."

"Fine. Go ahead. Benefit me."

He sniffed. A sure sign that somewhere, duplicity was at work. "Marcie's making good grades, isn't she?" he asked.

"You give her money for good grades," Joanne said, "you should know."

"A reward is recognition—a child needs incentives."

"It also keeps her perpetually infantile in expectations, Ralph. A college scholarship, career potential—there are other incentives besides ten dollars for each A, and five dollars for every B."

His voice altered to the proper mix of courtroom attorney and pleading innocence. "I don't pretend to be a psychologist, Jo. Other than what comes naturally, that which is needed to do well in my profession, I'm no psychologist. I wish we could discuss these things without fighting."

"I'm sorry, Ralph. I'm very busy. Could we get to the bottom line?"

"Okay, Jo. All right. I get the message. You keep it up, honey. One morning Marcie will announce she's moving out of your house into mine. When the day comes, you will blame me for her decision, naturally."

"I'm not too concerned about that, Ralph. Marcie can be devious and cunning, but she isn't stupid. She isn't going to compete with your pouty-lipped girl friends, or keep canapes fresh for your poker playing cronies on Saturday nights. Let's not worry about Marcie leaving me, Ralph. Unless you're worried that she *will* move in with you."

"My daughter would always be welcome—"

"Ralph," Joanne spoke sharply, "please get to the point. I am incredibly busy."

"Doing what, Joanne? Writing term papers? Grading on a new curve? We're dealing with our child! Can you spare a minute for that?"

She took a deep breath. "I'm sorry, Ralph. Please go ahead."

After an interminable silence, he said, "Marcie wants a car."

"Absolutely not."

"Actually, I agree. Not this year, surely."

"Not next year."

"But the *next* year, when she's eighteen—"

"When she's eighteen," Joanne replied, "she has a legal

33

right to do anything she pleases. Until then, there will be no car. She borrows mine on occasion. She borrows yours. We pay the insurance, buy gasoline—she can't afford a car, anyway."

"I realize that. I think we're in agreement."

Joanne muttered an obscenity.

"Sorry, Jo, I didn't hear you."

"So what is there to discuss, Ralph?"

"So," his voice lilted, "since that is so, I figured it wouldn't hurt if she borrowed my car."

"She already does that."

"I'm getting a new one and—"

"Ralph! You can't buy Marcie's love and allegiance. I know you suffer guilt and I know you—"

"Guilt?"

"Yes, guilt! I suffer guilt, why shouldn't you?"

"All right. In that context, all right."

"You know the temptations which beset a teen-ager these days. She needs—she wants and needs—restrictions. She may complain bitterly and vociferously, but down deep she's grateful for a parental excuse which relieves her of peer pressures."

"The car would remain mine," Ralph reasoned. "Marcie would have the use of it."

"Full-time, you mean."

"It would still be my car."

Joanne wiped her hands with a tissue, the phone clamped to her ear with a hunched shoulder.

"She could learn the responsibilities of possession," Ralph said, "without the liabilities of ownership, that was my thinking."

"Ralph, she's using the two of us against one another again."

"You always accuse her of that, Jo."

"She wanted you to call me about this, didn't she?"

"She suggested it."

"Once again, old mother comes off the heavy. Is that fair, Ralph?"

Long pause. "No."

"All right. Please tell Marcie we discussed it and the status quo will continue."

"I'll tell her we haven't come to a firm decision and—"

"No," Joanne demanded, "tell her definitely, *No*. Other-

34

wise, she'll drive me crazy for weeks, pushing incessantly until the decision is final and adamant."

Sniff. She waited. *Sniff-sniff*. Before their divorce, Ralph had gone to an allergist who told him he was suffering a psychosomatic reaction. This, Ralph had attributed to their marriage. Over the phone, she heard him blow his nose.

"Being a parent is not easy," he said, evenly.

"Made all the more difficult by a highly intelligent daughter," Joanne said. "She got your good looks and keen mind."

He laughed softly. "She's a good girl."

"I want to keep her that way."

Another long pause. "Everything all right in your life, Jo?"

"Yes. How about you?"

"Overworked. But that's the name of the game. I have an interesting case coming up with the State Attorney's office. Still under wraps, so I can't talk about it."

She waited, waited.

"You have enough money? Happy?"

"Yes." *Bastard*.

"Good," he wheezed. "I love you, Jo."

"I love you, Ralph." *Used to. Could still. Damn you!*

"Very well," tone professional again, "let me call Marcie. I'll take care of this, Jo."

She hung up, mouth tasting like yesterday's guacamole salad. Sweaters had formed on her teeth as they talked. She felt the distant drum of an approaching headache, muscles corded at the base of her skull.

Base of the skull. Blunt trauma, skull crushed by a blunt instrument . . .

She summoned Bea and directed, "Duplicate these sixteen files and send copies of everything to Bud Diehl in Jacksonville."

Bea examined the contents, a photograph, and grinned. "Hot diggity," she said.

"This is confidential, Bea."

The girl flashed hurt, dark eyes, "I know that."

"I felt compelled to say it. Sorry."

Left alone, Joanne made mental note of actions she might have to undertake. Police departments were not always cooperative. But crimes like this stirred such public outcry and put such pressure on investigators—they'd help, and they'd call to seek help, hopeful that their own cases could be resolved.

The telephone. Bea must not be at her desk. Joanne answered, "FSU criminology, Fleming speaking."

"Mom! The most wonderful thing—don't get angry, all right? Just listen. You know daddy's old Cadillac? Listen, mom—he's getting a new car because his accountant said the Caddy is depreciated to zero. It has only 26,000 miles and practically new radials in good condition and—"

"No, Marcie."

"Mom!" Marcie squealed. "He's going to sell it for nothing because nobody wants a gas guzzler."

"No, Marcie."

"Mom, daddy said it's up to you."

"And I say, no."

"Mom! Gar—gar!"

"Marcie," Joanne warned.

"I'm going to kill myself." Marcie fell away from the telephone screeching.

"Marcie," Joanne said, "your father loves you and he wants to please you. You are taking unfair advantage with these pressure tactics."

"I'm going to hang myself!"

"Don't be ridiculous."

"I'll drink some of that stuff that unstops commodes!"

"Which reminds me. Get some hamburger out of the freezer for dinner, will you?"

No sooner had Joanne hung up than the telephone rang again. She lifted the receiver prepared for combat.

"Jo, this is Bud Diehl in Jacksonville. Thought you'd want to know. The jaw with the capped teeth—it's the Ramirez girl."

"Oh."

"Got us one, haven't we?"

"Apparently," Joanne said, quietly, "we have."

Chapter Five

A lingering scent of insect repellent mingled with the odor of charcoal briquettes burning in a hibachi. Ken lay on a deck lounge, knees bent, heels drawn close to his posterior. He sipped beer, reading.

"Are you watching the fire?" Joanne inquired.

"Yep." He licked a forefinger, turned a page.

As a peace offering, Joanne had suggested a cookout, with Marcie free to invite her friends. She'd invited only Charlie Mason. The boy, son of a prominent surgeon, was like a friendly, clumsy St. Bernard, his presence impossible to ignore as he shifted constantly, crossing short stocky legs, wiggling a foot nervously.

Marcie was—*inflicting* was a good word—herself on the scene. She heaved monumental sighs, rolled green eyes skyward, stretched repeatedly and assumed positions as if deliberately to expose the cheeks of firm, youthful buttocks.

"Marcie," Joanne suggested, "haven't you anything to wear but those shorts? You've about outgrown them."

"They look as good as Ken's."

"His are slightly longer." But only slightly. Joanne saw Marcie's eyes dart to Ken's hairy inner thighs.

"Marcie tells me you do psychological profiles on sex criminals," Charlie attempted.

"That's part of what I do."

"Testifies in court, interviews sex maniacs, all that good stuff," Marcie added.

"You do?"

"That's part of my work," Joanne said.

The boy hooked a canine tooth on his lower lip, squinting through red eyelashes. His forehead was peeling from a recent sunburn.

"Crime and criminals," Marcie intoned, "that's the major topic of conversation around here. Sex and crime."

"Sounds interesting," Charlie ventured. Ken laughed, softly.

"I read your article in *Psychology Today*," Charlie said to Joanne. He bumped into the patio table, then grappled for teetering objects.

Well? You read it and what?

"I didn't understand it," Charlie confessed.

"Mom doesn't write for the masses," Marcie said. "She writes for the intelligentsia."

"For the person who already has some background in the subject," Joanne amended. She made a note on a graph she had drawn.

Marcie collapsed at Ken's feet, an arm on his bare knee. "What're you reading, Ken?"

He lifted the book: *Legal Aspects and Procedures of Constitutional Cases.*

"My father cancelled our subscription." Charlie spoke to Joanne. "He caught me reading some stuff he didn't like."

"Such as what?"

"About incest."

"Pro or con?"

The boy waggled a foot, thumping the table leg. He had a mannerism of waiting before reply—Joanne wasn't certain whether by deliberation, or because of slow mental processes. "I'm not sure," he said. "Dad snatched the thing out of my hands. The library didn't have that issue, so I couldn't finish it. What do you think, Dr. Fleming?"

"About what?"

"Incest."

"Uh—" Joanne saw Ken glance at her with scarcely veiled amusement. "I suspect incest is justifiably a taboo," Joanne said, cautiously. "For societal, genetic, and familial reasons. But the victim must be made to realize it is not so shameful that it should mark one's life."

Charlie Mason stared at her. Just as Joanne was congratulating herself on leaving him befuddled, Charlie said, "It's interesting that the degree of guilt is in direct relationship to the degree of danger to the coupling, genetically."

"What?"

"Most forbidden is father-daughter," Charlie expounded. "Less taboo is mother-son; even less is sibling incest—a direct correlation to the danger genetically, if conception should occur."

38

Over the slouched boy's shoulder, Joanne saw Ken pull down the corners of his mouth, eyebrows lifted.

Marcie hugged Ken's knee, a move too intimate to ignore.

"Have you finished making the potato salad, Marcie?" Joanne asked.

"Yes, mom." Marcie shook Ken's leg. "Is that a good book?"

"It serves its purpose."

Marcie announced to Charlie, "What we have here is an ongoing conflict between ideological poles. Mom is the idealist who believes criminals are products of their environment, misunderstood by a callous society—" Marcie now indicated Ken, "—while he is the foot soldier, frontline defender of the streets. He makes a bust, tallies a rap sheet, studies books that teach him how to make the arrest stick, and he thinks all bad guys should be locked up. Period."

"And what do you believe?" Ken asked, amiably.

"I believe," Marcie said, "law is created by a ruling class which subjugates the lower class for selfish purposes."

"You've been listening to your mother."

"Sounds Marxist," Charlie suggested.

"It is." Marcie stood. "Almost every law is to serve a ruling class and perpetuate their power, right, mom?"

"There are particles of truth in that."

"Did you know," Marcie confronted Charlie, "premarital sex is against the law?"

"It is?"

Marcie did a half turn. "It's against the law to have extramarital sex, isn't it, Ken?"

"The law as written," Ken said, "is sometimes far removed from the law as applied."

"That means they ignore sex unless they need the law to bust you. Like vagrancy laws—written as a convenience to cops and the ruling power structure, right, mom?"

"Marcie, I'm sure Charlie isn't interested."

"We know a lot of criminals," Marcie taunted, "don't we, Charlie?"

The boy grinned, chin down.

"The ridiculous thing is," Marcie sneered, "law is just a farce."

"We'd be in trouble without it," Ken observed.

"Mom's right," Marcie said. "But so are you! The law is

enforced with bias—you make the decision about an arrest right there on the spot, so you're a cop and a judge at the same moment."

"That's true."

"What's illegal today may be perfectly all right tomorrow," Marcie said. "Not long ago, blacks couldn't marry whites in this state. Now they can. It's all a farce."

"My, my," Joanne chided, "aren't we cynical?"

"I am," Marcie rejoined. "You should be."

Ken held up an empty botle. "Get me a beer, will you Marcie?"

"It's like lawyers," Marcie said. "They become legislators and judges and congressmen and senators—making laws. Then they return to private practice and make money figuring out how to get around the laws they've made."

"Better not let your daddy hear you say that," Joanne cautioned.

"He's the worst of them all!"

The girl's tone made Joanne look up. Marcie glared, blonde hair framing her tanned face, green eyes flashing.

"Marcie," Joanne said, quietly, "you have no basis for making such a statement."

"Yes, I do. He's working on a bribery case right now. A big shot politician who's been taking kickbacks."

"Marcie, I don't think that's something to be discussed. Your father said it was still under wraps and—"

"You know what he said?" Marcie snapped. "He said he had to give the really big criminal immunity. So he can hang all the other guys less guilty than the big shot. Bunch of crap, that's what the legal system is."

The girl stamped across the patio and into the house. Charlie knocked the table, unfolding, rising to follow.

To Ken, Joanne said, softly, "Ouch."

He put aside his book, stirred charcoal. Charlie returned to bring Ken a cold beer. "Marcie will be out in a moment," he said. Then, "Dr. Fleming, how do you do a profile on a criminal who is uncaught?"

"Using clues from the crimes," Joanne said. She was listening for Marcie's movements, inside.

"All criminals are the same?"

"To a large extent, Charlie. That's how police recognize a *modus operandi*. The criminal falls into behavioral patterns." Joanne heard a commode flush and she relaxed

40

slightly. A moment later, Marcie reappeared, tossing her head to throw back flaxen hair.

"Sex criminals are usually sick," Marcie joined the conversation. "Mom hears all kinds of juicy things, don't you, mom?"

"None of which I'm at liberty to discuss."

"She means," Marcie interpreted, "our ears are too young for such mature subjects. We daren't hear about dildos and condoms and—"

"Marcie!"

"The coals are ready," Ken interrupted. "Bring on the steaks, Marcie."

When the young people were inside, Joanne said, "We're invited to a beer and barbecue at Phillip Dupree's lake house this Saturday."

"You're invited," Ken amended, "I'm welcome."

In the kitchen, Charlie's voice rose through two octaves, "Marcie, that sucks!"

"That term," Joanne said, "is abominable and obscene."

Marcie brought out the steaks, then went back inside for plates and utensils, Charlie trailing behind.

"So can we go, Ken?" Joanne asked.

"If you want to."

"I think we'd enjoy it," Joanne said. "Anytime after four, Phillip said."

Ken placed steaks on the grill.

"We don't have to go if you don't want to," she offered.

"Did you tenderize these?"

"Yes." She moved next to him and Ken put an arm around her neck and squeezed.

"You don't mind, Ken?"

"Why should I mind? I'll be with the sexiest woman there."

"Okay, you two," Marcie yelled through a window, "break it up!"

Joanne groaned, "Will this adolescence ever pass?"

"Don't wish away precious years, Jo."

She returned to the patio table, gathering her notes, placing them into a valise.

"Getting anywhere on that?" Ken asked. He meant the sixteen file folders.

"They found a new victim," Joanne said. "Also one of the missing girls."

"Ummm." Ken turned sizzling meat, sipped beer.

41

"Want to know something eerie," Joanne mused. "I think the killer may be living somewhere in this area."

Ken sipped beer, watched fat fry.

"Mom!" Marcie at the kitchen window, "May I go to a movie?"

"This is a school night, Marcie."

"We haven't got but two more weeks, mom. Nothing is happening in class, I swear it."

Joanne looked to Ken and he lifted his shoulders.

"If you're in by ten," Joanne answered.

Boy and girl shrieked in unison and instantly, Joanne regretted her permissiveness. Why ten? Always before it had been nine.

"Wise decision," Ken commented.

"Was it?"

"Yep. Time to ease up. Wise decision."

She encompassed his waist with both arms, standing behind him. "The things I always admired about you," Ken said, voice deep, "your good mind, good sense, and the fact that you really try to be a good mama."

"You might get some debate from Marcie on that."

"Ask when she's thirty," Ken suggested. "See what she says then."

Joanne kissed his shoulder. "You make me feel better, always."

"Defender of the public," Ken said, soberly. "Front line soldier . . ."

Phillip Dupree's tri-level ranch style home dominated a knoll overlooking Lake Jackson. A plush carpet of Bermuda and St. Augustine grass stretched beneath spaced pines. Under a tent, four men turned racks of ribs over a pit, basting meat, juices searing. In a cauldron darkened by smoke, baked beans grew thick in a honey sauce.

"There's beer in casks," Phillip greeted them. "Also in bottles and cans—ignore the state tax labels. Some of it is imported from Colorado."

Ken took in the scene and excused himself, heading toward tubs filled with iced brew.

"Cowboy says Ken's a good man," Phillip remarked. "Says when Ken gets some experience he'll have a future as a deputy sheriff."

"Ken will be so pleased," Joanne smiled sweetly. Phillip

laughed and squeezed her arm. "Cowboy is here some-place. Trigger, too. Make yourself at home, Jo."

Tennis courts, a swimming pool, a home that must've cost two hundred thousand dollars. "Graft," Ken murmured, rejoining her. "No other way."

"Nobody seems to mind," Joanne whispered. "Half the politicians in town are here, and several judges from various courts."

"Why should they mind?" Ken walked close at her side. "Everybody here is probably benefiting from the same source."

"Are we?"

"Drinking his beer, eating his meat," Ken noted, sardonically.

The party moved through several stages. On the lawn and before dark, older attorneys, judges, and elder politicians mingled in social eddies with like members of their legal stratum. As the sun flowed over the horizon, a string ensemble began playing, lanterns winked and most of the senior citizens ebbed away in the night. It was a younger, more lively crew who remained to dance on a patio at poolside.

By ten o'clock, Joanne was laughing inordinately, drinking another beer, and Ken was propping her up surreptitiously.

"Now tell me what you do?" The intense young man leaned nearer to hear better.

"Psychological profiles of the criminal mind," Joanne enunciated. She swung her head to look at Ken. "I said it," she boasted.

"So what is that, exactly?" the young man asked.

"Let's say," Joanne said, "there's a sex criminal running loose somewhere. He's raping and murdering women. Let's say for a long time the women are listed as missing until finally somebody finds a body. You with me?"

"I'm with you."

"Then," she said, "let's say the body is strangled, suffers blunt trauma—you know what that means?"

"Yes, I do. Go on."

"Let's say there are lacerations, human bite marks—"

"Bites?"

"On the breasts and buttocks. Typical of this type of killer, actually."

"That's interesting."

"Then I do a profile," Joanne concluded. Ken kept a hand on the small of her back.

"From those few facts?"

"The more facts the better, of course," Joanne said. "But we can assume some things—sexual arousal during the commission of the assault and murder, the fact that the killer is sane—if we assume that, we can make a profile of some accuracy."

"How accurate?"

Joanne pursed numbed lips. "Lemme see," she said. "If enough clues are available, the profile can be uncannily correct. In a case I'm studying now, for example—I got a hunch."

She realized Sheriff Rogers and his wife sat nearby, listening. Phillip Dupree winked at Joanne. Laboriously, she winked in return.

"What case is that, Jo?" Phillip teased.

"Sixteen missing women—well," Joanne redirected, "now fifteen. They found one of them near Jacksonville. Maybe two."

"Oh, yeah! Right." Her initial listener adjusted his spectacles, slipping closer. "I read about that. Three bodies together. The—what's her name—the Hightower woman, right?"

"Right."

Others had come into the sphere of the conversation and Joanne took a deep breath. The topic seemed to have assumed more importance.

"So," the young man urged, "you're doing a profile on this unknown murderer, is that it?"

"Trying to."

Sheriff Rogers glanced at Phillip Dupree and they laughed.

"What kind of guy is he?" the young man asked.

"I don't have enough to go on, to be sure."

"But you have an idea—"

"Joanne," Phillip chided, "better ask if your remarks are off the record. That's Tony Eldridge with the *Democrat*."

"This isn't an interview," Eldridge said quickly. "I'm intrigued, that's all."

"Those eggheads with doctorates in criminology sound good, all right," Sheriff Rogers cautioned.

"But it makes sense," the reporter replied.

"Hogwash," Sheriff Rogers said.

"Now hold on, Cowboy!" Joanne scolded. Everybody laughed except Rogers, his wife, and Ken.

"Honey," Ken murmured, warning.

"Well, I'm a little weary of old-fashioned complaints based on ignorance and chauvinistic concepts," Joanne said.

"Whoo!" Phillip Dupree whistled.

"Very well," Sheriff Rogers challenged, evenly, "let's hear your theory on this unknown killer, Dr. Fleming."

Joanne looked at the circle of faces. She assessed her sobriety, her command of her senses. Why not? Yes, by golly, why not! She recounted the similarities of disappearances, the haunting likeness of the missing women. She pointed out the incidence of locale, near schools. Then, as a final argument, she outlined the known facts concerning the disappearance of Donna Hightower, and the condition of her body when found.

"When one of the skeletons was identified as another Jacksonville woman—I knew they were probably linked together," Joanne expounded. "Returning to the scene of one murder with yet another body is a sure clue to the personality involved. I'm willing to bet the third body is one of the other fifteen missing women. If so, the case becomes a classic example of sadist-murder."

"That's quite remarkable," the reporter stated. "But what does that tell you of the killer?"

"It's all postulation at this juncture," Joanne said. "But if I may employ poetic license, psychologically, I can make an educated guess."

"So, make your guess."

"He's a handsome devil," Joanne said to a silent audience. "Charming, witty, educated, above average intelligence. His mother would describe him as a thoughtful son; his father has been missing, or only a weak figure—and between the killer and the father there would be animosity, a competitive lifelong fight for the attention of the mother. This killer dotes on his mother. But deep inside, he hates her. He is drawn to her and repelled at the same instant, and the turmoil of guilt-love-hate-worship all whirl like a psychological tornado in his subconscious."

"He kills women to relieve this?"

"Yes," Joanne said, "he does."

45

"Many people have similar backgrounds and they don't rape and murder," the reporter said.

"That's the mystery," Joanne said. "Why did one child in similar circumstances grow up to become normal. But this one, and it could happen to any of our children—this one twisted at a crucial point. When the child was at the scratching, biting, aggressive stage of infantile development —the parents not showing love, the parents aggressive, too —something warped."

"So all we need is a description," Eldridge said, "and they could print this profile and catch the guy, maybe."

"That's true," Sheriff Rogers mocked. "Describe the man, Dr. Fleming, and we'll put out a bulletin on him."

Somebody laughed, but nobody moved away. Joanne thought a moment. "You know that poem, 'Monday's child is fair of face; Tuesday's child is full of grace—' "

"Right."

"I think of this killer as born at Monday midnight. Handsome, a quick, disarming smile. Wavy brown hair, maybe, and wears white sneakers, like tennis shoes."

"Why tennis shoes?" Phillip Dupree asked.

"For traction," Joanne said. "Sure-footed. Something he could discard that rots fast, inexpensive to replace. Blood stains. He'd want to get rid of the shoes and clothes."

"What color eyes, doctor?" Sheriff Rogers goaded.

"I'll guess—blue!—for no good reason except my former husband has blue eyes and I think of them as beautiful and menacing."

Amid laughter, Ken lifted Joanne to her feet.

"May I use this for an article, Dr. Fleming?" Eldridge asked.

"You may," Joanne said. "But don't quote me by name."

Chapter Six

THE article was false and infuriating. Inference and innuendo woven into a fantasy by some psychologist—he knew it was a psychologist, "His mother would think of him as thoughtful, his father a weak or missing part of this twisted child's life."

Seething, he read on. *Psychopath* was the word "she" used. Using "clues" from the body in Jacksonville, with gossamer hints of that alone, "she" presumed to know what motivated, controlled and "warped" this "psycopath."

No name, but "she" was quoted throughout.

He knew well enough the formidable foe a woman could be. He also knew how to control one. Any woman—*any* woman—get her in the right circumstances and she'd drop that mightier-than-thou facade.

"Brown wavy hair . . . blue eyes . . ."

He read that nervously, glancing about as if his mind were exposed. A wild guess, of course. Postulation, the article admitted. Dangerous postulation.

"Wears tennis shoes . . . to throw away."

He never threw them away. Canvas washed easily, quickly.

The headline was provocative, a sensational attempt to catch the eye: KILLER ON THE PROWL?

He scanned the paragraph listing judges, politicians, the sheriff and attorneys attending a barbecue at the Phillip Dupree lake house. Fine, let them talk. If they followed this woman's advice, he was in no jeopardy.

In fact, the article insinuated that "she" was not well received with her theories. A quote from Sheriff Rogers: "Describe the man and we'll put out a bulletin . . ."

Sarcasm?

He threw the newspaper to the floorboard where the passenger seat should have been. He had removed it. He needed the space. Behind him—he touched it—the tire iron lay beneath a crocus sack.

From here he could see the dark brown double doors of the Breaker Bar, a popular hangout for the college crowd. Between the nightclub and a motel next door, phosphorescent waves broke onto a beach of bleached white sands. From the Breaker Bar came a throb of disco, playing at deafening levels for wall-to-wall dancers, the air thick with smoke and the sweet aroma of pot.

He lifted his arm, looked at the luminous dial of a Seiko diver's watch—10:35. Twenty-five more minutes. Then it would be eight o'clock, Seattle time. *Mork and Mindy* would be over. Evening news past. Dinner dishes done. At eight, Pacific time, he'd call mama and sing her Happy Birthday.

He sat with an elbow in the curve of the steering wheel, clicking his upper teeth with the nail of a forefinger flicked off his lower incisors. He was not ignorant of psychology. He'd learned enough to know the science was woefully imprecise. It was like the study of law—more clinical than applied, and seldom concrete. One learned the ground rules and, with dismay, found that no factor was a constant, no rule inviolate. Yet, psychologists struggled to erect an image, gave out interviews like this one—hoping to delude the uninitiated.

It had been his observation that psychologists made the worst parents, the lousiest spouses, the most tortured citizens. *They* needed a psychologist.

He watched a girl come out of the Breaker Bar, music rising as if a tourniquet had loosened, staunched again by the closing door. She lit a cigarette, stood there in short-shorts, then strolled toward the beach.

He looked at his watch: 10:40. Time moved at a different tempo when anticipation was its keeper. But, commingling with anticipation was a niggle of dread he always felt when he was about to call home.

Mama would like the decanter. It would look great on the dining room credenza. As always, he had shopped carefully, devoted much forethought to the gift—imagining how mama would feel when she received it, what she'd say. But timing was everything. Thus, he must call precisely at eight, Seattle time.

Sweat traced his ribs, mosquitoes buzzing. He felt queasy, skin tacky. In the rearview mirror, he watched a

48

police car pass on busy Highway 98, patroling packed motels and bars.

At 10:59 he walked to a telephone. Earlier, he'd made sure he had ample change. Now, he dialed his number, fed in quarters.

"Hello?"

"Hi," he said. "Is mama there?"

"Is this collect?"

He covered resentment with laughter. "All paid up. Is she there, Malcolm?"

His stepfather shouted, "Edna!" Then questioned, "Where are you?"

"Virginia. Did she get my gift?"

"I think so. Edna! Long distance. Come on." Back to the telephone, "She's painting the hall."

"She is?"

"She never did like that green."

"That's the color she told me to paint it—"

"Well. You know your mother. She's cleaning her hands, hold on. Where in Virginia?"

"Roanoke."

"They have any timber there?"

"Oh, yeah."

"Mount St. Helens blew—did you see it on TV?"

"Yes, I did."

"Weyerhaeuser lost a quarter of their total national forest. I knew two of the men killed at the Number Four Camp."

"I'm sorry."

"Edna, goddamn it, the boy is waiting!"

He could hear Malcolm's heavy breathing. "Are you working?" his stepfather questioned.

"Yes."

"How's it going?"

"It's okay."

"Here's your mother."

"Hi, mama."

"You always catch me up a ladder or out in the yard."

"I thought you'd be done watching TV, dinner over and past—"

"I'm painting."

"The hallway, Malcolm said."

"Yes."

He subdued the ache of disappointment. "I called to sing Happy Birthday." But he didn't.

She said, "At my age, birthdays aren't something you want to think about."

"You're getting better, mama, not older."

She heaved a sigh pregnant with weariness.

"Did you get your gift?" he asked.

"Sure did," she said, flatly. "Thanks."

"I looked at Baccarat," he explained, "but the patterns weren't as good as the one I bought. They had Steuben, but five hundred dollars seemed a bit steep. I really liked the Waterford better, actually."

"Waterford?"

"The decanter. It's Waterford lead crystal. It didn't come broken did it?"

"I don't think so."

"You ought to check it over, mama. It's insured."

"When I get things squared away. Your father wants to know where you're working."

"Uh—it's only part-time, mama. I'm thinking about going back to law school."

"You'll lose credits if you don't go back in Utah."

"I know. But I like it here."

She didn't ask where "here" was. She said, "Your father wants to know if you remember the Number Four Camp —it's that logging camp on the river near—"

"Yes. I know it. Mama—are you doing all right?"

"Tired, but that's normal. I think your father wants to speak to you."

"Mama—"

"Did I tell you I knew two men killed there?" Malcolm's voice rasped.

"Yes, you did."

"If it'd blown a day later, I'd have been there. We were due to start cutting at Camp Four Monday morning. The mountain blew up Sunday. You saw it on TV, you said?"

"Yes, I saw it. May I speak to mama?"

"She's back in the toilet, hold on. Edna! Come'ere!"

Malcolm talked about the devastation, volcanic ash which "came down like dirty snow" and the state of the timber business as a result of the Mt. St. Helens explosion.

The operator interrupted, "Your time is up, sir. Please deposit another three dollars and sixty-five cents."

"Malcolm, is mama coming?"

50

"Edna, this boy is using up his nickels!"

"That will be three dollars and . . ."

He fed coins into the slot. Music from the Breaker Bar rose as a raucous, drunken couple wandered out into the night.

"Hello, Malcolm?"

"Let me see if I can find her," his stepfather grunted.

He heard voices afar, but apparently they had forgotten the phone was off the hook. When the operator demanded more money, he hung up.

He stood, sweat-soaked, swallowing noisily. Briefly, he considered trying to call again, but decided against it. He returned to his car and slammed the doors, chest hurting. He felt behind the seat for the tire iron. Cold, hard, reassuring metal.

A police car entered the opposite end of the parking lot, checking vehicles with a spotlight. He cranked up his motor, turned full circle, and found a place where he could park with his car tag hidden. He fell over on his side until the light arched past, the cruiser going on. Sitting up, he stared at the double doors of the Breaker Bar.

He placed a sling around his neck and cradled his arm. He inserted the tire iron. To any observer, it would appear to be a rigid support, a splint, a cast.

Inside the Breaker Bar, music reverberated with earsplitting volume. He sought a place to sit, passing through with the slung arm held by his "good" hand.

He saw her almost at once. Hair combed evenly to either side, she sat with chin up, an enigmatic smile on wide, full lips. Her companions were more plain, lacking applications of cosmetics which the girl wore, despite the fact she'd obviously spent her day at the beach. Like her friends, she wore shorts and a halter.

He chose a table in front of her and nearby. He ordered a beer. With peripheral vision he watched a man approach, bend to speak, argue briefly, then walk away rebuffed. She was untouchable, her demeanor said; she had merely deigned to sit with these lesser souls.

Many watched her. Some glances overt, others darting and quickly averted if she seemed to notice. She seldom noticed. A pillar of composure among screaming adolescents. A diva mute between arias; a movie starlet incognito; a jewel uncut but of indisputable quality. Yes, she was the *embodiment* of quality.

51

It was a subtle game of psychological dominance. Not once did he glance her way, thereby setting himself apart. She saw him. He felt it. He sipped beer, mouth bereft of saliva, his belly muscles aquiver. The beauty queen's coterie noisily shouted their drink orders, squealing as men's hands crept beneath the table to explore legs.

Impossible to ignore. Yet he ignored her.

A gentle throb in his groin, the music a maddening pulse, dancers gyrating in speckled light reflected from a revolving orb—it became her and him, as if they had been alone in this room.

When she got up to go to the ladies' room, he studiously avoided looking, but from a corner of his eye he missed nothing.

"Want to dance, handsome?" a girl yelled at his ear.

He shook his head, smiling. Stung, she started to turn away, then encouraged by his grin, she pleaded, "Come on, dance!"

He lifted the injured arm and shrugged. She twisted a sour expression, thereby excused, and left to rejoin her companions. The beauty queen had missed none of it.

A game of visual cat-and-mouse, each sorely aware of the other, neither yielding with a direct look—they were two isolated beings out of their element. She gazing not at but beyond him; he following an orchestral beat with gently tapping fingers on the table, his beer gone warm.

Beneath his shirt, the hair of his chest gathered perspiration and he felt sweat run down the calves of his legs. The ache in his abdomen grew, his mouth felt copperish as if he held pennies on his tongue. But his expression remained unconcerned, his lips a simulacrum of her own smile, his chin lifted—the electricity between them like a laser combing space, one world seeking another. He felt a sympathetic resonance and it was as if—in the emptiness of a far galaxy —he had touched her with the knowledge that there was, somewhere out there, a kindred spirit.

When she reached up, head tilted, to push back coiffured hair, he knew he was winning. When she dared adjust her gaze nearer though still not on him, he was certain of success. Against his forearm, the tire iron assumed only his body heat, yet felt hot to bare flesh.

Another girl approached, begged for a dance, and he declined with a beguiling smile, a sorrowful shrug, and it was the hurt arm he gave as his excuse.

"How'd you hurt it?" she yelled.

"Skiing."

"Skiing? Where?"

"Aspen. Colorado."

"I've been to Aspen."

He grew cold to discourage her, nodded politely, until finally she blinked good-by and left. All the while, the beauty queen had ventured to study him overtly, assuming his attention was elsewhere.

He left a dollar on the table. He made his way through the crowded room, finally emerging into the relative cool of outdoors. His lungs were aching, his chest constricted. He readjusted his trousers, his excitement barely controllable.

In his Volkswagen, he sat watching. She would not rush after him, of that he was certain. In fact, had she done so, it would have robbed him of the pleasure of waiting, waiting.

But, when she did come out, her friends screeching around her, she alone scanned the lot. He saw them pile into a customized van, with much slamming of doors. When their motor started, he started his own.

They went to a drive-in, ordered hamburgers. Several of the girls noisily sought a rest room. At last, as midnight waned and his watch approached one, they went to a motel. They had a common room, a normal arrangement with students seeking economy as well as camaraderie.

He watched from across the street as they went up a flight of outside stairs.

He pulled into the lot and parked, left his keys in the ignition, and got out. A slight haze gave halos to street lamps; the metal stair rail was damp with miasma. He went up to the second level, circling on silent rubber soles, and stood in the shadows near a Coca-Cola machine, waiting.

When she came—lured as if by some primal scent—he was there. Still in her shorts and halter, the motel room door left ajar, she pushed quarters into the drink machine.

She heard nothing.

She was senseless and in his arms without a whimper. He carried her downstairs to his car. He dumped her onto the floorboard, where the seat had been, her head to the front, her legs behind the driver's seat. She groaned, but didn't move.

He pulled out and drove away without great speed.

53

But he could have stopped himself. At any point, he could have halted. His moves were, he told himself, the purposeful actions of a professional. Tomorrow, the papers would call it "daring" and the girls upstairs would say it happened "in the wink of an eye."

He put a hand on her as she stirred.

Good.

He turned north, going toward State Highway 20 to the open expanse of pine seedlings and back roads creating a maze of firebreaks.

She moaned again and he soothed, "You're all right. Lie still now. You're all right."

Chapter Seven

WHEN Dr. Thaddeus Kreijewski was peeved, he sounded like a bellows. At this moment, he snorted, stroking his salt-and-pepper Vandyke, his eyes hidden behind the glare of light on his spectacles. "Disappointed, disappointed," he intoned.

"I'm sorry, Thad."

"You of all people know the value of public relations, Joanne. But this—" he thumped the newspaper article with the back of a hand, "is really disappointing."

"My name isn't mentioned," she said, lamely.

"Doesn't have to be!" His coarse eyebrows rose. "The word criminology is here. The term, 'psychological profile' is here. That says it all. As a matter of truth, I wish your name were mentioned. Then at least *all* criminologists wouldn't be shrouded under the same blanket of speculation and sensationalism."

He meant the "wavy brown hair and blue eyes"; he meant the headline: KILLER ON THE PROWL?

"We are reduced to shamanism," he stroked, snorted. "Little more than necromancers conjuring up the dead for facts concerning their demise."

54

"I don't think the general public will respond quite that strongly."

"The general public is not my concern," he said. "I am far more worried about any young person out there who may be considering coming to Florida State University to attend the school of criminology. Far more concerned. This article has twin faults: those who come because of it will be expecting a course in crystal-ball gazing; those who know what criminology is will be driven away by the unprofessional misuse of facts. Lack of facts!"

"I'm very sorry, Thad. I wasn't being guarded and—"

"You were misquoted."

"No," she confessed. "I said all that. But I wasn't thinking of the end result. However, I would stand behind my statements if pushed to do so."

He swore in Polish. It was his tone and expression which carried intent. Joanne clasped her hands to still them.

"You did not explain how a profile is composed. You did not add a strong disclaimer. You did not even accept responsibility for the interview."

"I see that now."

He tweaked his beard, a tic forming under one spectacle. As he gazed at Joanne, the reflection of fluorescent lights appeared to replace his pupils. "I don't know what can be done to undo this," he said.

"Thad, I made a mistake, but it isn't a calamity. I think you're overwrought."

"Um," he said. "Um, um, um! I spend fourteen years elevating a small college department of criminology. I come to this provincial—" he paused, face contorted, "town! What are the odds, I asked myself, of making this school one of the best, with Michigan State and the State University of New York at Albany as my competition?"

"And you have done it."

"I bid five spades when I came here."

"And won."

"We have finally been recognized, justifiably so, as the best school of criminology in the nation. The world."

"I know that."

"Now this."

For a moment, she feared he might actually shed tears. His voice choked. "Joanne, why would you say 'wavy brown hair and blue eyes'? You can't possibly draw such a conclusion from any known facts short of an eyewitness."

55

"I know, Thad. I say I was—not thinking."

"And this—" he adjusted the extension of his arm to the focal point of his glasses. " 'He's a handsome devil,' she said. 'Charming, witty, educated, above average intelligence. Monday's child born at midnight, fair of face and full of grace.' Joanne, this is blatant poppycock."

"It is an assumption, Thad, I have to admit that. But I have reason to believe—"

"That he's *handsome*? Witty? Charming? Jehoshaphat!"

"Based on the victims, girls who would be skeptical of a man's advances—"

"You don't know the method of assault. You're guessing."

"I think the article says it is 'postulating,' " Joanne countered.

"Who knows what postulating means?" he cried. "The education of the average American reader is eighth grade. They'll think he's holding a pose."

Enough. Joanne arose stiffly. "I apologize, Thad. But I happen to believe I'm right on the money in that article."

"I'll accept that," he said. "Prove your theory."

"I have no proof as such."

"Then point made." He motioned her out, brusquely, answering the ring of his telephone. But she no sooner reached the exit when he called her back.

"Sheriff Rogers," Thad said, phone covered. "He'd like all the evidence we have so he can pursue your murderer."

Joanne took the phone. "Good morning, sheriff."

"Stirred us up a stink, Jo."

"How's that?"

"The telephone has been ringing all morning. Fathers with daughters in school, folks who claim the killer is a neighbor."

"Tell them to read the article carefully, sheriff. It doesn't claim the killer is in Tallahassee."

"This is an election year, Jo. Suppose the killer *is* in Tallahassee?"

"There have been no murders of this type in your jurisdiction, sheriff. You're off the hook."

"Shall I refer all such calls to you?" he threatened. "Or should I call in the reporters and suggest this was the drivel of an inebriated woman?"

"All right," Joanne said, evenly, "I'll call the reporter and do a follow-up."

"No you don't," he warned. "Better to let this hoax fade away than to reinforce it."

"I would avoid use of the word 'hoax,' sheriff."

"What do you suggest, Fleming? You have claimed a killer is on the prowl. You have attributed more than fifteen murders to this man. People are frightened."

"I'll have to think about this."

He hung up and she turned to replace the phone. Dean Kreijewski was looking at her. "Distraught?"

"Highly."

"Um," he grunted.

She returned to her office, face flushed. When she entered, Tony Eldridge from the *Democrat* was there and Bea didn't appear happy.

"Messages," Bea said, cryptically.

"May I talk to you, Dr. Fleming?" Tony asked.

"Come in." Joanne leafed through her calls—two psychiatrists, forensic specialists at State, a practicing criminologist—

"Dr. Fleming, our article has stirred a great deal of interest," Tony said.

"Yes, it has."

"My editor suggested we do another article and I was wondering—"

Joanne raised a hand, "Mr. Eldridge, I'm afraid I've done us both a disservice."

"Dr. Fleming," Bea on the intercom, "Bud Diehl calling."

"Excuse me," Joanne said, lifting the phone; "Hello, Bud."

"Jo, that third body hasn't been identified. I'm sending a telex to the police departments with jurisdiction."

"Good, Bud."

"I guess you got a call from Panama City?"

"No."

"Night before last a college girl vanished on the way from her motel room to a soft drink machine."

"Any witnesses?"

"Not yet. It was after one A.M. There were blood spatters around the drink machine. They're running type on it today."

"Thanks, Bud." Her stomach knotted.

When she hung up, Bea was at the door. "Shall I hold your calls?"

57

To Eldridge, Joanne said, "I can talk to you if you will excuse the interruptions. Otherwise, we'll have to set up an appointment."

"If you don't mind, I don't."

"In which case," Bea reported, "Marcie is on the line."

"Yes, Marcie?" Joanne said, crisply.

"Mom, I'm going over to spend the night with a friend."

"Is that a statement or a request?"

"Whichever cuts it."

"Neither cuts it," Joanne snapped. "You still have a week of school, Marcie."

"Mom, nothing's going down!"

"We'll talk about it tonight." Joanne hung up.

The reporter pushed up heavy eyeglasses with the eraser of his pencil. "What I had in mind was this, Dr. Fleming —more of an in-depth piece about the psychological quirks which create such a killer as you've profiled."

She was considering this on one level, but her mind was churning. Dean Kreijewski should be consulted. Sheriff Rogers would be furious, and for that she couldn't blame him. Yet, the missing girl in Panama City—and with nothing more known, she felt tingling intuition again—perhaps the public should be alerted, albeit more responsibly.

". . . something about the kind of parents he probably has," Tony Eldridge was explaining. "Most people cannot conceive of a man so brutal and yet, as you tell it, he's sane."

"Yes," Joanne noted. "Sane."

"Perhaps we should begin with a definition of sanity," Tony said.

"Dr. Fleming," Bea's voice from the intercom, "Ken calling."

"Hey, Jo," Ken's voice was deep, calm, "how's it feel to be the talk of the town?"

"I'm bleeding," Joanne said.

"I came by your office and saw the reporter there."

"Any suggestions?"

"Promise to keep him posted and send him home."

"That's a good idea."

"How about lunch?"

"Can't."

"Dinner?"

"Maybe."

"Bye."

"Bye," she said. Then, smiling, "Tony—may I call you Tony?"

"Certainly."

"Tony, could you hold off this interview? I'm sorry but I'm snowed under this morning, as you can see. It doesn't promise to let up."

He stood. "May I make an appointment with your secretary?"

"Why don't you call next week?"

His stance altered slightly and Joanne recognized a hardening of attitude.

"Something is about to break, isn't it?" the reporter questioned.

"I don't know."

He nodded. Joanne considered trying to induce complacency with a vow of future information. But she saw by his face, he already sensed a developing news story.

"Thanks for your time, Dr. Fleming."

"Thank you for coming."

As he departed, Joanne sank lower in her chair.

"Ken calling," Bea announced.

"Hey, Ken."

"I saw him leave."

"Where are you?"

"Next door office."

"Come in, you joker."

A moment later, he entered, baseball cap at a jaunty angle, winking at Bea in passing.

"My professional butt is in hot water," Joanne said.

"Yep."

"I'm sure I deserve it."

"Yep."

"Thanks for the support."

"Hey," he crooned, "I'm with you. You can be happy you didn't do a strip at that party, that's all."

"I've been duly chastened."

"Bunk," Ken said, seriously. "That reporter saw you were in no condition at the party to grant an interview. Yet he made his article read like one. He was there to do a society column and things were dull, so you livened up his evening."

"Meaning he used me."

"Absolutely."

Joanne took another call. "Hello, Fleming speaking."

"Jo, this is Ralph."

"Yes, Ralph."

"Is that killer story your doing?"

"Yes."

"Well you asked for it," Ralph sniffed. "State Attorney wants me to request any and all evidence you have."

"I have no evidence. Tell him to call Bud Diehl, homicide, Jacksonville."

"Uh-uh, honey," Ralph snuffled. "He knows a cream puff when he sees one. He wants *you.*"

"Forget it."

"Suit yourself." Ralph was too amenable for comfort. He sniffed again.

"I'm not a detective or a politician, Ralph. Tell him that."

"Right-o. I'll tell him."

"Ralph, what's going on?"

"Politics, Jo. Good old politics. Sheriff Rogers was on the noon news reassuring the public that if there was a rapist-murderer here, he'd get what the Swain rapist got—fifteen years in prison."

"Fifteen years!"

"Thank God I didn't represent that poor bastard."

"I have to go, Ralph."

She met Ken's gaze. "They gave Swain fifteen years."

"That's what I heard."

"Justice," Joanne said bitterly, standing. "Come on, I'll take you up on the offer for lunch."

The Cypress Rooming House was on College Avenue, up a hill from the FSU campus, near the Tallahassee business district. Here, he was "Bob Brantley," a night student who sold hearing aids by referral from magazine ads. Which, indeed, he did, periodically. His best sales pitch was a low-key monotone that was better persuasion than anything he could say.

Without air conditioning, the rooming house became insufferable by noon, and most students found reason to seek cooler locales. The building, a two-story structure, was loosely run by an overweight matron who admitted new tenants with one admonishment: "Girls on the first floor; after eight P.M. you stay on the second floor—no mixing." The home-style meals offered twice a day were all-you-can-eat and wholesome, so the building remained booked and the permanent residence for twenty-five erstwhile students.

He sat in a wicker rocker in his small, private room, dressed only in jockey-type underwear, reading again the tattered remnants of the article. "By Tony Eldridge."

An oscillating fan swung in a half circle, drying perspiration. He would dress as soon as his body cooled from a tepid shower. His choices: "hot" and "tepid." There was no "cold" in the faucets.

He'd been simmering emotionally, as well as physically, debating how to approach his "problem." He had considered various plans, including outright assault, which was oddly repugnant. It suggested the wrath of vengeance, a loss of control. But one thing was certain, this woman's ego needed to be leavened. There were too many of these psychologists, or whatever she was, flaunting pseudo-factual fantasies about "psycopaths."

What she needed was a good lesson.

Well.

He was the one to give it to her.

Get her out of the rarified strata of academia, put her under the right circumstances—she'd squeal, just like they all did.

He grabbed himself, squeezing, teeth clamped.

He would be aloof. Completely detached and aloof. Not emotionally involved, that was it. The trick would be, get *her* emotionally involved while he remained surgical and analytical, completely in control.

She'd know something about psychology then.

He dressed in Perma-pressed polyester slacks, matching socks, Hush Puppy loafers and a knit shirt. Immediately, he was soaked with perspiration. Outside, heat radiated from concrete and cobblestones, undulating waves rising to scorch his eyes and nostrils. It got hot and humid in Oregon and Washington, but nothing like this.

He walked two blocks to a pay telephone, which some industrious student had manipulated so it gave free calls. He dialed the Tallahassee *Democrat*.

"Tony Eldridge, please."

"Yo?" Tony cried. "This is Eldridge, can you speak a little louder?"

"Listen, Tony," he kept his voice down, "this is Bob; we met at Phillip Dupree's party."

"Who?" The reporter was yelling over the din of his surroundings.

"What was that lady's name? The one talking about the mind of a criminal? Somebody ought to write an article on that."

"You mean Fleming? I *did*. Didn't you see Monday's paper?"

"No, I didn't. Well, I've forgotten her first name. I thought maybe I could do an article about her. You already wrote an article?"

"Monday's paper—could you talk a little louder?"

"You mind if I do a story too? A different angle, of course."

"Help yourself. Listen, what'd you say your name is?"

"No, no, I asked what was *her* name?"

"Fleming. From FSU—Joanne, I think. Now tell me again, who are you?"

He mumbled, then louder, "Tampa *Trib*. I'm only visiting. I'll read your article—Monday's paper, you say?"

"Yeah—"

He hung up. Fleming. Joanne. FSU.

That's all he needed.

Chapter Eight

WHEN Joanne asked Ralph for a dinner meeting, he had stalled, checking his calendar, grumbling before yielding. His resentment was irritating, but justified. Once he had accused, "I can tell the magnitude of your need by the place you suggest we meet." Tonight, out of deference for his preference for steak, Joanne had suggested the Brown Derby, off North Monroe Street. She was already seated at a secluded table in a rear corner when he arrived punctually at seven.

He lifted the tablecloth, saw her briefcase and asked, "What ulterior motive, Jo?"

Before she could reply, he addressed the waiter, "Two

martinis very dry. No. Make that Tanqueray on the rocks with a side dish of olives."

"Yessir."

"*Tanqueray*, young man."

"Yessir."

Ralph cocked his head and gazed at Joanne. "So?"

"If you'd prefer to be social first, we may, Ralph."

"My abdomen is doing a figure eight. If you will drop the bomb, I can at least try to relax. Is it Marcie?"

"No."

"What then?"

"The Swain case."

"Swain? You mean the rapist."

"Yes."

"Oh, damn, Jo."

"It's a travesty of justice, Ralph. Fifteen years at Raiford is in itself criminal. I think I've found at least one cause for appeal and—"

She reached for her briefcase but Ralph took her wrist. "Jo, justice was done. He was guilty."

"He was indigent," Joanne said, sharply.

"He had good representation. I know that young attorney. He's sharp, well educated, capable—"

"—inexperienced, awed by Judge Alcorn, and underpaid for the defense of Swain."

"That doesn't mean Swain isn't guilty."

"He is guilty," Joanne labored, evenly, "but he is not the menace to society his sentence would indicate. He'll have to serve at least three years before he faces a parole board. They tried him like a hardened criminal."

"Jo." Ralph's blue eyes darted here, there, returned, "I don't have time to take this on. I'm up to my Adam's apple in a very big case that requires hundreds of hours of tedious meetings with accountants, Florida enforcement, the FBI—I can't take on the Swain case and do it justice."

They lapsed into silence as the drinks arrived. Then, Ralph said, "Besides, they'll appeal the thing almost automatically."

"That's a good word for it, 'automatically.' Swain needs somebody clever enough to turn this thing around."

"Damn it, Jo. I'm not on the public dole. I'm trying to pay two junior associates and three secretaries. I have a nut of four hundred a day just to break even."

63

Joanne sat back, holding her martini with both hands, staring at it.

"Besides," Ralph reasoned, "Swain would have to fire the public defender and I'd have an enemy forever in that young lawyer. He needs the money. He needs the practice. He needs the case! Talk to him."

"I did. He can't afford to devote any more investigative time to the matter."

"Well, neither can I." Ralph glared across the room. "You have to be a crusader, don't you? You make me feel like a bloodsucking leech. I can't jump into every miscarriage of the judicial process. You know that Judge Alcorn would be unhappy about being overturned on a case as . . . as nothing as Swain."

"Okay," Joanne said, bitterly.

Ralph sniffed and sipped his martini. Sniff. He downed the drink and snapped his fingers for the waiter. "Is that Tanqueray?"

"I specified Tanqueray, sir."

"You go back there and tell your bartender I want *Tanqueray*. This time make it a double."

The waiter gone, Joanne said, "Ralph, this is Tanqueray."

"Who can tell when there's more water from ice cubes than gin?" He sniffed, took a deep breath and sighed. "One damned thing after another," he said.

"I'm sorry, Ralph. I know it's an imposition to ask this of you."

"It is, Jo. I'm in something so important I can't sleep nights and I don't know what to do about it."

"Want to talk about it?"

"I can't."

The waiter returned, awaiting Ralph's first sip. Ralph nodded, looked up at the young man and nodded again.

"The thing is," Ralph lowered his voice, "miscarriage of justice comes in degrees and intensities. Swain got shafted. I see it. Any sensible person sees it. Guilt does not connote societal responsibility. I'll accept the theory that poverty, deprivation and poor education contribute to crime. But what of the privileged sonofabitch who becomes a criminal? He's the one who should really get burned by the law. He abused the law, the social order, and for no good reason except he's greedy."

"You're beginning to sound like me," Joanne said.

"I don't take that as an insult."

"None intended."

"Well, I can tell you this." Ralph lowered his voice further. "I'm sitting on a very hot situation. The bastard is guilty as original sin, but he's powerful. If I strike a deal with him I can bag a lot of secondary people and let myself off the hook politically. But if I go for the bigwig, and if I don't nail his coffin shut, I'm dead in politics from now until hell is an ice rink."

"Marcie said you were giving him immunity."

"Marcie! What does Marcie know?"

"She said you were giving immunity to the big shot, settling for the little fish."

Perspiration beaded Ralph's brow and he looked gray. "This is the biggest secret since the Manhattan Project. There aren't five people in the whole state who know what we're investigating. How did Marcie hear about it?"

"I don't know. I thought you might have told her."

Ralph gulped gin. "She could blow this whole thing. I could be ruined and don't even know it. I could be a corpse sitting here right this minute and I just thought I heard my heart beating."

"You know how Marcie is, Ralph. She's her father's daughter. She may have overheard a telephone conversation, or—"

"No, no," he protested. "Impossible! I wouldn't have discussed this with anyone. No one! Everybody on the street probably knows about this."

"I doubt that, Ralph."

"We've got to shut Marcie's mouth, Jo."

"You want to put out a contract on her? I'll take it, if the price is right."

"No kidding, Jo." He was ghostly. "If Judge Alcorn gets a whisper of this—"

"Alcorn?"

He slapped his forehead with a palm. "I'm ruined," he wheezed. "Seduced by a divorced woman and destroyed by the fruit of my loins. I'm ruined."

"Ralph," Joanne said, genuinely, "let's drink our drinks, eat our meal and talk this through. Marcie is a smart girl. If she really knew anything she would've said nothing. So what we can assume is, she's guessing."

"You think that?"

"I know that."

"I hope so. Do you think she suspects it's Judge——" Ralph looked around, furtively, "What's'isname?"

"No. I'm sure she doesn't know."

"Now you see my situation." Ralph talked with lips immobile. "He's up for Supreme Court justice. He's probably the single most powerful man in the Florida Bar. But——and goddamn it, I want to weep when I say it——he's a common criminal."

"In what way?"

"Money. Bribes. Kickbacks. The scandal is going to bring down this administration."

"I see."

"That's one reason I can't take the Swain thing. I can't risk it, Jo. I can't take a chance on Alcorn crying 'prejudice' or 'vengeance.' "

"That's ridiculous."

"Of course it is," he wailed softly. "But I still can't risk it."

"Then perhaps you could counsel Swain's attorney, the young public defender."

"He won't permit that."

"He says he'd be grateful."

"You already discussed this with him?"

"Yes."

Ralph shook his head, pained. "I don't know why I try to resist," he said. "You're a psychologist. I am putty. All right."

"You'll do it?"

"Advise, yes. Actual appeal, no."

"Fair enough."

Ralph circled the rim of his glass with a forefinger, pensive. "Would you go for the biggie, Jo? Or take the smart route?"

"The biggie may be the smart route."

"Not if I stumble."

"You won't."

"I'm not so sure. I'll be up against one of the toughest legal brains in the state. Alcorn will have a battery of the best, and most eager, defense attorneys."

"You can beat them."

"I don't know."

"Listen, you." Joanne seized his cuff. "You're the finest attorney in this state. In the South! You are careful, meticulous, methodical and precise. You, of all people, know this is true. You will present a case so tight, the judge will be done before he tries to muster a defense. In fact, he *won't* have eager and able attorneys, they'll be scared to accept because you prepared the prosecution. They're ambitious, but they aren't dumb."

"You really think so? No smoke?"

"No smoke. And I *know* so."

Appreciatively, Ralph leaned over and kissed her. In silence, they drank their martinis, ordered more.

"That child of ours," Ralph mused. He laughed, softly.

"She's turned from the same stone as her father," Joanne said. "She's brilliant, independent, and capable of driving me to despondency as she carves out her own identity."

"I guess I stand accused."

"It isn't a condemnation, Ralph. She can also be gentle, warm, loving, kind, generous and so excruciatingly adorable she makes my heart ache. That's like her father, too."

He kept his head down, but peered at her, sheepishly. "On my death bed," Ralph murmured, "I'm sure I will dread going to hell for the things I've done to you."

"Of course you will. I intend to stand beyond the glass of the viewing room, watching you sizzle in perdition."

"Yeah."

"However," she took his hand, "I'll petition for oil-burners so the devil won't make you shovel coal."

They contemplated one another, a familiar lump in their throats. Later, over superb steaks and a fine claret, they discussed Marcie's college years looming just beyond the horizon. Joanne relented to Ralph's persistent questions and outlined her thoughts on the murderer described in Tony Eldridge's article.

"Chilling," Ralph concluded.

"Yes, it is. He's a man distorted by environment, with a personality convoluted by parents who probably would not know what they've done. He's the most deadly of predators. Something sets him off—the physical appearance of his victims, perhaps. Something. Then, at that instant, he becomes completely murderous. Otherwise—and I'm only guessing—he's probably a man who lives an existence without conflict. Except within. Within, he's tortured."

"Because of his crimes?"

"No. He feels no contrition for the murders. He looks back on the acts of torture with the detached air of someone who observed a particularly violent and emotional movie. It's real, but unreal. He probably examined his own thinking about it and is mystified, maybe even slightly disturbed, because he sees no compassion within himself. Yet, he knows he has been compassionate under certain conditions, with certain people."

"Crazy, then."

"No. Sane."

"This is where I differ with you psychologists," Ralph said. "You describe someone like this maniac, then you say he's not insane. How could anyone do such things and be sane?"

"If he is insane," Joanne said, "that settles that. He's not responsible for his crimes, by reason of insanity. If he's insane, he cannot control his passions, he is a victim of his compulsions. Insane, he might not remember the assault itself. But insane criminals generally get caught quickly because they make no effort to hide their crimes. I believe this man is sane. He can strike, or not strike, as he wills. In the face of danger, he can withdraw. He has control. He remembers it all. In fact, he fantasizes about this aspect or that of his crime. It is his sanity, his control, which makes him so awesomely deadly. As you know, when a criminal knows right from wrong, when he's capable of *not* committing a crime to protect himself—he's legally sane."

"Well," Ralph extended a leg to reach in his pocket, "I'm glad that's your line of work and not mine. You're very good at it, as you well realize. But having to study such people is depressing."

"Somebody has to do it."

"Yes, I suppose." Ralph gave the waiter a credit card. "But—and I've asked myself this repeatedly—why you?"

"It's interesting work."

"I can understand how somebody evolves into an unpleasant line of work," Ralph said. "Such as being a coroner, doing autopsies. Life has a way of sucking us into vocations almost against our will. But you set out to study criminology. You deliberately specialized in sex crimes."

Why did she feel defensive? Ralph wasn't belittling, berating. Yet, his gaze was unnerving. He shrugged his shoulder, correcting his posture. "It doesn't matter," he said. "I was only curious."

"I don't know why I do it," Joanne blurted.

He signed the check, took back his credit card. "See, that would worry me," he said. "I'd want to know what made *me* tick, before I worried about anybody else."

"You know what they say about psychologists," Joanne laughed. "They need to see a shrink."

She couldn't assess his expression, standing in the shadows outside the restaurant, his face dark. "I enjoyed it, Ralph."

"Do it again sometime," he said crisply.

In that instant, as it always did upon parting, the last fragment of familiarity fell away. A moment ago, close friends and confidants; now, business acquaintances going separate ways. Once spouse and lover—now old flames who'd briefly reminisced. She watched him drive away without a backward glance. In the dark, she choked down recriminations. There were, she told herself, "two sides" to every story. There always were.

She'd heard his side often enough. By now she could recite it. Joanne unlocked her vehicle and suddenly threw her briefcase across the front seat with such force she heard vinyl crack.

Alone, she burst into tears.

The window air conditioner humming, drapes drawn and the bedroom door latched, Joanne lay staring into the dark. Ken massaged her thigh, breathing heavily, his moment near.

Swain . . . rapist . . . her mouth was acid as she contemplated defending the man. She would, of course: that was the professional thing to do.

"In all things psychological, be methodical and detached, Joanne . . ." Papa's voice from the past, his brooding dark eyes assessing the daughter at his knee. "If there is a single failure of the psychologist," papa said, "it is the inability to become detached and remain professional. Do always the professional thing, regardless of your personal emotions and—"

"Jo, you all right?" Ken asked softly.

"Yes, Ken."

He continued.

Marcie was spending the night with a girl friend. With "nothing going down" during this final week of school, there really was no reason to refuse the child her request. So Joanne had consented.

". . . do always the professional thing . . ." Joanne squirmed with the thought.

"Jo?" Ken's breath was moist on her neck. She'd broken rhythm.

She stroked his back, soothing, "I'm fine."

More aware of her movement, more compliant and attentive, she wanted to hurry him, without haste. *Attorneys defend men they abhor . . . surgeons save despicable beings . . . the professional psychologist had a responsibility, too*—the muted thud of a car door made her jump.

"Jo?"

"Sorry."

For a moment he lay still, then withdrew.

"Ken—I'm sorry."

He sat on the side of the bed, back to her. She reached out, touched his bare leg. "Ken, I'm sorry. Forgive me."

"It's all right." He arose, went into the bathroom. Joanne heard the commode flush, a pelt of water as he turned on the shower. *Damn it.*

Going to the bathroom door, eyes narrowed against the glare of light, Joanne said, "If you want a bath, I'll bathe you."

"It's okay." He pulled the curtain closed, shutting her out.

"Please forgive me, darling."

"Don't worry about it."

She stood there, nude, silently cursing herself. Ken poked his head around the curtain, water dripping from thatched brows. "Little girl," he said, "daddy isn't through playing house. Daddy just knows when to wait awhile."

She put her fingertips against his wet face and nodded, without smiling.

"Jo, can you sit in here with me?"

She took the only seat available.

"Know what I've been wondering?" His voice rose behind the curtain, his form barely seen through opaque fabric.

"What have you been wondering?"

"Whether you'd like living in Detroit or someplace."

"Not Detroit, no."

"How about Cleveland, Chicago or New York?"

Joanne pinched the bridge of her nose between thumb and ring finger.

"No deal, right?" Ken called.

70

"I like Tallahassee, actually."

"Right. That's what I thought."

After a very long time, Joanne inquired, "Would you drink coffee if I made some?"

"Sure would," he said.

"I'm going to the kitchen, then."

She threw on a terry cloth robe, cinched it at the waist and walked the long carpeted hall to the kitchen. Angry with herself, she made a clatter of this and that, shoving aside utensils in the sink to fill a percolator with water. Then in frustration, she seized the edge of the counter, eyes closed, groaning aloud.

Maybe Ralph was right, it was herself she'd better learn first.

But wasn't oneself the topic all psychologists considered most often and at greatest length? The longest running, constantly considered show in town—Joanne Fleming, as reviewed by Dr. Joanne Fleming!

Disappointment with herself twisted into anger at Ken. He was taking a job in another city. Leaving her. Wasn't he? That veiled offer to go along was neither a proposal of matrimony (which she didn't really want) nor was it a plea for illicit companionship. "Think you'd like to live in Detroit . . ."

"Damn him!" Joanne said aloud.

Her own voice made her open her eyes. The percolator, "do not immerse," was overflowing.

She sagged against the counter, gazing out the kitchen window into the night.

A shadow in the yard caught her eye and Joanne leaned close to the window, peering.

A dog? Too large for a dog. She went to the light and extinguished it, returning to the window above the sink. Her eyes adjusting to the darkness, she searched the shadows. Nothing.

But—along the low fence bordering rose bushes, there was a patch of moonlight, an almost imperceptible patch of—

Somebody?

Some *thing*.

A rag perhaps, thrown over the fence to dry after Marcie washed the car this afternoon. The driveway was adjacent to the fence. Yes, that was it. A washcloth hung out to dry.

71

But, as she thought this, it moved.

With the windows closed, she couldn't be sure—the trees gave no evidence of a breeze. Shadow patterns fell in a chiaroscuro patchwork across patio and yard. Through the farthest hedge to the rear, a light from the next street over winked amid the bushes.

Nothing.

Nevertheless, she stood waiting, as if to outwait something, breathing almost not at all—watching.

"Hey!" Ken called, and Joanne wheeled, startled, as he flipped on a light and confronted her, nude, grinning. "How come you're in the dark?" he asked.

"I thought I saw something out back."

Ken glanced through the window, reaching for her. "I don't see anything. Give me a kiss and a cup of coffee."

As he hugged her, she laid her head on Ken's chest—but she was still watching.

"Ken!" Joanne shrieked.

He jumped back.

"There was a face at the window," Joanne cried.

Ken ran to the rear door, threw it wide, and naked, stood on the patio as though ready for combat.

Trembling, she followed, watching him poke through shrubbery.

"Are you sure?" he asked.

Was she sure? Her own reflection, perhaps. A child playing Peeping Tom—

Ken returned, took her in his arms. "You know something, Jo? I think you're spending too much time with your work. It's getting to you."

Somewhere out front, down the street, she heard a motor start—a familiar sound, since many students had them . . .

A Volkswagen drove by, motor puttering, and faded into the night.

Chapter Nine

KEN stood on a small utility ladder to reach the patio light. The globe removed, he replaced the corroded fixture and began reassembling the exterior covering.

"What's happening, Mr. Blackburn?" Charlie slammed the back door, bumped against the ladder and stood gazing up at Ken.

"What say, Charlie?" Ken pointed at his toolbox. "Hand me a Phillips screwdriver, will you?"

Marcie put a pitcher of iced lemonade on the redwood table. "Mom, we need to talk."

Joanne closed her book on one finger, holding her place.

"Woman-to-woman," Marcie said.

"Is this something we can discuss here?" Joanne asked. "Or should we go inside?"

"Everybody I know is having sex," Marcie said.

"I doubt everybody," Joanne replied.

"Most everybody but the lame and halt," Marcie insisted. "Anyway. So I'm thinking about having sex with Charlie."

Charlie dropped the toolbox.

"You can only fight off a biological urge so long," Marcie noted. "We spend half our time wrestling, the other half debating. I like Charlie all right. Not love. But love isn't what it's cracked up to be anyhow. I mean, love isn't needed for sex, right?"

"Perhaps we do need to go inside," Joanne suggested.

"No, no," Marcie dabbed lemonade from her lips, "seems to me this ought to be a communal discussion."

"Communal?"

"Charlie thinks I ought to protect myself," Marcie declared. "Which is to say, he refuses to wear a prophylactic."

"Marcie—" Charlie squeaked.

73

"Marcie," Joanne countered, "don't you think this is something better discussed in private?"

"Something gets lost in the translation if we do that," Marcie said.

"What?"

"You discuss it with me, I repeat it to Charlie. He comes up with arguments why we ought to do it anyway, I come back for your rebuttal—it would be easier to go on and get this out of the way here and now. So. I was thinking about taking the pill. What do you think about that?"

Ken took apart the light fixture again. Joanne watched Charlie gather the tools, replacing them in the box.

"A girl has to start sometime," Marcie lamented. "The pressure is terrific. But I don't know . . . it seems awfully sweaty and sticky to me. Still, every other girl is putting out, Charlie says—"

Charlie's eyes rolled back.

"How old were you when you started putting out, mom?"

"It is not your question I object to," Joanne said, "as much as the terminology."

"Oh." Marcie looked across the yard. "Well, then," she said, "at what age did you begin to indulge in premarital sex?"

"I was married," Joanne said. Marcie's expression made her add, "Almost. Your father and I were engaged."

"He was the first?"

"Yes."

"Things've changed," Marcie said. "But that explains your lingering attachment to daddy, emotionally. A girl always has a lifelong attachment to the man who breaks her hymen."

"Marcie!"

"Which is one reason I've held off with Charlie, if you want to know the truth." She turned to the beet-red boy. "No offense, Charlie. But since the experience will mark me emotionally, for life, I'd like it to happen somewhere besides on the hood of a Triumph convertible mired up to the axle in red clay on a rainy night."

Ken withered Charlie with a glare.

Mustering aplomb, Joanne put aside her book. "The decision to begin is, as you've said, lifelong. It isn't the act of sex that should concern you, so much as the emotional residue which redounds from it."

74

Marcie winked at Charlie. "She makes it sound pure, doesn't she? Go on, mom."

"In any relationship," Joanne counseled, "it is the emotional, not the physical, which should be of paramount concern."

"Like you and Ken," Marcie said.

Uncertain, Joanne said, "Yes. Like us. But a relationship between any two people has its cost and profit. We pay emotionally whether we're dealing with boyfriends, husbands, heterosexuals, or otherwise. Thus, it is always wise to ask the final question first. That is, what profit or loss will come of this action."

"Right," Marcie said.

"Sex is more than physical, Marcie. Much more. In a James Michener novel I read a great line: 'Contrary to popular opinion, most intercourse in marriage is conversation, not sex.'"

Ken poured a glass of lemonade and gave it to Charlie. He poured another for himself and sat at the table.

"It's difficult to say no." Marcie looked pained. "Charlie wants to do it so bad he's got hot rocks and—"

"Marcie," Joanne said, firmly, "perhaps first you should learn the terms which describe your thoughts."

"His testicles hurt," Marcie amended. "I *like* Charlie. I don't want to make an enemy out of him. I want us to go together. I just don't especially want to put out. It's all we talk about! Charlie says we ought to get it out of the way so we can go on to more substantial things."

If Charlie's throat had been cut, he wouldn't have bled a drop—his flush had gone stark white. Joanne took his wrist, pulling him to sit beside her. She put an arm around the tortured boy's shoulder. "This subject," Joanne said, "is the oldest single topic since Adam and Eve. All the persuasions, all the arguments, all the debates you can conjure—all have been used millions of times by boys and girls since the beginning of man."

"I want to do what's right," Charlie croaked.

"Of course you do," Joanne said. "So does Marcie. And doing what's right is not always an easy choice. Nor, for that matter, is 'right' always right, or wrong. The time, place, age, person, and emotional stability of the two people make 'right' wrong, or right again."

"I don't want to get knocked up," Marcie said.

"Marcie. Terminology, please."

"Pregnant," Marcie corrected. "But one of these nights, I'm going to give in. I may not have had enough sleep, or I may be weak from not eating—"

"From not eating?" Ken said. "That I doubt."

"Or, I may just be horny myself," Marcie admitted. "Women go into estrus, too, you know."

"The human seems less susceptible to that than other animals," Joanne said. "However, the responsibility for doing this—or avoiding it—should be shared by both you and Charlie."

Charlie stared at his feet, Joanne's arm still around his shoulder.

"There are alternatives to copulation," Marcie sighed. "But if you're going to do *those,* why not go all the way?" Marcie looked from her mother to Ken. "You do know what I'm talking about."

"Surprisingly, yes," Ken said.

"But Charlie gets sick to his stomach, sometimes," Marcie reported. "I can't help wondering whether it's fair for me to make him go through that."

"I could take a cold shower maybe," Charlie offered.

"Boys don't think about the terrific emotional baggage we girls have to carry," Marcie said. "We have to face menstrual cramps and possible pregnancy. I don't want to be frigid, but I also worry—and *would* worry, even if I were on the pill."

"It's something to worry about," Joanne agreed.

"Then I'd face the agony of marriage, which I'm not ready to face," Marcie continued, "or abortion which I don't object to, but I don't know if I could go through with it, if it were me."

"These are very adult considerations," Joanne said. "This is part of the emotional thing we're talking about."

"Before you're married," Marcie mocked a minister's sepulchral tones, "desist and be chaste. Be not polygamous. Marry and be monogamous. But after the divorce—hey, go at it."

Ken's face set.

"Being married," Marcie said, "present or past tense, is a license to be promiscuous. So, in the face of that silly contradiction, most girls these days say nuts, and go ahead and have sex."

Ken lifted a thick finger as if asking permission to speak. When Joanne nodded, Ken twisted to face Marcie. "After all the talk is over," he said, "are you going to go ahead, anyway?"

"I don't know yet."

"I suspect all this talk won't change a thing," Ken predicted. "So, let me tell you: going to bed with some guy is not 'this one time.' It's forever. It's like being pregnant—that's forever, too. The same with being married. Even after a divorce, the marriage has happened and never again as long as you live, *never* can you wear the traditional white dress which says you're a virgin. Your clothes may be white at the next wedding—but inside, you aren't dressed in white. That may or may not be important, but it's true. Nobody can tell you what to do about this."

"Ken," Joanne attempted, "I think—"

"Nobody," Ken persisted. "It's like jumping off a tall building. Once it's been done, you can't go back. With that in mind, you do whatever you're going to do. Whatever your decision, you have to live with it."

He turned to Charlie and added, "Believe it or not, so do you."

"I believe it," Charlie nodded rapidly.

"End of discussion," Ken concluded, "unless you want to go to a doctor and get an examination and go on the pill."

"I'll think about it," Marcie said.

"Let us know," Ken stated. "We're interested. We would help you. You understand that."

Marcie threw her arms around his neck and held him. Then, with a tearful kiss, she jumped up and ran into the house. Ken jerked his head sideways dismissing Charlie so the boy could follow.

"Thank you," Joanne said. Ken shrugged.

"I was at a loss for words," Joanne claimed. "As long as we stay on the philosophical level, I'm all right. But when my daughter is talking—"

"I know."

Inside, the two youngsters were now chatting, laughing. Ken studied Joanne's expression which, she was sure, correctly mirrored deep concern.

"Jo," Ken said, "you can't impress your value system on that girl. Marcie is right—things have changed. It's a tribute to you, to both of us, that she feels free to bring the subject into the open as she did."

"Perhaps you didn't notice," Joanne said, "but you have

77

used the words 'we' as in . . . will help . . . and 'us' as
in . . . the two of us together. Should I presume anything
beyond the helping hand of a friendly neighbor?"

He didn't smile.

"Have I touched a sensitive nerve?" Joanne asked.

"I suppose you did."

"Ken," she grinned, "I wasn't trying to trap you into a
promise. I wasn't even after an insinuation."

"And," he said, standing up, "there was none offered."

In the living room, the TV on, but without sound, Joanne
broached her subject cautiously. "Ken," she said, "I detect
a void between us. A misunderstanding. More precisely,
no understanding. I'm referring to our conversation on the
patio this afternoon."

Eyes dark, brooding, he gazed at her.

"I think," she said, "we should have an understanding
on this marriage thing."

Maddeningly, he waited in silence. Joanne intertwined
her fingers, sitting on a hassock at his feet. "By that," she
said, "I mean . . . you don't want to . . . that is, do you
want to marry me?"

"Do you want to marry me?"

"I don't know. I don't think so. Not actually. No. Do
you want to marry me?"

"What makes you ask, if your decision is made?"

"Don't be obtuse, all right? That business about 'Would
you like to live in Detroit,' for example. What was that?"

"Why do you ask me where I want to eat dinner?" Ken
responded. "I wanted to know what you're thinking."

"Why should I be thinking about Detroit? Or Cleveland
or Chicago or New York, for heaven's sake? Except because you're there."

"If I were there," Ken said, "what would you think?"

"Damn." Joanne stood. "This is going nowhere."

"Where do you want it to go?" Ken challenged.

"How would I know? You make references to we and
us and ours. You bed and board with me at every opportunity. You imply that you care for me, and for Marcie.
Marcie looks upon you in a favorable accepting way."

"Meaning she doesn't resent me."

"Meaning," Joanne said, "she doesn't have any firm
basis for decisions. Should she love you? For that matter,

should I? If so, all right. If not, all right. But as it is, none of us can get a handle on our relationships."

"Do you love me?"

"Ken—I'm—well, I'd miss you if you weren't here. I appreciate you. I enjoy you. Does that constitute love?"

"Okay."

"Okay, what?"

"Okay, I'll accept that."

"Accept what, damn it!"

"Whatever you want accepted." Ken rose and strode from the room. Following, Joanne said, "Ken, maybe you don't know what to think, is that it? You're afraid you're abandoning me, Marcie—is that it? Or, perhaps you feel like *we'll* feel we've been abandoned."

"Would you?"

"How about a straightforward frontal assault," Joanne snapped, "instead of these sidestepping innuendos. Do you love me or not?"

"Like you said, Jo," Ken's voice was low, "I don't know."

"Neither do I."

"Then we're even." Ken took a can of beer from the refrigerator and popped the top.

"I suppose I'm frightened," Joanne confessed.

"So am I."

"You?"

"Scared to death," he said. "Since we're discussing it, I'll tell you something—my first marriage was such a disaster, such a horrible, horrible mistake—I don't trust my judgment anymore. Now, when I see a potential problem, any kind of problem, I want to be mighty sure I can solve it before I take it on."

"And you think you see a problem with me?"

"It isn't important as long as we aren't married."

"What does that mean?"

"Look," he sat on a bar stool, "tiny little things are completely irrelevant between friends. But microscopic faults can become monstrous when you're married. I don't know, maybe it's immaturity on my part, but I'd be scared to marry you."

"Why?" she demanded.

"It isn't important, Jo, unless you're talking matrimony. Why worry about it?"

79

"Ken. Listen. This is not to suggest I want to get married. But, sometimes another person sees things we don't see in ourselves."

He sipped beer.

"I wish you'd tell me what you mean. I don't want to lie awake nights tearing my psyche to shreds seeking flaws. Tell me and put me out of my misery."

"Fair enough," Ken said. "We'll begin with what you object to in me."

"I don't object to anything."

"Obviously untrue. Otherwise you'd be madly in love with me and eager to be my wife."

"That's absurd."

"I'm a lowly deputy sheriff," Ken said. "I'm several grades below the social level to which you've become accustomed. My grammar may slip now and then. I'm a product of my former self—a tough Miami barrio cop—and although I'm struggling to improve myself, I'm basically just a cop. I see myself pretty good."

"Reverse psychology, right?" Joanne accused. "Now I give you a sales pitch on what a wonderful fellow you are. Ralph is a sucker for that. I tell him how much Marcie is like him and he melts before my eyes."

"You aren't lying when you say it."

"No, but being frank and honest isn't my reason for being frank and honest with Ralph. Okay. You're intelligent, witty, caring, gentle, sweet, ambitious—"

He stood so abruptly, the stool toppled. "Hey," Ken glowered, "do us a favor. If you want to play games, fine. But let's not forfeit credibility. I'll consider it a tribute to my intelligence if you don't overdo it. You win. Let's quit."

"Ken?" She followed him into the living room again. "I didn't mean to sound sarcastic. Actually, you are a wonderful man. I'm very fond of you. I'm trying to avoid losing you—but I don't have much to offer to induce you to stay."

"We aren't juvenile lovers," Ken said. "It isn't necessary to manufacture a fight to make parting easier."

She sat on the hassock and put a hand on his knee. "Ralph nearly destroyed my self-confidence when we were married," she said. "Never overtly. In subtle ways, he picked and picked until he'd picked a crack in my estimation of myself. Before we divorced, I was in ruins. I was

80

convinced I was dull, drab, had little to offer, made a terrible bed partner and was a millstone around his neck. It doesn't take much to destroy this veneer I've reconstructed, you know. Under it I'm still a shattered remnant of what I used to be."

He gave a nod. "My story, same song, second verse."

"You're wrong to think I look down on your job, or your background, Ken. It simply isn't true."

"Perhaps I look up at your job and background," Ken said. "Either way, there's a difference in elevation."

"Doesn't have to be. I measure a man's success by the satisfaction he has in himself. Not only are you satisfied, you're a man on the rise."

"Not in Tallahassee. I'll have to go north to a major city to pursue my career. Which brings us back to the conclusion that we're dog paddling, staying afloat but going nowhere."

Lack of reply was, of itself, a reply. He patted her hand, face rigid. "Therefore," he suggested, "let us enjoy one another. Let us not dwell on one another's faults."

"Are you going to leave me to suffer endlessly over what you've been talking about? Or will you tell me what this 'problem' is, where I'm concerned?"

"It isn't important."

"As long as we're not getting married, it isn't."

"That's right."

"Tell me."

"Jo—"

"Tell me."

"Okay." He had a gleam in his eye. "I never have understood how you got freckles on your fanny."

"Tell me," she insisted.

The gleam evaporated.

"Tell me, Ken."

"I guess this ends it," he said, softly. "Maybe all good things tend to self-destruction, I don't know."

"Tell me."

"It's your attitude on sex."

"Marcie?"

"No, you. You and me."

Shocked, she laughed.

"You never fully enter into it," Ken said. "You agree to participate, but without genuine spirit. You accept loving, but without the true satisfaction of enjoyment. It's as if you are cooking a meal by a recipe, add this or that and bake. But you don't . . . seem . . . to . . . enjoy it."

"That's not true."

He sighed, "Isn't it?"

"No. Not true."

"Then rape me."

Chapter Ten

JOANNE paced the floor in front of her desk, dictating.
"Society attempts to regulate individual sexual attitudes and behavior," she said. "This is accomplished through education, religion, social pressures, medicine—and of course, by law."

She waited as Bea completed cursive strokes and flipped her stenographer's pad to a fresh page.

"A prolonged penitentiary sentence is often an attempt to bend an offender to society's regulations," Joanne continued. "A prison sentence is termed justified since it will prevent the dangerous offender from attacking again. The purpose of such incarceration is, simply, to incapacitate rather than to punish. We would like to think that, during such penal terms, rehabilitation is possible through psychotherapy. Unfortunately, this is seldom true."

When Bea looked up, Joanne said, "Send a copy to Ralph, Bea. Attach the profile I did on Swain and any other pertinent papers."

"All right, Dr. Fleming."

Joanne sat at her desk, contemplating her moves on Swain's behalf. There was always the awesome chance she had misjudged the man and he was genuinely dangerous. Still, she reassured herself, fifteen years was entirely inappropriate.

Sex as a crime fell into two categories. First, physical aggression such as forcible rape, including violent homosexual acts and indecent assault. The second category included nonviolent but illicit intercourse such as homosexual relations between consenting adults which was offensive to the community at large—to relatives of the participants or in terms of religious precepts—but not to the "criminals" involved.

Swain's acts were more "illicit intercourse" than rape. But she hadn't been able to substantiate that, in a legal way.

She examined her desk calendar. Today was the Women's Club luncheon at which she was to speak. She hadn't given it a thought until this moment.

Oh, well. She leaned back, swiveled her chair to face the window. She'd give the ladies her usual lecture, a talk Ken described as "Ain't life gland?"

More than most care to admit.

"Telephone, Dr. Fleming," Bea said, through the intercom.

Joanne answered, "Fleming speaking."

"Dr. Joanne Fleming?"

"Yes."

"Age thirty-six; daughter, Marcie; former husband attorney Ralph Fleming?"

"Who is this?" Joanne asked curtly.

The telephone clicked, a dial tone burring. Joanne depressed her intercom key. "Bea, who was that calling?"

"He wouldn't give his name."

Joanne tapped her desk with a forefinger. *Age thirty-six; daughter, Marcie; former husband—*

She dialed home. "Marcie?"

"Hi, mom."

"Are you alone, darling?"

"Charlie's here."

"When are you going to your father's?"

"In about fifteen minutes. We're going to his place at Panacea, not here in Tallahassee."

"I know."

"Anything wrong, mom?"

"No. Nothing wrong. Have fun."

"Thanks. Hey, mom—I love you."

"I love you, silly filly."

Joanne hung up, shook off apprehension. She took another call. Bud Diehl, Jacksonville.

"They found the Lake City girl, Jo. The parents identified a ring that the child was wearing."

"Oh dear, Bud."

83

"The body was under a lean-to in an abandoned pigsty," Bud droned. "Decomposition nearly complete. But there were signs of a fracture at the base of the skull."

"Bless her heart," Joanne murmured.

"I'm calling a three-state conference of all interested parties, Jo. At the Civil Defense building, nine A.M. next Wednesday, Thomasville, Georgia. Could you come?"

"I'll try."

"I chose Thomasville because it's only thirty-three miles from you, Jo."

"I'll be there then. Oh, Bud—anything new on the Panama City missing girl?"

"I don't think they're convinced of foul play, despite blood around the soft drink machine."

"Why not?"

"Trouble with her parents over several marriage proposals by an older man they can't locate."

"Maybe she is a runaway then."

"Maybe."

Bea came in and put the typed deposition on Joanne's desk for approval. "The conclusion is weak," Bea observed.

"Unfortunately, I agree." Joanne read the words. "Add this, Bea: 'Under sex-psychopath laws, Mr. Swain has been trapped by legislation designed for the protection of society, when in fact Mr. Swain poses no threat to society. Rather than subject Swain to the inuring influence of a penitentiary, society would be better served if the defendant were compelled to undergo therapy and probation with supervision.' "

Bea took the notes and returned to her typewriter.

Joanne dialed home. She listened to the ring, waited . . . waited . . . no answer. Marcie had gone. Joanne shuddered and, surprised, identified it as relief.

"You're due at the Women's Club in half an hour, Dr. Fleming," Bea reminded.

Joanne took a quick, disheartening swipe at her unruly hair, straightened her skirt and grabbed her pocketbook.

"Ken on the line," Bea said as Joanne walked past.

"Call him later," Joanne replied. Down the hall in quick, hollow steps. She winced at a rush of heat as she left the building and hurried toward the parking lot. On second thought, it wasn't all that far, she'd walk.

Sunlight attained intensities here that blinded. She detoured to get sunglasses from her car, then walked unhurriedly toward the Howard Johnson's restaurant three blocks distant. The campus was quiet, almost deserted. Summer session had not yet begun. She strolled down Tennessee Street in sparse shade. This may have been a mistake. Sweat oozed between her breasts. Dust swirled from passing traffic and powdered her skin.

At a corner, she paused. Uneasy, she turned to glance back the way she'd come. Several students ambled along behind. Crossing the street, Joanne turned abruptly—she was alone. Ken was right—her work was making her paranoid.

Suspicion is a handmaiden to alertness, papa used to say. In primitive man it was his key to survival.

Like a patron in a crowded arena who senses eyes at his back, Joanne felt a prickle of awareness. She hastened her step, anticipating the air-conditioned comfort of the restaurant. Yet, once through the door, she backed against a wall of the foyer to watch the street.

Nobody she knew. A man in a small, battered foreign car, oblivious to his surroundings. The car putted away.

She'd better spend her time thinking about points for this unprepared speech. Sex crimes . . . penalties . . . inequities . . . remedial actions. . . .

Her speech was awful. Poorly organized, loosely delivered. One elderly member dozed at the head table. When Joanne saw that her audience wasn't interested in the legal aspects of sex crimes, she shifted to her old stand-by: how to avoid rape. But even that fell on yawning women, the type who presumed that such things happened to "girls who invite such."

She wouldn't have tried so hard, but for Tony Eldridge who was sitting to one side taking notes. If her ineptitude was to attain the dignity of print, surely she had to make it more exciting than this! She resorted to the surest ploy of the beleaguered orator: "Are there any questions?" Let *them* choose the topic they wished to hear.

No hands. Joanne smiled at Tony.

"Many of you probably fantasize about rape." Joanne couched vicious intent behind a genial expression. The lady asleep shifted, her head now thrown back, dentures loose in a ghastly overbite.

Anxiety had sent Joanne's voice to a higher register. She deliberately brought it down again, her hands perspiring, face flushed. Tony Eldridge closed his notebook, studied his wristwatch.

Amid a scent of Yardley and patting powder puffs, Joanne labored to a conclusion and took her seat. These ladies didn't care. Why had she allowed herself to get into this?

When Tony Eldridge's eyes met hers, Joanne smiled, nodded. His expression unchanged, he gazed past her.

Ralph's voice sounded distant on the telephone. "Jo, this is Ralph."

"Ralph, I'm sending over a deposition to attach to the Swain appeal."

"Forget it. The appeal has been denied."

"They denied it?"

"Flatly and without comment."

"But, why?"

"Now why do you think?" Ralph snapped. "Because there's a headline in today's newspaper which says, and I quote, 'Albert Alcorn For Supreme Justice.' That's why."

"That kills it?"

"Dead as a doornail."

"Can't you by-pass that court and—"

"Dead," Ralph said emphatically, "as a doornail."

"Oh damn it, Ralph."

"Therefore I have petitioned for a rehearing on the basis of new evidence."

"You did? Wonderful! What new evidence?"

"There isn't any," Ralph said. "But this continues the case until the thing on Alcorn breaks. By then, the appellate court may not be so eager to kowtow for political purposes."

"Good, Ralph. Very good."

After a long pause, Joanne said, "Then you're going for the biggie, after all."

"Pray for me," Ralph said.

"Have fun with Marcie."

"Yeah, thanks—what?"

"I said, have fun with Marcie."

"Marcie! My God. I can't make it, Jo. I completely forgot it."

"Uh-oh," Joanne breathed. "She's already gone to Panacea. Did you ever get a telephone put in down there?"

"That'd defeat my purpose for having a getaway. Aw, nuts!"

"Wait a minute," Joanne said, "I'll drive down and tell her."

"She's going to be disappointed."

"In fact," Joanne offered, "I'll spend the night, so she and her boyfriend can stay there. If that's all right with you."

"Certainly. I'd appreciate it."

Joanne dialed Ken. Out of touch. Slightly disturbed at having been so magnanimous, Joanne told Bea she was going home, "and then to Panacea."

"Have a nice weekend," Bea grinned. "I for one am going to Wakulla Springs, sop up some sunshine, introduce my body to a variety of male tourists and—"

"Spare me," Joanne said.

She drove home, worrying about Ken. This was one of those communication gaps which stirs misunderstandings. Earlier she hadn't taken his call; now she couldn't reach him.

She entered the mustiness of a closed house, doors and windows shut, air conditioning off, as she had instructed Marcie. Immediately, she tried to call Ken at work, then his apartment. Not there.

Joanne drew a map, giving explicit directions to reach Ralph's cottage down at Panacea. Hanging this on a cupboard with transparent tape, she added a note explaining the predicament, extending an invitation, "come on down, Ken."

She went to her bedroom to pack an overnight bag. Instantly, she sensed something amiss.

A methodical, almost tedious attention to detail was an inherent trait. Her desk drawer at the office—she could tell at a glance if Bea had been in there. Exactly six paper clips, her pencils arranged in order of length and hardness of lead, sharpness of point. Her home was not so orderly overall, but the bedroom, and specifically her dresser, were inviolate. Marcie would never, had never, plundered through this room. It was an unspoken agreement between mother and daughter—bedrooms were private.

For a moment, she couldn't be sure what was different. Senses keen, she turned, examining the sewing machine set up in a corner, her desk beside it. The closet door was ajar. That was one thing. The bathroom door was half closed, that was two things. The dresser—a bottle of perfume almost precisely where she kept it, but nonetheless off an inch.

Easy now.

She pulled open a drawer. Her jewelry was here. The next drawer: neatly folded underwear, rumpled slightly. So minor as to be unnoticeable to anyone else, but it had been disturbed, she was almost sure of it.

Her first angry thought was, Marcie had been rummaging around. But as Joanne walked, tiptoed, to the closet, pique became wariness. She stood to one side and pushed open the closet door with her fingertips. Dresses, suits, winter garments all there, but not in the perfectly symmetrical order that was almost an obsession with her. A jacket slightly askew. Joanne straightened it. A wooden hanger separated from the others by a wire hanger. She never did that.

"Picky, picky, picky," Ralph had screamed once. "God, I could stand you better if you'd make one mess in your life . . ."

She looked under the bed. Checked front and back doors. Locked. No indication of forced entry. Yet throughout the house she detected tiny things: an object out of line; her cookbooks in the kitchen in reverse order—Italian-French-Chinese.

She walked on the balls of her feet, near a wall, to avoid a section where the floor creaked. Outside Marcie's room, Joanne paused. She turned the knob, pushed the door open. Still in the hall, she bent to peer down under Marcie's bed. The closet was open, cluttered. This was not her territory; she'd have no way of knowing if anything had been stolen. Joanne entered, looked around. The window. Unlocked! Marcie—

She secured the latch and looked across the backyard. Less motivated than her mother, Marcie was not prone to regimentation. Her window sills were dusty—except this one. Joanne walked quickly to the kitchen, out the rear door and back to the area beneath Marcie's window.

Twigs of an azalea were broken. She pulled aside the foliage. In a pine-chip mulch, she saw two indentations, as a ladder would make. Joanne stood, searching. Ah, on the patio! A utility ladder Ken had used a few days ago to change a light fixture.

And on the feet of the ladder—bits of pine bark.

It took will to reenter the house. She went first to her silver drawer. Nothing missing. Down the hall again to Marcie's room.

Under the window in the nylon pile of the carpet were tiny pieces of bark.

Charlie could have come visiting after hours. Marcie might have used the window and ladder for a midnight escape. She wasn't above such shenanigans. Yet Marcie wasn't likely to invite invasion of her own privacy by invading her mother's bedroom.

So, someone must have been here. For what? Nothing missing. Jewelry, a few pieces of art; the most appealing would be her sterling silver which fetched a good price these days. And it was safe, intact.

Heart bounding, she walked the hallway with an eerie sense of being onstage. As if, right this moment, she were being watched by an unseen camera in one of those asinine commercials on TV.

She went to the living room and barely moving a drape, looked out. A neighbor's dog playing with a child. A young man mowing a lawn down the street. Everything so suburban, so normal.

Joanne called Ken again.

"Sorry, Dr. Fleming," the dispatcher replied, "Ken's at the far end of the county on a call from some farmer. Evidently he's away from the patrol car. I've got your message for when he calls in."

A shiver. Joanne retraced her route, room to room, double-checking locks on all the doors and windows. Hurriedly, she threw a bathing suit and change of clothing into a small weekend bag. Checked the garage door, one last time. It *was* bolted.

In her car, she inadvertently flooded the engine and it became difficult to start. But, with the motor finally roaring, she backed out of the driveway and turned toward a by-pass which circled town.

Joanne and Ralph had acquired the cottage at a time when they couldn't afford it. One of his first clients had been unable to settle a legal fee and offered to sell the dwelling at a low price. The retreat was, during those happy years, a source of solace, privacy, and proof of their future prospects. They had struggled to make the payments

—sixty dollars a month—and each weekend found them there, painting, repairing, cooking out and feeling affluent.

The original building now formed the core of a more pretentious structure. Over the years, as money problems eased, they added decks, patios, a veranda, walkways to the boathouse, and several spacious bedrooms on the "water" side. In the divorce settlement, Joanne got their principal place of residence, Ralph got the cottage. Joanne hadn't been here since.

Her heart wrenched as she turned into the driveway, a crunch of oyster shells bringing a rush of bittersweet memories. She shut off the motor, sat staring at this repository of youthful dreams, naivete, and hope. Charlie's car was here.

She circled the house and realized they were gone. Ralph wouldn't have arrived for another couple of hours, so Marcie and Charlie wouldn't be waiting expectantly. Joanne strolled toward the boathouse. Ralph's pride and joy was an inboard cruiser capable of speeds up to forty miles per hour on calm waters. It was not there.

"Water skiing," Joanne guessed aloud. She walked the private pier, looking east, then west for signs of the youngsters. Across the inlet lay Bald Point, a favorite swimming area; around a bend, the Gulf of Mexico spread south to a far horizon.

Suddenly, she felt alien, as if trespassing. She knew there was a key hidden above a rear door. She was not on unfriendly ground. Still, she almost decided to leave and come back later, about the time Ralph would have arrived.

Out front, beyond the house, she heard a car motor. Volkswagen. Marcie must have invited friends. The summer crowd would be arriving about now. With Ochlockonee Bay as their common interest, and with only these few summer months to meet and renew acquaintances, an odd sort of friendship evolved along the Gulf resort area. They did not ask penetrating questions, nor did they offer insights into themselves. They gathered for cookouts, fishing parties, beer and poker sessions. They called one another by first names. Yet, for all that, they knew virtually nothing beyond name, occupation and home towns.

She dreaded meeting any of them for fear, even after all these years, they would blunder into a social faux pas, asking, "How's Ralph, Jo?"

She peered through gathering afternoon showers, dark shade beneath thickets of semitropical growth. The thick roots of a banyan tree blocked her view of the driveway. Joanne walked in that direction.

"Hello," she called.

The Volkswagen motor roared, tires scratching in the oyster shells, rubber squealing as the vehicle hit pavement. Joanne bolted for the roadway. As she reached the macadam, she caught a glimpse of the small car disappearing around a curve, going toward the main highway.

Belatedly, she realized she had left her car windows down, her pocketbook on the front seat.

Yet, even as she hurried to check, Joanne had the same feeling she'd had at home.

There was nothing missing.

Chapter Eleven

IT'S typical of daddy to forget." Marcie set up a Scrabble board.

"He's very busy on something critical," Joanne said.

"Always," Marcie grumped. "Busy and critical. Before daddy abandoned wife and child—Charlie, you're bumping the table!"

The boy moved back, bumping into a lamp.

Joanne delivered three Greek salads with a bowl of saltines.

"Is the air conditioner broken?" Charlie inquired.

Marcie mimed her father. "Air conditioning would turn a sea breeze into city wind."

"Who plays first?" Joanne asked, selecting seven letters, consonants all.

"I am," Charlie said. Immediately he played: *rejects*.

"Charlie!" Marcie wailed. "Mom, look at that. Fifty plus double score. Charlie, that sucks!"

"Marcie," Joanne pleaded, "could you please drop that phrase from your vocabulary?"

"Fifty plus double score," Marcie fumed.

Smirking, Charlie crossed his legs and the table jolted. "You expecting anybody, Dr. Fleming?"

"No. Why?"

"Thought I saw somebody."

"Where?"

"At the window."

"Which window?"

"Behind you."

Joanne looked past Marcie's shoulder into a mirror which reflected the window. It was open, screened, dark.

"When?" Joanne asked.

"Just a minute ago."

"Why didn't you say something?" Joanne demanded.

"They left," Charlie said. "Your turn, Dr. Fleming."

Joanne played for a low score. She watched the mirror obliquely. "Marcie," Joanne asked, "you haven't been in my bedroom at home, have you?"

"No." Marcie studied her letters.

"Maybe Ken . . ." Joanne thought aloud.

"Ah-hah!" Marcie played all seven letters, fifty plus a triple letter, and passed Charlie's score.

"Hey, that's great, Marcie!" Charlie conceded.

In the mirror a shadow, the faintly illuminated outline of —Joanne froze, watching.

"The game of champs, right, mom?"

There were no weapons in the house. Ralph was more afraid of an accident than of any intruder. Joanne watched the window—the shadow was gone. She arose casually, went to the kitchen cupboard and got a long, sharp filet knife. She returned, used the knife to slice a piece of cheese, and put it where she could reach it easily.

Charlie scribbled on a pad. Joanne watched the mirror, the window.

"Best I can do." Charlie scored well, drew more letters.

Joanne played the easiest thing available, ignoring Marcie's wince. "All consonants, right mom?"

"Afraid so."

Then, again, a form took shape at the window and Joanne's heart rose in her esophagus. Closer now, near enough to see white of flesh, the contours of cheeks and nose.

"Charlie!" Joanne cried, "there's somebody out there." The boy fell backward, scrambling to his feet as Joanne rushed to the door with knife in hand.

She threw open the portal and screamed—

"What's going on here?" Ralph asked. He put luggage inside the door, turned to get fishing tackle.

"Why don't you announce yourself, for heaven's sake?" Joanne shrilled.

"I was about to knock, Jo. And what are you doing with that knife?"

"You're lucky she didn't gut you," Charlie said.

"Welcome, father," Marcie called.

"I got to thinking," Ralph explained to Joanne. "Life is flying by, time is short enough in this world. Business can wait, that's all. My daughter merits some time, too."

Marcie grinned, "How about a hand of Scrabble, daddy?"

"So," Ralph sniffed, "you can go on home, if you want to, Jo."

"Hold it," Marcie commanded, "not before we have a four hand game of Scrabble, okay, mom?"

"It's already getting late." Ralph rubbed his nose. "Maybe you should consider going, if you want to, Jo."

"Trying to get rid of me?"

"No, no." Ralph put his fishing gear in a corner. "Thinking of you, that's all. There's fog building on the highway and I always worry when you take that long drive alone."

"You could spend the night, couldn't you, mom?" Marcie asked.

"No," Joanne said. "I'll go back. But first, we'll play one game together. Now, Charlie, you're up against your equal."

"Good," Charlie beamed. "Sit down, Mr. Fleming."

Ralph loosened his tie, face flushed. Then, he pulled the tie off and tossed it onto an empty chair. "One quick game," he said, "then you really should think about getting back, Jo." Sniff. "Or spend the night."

"I'd prefer to go back. One game," Joanne agreed.

"Any more of that salad?" Ralph asked.

"Take mine, Mr. Fleming," Charlie said. "I'm not hungry and I haven't touched it."

"You don't like Greek salad, Charlie?" Joanne questioned.

"It's okay. I don't care much for anchovies."

"Umm," Ralph ate one, "delicious."

"Kind of like flat worms with hairs," Charlie observed.

"Play, daddy," Marcie prodded.

They fell into silence. Ralph adjusted his seven letters, glanced at his watch. He smiled at Joanne.

"How's tricks, Mr. Fleming?" Charlie asked, genially.

"Fine," Ralph said, playing *piscator* off Marcie's word.

"Now that," Charlie said, "is a great play."

"Don't forget your handicap, daddy," Marcie warned.

"Oh, yes." Ralph gazed at the ceiling. "I must also define any word I use. 'Piscator' means 'fisherman.' "

Marcie tallied the letters, wrote the score. Joanne caught a movement in the mirror and looked at Charlie.

"Your turn, Charlie," Marcie said.

Joanne slowly brought her eyes back to the mirror, the reflected window. Her imagination. Had to be. Getting jumpy. Scaring these youngsters. *Cut it out, Joanne.*

Out of the dark, beyond the screen—no, it wasn't her imagination—something—somebody.

"Ralph," Joanne quavered.

"Umm?"

Thick hair, eyes shadowed—Joanne jumped up, wheeling, "Ralph! There's somebody out there!"

Ralph grabbed the knife and went for the door, Charlie close behind. Into the night, man and boy rounded the corner of the house.

"Ralph?" A woman's voice.

"Uh-oh," Marcie wheezed.

"Darlene!"

Heart still pounding, Joanne heard introductions mumbled, Charlie's voice, "Good to meet you."

"One of daddy's girl friends," Marcie sighed.

The woman had come prepared to stay. She entered, dressed for travel in a wrinkle-free suit, and put a cosmetics case inside the door next to matching tote bag. Face flaming, Ralph flustered, "Darlene Sands, I'd like you to meet my wife, Jo."

"Former wife." Joanne shook hands.

"Former, yes," Ralph smiled thinly. "And this is Marcie."

"Former daughter," Marcie said.

"I've heard so much about you." Darlene spoke with a slight accent. "As beautiful as your photographs, too. She looks like you, Ralph!"

"We all have our problems," Marcie said.

"Have I interrupted dinner?" Darlene questioned, full lips pursed.

"No, no," Ralph said.

"I have several bags in the trunk of my car, Ralph," she said. "If I could change into something more comfortable?"

Ralph looked tortured, a grin with a grimace. "Sure you can. The bath is—"

"I remember." She took her tote bag and cosmetics case.

"I'll help you, Mr. Fleming," Charlie volunteered, following. "Boy, she's a knockout."

"Height in inches," Marcie said to Joanne, "plus twenty, equals IQ. And daddy doesn't go with basketball players."

"Marcie," Joanne reprimanded without conviction.

"Am I right?"

"I admit, most of them are not intellectually stimulating."

"Maybe it isn't his intellect he wants stimulated." Marcie's lips curled. She gave a quick shrug, "Oh, well. It was too good to last, anyway. I thought for a minute we'd all be together and—"

"Much better." Darlene came out in pressed cotton slacks, shapely breasts faintly visible beneath a too-sheer blouse. "Scrabble," she observed.

Ralph and Charlie came through carrying several suitcases which they took to the master bedroom.

"How about a five-hand game of Scrabble, daddy?" Marcie hollered at large.

"Sure," Ralph responded. "If Darlene wants to play, sure."

"I'm not very good with words," Darlene confessed.

"Take my place," Joanne offered. "I'll be leaving shortly, anyway."

But Marcie insisted and Joanne found herself pulled into the game. Darlene sat close to Ralph. Conversation ceased, all of them contemplating their own letters.

In the mirror—something moved.

Joanne stared at the reflected window. "My turn?" Ralph inquired.

"Play," Marcie ordered. Ralph placed his word: *usufruct*.

"Can you use dirty words in this game?" Darlene asked.

Clearly, a *face* at the window. Trembling, Joanne stared.

"Mom?" Marcie was held by Joanne's expression.

The face came nearer. Without doubt it was—

The image withdrew.

"Such a secluded place," Darlene observed to Marcie and Joanne. "Does it frighten you?"

"Not as a rule," Joanne said, curtly.

"When I flew into Miami this evening," Darlene explained, "I called Ralph and I mentioned how quiet and peaceful it was here."

"Are you a jet setter?" Marcie asked, bluntly.

Darlene laughed. "I had no thought of coming," she said to Marcie, "but, you know your father."

"Yes, we've met."

"Ralph," Joanne gathered her belongings, "I'm going on. It's getting late—"

"Must you?" Ralph feigned.

"On the other hand, I could spend the night," Joanne said, acidly.

"But then, it's only an hour's drive," Ralph answered quickly.

"So I'll go."

"Bye, mom."

"Bye, darling." Joanne kissed the girl's warm cheek. "Pleased to meet you, Darlene. What kind of work do you do?"

"I'm in music."

"Selling it? What?"

Darlene smiled. "In a way, yes. I have only now completed a twenty-eight-country concert tour. I am a pianist."

"What orchestra?" Joanne felt her smile crumbling.

"I play alone. With a few strings to accompany me, usually. But generally, alone."

"Sands!" Charlie rubbed thumb and index as if to snap fingers. "I read about you in *Newsweek!*"

"How old are you?" Marcie blurted.

"A secret I will tell to this room only," Darlene winked at Ralph. "I'm forty, Marcie."

"Older than daddy?"

"Age is a state of mind and artery, dear."

When Joanne reached Tallahassee, she pulled into the unlighted parking lot of a restaurant. She fumbled for coins and walked to a pay telephone, the car motor still running. She dialed Ken's number and waited.

"Yeah?" Ken growled into the receiver.

"Ken, could you meet me at my house?"

"Something wrong?"

"I don't want to go home alone."

"What time is it?"

"After midnight."

"After one," Ken yawned. "Right now?"

"In about fifteen minutes."

"You all right, Jo?" Awake and on duty now.

96

"Little spooked."

"Okay. I'll be there."

"Thank you, Ken."

Joanne hung up, hurried to her vehicle. At a motel across the highway, laughter, the tinkle of a discarded can. She bit her lip, disappointed, hurt. Ralph had lied. He came not for Marcie, but for Darlene. Most painful was her shock upon learning this was not the stereotype of Ralph's girl friends. The full, permanently pursed lips, sexy figure, but with talent and brains and some renown.

At last, her own driveway. When she drove in, Ken was there to greet her. Joanne burst into tears and without questions, he held her close.

"A horrible day." Joanne unlocked the kitchen door. "I think I'm being watched and—"

"Watched?"

She recounted her eerie walk to the Women's Club meeting. "I think somebody has been in my house."

"Anything stolen?" Ken asked.

"Not so far as I can determine."

Ken walked through, turning on lights from room to room.

"You know how I am," Joanne said. "I keep everything in a precise place. But the closet door and bathroom door were ajar. And my perfume was moved. And there were imprints in the ground under Marcie's window and her window wasn't locked."

"Nothing damaged?"

"Nothing I could see." Joanne followed him into Marcie's bedroom. "The utility ladder had bark on it and there's bark on Marcie's rug."

Ken stooped and pinched some of the pine bark from Marcie's floor. He rubbed it between his fingers, smelled it.

"Then Ralph scared me, showing up," Joanne continued. "Then a woman friend of his scared me again, looking in the damned window. And then another man—and I was sure this was the same one who's been following me all day."

"What'd he look like?"

"It was dark."

"About my size?"

"I can't be sure."

"My weight and height?"

"Maybe. I don't know, Ken. It was dark."

"Did you see the color of his hair?"

"I don't know—brown, I think. Wavy brown."

"What color were his eyes?"

"I said it was dark!"

"What color do you *think* they were?"

"I—blue, I think."

"It was me."

"What?"

"It was me. I looked in, saw Ralph, and left."

"Why did you do that?" she shouted. "Sneaking around like a thief. Why didn't you say something?"

"What was I supposed to say? 'Hi, Ralph, I came by your house to see your child and former wife?' It wasn't my terra firma. So I left."

"Dear God!" Joanne cried. "I'm shaking like a dipsomaniac!"

"I told you," Ken said, evenly, "you're thinking too much about your work. You've got to take time off."

"I can't."

"Why not?"

"There's a three-state conference coming up next Wednesday. All departments concerned with the missing women."

Ken's tangled eyebrows knitted as he frowned. "Suit yourself. But you keep on in this state of high tension and you'll be in a hospital."

She put her head on his chest, thankful for his presence.

"Spend the night?" she asked.

"Thought you'd never ask."

He lifted her chin with a finger and kissed her lips tenderly. How could such a powerful man, the face and jaw so strong—kiss so exquisitely?

"Know something?" Joanne whispered.

"What?"

"I think I love you."

He grunted, pulling free. He went through the house, turning off the lights.

"Is that all the response I get?" she called. "I tell you I think I love you and you burp?"

"I'm not responding to a case of infatuation." Ken came into view down the hall. "When you know for sure, I'll have a statement."

In the shower, Joanne heard Ken moving around in the bedroom. When she came out, wrapped in a towel, he was gone. The light in Marcie's bedroom was on. Joanne walked to the hall and stood watching. Nude, Ken was examining the window sills. He held a cupped hand with particles in his palm.

"The only clean window is the one that was unlocked," Joanne commented.

"Marcie could've been sneaking out."

"That occurred to me."

"She may not admit it, if she did," Ken said.

"I realize that."

"I wouldn't ask her," Ken advised.

"Why not?"

"It would force her to lie, if she has been doing it. If she hasn't been sneaking out, it would only frighten her."

"I suppose you're right."

"I'll ask somebody at the lab to check these pieces of bark."

"What would that tell you?"

"Probably not much."

"Forget it." She brushed his palm clean.

"Take off a few days after the conference, Jo. I'll take some leave. We'll go to the Smokies for a few days together. Marcie is going to be with her dad awhile."

"I'll see."

They went into her bedroom again and Joanne turned slowly, looking for new evidence of intrusion.

"I'm glad Marcie is down at Panacea," she said. "I feel better with her out of town."

Ken patted the bed, soberly.

Joanne flipped off the light, met his hand in the dark. *Yes. Much better that Marcie was not here.* All she needed to worry about now was herself.

A moment later, her head on Ken's burly arm, Joanne listened to the somnolent breathing of a sleeping man. . . .

Something scraped against the house and she jumped. Ken's breath caught, eased, pulling her to him.

It scraped again, but she didn't let herself respond. Enough was enough.

Chapter Twelve

JOANNE studied a case report, consulted notes, then activated a dictating machine with the foot pedal.

"The defendant may be described as a masochist," she recited. "Masochism is the converse of sadism. The term for this deviation is named for an Australian author, Leopold Sacher-Masoch, whose novels in the late 1800's covered the subject. Masochism is the seeking of what is normally painful to a person, and from which pain the subject derives sexual pleasure."

"Dr. Fleming," Bea interrupted, "Mr. Fleming is calling."

"Yes, Ralph?"

"Honey, may I drop by and pick up some extra clothes for Marcie? She asked specifically for shorts and 'middie' blouses, whatever that is."

"They're indecent without bras. Make her wear one."

"I'll try. When would it be convenient, Jo?"

"This evening." Joanne debated how to ask her question without asking. "Is Marcie down there alone, Ralph?"

"Oh, no." He snuffled.

"Charlie is there with her?"

"Uh—no, he's gone. With his family to Cape Cod for the summer, I think."

"So, Darlene Sands is there."

Sniff. "This evening, you say?"

"I'll be home after five."

"Any possibility of being there earlier?" Ralph asked.

"Why?"

"It'd be more convenient for me. That's all."

"It's a long way to commute, right?"

"I use the hour for introspection. Time alone to . . ." sniff, ". . . think things through."

"I'll put the clothes in a box by the garage door during my lunch hour, Ralph." *You creep.*

"Fine, fine, Jo. Talk to you later."

She held a finger on her notes, jaw aching around clamped teeth. She stabbed the intercom button. "Hold all calls, Bea."

Then, with supreme concentration, she returned to the case report and her deductions. "Masochism is often associated with fetishism," she dictated, angrily. "It may be exhibited in a desire to be bound, enslaved, and dominated. It may involve debasement, degradation, even castration. In a milder form, it may be seen in religious flagellation."

She paused.

"And I must be one to put up with Ralph Fleming," she said. *Damn it.* She reversed the dictating machine to erase her comment. Then, with a sigh, she put aside the microphone and leaned back, staring at the ceiling.

As she thought of Ralph—she sniffed.

"Like most things we do, getting a tan is a pain," Marcie said, spreading lotion. "We grow old looking like the tongue of a shoe, but we do it because men think tans are sexy."

"American men," Darlene amended. "Not all men. Among the darker peoples of the world, white flesh is prized most."

"Really?"

"Men want what they don't have," Darlene said. "If everything around them is white, they want tan, and vice versa."

"Charlie thinks tan is *it*." Marcie dabbed her nose with zinc oxide. "I don't know why I bother."

Darlene laughed, "We women have been saying things like that since the first man."

"Listen, Darlene." Marcie turned on her deck chair to face the woman. "I've been thinking about having sex with Charlie. What do you think?"

"It's not for me to think."

"Mom said she and daddy had sex when they were engaged. That's supposed to make it all right. But what if the engagement had been broken off? Would mom have been a fallen woman? Sullied and undesirable?"

Darlene reached up with one finger and adjusted sunglasses over closed eyes.

"I could say Charlie and I are engaged," Marcie reasoned. "But somehow that doesn't make it better to me."

"The missing ingredient is love," Darlene said.

"Well. I don't love Charlie."

101

After a moment, Marcie observed, "I can't believe you're forty. You have a terrific body."

"A marvel of modern science."

"What?"

"The breasts are silicone, the flat tummy is a result of something called abdominoplasty which you can get from a competent surgeon for about four thousand dollars."

"A stomach lift?"

"Exactly."

"No scars?"

"In the pubic hairs. But by the time a man gets there, scars won't deter him."

"Did you get a face lift, too?"

"Not yet."

Marcie pondered the form lying before her.

"They can tighten other things too," Darlene added.

"All for men."

"Yes. For men."

"It's so frustrating!" Marcie wailed. "And complicated. They want a young body and an old mind."

"Yes."

"You're perfect for daddy," Marcie grumbled. "He likes them young and sexy, but being older than him, you satisfy his need for a mother figure."

Unruffled, Darlene said, "All men are seeking a mother. They want to dominate, yet to be dominated."

"How do you know which to do when?"

"That," Darlene sighed, "is an advantage of the old mind. It comes with experience."

"Darlene?"

She answered, eyes still closed, "Yes?"

"When did you start fornicating?"

"Very young. I grew up in a bad neighborhood. Most girls there were victims of their contemporaries. Sometimes unkindly. I was lucky."

"How?"

"My first lover was a much older man."

Marcie sat forward, voice lowered. "Will you tell me about it?"

Darlene groped for a hand towel which she used to blot her face and chest. She sat up. "It was in Milan," she said. "My first concert tour, when I was a child. I had left Chicago and gone to London for further tutoring. My parents received an offer for the tour, which was to be a youth extravaganza. So I went. For a period of rest, several weeks, we stayed in Milan. The orchestra, the Vienna Boys Choir, me."

"Alone?"

"In the company of a hundred young people. But alone. After Chicago, which had been home and a trap, music had mysteriously lifted me from my element and thrown me into the world. I was vulnerable. I was too afraid to make friends, and I must have given an impression of maturity because I seldom spoke. I was shy. This appealed to the man."

"How old was he?"

"Twice my age."

"How old were you?"

"About your age."

"An intercontinental affair," Marcie marveled. "At sixteen!"

"He was handsome, thoughtful, sophisticated," Darlene's liquid brown eyes were as distant as her memories. "He was . . . gentle. I thought he loved me. That probably wasn't true. But it was important at the time."

"Did it hurt?"

"Yes. And no. Like striking the elbow which causes pain and pleasure simultaneously."

Marcie inched nearer. "Go on," she said.

"We walked narrow winding streets hand-in-hand. We sipped wine—even children drink wine over there—and we sat in candlelight looking into one another's eyes. It was very romantic."

"What finally happened?"

"Finally? As with all love affairs. It was Hemingway who said, true love is doomed—one must always die before the other. Sometimes, it is better that love dies before the body."

"Love really makes it better?"

"I think so."

"So I should wait?"

"That is not a decision anyone can make for you." Darlene stood, wiped her smooth firm legs with the towel.

"That's what mom's boyfriend said. But it's tough to do. Charlie is horny and we're always wrestling and sweating. He's so immature. I wish I could find an older man."

Marcie followed Darlene into the cottage. "An older man who is gentle and knows what's he's doing," Marcie went

103

on. "Charlie could stab you to death before you know he's making a mistake."

Darlene's eyes flitted from side to side, probing Marcie's expression, left, right, left, right.

"Trouble is," Marcie said, "how do you *get* an older man? The ones that you'd want, know better. They say, 'Jailbait' and 'San Quentin quail' . . . and the ones that *would* do it all have dirty fingernails."

"That's about the size of it," Darlene agreed. "Would you like some lunch? I'll see what's here."

"Sure."

Darlene looked in the refrigerator, saying, "Peanut butter, beer, one egg."

"This is a bachelor pad," Marcie explained. "Listen, Darlene. So. How do you attract an older man? No scum. A real man?"

Darlene opened cupboards, searching. "One must be more than available," she said. "One must create an air of mystery. An aura. I see canned soup and more beer."

"That's about all there is." Marcie leaned on the kitchen counter. "You create an aura?"

"Nothing attracts like nonchalance," Darlene said, stooping to look below. "An aura of detachment—aloof. Hands away, fellows. Like that."

"Snobbish," Marcie deduced.

"No." Darlene stood, scanning counters. "Not so much unavailable as selective. Discriminating. There's a distinction."

"I see that. But I'm not sure I could pull it off."

Darlene touched Marcie's face in passing. "It comes with the old mind."

"Which means growing pains are the only way to grow."

"It seems to be nature's way. Marcie, there is nothing here. Let's go to a restaurant."

"Great!"

As Darlene showered, Marcie continued the conversation, sitting on the commode awaiting her turn. "Mom has let herself go to pot," Marcie stated. "She worries herself skinny. Even her clothes look old—suits, slacks, skirts—practical things. Not cheap, either. But matronly, you know what I mean?"

"Your mother is a businesswoman," Darlene replied, beyond the shower curtain. "She has an image to uphold, as I have an image to uphold. Her image is no less admirable."

"I guess so. But mom doesn't try to be appealing. I get irritated with her because she won't try. No wonder daddy went looking."

"What a man seeks while looking," Darlene said, "is seldom what he wants in a wife."

"Her panties," Marcie countered. "Full bloomers that come up around the waist—no bright colors, always cream, beige, tan, shell. No bikinis for mom, no sir."

Darlene threw back the curtain, pointed at a towel. Marcie handed it over.

"Mom has made the effort at one time or another," Marcie conceded. "She must've tried somewhere along the way."

"I'm sure of it."

"Like the business of being a gourmet cook," Marcie recalled. "That was terrible. Chickens cooked in orange juice. Awful stuff."

"Being a great cook, like being a great musician, requires constant practice, Marcie."

"Yeah," Marcie yielded. "But with mom it's like a syndrome, the story of her life. She bought cookbooks, Chinese, German, French—she clips recipes from magazines like she's trying to stay current in all the culinary arts. But our freezer is full of TV dinners and the cupboards are instant everything: rice, potatoes, hot chocolate, tea—"

"Your mother is a busy woman."

"It's more than that," Marcie said. "She buys books she never reads. Our Bible is on an end table in the living room as if we read it every night. The publishing company's brochure is still in it. She has a lot of record albums, Strauss waltzes so old they crackle while playing. She goes for Perry Como and Frank Sinatra love songs. That's okay. But she also has classical music. Bach, Beethoven, Chopin —and after all these years they still look new. It's like she wants to be different. But doesn't have the strength, or the will, or something."

Marcie sighed. "There's a sewing machine in mom's bedroom, always set up and ready to go. She saves bags of old clothes she's cut up in swatches, like she's planning a patchwork quilt someday. The only thing is, she never sews. Still, the sewing machine sits there."

"It sounds to me," Darlene said, "as if your mother went through a period of trying to please someone else.

Now having found herself, she no longer pretends to be other than what she is. Don't you think?"

"I don't know."

"Her book is probably the best indication of the woman within."

"You read her book?"

"It was very popular in France and England."

"I couldn't get past all those heavy psychological terms."

"Someday you will," Darlene said. "Then, what your mother wrote will be relevant and her wisdom will be obvious."

"You think so?"

"Go ahead now, take your shower. I'm famished."

Marcie shed her bathing suit and examined herself in the mirror. "What did you call that operation? I'm already getting a pot."

Darlene laughed in the bedroom. "With a body as perfect as that, don't worry about it. One should not fight nature except as an extreme measure."

"But you did it."

"Yes, so I did."

"Keep it sexy, right?" Marcie hollered above the shower.

A few moments later, Darlene spoke just beyond the curtain, "Marcie?"

"What?"

"There's a price for every vanity. The truth is, I had an abdominoplastic operation for professional reasons, not for any man."

Marcie stood with water streaming onto her scalp.

"The truth is," Darlene said, "I wish I'd never done it. But younger pianists book better and I have always been known as a prodigy. Old piano players are no longer prodigies."

"It made you look good," Marcie acknowledged.

"But I am, as you say your mother is, trying to be something different. I am doing it not only for myself, but for my agent, the recording companies and public relations people. We're a great deal alike, your mother and me."

Marcie stood motionless in a torrent of water, trying to think of a suitable reply. In the end, she said nothing.

Darlene shifted into neutral, hesitating at the main highway. "Which restaurant do you prefer?" she asked.

"They're all good," Marcie said. "Faivers is built out over

the water, so the view is better. Daddy says the one without a view has to try harder."

"I agree with your father." Darlene crossed the highway and pulled up to The Oaks restaurant.

Seated inside, they ordered lunch and sat drinking iced tea. "I really appreciate being able to talk woman-to-woman, Darlene."

"I've enjoyed it."

"I try to talk to mom," Marcie said. "She stays super cool on the outside, but inside she suffers. I can tell by her eyes."

Darlene nodded, looking out a window at a battered Volkswagen parking beside her car.

"How did you meet daddy?" Marcie asked, following Darlene's gaze.

"At a concert in Washington. He was there with a political convention. We had a mutual friend, one of the Florida senators."

"When was that?"

"Now he," Darlene mused, softly, "is handsome."

Marcie saw a tall young man step from his small car, lazily extending arms overhead. He'd gotten too much sun, but it was sure to tan. He stood beside Darlene's automobile, stretching his legs and back.

"When did you meet daddy?" Marcie asked anew.

"It's been seven years, I guess."

"Before the divorce," Marcie calculated. The young man combed long wavy brown hair with even strokes, using Darlene's car window as his mirror. He tossed his comb into his car and slipped on a pullover knit shirt.

"Oh, Marcie," Darlene smiled sadly, "to be your age again."

"What would you do differently?"

"More of the same." Darlene followed the man's passage across the parking lot to the front doors. Marcie turned slightly to see for herself. The man spoke to a waitress. She brought him to a nearby table. As he read the menu, bare legs golden, Marcie watched Darlene use peripheral vision to assess muscular calves, bronzed forearms.

"I think he lives in Tallahassee," Marcie said.

"Umm?"

"I've seen him before."

"Who?"

107

Marcie leaned across the table, eyebrows lifting. "Him," she emphasized.

But Darlene wasn't listening. She puckered full lips, looking into the dining room, beyond him. He, oblivious, focused deep blue eyes on a menu.

Never once did he glance their way. He sat, one hand properly placed in his lap, eating with slow even movements of the jaw. He was not thinking of Darlene, that was obvious. Or, as with so many handsome men, he had become accustomed to admiring women.

"He reminds me," Darlene spoke as if to herself, "of the man in Milan. Regal, assured, like a prince."

Irritated and not sure why, Marcie ignored him. One mooning female was enough for anybody. Darlene had begun speaking in a voice designed to project, mentioning famous people, foreign cities.

When he finished his meal, he arose abruptly and went to the cash register to help an elderly lady with her packages.

Darlene murmured something in French. Marcie said, tersely, "I don't speak the language."

"Handsome," Darlene translated. "Courtly. A beautiful man."

"He's okay."

"And," Darlene added, "a *gentle* man."

Chapter Thirteen

BUD Diehl left his automobile in Tallahassee, joining Joanne for the drive north to Thomasville, Georgia. Joanne considered the thirty-three-mile trip one of the most beautiful in the nation, wending through gently rolling virgin woodlands under a panoply of oaks bedecked with Spanish moss. Historically, since the Civil War, the area had been dominated by massive plantations originally seized by carpetbaggers come to plunder a defeated people. For a hundred years, the owners prospered under a cent-an-acre taxation—which had finally begun to change. Now the tracts were splintering, giving way to fashionable housing developments north of the Florida capital.

Joanne drove, Bud Diehl slouched against the far car door. The detective had almost failed to meet the Jacksonville requirements for police training when he tried to enlist fifteen years ago. He was shorter than Joanne and weighed only a few pounds more. Prematurely bald, he compensated with a huge walrus mustache which he constantly fingered as he thought or spoke. More cerebral than physical, Bud Diehl practiced a self-effacing demeanor. Quiet-spoken, with sleepy eyes flecked by yellow darts, he was in fact a competent, intuitive man with the tenacity that drives a prey to the ground.

After their first meeting—a summer seminar Joanne taught at the University of Florida—mutual respect had grown through telephone calls and correspondence.

"There were scattered bones and some hair which proved to be two women," Diehl was saying. "The bones were not completely oxidized, and their deaths were judged to be sudden, possibly by suffocation, according to lab reports."

He chewed the inside of one cheek. "What's troubling me most," he said, softly, "is the people investigating these deaths."

"What do you mean?"

"You know how it is, Jo. Dealing with inexperienced smalltown cops. If they don't have a smoking gun case, they don't know where to begin. They mess up evidence through carelessness. Even the really good men like Mathisen in Orlando, or Reeber in Pensacola—they're homicide, not sex crime investigators. They do everything by the numbers and follow procedure, but they aren't trained for this type of crime. That's why I wanted you at this conference."

He twisted a tip of his mustache. "They found a couple of bodies down in Dade County, still unidentified. Females. They've circulated the dental charts to missing-person publications around the country, but so far nothing."

"We need witnesses," Joanne said. "We need a modus operandi—more than what we have."

"Yeah. Turn right at the next street, Jo."

The slate-sided buildings of the former Veteran's Hospital were vintage World War II. Now, in deep underground shelters, this was the southeastern center for Civil

Defense. Inner sanctums of the complex were connected with NORAD in Colorado, distant radar stations across the Arctic, the White House. Neatly trimmed lawns sprawled amid camellias, azaleas, and rose bushes. A sweet scent of oleander wafted beneath the pines.

Bud escorted Joanne into a meeting room, an old cafeteria with poor acoustics, and introduced her to Georgia Bureau of Investigation men who were hosting the conference.

"This is Detective Samples from Portland," Diehl said. "He's keeping us posted on the thirty-seven cases in the northwest."

"Did anyone out there do a profile?" Joanne asked.

Samples smiled sardonically, "Several dozen, to fit the clues available at the time."

"Let's sit, Jo," Diehl said. "They're about to begin."

Overhead circulating fans whumped gently, warm air thrown downward as one man after another droned in monotones that left heads nodding. Joanne kept notes, but added little to her store of knowledge, until Detective Samples was introduced.

"Since nineteen sixty-nine," Samples said, "there have been thirty-seven similar cases of missing women in the Pacific northwest. The first known incident occurred in Seattle, followed at a rate of one a month for eleven months. Other disappearances were reported in Oregon, California, and across the border in Vancouver. Then there were no more reports in our area, but Utah began having them. Of nine Utah girls, three were found slain and abandoned in the same spot. Four more were discovered in remote canyons. The M.O. involved beating to the head, mutilation of the body, and strangulation."

Joanne made a note, glanced at Bud Diehl sitting on his lower spine, twisting his mustache.

"Then the Utah authorities stopped getting reports," Samples said. "Now you folks are having the problem. We think it may be the same felon. For that reason, I was asked to come here and make myself available to you."

"Any witnesses?" Joanne asked.

"Nothing positive," Samples replied without looking her way. "We did have a report from a woman, age twenty-three, who said some guy in a Volkswagen tried to kidnap her from a shopping center. She said he raised a tire tool over her head and threatened to kill her if she didn't sub-

110

mit. As it was, she escaped when a car full of college boys came to investigate her screams."

"How did she describe her assailant?" Joanne questioned.

Samples kept eyes averted, answering, "Tall, heavy-set, mid-twenties, uncut hair—"

"Uncut?" Bud Diehl asked.

"Like a hippie," Samples said. "Shoulder length."

"Color?" somebody called.

"Sandy to brown."

"What makes you think that assault may be connected to the missing women?" Bud asked.

"Actually," Samples shuffled papers, eyes down, "we don't have much . . . we're grabbing at straws. Except four years ago a couple of women were apparently kidnapped from a lake near Portland—within an hour of one another, incidentally—and later their bodies were found together. There were forty thousand people on that lake-front and this happened in broad daylight. The witnesses varied on a lot of things, but all agreed he was carrying his arm in some sort of a sling, telling women he'd hurt it skiing."

Samples winced, looked over their heads. "His line was, he needed help putting a boat onto his car. One woman went with him to his vehicle, which she described as an old model VW. The passenger seat was missing, she said. There was no boat. The man said his boat was 'up the hill' but she didn't go with him because she had to meet friends a few minutes later. However, she later saw the guy pitching the same line to other girls. She saw one girl leave with him and that was the last anybody saw her alive."

Joanne lifted a hand. "Detective Samples, have your people been operating under the assumption that these are sex crimes?"

"We are now."

"But not at first?"

"No."

"Why?"

"For one thing, until we began finding bodies, there was no proof of a homicide." Samples scrutinized the air. "Then, when we found bodies, they were decomposed. The disappearances were strung out over several jurisdictions and the individual departments had no reason to assume they had a roving killer."

111

"Would you suggest then," Joanne postulated, "that henceforth these gentlemen should go on the assumption the crimes are by a sex criminal?"

"Yes, I suppose."

"I agree," Joanne said. "Which means that extra care must be taken in future investigations of any new bodies discovered. Coroners and homicide officers must be apprised of the fact that the investigation should receive sex-crime status."

"That's a heap easier said than done," one officer commented. A patch on his sleeve identified him as chief from a small town. "When I find a body, I can't leave it lay," he said. "We sack it up and haul it in and call GBI. By that time, evidence is lost."

"Have you found more than one body?" Diehl queried.

"Every now and then," the officer said. "Most of them don't fit this. Hunters self-shot by accident, a husband kills his wife, heart attack victims—but looking at a pile of bones, it isn't easy to see if the corpse is male or female, killed violently or otherwise."

"That's true," a Georgia bureau officer stated. "We send in somebody from State Forensic and it may take a month or more to determine cause of death."

"Especially if it's strangulation," someone added.

"Somehow," Bud Diehl stood, "we must find a way of coordinating our efforts. Not only past cases, but future ones. I invited Dr. Joanne Fleming here to give us her opinion of the kind of man we're up against."

Samples yielded, and beneath the table Joanne saw him wipe his palms down his trousers. As Bud listed her credentials, Joanne assimilated thoughts. Her task was more than presenting a profile on an unknown sex offender. She had learned from experience that these pragmatic officers had to be "sold"—convinced that what she said had credence.

She spelled out the personality traits which would apply if the murderer was classified as a psychopath. She used another term, sociopath, meaning much the same thing, and defined it in laymen's terms. She then drew on known facts, the Jacksonville woman, the bites on her body, positive results of acid phosphatase tests which indicated sexual attack.

"We can't be positive of anything with the evidence at

hand," Joanne said. "But I thought perhaps it would be useful if we had an educated guess from which to work."

She listed the six traits which would classify their criminal as "sadist-murderer."

"Periodicity," she said. "Striking on a regular cycle. As Detective Samples stated, one a month—that's typical. The killer suffers no penitence, no conscience. Other than that, however, he is perfectly normal."

"Sane?" Bud Diehl interjected.

"Yes. Sane."

Samples gazed at a far wall, but his expression altered. Disbelief. Joanne saw it in others, too.

"Psychiatric evidence abounds on this type of criminal," Joanne continued. "The killer is a man who feels threatened by people unless he can structure the outcome of the relationship. Thereby, passive-aggressive tendencies evolve. The killer feels hostility toward any authority figure, and forced to subdue this, inner conflict intensifies. Toward men, for example, he may be genial, hedonistic and masculine. With certain women he may be the epitome of gentility. Yet, another female sparks some deeply imprinted conception and in cold blood he will rape, torture and murder. In the beginning, the killer considers himself in control. He tells himself the women "deserved" what they got. He thinks about this or that part of his assault, their responses, their terror indicates his mastery; he maims them as a means of debasement. Throughout, he is sexually aroused."

Samples doodled on a pad, jaw muscles bulging. Others occupied themselves with a jiggling foot, hands rubbed together, peering at the ash of a burning cigar.

"There are tests, developed over the years," Joanne said, "which have proven accurate in diagnosing such men. One is the Minnesota Multiphasic Personality Inventory. We call this an 'objective' test, as opposed to a 'projective' test . . ."

Too deep. Too pedantic. Joanne shifted gears, mentally. "The point is, people with certain psychological disorders will answer in certain predictable ways. There's always a chance of testing error, but even that has been virtually eliminated with use of a computer such as the CDC6500 at FSU. We can statistically diminish human error . . ."

Over their heads. Joanne took a breath. She needed something to strike a nerve, something they could relate to. "Gentlemen," she declared, "you are facing a criminal who thinks he's smarter than you are. He has the advantage of anonymity. He doesn't have any logical connection to his victims and his crimes are therefore the most difficult to solve. He strikes without warning, returns to his lair in some distant city and——"

Samples sat upright, staring at her.

"He leaves few clues, if any," Joanne continued. "He scoffs at you as a bunch of uneducated cops, fumbling the evidence. His greatest asset is your lack of comprehension as to the kind of man he is. You're dumb—in this man's view. While he sees himself as analytical and intelligent—he perceives the police as ignorant rednecks spitting tobacco and chewing on a weed stem."

As Joanne started to sit, Samples waggled a finger. "Dr. Fleming, what's this business about returning to a lair?"

"He goes out of safe territory, strikes, and returns," Joanne said. "That's my guess."

"How big would his safe territory be?"

"A city. A county. Even a state."

"Then," Samples asked, "would you assume he leaves an area once his safe lair has been spoiled?"

"I think that's a fair supposition."

"Which suggests," Samples said, "the last murder in a region may have been in his safe territory?"

"Quite possibly."

"Hot damn," somebody said. "Where's a map?"

"Tallahassee," Joanne said.

"What?"

"That's the center point so far. Tallahassee is about midway between Jacksonville and Pensacola. He's struck nearer and farther, but never in Leon County, Florida."

"When I go back to Seattle," Samples told the man next to him, "I'll concentrate on the last place a girl was taken. It's worth a try—and I have a feeling about it. Up to now, we had no idea where to start."

"One other thing." Joanne waited for attention. "You should know that this man's psychological disorder may worsen."

"In what way?"

"Like a man experimenting with drugs, he develops a tolerance, then goes to stronger narcotics. Eventually it takes more to recreate his original euphoria. It is not inconceivable that the killer will resort to an orgy of violence."

They pondered this awesome prophesy. Then Bud Diehl spoke. "We've *got* to coordinate our efforts."

Joanne put papers in her briefcase. *Task accomplished.*

In a soft amber glow of candlelight, Bud Diehl sipped some beer from a stein and withdrew, foam on his mustache. "Now that," he said, "is good."

Ken nodded, winked at Joanne.

"I wish I enjoyed beer," Joanne said. "You men always make it seem so deliciously satisfying."

"And 'tis," Bud belched into a closed fist. "You rang their bell today, Jo. That line about ignorant rednecks— it's true, but they don't like hearing it."

"Anybody we know?" Ken asked.

"Most everybody," Bud chuckled. He recounted events at the conference. "Then," he concluded, "Jo says 'Tallahassee, that's the center point.'"

"Uh-oh," Ken sat back.

"What?" Joanne demanded.

"What'll come of that remark, Jo?"

"They'll start working together, I hope."

Ken's eyes reflected a flicker of candle flame.

"What?" Joanne asked again, testily.

"You must love controversy," Ken said. "You barely scrape out of one, and here you go nose-diving into another—"

"What?" Joanne snapped.

"You practically told them this killer is living in Leon County, didn't you?"

"I said no such thing."

"You didn't?" Bud Diehl licked a hairy lip.

"I did not. I said this is center point, geographically. He could be anywhere."

"Well, Jo," Bud muttered, "naturally, we assumed Tallahassee is his safe haven. That isn't what you meant?"

She hesitated.

"You did mean that," Bud insisted.

"Yes."

Ken looked away.

"It's a reasonable guess, isn't it?" Bud persisted.

"Yes."

Ken's expression made Bud inquire, 'Something happening I don't know about?"

"Ken is worried about Sheriff Rogers, when and if he gets wind of this."

"He got wind about two minutes after the conference," Bud said. "I called Rogers immediately. We asked for any assistance he could give."

"I see," Joanne remarked.

"Why should that cause trouble?" Diehl said. "Cowboy loves a parade. He'll posture and denounce, and all the while he's sitting on a publicity pyramid."

"Let us say a fervent prayer that you're right," Joanne worried. "Cowboy Rogers doesn't see eye-to-eye with me."

They watched as a waiter placed their steaks. Slicing into charred meat, delivered as ordered, Bud Diehl carved with elbows out-thrust. "You know, Jo, I can't help fretting over what makes this killer tick. It's a little too simplistic to lay it on his mama and papa."

"It is indeed."

"I grew up in an orphanage." Bud talked around a nugget of steak. "I didn't know a thing about my parents except they abandoned me. I got shoved around, abused by older kids, finally got sent to a foster home run by a woman who saw me as fifteen dollars a week. Her profit depended on how cheaply she fed me."

"Tough," Joanne conceded.

"Yeah." Bud patted his mouth with a napkin. "It was. I went through a childhood that would twist anybody. But I never had a desire to rape or kill anyone. So what really makes a killer like this man we're after?"

"Off the wall?" Joanne warned.

"Shoot."

"Some authorities believe it's a matter of chemical balance in the body, glandular secretions."

"Meaning there's an evil chemical and a good one?"

"Fundamentally, yes." Joanne paused, thinking. "I did research on a grant at the Federal Correctional Institute. I had to secure urine samples from inmates who volunteered for the program."

"Urine samples!"

"Yes. This grew out of research by scientists at the New York Psychiatric Institute who were studying love."

Bud gagged, then laughed.

"There's some evidence," Joanne continued, "that love is an outgrowth of a chemical called phenylethylamine. Urine samples are used to gauge the level of phenylethylamine."

116

"Aw, Jo—come on."

"They'd been studying people who fall in love habitually and disastrously. The theory is that a so-called 'loving brain' produces more phenylethylamine than normal. The result is ecstacy, tremendous drive without benefit of sleep, birds singing, bells ringing—in short, symptoms seen in lovers."

"You're putting me on, right?"

"No. It's true."

"Sounds like a pretty satisfactory condition to me," Ken observed.

"It's the aftereffect that isn't," Joanne said. "When the lovebonding breaks, the subject is plunged into depression, becomes lethargic, cries inconsolably. Such people often compensate by overeating. Chocolate is one thing they seem to crave. Chocolate, by the way, contains large amounts of phenylethylamine."

"I've said before," Ken smirked, "love is gland."

"And you're more right than wrong. People who have an unstable control mechanism which causes starts and stops of phenylethylamine seem to suffer more than those with stable flows of this amphetamine-like substance. In milder cases, the victim caroms from one infatuation to another. In the extreme, unrequited love may bring about self-inflicted injury."

"That relates to our killer?" Bud asked.

"It might," Joanne said. "The day may come when psychopathic criminals undergo injections as a part of rehabilitation. Rather than prison, someday scientists may correct the chemical imbalance which fosters sociopathic behavior."

Bud munched food, mustache waggling. "Somehow," he murmured, "the possibility of a murderer guilty by reason of chemical imbalance is more frightening. It seems so—futile. So unnecessary."

"A modern day horror story," Ken observed.

"Obviously," Joanne said, "a criminal is the product of environment, societal pressures, parental influences, maybe poverty—as well as any glandular dysfunction. But it may help explain why one child survives adverse conditions and becomes a detective, while another becomes a sadist-murderer."

117

Chapter Fourteen

"M ARCIE," Ralph said, "you can't stay down here alone. Your mother wouldn't permit it."

"Part of my problem is mom's treatment of me as a child."

"You are not yet adult." Ralph lifted his chin, fashioning a Windsor knot.

"That's old-fashioned, daddy. Nobody wears ties like that anymore."

"I'm not a college student, Marcie. Please, get your clothing together so we can go. I have a critical meeting this morning."

"Daddy, let me stay here. It's boring at home during the summer. The kids are all down here, not in Tallahassee."

"I'm not going to invite your mother's wrath, Marcie. While you were here with Darlene, that was all right. But now, Darlene is gone."

"You think that made mom rest easy?"

"Darlene is a responsible adult and—"

"Mom hates Darlene!"

"You don't hate somebody you scarcely know, Marcie. Get your clothes."

"Mom can't stand the woman, daddy! She's jealous. She resents Darlene. She sees through her."

"Your mother may be jealous, that's normal. As for seeing through Darlene—"

Marcie's guffaw made him turn, face coloring. "So long as I'm with a mature person, right, daddy? Anybody over thirty is mature."

"Marcie, this psychology is a weak imitation of your mother's. It won't work. Get your clothes."

"You know what Darlene talks about? Sex. She eyeballs young men all day and then comes home to make a fool of you. In case you don't know it, Darlene is a horny old—"

He crossed to her in two angry strides. "Girl, you aren't

too big for a spanking and you're asking for it. Get your clothing. *Now.*"

"She's got the morals of a—"

He seized her shoulders and shook her. "Get-your-clothes."

Gathering garments in the next room, Marcie yelled, "If I did what you and mom do, I could understand! I wouldn't blame you if you treated me like a libertine. But I keep my pants on—"

Ralph loomed in the doorway, face livid. Marcie shoved dirty clothing into a bag.

"Marcie," he said, evenly, "never again speak of your mother in that way. She doesn't deserve that from you, or me, or anybody else. Henceforth, you will confine your opinion to me alone, and that I may permit. But never again speak of your mother in that way. Is that understood?"

"I'm sorry, daddy."

But as he left her, Marcie grumbled, "But I'm right."

Driving toward Tallahassee, her father's jowls retained the rubescence of anger. Tiny broken blood vessels formed a delicate web on his cheek.

"If I had someone with me," Marcie reasoned warily, "would that make it all right to stay in Panacea?"

"Depending on the person."

"An adult."

"Depending on which adult."

"Why not you?"

"You know I can't do that. I have to work."

"You could drive down each evening, couldn't you?"

"Commuting two hours a day is a little arduous, Marcie."

They drove without conversation for several miles. Marcie said, "Is it all right if I stay with you at your apartment in Tallahassee for a few days?"

"You may do that, if you wish. If it's all right with your mother."

"She won't care."

"Fine, then." His hands left perspiration on the steering wheel.

"This is so silly," Marcie said. "I'd be enjoying myself in Panacea and I'd be all right. There isn't a bit of difference between being alone in Panacea and being alone at your apartment. Or being alone at mom's! That's the kind of unfair logic I face from you and mom all the time."

119

"Marcie, I'd be late almost every night, driving down to Panacea. Nine o'clock or later, every night."

"And I'd be all right."

"Actually," he said, "I think you would be. But I find myself caught between your demands and your mother's. I understand and empathize with both of you. Frankly, I resent it, Marcie."

Sensing victory, Marcie wheedled, "Daddy, please. I'm sixteen years old."

"Marcie, I'll compromise to this extent: if your mother approves, I'll agree."

"Why shouldn't she approve?"

"Because I'll be late getting down there in the evening."

"Daddy, can't you make this one decision without mom? You know she'll object on general principles. That's how she is. If you must discuss it with her, please don't cloud the issue with the time you'll be away. Accent the positive, not the negative."

Ralph grunted, pulling into the driveway. "All right, Marcie—compromise is what politics is all about. I'll yield. Tell your mother yourself, and let me know her response. If she says it's all right, I'll pick you up here this evening promptly at eight and we'll go back down to Panacea."

"Thank you, daddy!" She kissed him, grinning.

"God help your future husband," Ralph said.

Joanne dried dishes, putting them away as Marcie pleaded her case.

"Has it occurred to you that your father and Miss Sands might wish to have some time alone, Marcie?"

"She's gone."

"Oh?"

"Left last night. Going to Paris. Good riddance, too."

Joanne veiled her interest, put away cutlery.

"She's just like all the others, mom. She's a sex object."

Joanne shot a glance at the girl, rounding her nails with an emery board.

"At first," Marcie said, "I thought daddy was drawn only to the sensuous giggly ones. Then, when we found out Darlene was famous and talented, I thought we were wrong. We weren't."

"Do you mind explaining that?"

"She's just a piece of fluff, mom. Talks about sex constantly, looks good because she's had a stomach lift, her breasts are mostly silicone injections—"

Joanne let the secret of enjoyment show. Marcie grinned. "She tries to pick up young studs."

"Oh, dear."

"I told daddy she was making a fool of him."

"That wasn't the most prudent observation to make, Marcie."

"Hello, hello," Ken's voice at the back door.

"She's old enough to satisfy daddy's need for a mother-figure and looks good enough to satisfy his sexual appetite."

Ken turned on a heel to leave again. "Come on in," Joanne urged.

Ken kissed Marcie, then Joanne. He reached in a cookie jar and withdrew a fistful of vanilla wafers.

"It'll be good to have time for quiet, mature contemplation," Marcie continued. "Daddy will be driving down every night. We'll have time to get better acquainted."

Ken peered at Joanne, expressionless.

"I suppose it's all right," Joanne agreed.

"Thanks, mom. Daddy will pick me up at eight, tonight."

"That's late to leave, isn't it?"

Marcie strolled toward her bedroom. "Daddy's trying to get things squared away so he'll have more time. See you, Ken."

"Did you get the drift of that?" Joanne asked.

"Only that you are, somehow, in some way, being had."

"I suspect."

"I wouldn't worry about it."

The telephone rang and Marcie called. "Long distance, mom!"

"Jo, Bud Diehl." His voice was whispery. "I hate to disturb you at home. Do you have a minute?"

Joanne got a pad and paper and sat on a high stool at the counter.

"The girl that disappeared in Panama City," Bud said, "she'd gone from her motel room to a drink machine, remember?"

"I remember."

"Specks of blood at the machine, which proved to be O-positive," Bud recounted. "They ignored it, classified the girl a runaway because she'd been under pressure to get married from a man somewhat her senior."

"Did they find her body?" Joanne asked.

121

"No. But they located the boyfriend. Working on the Farley nuclear power plant up near Dothan, Alabama. Anyhow, he passed a polygraph. The girl hasn't been with him and he hasn't seen her. They're treating the case as one of our missing girls now, and foul play is suspected."

"All right."

"I got a copy of the interviews from the Panama City police, Jo. I want to read you part of it."

"Go ahead."

"Okay," he said. "The girls were all from Chi Omega there at FSU. One of the girls reported this conversation in the motel room after they came in from the Breaker Bar:

"ANNETTE: Are you telling me nobody there appealed to you?

VICTIM: Nobody. Those aren't my kind of people. I really don't enjoy that scene.

ANNETTE: How about the handsome dude with his arm in a sling?

VICTIM: He didn't seem to be open for much conversation."

Joanne sat, pencil poised. Bud said, "Are you there, Jo?"

"I'm here."

"Remember what Samples said about—"

"I remember."

"Okay." Bud turned some pages. "They released the story to the newspapers in Panama City, asking for any witnesses. It's tough, because so many patrons at that particular bar come from out of town. But they did get this from a local girl who said she'd approached a man about dancing. This is what she said: 'He was the only person there who didn't seem to be having fun. I don't know whether you'd say he was suspicious or not, but he wouldn't dance. He couldn't, really. He'd hurt his arm skiing in Colorado.' "

Joanne shuddered. She still had written nothing.

"What do you think, Jo?" Bud asked.

"What does Detective Samples say?"

"He thinks it's the same one from Oregon-Washington-Utah."

"He could be right."

"We're asking all the Pacific Northwest cities to send us anything they have. I've been elected to coordinate this thing."

122

"Thanks for calling, Bud."

"Beware detectives bearing info," Bud chuckled. "I'm after something."

"Oh. All right."

"Like I said, Jo, the girls were from Chi Omega. Would you consider going over and talking to them? There are four."

"I don't mind, Bud, but Sheriff Rogers might."

"He's bitching already because he's short on deputies and we're imposing. No missing girls in his jurisdiction, he says. If the truth is known, though, I'd prefer a psychologist's point of view. Maybe some of the girls would submit to hypnosis. Will you do it?"

"You know school is out for the summer, Bud. They may be gone."

"Two are," Bud said. "I called. But two are still there. You have a pencil and paper?"

She took down the names. With a soft farewell, Bud hung up and Joanne realized Ken was standing behind her.

"He wants me to interview them," she said.

"Sheriff Rogers isn't going to be happy, Jo. He's already complaining. He called me in today and asked if I couldn't control my shrink girl friend."

Marcie came through, suitcase in hand. "Daddy's here."

"Have fun, darling,"

"Bye. Bye, Ken."

"Bye yourself," Ken said. "Keep your nose clean."

Marcie returned for another bag, commenting in passing, "You ought to see what daddy's wearing. He's dressed for golf." Into the bedroom, back with another parcel. "Why do all golfers dress like birds?" Marcie questioned. "Canary yellow, parrot green, bluebird—"

She kissed Ken full on the mouth and laughed. She hugged Joanne, kissing, saying, "Munch-munch-munch."

Alone, Joanne sighed, "There's always such a void after that child departs."

"Which leaves just you and me."

"First," Joanne said, "lock the doors."

Beyond the cottage, a soft ripple of bay waters lapped a pier; a gentle breeze stirred fronds of date palms and palmettos. He tied the laces of his tennis shoes in a double bow, to keep them from catching sandspurs. He'd come on foot, the Volkswagen left in the lane of an unoccupied house a quarter-mile distant. Now, with the feline stealth that came easily to him at times like this, he picked the placement of each foot, careful not to snap a twig, rustle a leaf.

From open screened windows came two sounds: the late news on TV in the den-dining room area; the muted thump of popular music from a radio in a back bedroom. He stooped to avoid a shaft of yellow light from above as he circled the building. Warily, he rose to peer inside. The father was lying on a sofa, mouth agape, sleeping with a magazine on his chest.

He stooped again, passed the cypress deck, and approached the bedroom. Slowly, slowly, he rose to peep inside.

The girl stood unconcerned and nude, gazing at her body in a full-length mirror. She lifted her shoulders, tummy sucked in, and twisted slightly to see the effect. She extended her chest, turned again, this way, that way, looking at firm flesh. Then, cupping herself, she formed a valley by pushing the breasts higher and closer together.

He kept his breath to evenly drawn inhalations. She slapped her buttocks, watching for signs of ripples, dimples. Then, with a groan, she relaxed and sagged.

She'd parted her hair down the middle, combed evenly to either side.

The girl faced her image. She squatted, knees spread, the pose grotesque—and exciting. She stood again, feet placed as though for a ballet exercise. Again, she squatted, thigh muscles rising, calves drawn taut.

He put a trembling hand on the side of the house, watching, staying in the shadows.

Here, secluded from the highway, well back from the bay, she was so certain she was alone and unseen. It was at these times that girls did the most exciting things—he'd once watched a girl masturbate with a vibrator. Later, he had returned—

But that was Portland. This was now.

She altered the position of her feet, a heel to the instep of her other foot. Again, she squatted, this time with arm outstretched, palm down, fingers pointing.

Shivering, he darted a glance at the patio. Somewhere afar, a dog barked. He stepped back from the window, looking into the night, listening. An automobile drove past out front, tires singing on warm pavement.

124

Now she stroked her legs, each calf with both hands. She went into the bathroom, out of view. He heard water running. He crept around a corner. The smaller, higher window of the bathroom was above a Spanish bayonet; the spiked leaves which gave the plant its name made access difficult. He looked for a ladder, chair, box.

There was a trellis, made of galvanized pipe joined by tees. He pulled vines loose from the structure, picked it up and hauled it to the high window. Quietly, he leaned it against the concrete block wall, tested it with a gentle push. A step at a time, he moved higher.

Shaving her legs. Humming along with her radio. She stroked, rinsed the razor, stroked anew. Blood trickled at her ankle, dropped into the tub making ruby spatters on porcelain.

He was shaking, breathing more rapidly, his heart pounding. The trellis slipped slightly as he readjusted his position for a better view.

The girl halted, listening.

An electric thrill coursed through his body. He deliberately jiggled the trellis again. She lifted her head, razor in hand, like a deer at a glen alert for hunters—listening—listening—

"Marcie!"

"Yessir?"

"I'm going to bed, darling."

"See you tomorrow, daddy. You want me to cook breakfast?"

"I'll eat when I get to Tallahassee. You sleep late."

"I love you, daddy!"

"Love you, Sweetheart. Good night."

Hands sweating, his legs aquiver, he straightened his knees to lock them, staring, his face close to the screen.

She continued her task, humming softly, and rinsed the razor under a faucet. Not four feet away—so near he could see goosebumps erupt when first she had been frightened.

She sat on the commode, feet on tiptoes, knees together, and gathered a massive wad of toilet paper which she held. Then, with a dab, she flushed the commode, turned off the light, and left him staring, shaking, mouth dry.

The bedroom light went out.

He eased down from the trellis, carried it back to where it had been, and laid it on the ground. Chest heaving, he waited for his eyes to adjust to the dark again. The barking dog yelped, fell silent.

Briars scratched at his trousers. He side-stepped free. Leaves crunched underfoot, twigs snapped—but he no longer cared. He was running now—long strides to work off tension, to ease the ache in his groin.

As always—the best part was the peeping. The watching, unseen—the delicious exhilaration of spying on someone who, unaware, acted perfectly naturally.

He'd been here before.

He'd come again.

Chapter Fifteen

THE tape recorder was intimidating but essential. Patty Neel, a sorority sister of the missing Panama City girl, looked from Joanne to Ken.

"She's dead."

"Why do you think that?" Joanne asked.

"I feel it. I know it. She went out to get drinks, and when she didn't come back, I knew something awful had happened. We tried to tell the police, but they acted unconcerned about it."

Ken had insisted on coming, and with some reservation, Joanne had agreed. Now, as he smiled at the nervous girl, Joanne was glad he had. Ken made the tape recorder unobtrusive, nodding with sympathetic understanding.

"Rose wouldn't just wander off," Patty declared. "She wasn't enjoying herself when she was with us, but she certainly wouldn't have gone off alone."

"You were close friends?"

Patty wrinkled a pug nose, seemed pained. "Rose was—not easy to befriend. She was distant. She'd sit in on long talks with other girls, but she didn't volunteer anything about herself. She was Jewish, for one thing. A Christian Jew, she said. But she was coming from a different place, mentally. Why she stayed at FSU was a mystery to me. She wasn't happy here."

"She encountered prejudice?"

"Not really. Not that I know of. But she felt—inferior. Yet she felt superior at the same time. I know that sounds contradictory. She acted shy, but she wasn't shy. Do you understand?"

"I'm not sure."

Patty stroked her hair with one hand, pushing auburn strands over a shoulder. "Rose rarely talked, and when she did, it was sarcastic. She had a way of turning off people who didn't know her. But then, when you decided you didn't like her, she'd do something so thoughtful or generous . . . it kept you off balance."

"Could you give me an example?"

"I had influenza over the Thanksgiving holidays," Patty recalled. "I wasn't able to go home. I come from Key West. Here I was cooped up in a nearly empty building, honking my nose and breathing vapors of Mentholatum, and feeling wretched. Rose had already gone home to New Jersey. Her father is a union organizer and Thanksgiving is a big social occasion for them. As soon as Rose got there, she told her father she had a sick friend and caught the next plane back to Tallahassee. She came walking in with barbecued chicken and we had Thanksgiving dinner together."

"That was thoughtful."

"Yeah, but the next week, back to normal. Walking past me like I wasn't even there. Funny like that. Hard to figure."

"Patty, let's talk about the evening Rose disappeared."

"Five of us drove down to the Breaker Bar in Panama City, which is a hangout for college kids. Everybody was having fun, except Rose. She didn't drink, she didn't smoke, she wouldn't dance. The fellows would come over and she'd turn them off—typical Rose. We tried to get her to ease up, but she wouldn't give an inch. We were all angry with her, but we were covering it up. Until we got to the motel."

"What happened there?"

"I hate to tell this." She stroked her hair, threw it back. "It sounds like we had a fight, which we didn't."

"What happened?"

"The whole evening was a fiasco. Nobody made connections with anybody and it was Rose's fault, really. When we got into the motel room—we all share one room—somebody said Rose was frigid."

Patty's lips twisted, chin dimpling. "Rose gave her usual performance. She said she hated the kind of scene at the Breaker. She implied there was nobody good enough. In the two years I've known Rose she rarely dated, and always Jewish boys."

"Patty, in the nightclub—was there anybody you would consider suspicious, or different?"

"The usual crowd. College kids mostly. The music is loud. It isn't a place where senior citizens would go."

"Was there anybody who attracted your attention—someone out of sync with the others?"

"One fellow from Colorado."

"Colorado?"

"I heard him tell a girl he couldn't dance because he hurt his arm skiing in Colorado. He had it in a sling—a cast, I think."

"How old was he?"

"Twenty, maybe. It was too dark to see and the lights are colored red and blue. There's a globe with mirrors that throws specks of light all over the room. That distorts features. You can't see well even if you're face-to-face."

"How was he dressed?"

"Shorts, casual shirt, no socks."

"What colors?"

"I can't even guess—the lights flash and turn. Nothing looks like the real color."

"Did this fellow with the hurt arm leave before, or after you?"

"I don't remember."

"Did you see him stand up?"

"I don't remember," Patty said, softly. "I've tried to think of things like that and I don't remember. We all talked about it later. I don't know. I just don't know."

"Did he have a beard?"

"I don't think so. Kind of ratty looking hair. He'd been on the beach all day like everybody else, I guess."

"Close cut? Long?" Ken interrupted.

"I wish I could say," Patty said. "But I don't remember."

*　　*　　*

Judith Sizemore was the student who first went looking for Rose when the sorority sister did not return. "Five minutes," Judith said, adamantly. "No longer. I went out to the drink machine . . . and nothing. I knew we had trouble."

"Perhaps Rose had taken a walk on the beach to cool off," Ken suggested.

"Not Rose. The wind blew her hair, salt made her itch—she wouldn't go near the water."

"Were you close to Rose?" Joanne inquired.

"No."

"Did you like her?"

Judith fluttered short eyelashes. "Rose could mess you up just being there. She did it that night."

"Drove away the boys," Joanne suggested.

"We did our best to warm her up, but she was an Arctic iceberg. Kept her legs crossed, fixed smile, arms folded: the message was clear enough. Buzz off."

"Why were you so quick to go looking for her?" Ken asked. "Did you suspect something was wrong?"

"To tell the truth, I don't know why I hurried out. But I did and something told me—watch it. I insisted we call the police right away even though the others wanted to wait."

"Judith, do you remember the man in the Breaker Bar who had his arm in a sling?"

"Certainly do."

"Can you describe him?"

Her eyelashes fluttered. "Five feet nine," she reported. "Gray eyes, mid-thirties, unshaven. White shorts, tennis shoes, white cotton socks. His shirt was tan, a pullover. He had his arm in a yellow bandana. And a gun. Don't ask me how I know. But he had a gun in the bandana."

"How *do* you know?" Ken smiled.

"He went to the men's room, and when he came back there wasn't any water on his shorts. You tell me how to wash your hands with an arm in a sling and not get water on yourself. Or, for that matter, how to zip and unzip."

"I see."

"Blondish hair, good tan," Judith continued. "Weighed about one-seventy."

"Would you recognize him if you saw him again?" Ken asked.

"Absolutely."

129

Later, walking to their automobile, Ken grunted, "You got nothing in there."

"I realize that."

They drove to Joanne's office, and she called Bud Diehl in Jacksonville.

"About all they agree on," Joanne reported, "is that he had his arm in a sling. After that, neither girl said anything that would stand up as testimony, even if you had a suspect."

"You think hypnosis would help, Jo?"

"No."

"Might be worth a try," Bud pressed.

"The girls had no reason to be alert or suspicious. The light was dim, revolving mirrors threw multicolored reflections over clothing and faces."

She relayed the lengthy description offered by Judith Sizemore. "All of which should probably be discounted, Bud. Most of her information is the result of unconscious transference."

"Which is?"

"The mistaken recollection of one person with another person seen at a different time under different circumstances. A teller sees a customer a few times, but not often. The bank gets robbed. She is shown mug shots and selects one. The one she selects is not the robber, but a face similar to the customer she's seen only a few times. That's unconscious transference. It's a major cause of mistaken identity claims by witnesses.

"These girls," Joanne continued, "had no reason for remembering the man with his arm in a sling. They were peeved with their friend, unhappy about their evening, and all they can remember for certain is—the arm in a sling, which was out of place. That much is probably accurate. Everything else is most likely unconscious transference."

"Damn," Bud whispered.

"Your best bet," Joanne said, "is to find a body and treat it as a sex crime from the first instant. It would help to know the sequence of the assault. I need to know *what* he does to the victims."

"God forbid that there are more."

"If he's the man I think he is," Joanne said, "there will be more."

*　*　*

Marcie shifted her three-speed and settled on the bike seat, pedaling only enough to maintain momentum. The wind was dry and warm. She could feel freckles popping out on her ears, but her tan was now deep enough to absorb such blemishes. She veered to the edge of the road to allow a Volkswagen to pass. Without a glance, he drove around her and continued on toward The Oaks restaurant and the Ochlockonee bridge.

She'd seen him several times recently. Always alone, deep in concentration and unaware of her. She'd also seen other women sneaking peeks at those rippling biceps and the golden hair of his chest and forearms, bleached by wind and sun. Marcie shifted gears again, gaining speed. He was now several hundred yards ahead, steadily drawing away.

. . . like a prince, Darlene had said.

Marcie had fantasized about meeting him. In her reverie, he spoke with an accent, expounding on music and literature, offering to take her skydiving, or soaring in his hang glider.

Up to now, he had paid no notice to her or any other woman. Maybe he was queer. They were always gentle with women, whispering girlish things, throwing back their heads with feminine giggles. A girl could feel safe with them, usually. A tender neuter, that's what she needed. Somebody not interested in sexual conquest, not eager to wrestle and sweat. Someone she could trust implicitly, lower her guard for once—someone to whom she could say whatever came to mind, without fear of his misunderstanding.

If he *was* one, thank goodness he didn't swish around with his butt tucked and feet splayed. He didn't gesture with his little finger and didn't speak in contralto. She'd heard him speak to waitresses at The Oaks—they liked him. They warmed to his smile, and it was a nice smile, really. He'd been seated next to Marcie several times.

It was curiosity, as much as anything, so far as she was concerned. Like having a new neighbor; you wondered—

She saw him cross the main highway to The Oaks. He parked, but didn't get out, head down as if reading.

Oh, well. She wasn't going to The Oaks, anyway. She had already decided to pedal across the long bridge spanning Ochlockonee Sound, to a favorite spot on the far side, a picnic area with tables and benches. It was shady,

131

cool, and the water was nice for wading. Even surrounded by tourists, she would be left alone to think private thoughts.

Marcie pulled into traffic, pedaling furiously to keep pace but wary of fishermen along the rail who often leaped backward in the exuberance of their catch. It was a wonder they didn't commit suicide, stepping into a flow of traffic while grasping for a flipping fish at the end of their lines. Fishing was such a smelly business. But Charlie liked it, and daddy, so she went sometimes. Chances were, it was like nail polish and lip gloss, you did it for men, not yourself.

Somebody yelled "shark" and Marcie halted to gawk with all the others. But it was a porpoise lolling beyond the channel marker. As she stood there, the Volkswagen passed slowly. He didn't look her way.

When she got to the picnic grounds, a site maintained for visitors by the Florida Highway Department, Marcie saw the VW parked, backed against bushes. Again, he appeared to be reading, eyes hidden behind dark glasses, head down. She wedged her bike between a sapling and another tree. She hung her sandals on the handlebars. Not many people here today. She walked barefoot into the water, watched hermit crabs scuttle for safety.

Now and then, although rarely, she found a coquina washed in by storms from the Gulf. Bald Point was a far better site for shelling, but she hadn't felt like cranking out daddy's powerboat, running over there, then having to wash it down and suspend it in the shed again. Marcie walked slowly along the shoreline, looking for periwinkles. A good specimen always had a live inhabitant —and she'd never been able to kill the tiny snail for the sake of taking a shell.

She rounded a curve in the land; rhythmic thumps of car tires on the bridge were muted now by mangroves and reed grass. A horseshoe crab the size of a dinner plate stirred sediment and disappeared into underwater weeds.

"Lose something?"

Him.

"Looking for shells."

"What kind?"

"Anything in one piece, really."

He was closer to shore than she, the bottoms of his shorts wet as if he'd been kneeling. "You collect them?"

132

"Off and on. Do you?"

He smiled, blue eyes crinkling at the corners. "I love to look at them, but I always put them back."

"Yeah," she grinned, "me too!"

He stooped, scooped a handful of particles, examined them closely. "Sometimes the best ones are very tiny."

"That's right."

Fifteen feet apart, they walked slowly to keep from kicking up clouds of silt. Now and then, one or the other would find something, comment, and drop it back in the water. Marcie turned, casually, wading back toward the bridge and picnic area.

"Here's some," he called.

"What kind?"

He motioned for her to come, but Marcie stood, asking, "What kind?"

"A mixture," he said.

"I'll look another day," she said. "I'm going on."

"See you."

"Right. Bye."

But when she got to the picnic area, Marcie dawdled, waiting. She tinkered with her bicycle, adjusted the nuts with a wrench she carried.

She heard the roar of a Volkswagen motor and, surprised, watched him pull away, up an embankment onto the highway. She'd been waiting for him—so how, she asked herself, did he get around her without being seen?

Through the bushes, obviously. A difficult way to go. Why not follow the same watery route she'd taken? She got on her bicycle, miffed with herself for not being more friendly. She'd had her chance and blown it!

She hauled herself up the highway, leg muscles quivering with effort, then turned toward home over the bridge. Nuts. She could have at least passed the time of day a few minutes . . .

Pedaling fast, she saw the VW far ahead, poking along so slowly other cars were blowing their horns. Then, with a gust of blue exhaust, the VW raced on, turned into The Oaks parking lot.

Marcie eased off, slowing.

Ah hah. Another chance.

She saw him sitting, head down, and yet now, she didn't fancy that he was reading, unaware.

Impulsively, she turned not into the restaurant lot, but

133

toward home. She shifted gears, gaining speed, following the narrow highway eastward.

Daddy wouldn't be in for several hours yet. Last night he didn't get here until midnight. This morning, haggard and irritable, he'd departed early, grumbling to himself about "impositions."

The wind whistling in her ears, Marcie heard a familiar noise behind her—the distinctive small motor of a Volkswagen, winding from second to third, whining as the gear was pushed to its limit.

Grinning, pedaling as fast as she could, Marcie left the main highway and all other traffic far, far behind . . .

Chapter Sixteen

LEGS pumping, butt lifted, leaning low over the handlebars, the girl was going faster than thirty miles an hour. He gained speed, closing in on her. Now, depressing the clutch, he let the motor drop to idle and coasted up behind her, hand on the horn.

Just as he blew, she veered across the pavement toward her driveway. Startled, to avoid a collision she thought imminent, she jerked the bike. Narrow tires struck soft sand, the bicycle twisted and the girl fell, legs entangled in the frame.

He brought the VW to a stop and ran back. "Are you hurt?"

"My elbow." Blood rose from abrasions. "And knee."

"I'm sorry. It was an idiotic thing to do."

"That's what we get for playing silly games," she said.

He helped her to her feet and, limping, the girl allowed him to support her. "You are hurt," he noted. "We need to find a first-aid kit."

"There's one in the cottage." She flexed a leg, testing.

"Come on," he offered, "we'll get you patched up."

She reached for the bicycle.

"Never mind," he said, "I'll come back for that. Come on."

Wincing, her arm in his grasp, she laughed, skip-hopping toward the cottage. "There goes the perfect tan," she complained. "It's only skin deep."

They circled around back, went up the steps of the deck, and she pulled open the unlocked sliding doors. Inside, she sank into a chair, directing, "In the medicine cabinet, in the bathroom. My daddy is prepared for anything."

He heard her suck air between her teeth. He passed through the master bedroom—the king-sized bed rumpled and unmade, pillows lying on the floor. On the lavatory were bottles of men's cologne and after-shave lotion. An electric razor was on the flush tank top of the commode. He found iodine, gauze, adhesive. In the medicine cabinet, also, were a snakebite kit, tranquilizers, and several bottles of Bufferin.

"This is going to burn," he warned. "You can holler if you want to."

Before he touched her, she screamed. "There," she announced, "go ahead." As he daubed the violent red medicine, she whispered, "Ouch, ouch, ouch—blow it."

He blew, lips close to her knee.

"Ouch-ouch—blow, blow!"

He blew more rapidly.

"You'll hyperventilate and I'll have to revive you," she said. When he looked up, there were tears in her eyes.

"Now the elbow."

"Don't kiss it," she ordered. "Mom says if you kiss your own elbow you change from girl to boy. I'm scared if anybody else kissed it I'd only go halfway."

He laughed, applied iodine and blew, cheeks puffed. Finally, he sat back. "It would have been a great loss, had you been a boy."

"Word for word what daddy says."

"What kind of work does your father do?"

"Lawyer." She straightened her legs as he cut gauze and adhesive tape. "He practices in Tallahassee."

"I'd hate for him to catch me at his daughter's knee."

"He doesn't get in until late."

"What about your mother?"

"They're divorced."

"I'm sorry."

"It's okay. They've got a relationship worked out. I'm the only one still suffering."

He gazed up into her green eyes. No self-pity, thank goodness.

"Having divorced parents is sort of like having one of them die," she said. "Only it keeps happening over and over."

He pressed the tape against her skin, examined his work. "I don't know how long that will stay."

"Suits me. You can skip the elbow."

"I think it should be protected."

"Well. All right."

"I'm no doctor," he warned.

"What *are* you?"

"A touch of this, a bit of that. Student."

"FSU?"

"Yes. Criminology."

"Uh-oh. Do you know Dr. Fleming?"

"I know the name."

"That's my mom."

"I don't have any courses under her." A moment later, "What's her field?"

"You'll laugh."

"Try me."

"She specializes in sex deviations. Sex criminals."

He concentrated on his work. "I wonder what she'd have to say about my sexual deviation."

"I don't know. What is it?"

"When I was a child, I liked to sneak around peeking into women's windows, watching them undress. It worried me that I got such a thrill from it."

"I expect that's fairly normal. Girls do that, too."

He was genuinely surprised, "They do?"

"Sure. If it's there—look. That's normal enough."

"I'll go get your bike. You stay put and let the muscles relax, so you won't stiffen up."

When he reached the road, he looked back—from here the house was difficult to see. He turned the bicycle, put the front wheel on a tree root and stepped on the rim, jumping slightly. Lifting the bent wheel, he attempted to turn it. It rubbed the frame and stopped. He carried the bike to the rear deck.

"I'm afraid the wheel is bent," he called.

136

"Phooey! It'll be the weekend before daddy can get another one, if then." She appeared at the back door.

"I'm terribly sorry."

"I've walked before," she said. "I can walk again."

"Nonsense! I'm here for awhile and have a car. I'll drive you anywhere you want to go."

"I wouldn't want to be a bother."

"No bother at all. I'm glad for the company. I've been lonely ever since I got here—this may be my luckiest day. Where shall I leave the bike?"

"In the shed by the boathouse."

He felt her eyes, following, assessing.

When he returned, he said, "We can begin with lunch. How about it? On me."

Hesitation. She averted her eyes. "Maybe some other time."

"Okay. What's your number and I'll call you later?"

"We don't have a telephone here."

"Then," he grinned, "I'll have to drop by off and on."

He started to walk away and she called, "Hey! What's your name?"

"Don," he said. "Don Whitney."

"Like the mountain?"

"Exactly."

"Good to meet you, Don."

"Good to meet you, Miss Fleming."

"Marcie," she said.

"Good, Marcie. See you later."

Heart pounding, abdomen taut, he controlled his strides, aware that she was watching. Nonchalantly, he whistled as he walked.

It couldn't be more perfect.

Joanne poured coffee for Ralph and herself, put a glass of iced tea before Ken. From the utility room came the blare of a radio accentuated by a washer and drier as Marcie cleaned her clothes, singing aloud as she did.

"How goes it, Ralph?" Ken inquired.

"Hectic."

"Are things going to suit you?" Joanne alluded to his investigation of Judge Alcorn.

"Tediously, but steadily," Ralph said. He gazed in the direction of the laundry room and Marcie's voice, off-key.

"You look like you've been through the grinder, Ralph," Joanne stated.

"I'm fine."

"You have circles under your eyes, you're pale."

"I'm fine, Jo. The coffee is good."

Marcie came in, arms loaded with clean clothes. She put them on a counter to sort and fold.

"You aren't getting enough sleep, Ralph," Joanne said. "You know what happens to your allergy when you do that. You need your strength for what you're doing."

"I'm all right, Jo. How's it coming, Marcie?"

"Another thirty minutes, daddy."

Ken sat with his right ankle resting on his left knee, the foot jiggling. His only sign of discomfort.

"You could leave Marcie here, Ralph," Joanne suggested. "There's no need to commute that long distance, daily."

"Everything is fine, Jo."

"She's been down there nearly two weeks, Ralph. It wouldn't hurt her to stay home awhile."

"I could stay at your apartment, daddy," Marcie offered.

"No, no," he sniffed, "I'm not unhappy driving to Panacea."

Ralph drew a breath. Sniffed.

"On patrol," Ken said to Ralph, "I went by your place the other evening. The lights were on after eleven. Hope everything was all right."

"Thanks for watching," Ralph smiled tightly. "I probably forgot to turn them off during the daylight."

"I think you were there," Ken said. "I saw your car."

"Marcie," Ralph straightened his back, "I'm in a bit of a rush, baby. I have a critical meeting this afternoon before we can leave. Maybe I could come back for you?"

"I'll be through in a minute, daddy."

Ralph blew his nose.

Joanne followed Marcie to her bedroom. "Marcie, is everything going all right down at the cottage?"

"Sure, mom."

"It would be a nice thing to offer, staying here so your father can get caught up on his rest."

"He's not losing sleep on my account, mom."

"He's working on something very important," Joanne said. "He needs to be fresh and alert for it."

"Daddy's not suffering, mom. We're enjoying it."

138

Intuitively, Joanne mused, "Found you a fellow down there?"

Marcie shrugged, "Lots of them. Mostly kids I go to school with."

"Nobody new?"

"Naw," Marcie said. "Funny thing is, I miss Charlie."

Joanne smiled sympathetically and hugged her. As she turned to go, Marcie said, "Mom, what does it mean when a fellow peeks into windows at women?"

Joanne's spine tingled. "You mean what psychological implications?"

"Yes."

"Scopophilia is—"

"What?"

"That's the term for it," Joanne said. "It means voyeurism. It's akin to exhibitionism where men, and occasionally women, expose themselves to strangers."

"Is it a sickness?"

"As always," Joanne said, "that is determined by a variety of factors. Mostly, the age of the person, and the intensity of obsessiveness. How old a person?"

"A kid."

"That's normal. Curiosity."

"What if it doesn't stop?" Marcie asked.

"First, it's trespassing and it's illegal," Joanne noted. "One could be mistaken for a prowler and get shot."

"I mean, psychologically."

Joanne sat on the foot of the girl's bed, watching Marcie pack fresh clothing. "Voyeurs who don't achieve satisfaction from pornographic films and magazines—that's the extreme of which you speak?"

"Yes."

"Such a person may go to great lengths to peep," Joanne said. "There've been cases where they fell from tall buildings and even off moving trains, trying to peek at women."

"What causes it?"

"Psychiatrists believe voyeurism is derived from an infantile desire to look. Biologically, that's not unusual. Young children are entranced with their mother's private parts, and they're very interested in all sexual matters. Most psychiatrists would probably say that voyeurism comes from a repressed experience of the primal scene— that is, watching parental intercourse. Freud thought the voyeur was trying to overcome a fear of castration."

139

"That's silly."

"Castration can be mental, as well as physical, Marcie. Fear of emasculation or loss of masculinity. Actually, voyeurism and exhibitionism are an important part of preadolescent sex play, according to Dr. Kinsey. When voyeurism doesn't diminish with age, we assume that, like most deviations, it stems from immaturity."

"Is it dangerous?"

"If somebody falls from a high place trying to sneak a peek, it can be. Or if he gets shot at a window."

The girl's furrowed brow prompted Joanne to add, "Voyeurs are called 'Peeping Toms' which is taken from the legend of Lady Godiva. Why do you ask?"

"I heard about a boy I know, peeping in windows. He seems so nice. I wondered."

"I wouldn't worry too much about it. In normal men, a desire to look is a part of sexual attraction and it's a preliminary before making further advances. Voyeurism is considered a psychosis only when a subject derives his primary sexual satisfaction from the looking at nakedness or intercourse. To such a voyeur, imaginary involvement in the scene is more gratifying than it would be if he were actually a part of it. It is one of the lesser psychological problems to worry about."

"Thanks, mom."

"What happened to your friend?"

"Nothing yet. Maybe he'll grow out of it."

Joanne turned at the door. "Biologically," she said, "voyeurism and exhibitionism are the seeking of love. It occurs most often in men who live in a female dominated environment. Sometimes, when a man is under the thumb of a domineering woman, when he is made to feel subservient to his wife or his mother, he might begin exposing himself to strange women as a means of proving his virility. When the desire to prove his masculinity becomes an overpowering obsession, it's a sexual deviation which requires psychoanalysis."

"Thanks, mom."

"Your father is waiting, Marcie."

As they entered, Ralph rose. "Ready, baby?"

"Bye, mom." Marcie bounded out. Joanne grabbed Ralph's arm.

"Ralph, did you ever get curtains for the bedrooms at the cottage?"

"Not yet."

"I think you should."

"Got to go, Joanne."

"Right away, will you?"

"Jo," his voice lilted, "stop worrying!"

Ralph glanced at Ken, kissed Joanne perfunctorily and went to join Marcie in the car.

Ken was still seated at the table. "Made a mistake," he said.

"What?"

"I mentioned to Ralph how comfortable the recliner is in the living room and how every time I sit down there I doze off."

"So?"

"He said, 'Yes, that's always been my favorite chair, too.' "

Joanne shook her head, soberly. "Don't worry about it."

Ken stood, rotated his shoulders to ease back muscles. "So, what's to hold us up now?"

"Hold us up from what?"

"Hightailing it out of here. To the Smokies."

"The Smokies," Joanne said dumbly.

"We are going to the Smokey Mountains, aren't we?"

"Ken—I—"

"Come on now, Jo. I had a hard time getting vacation approval with the deputy staff so low. You said we'd go after the conference."

"I didn't say that, Ken. You suggested it. I didn't respond positively."

"Jo—" Ken growled.

"Ken, this is a terrible time to go."

"Jo—"

"I'm overloaded at the office, I have to finish a report for Judge Alcorn on a man who is accused of assaulting a masochist personality—I really can't go now."

"Jo, I thought it was settled that we were leaving today —my bags are in the car. Pack up and let's shove off."

"Ken, honey—" she reached for him and he drew away.

"Look, Jo. I'm not going to sit out a vacation in my apartment. I've made reservations at a little hotel in Rabun Gap, Georgia, where we stayed once before. We've got reservations at Front Royal, Virginia. Beds with vibrators —quiet, beautiful view—"

"Ken, I'd like to, more than anything in the world, I'd like to. But—"

"The relevant part of any statement follows 'but,' " Ken snapped.

"But," Joanne persisted, "I just can't. I mean, not now. Couldn't you put off your vacation?"

She watched self-control reasserted. "No, I don't think so. I'll go alone."

"Ken, I'm sorry."

"Sure."

"I'd be wrought up over work I'm leaving."

"Sure, Jo."

"Another time, perhaps."

"Right." He rinsed his tea glass and put it in the dishwasher.

Joanne watched him play out the scene, giving her a kiss without passion. Then, alone in an empty house, she fought tentacles of depression. *Joanne, you are a fool.*

She subdued a desire to rush after him. She had her work, a career, responsibilities.

Eyes burning but dry, she decided to take a hot bath. That always made things right.

Chapter Seventeen

JUDGE Albert Alcorn addressed Joanne and District Attorney Phillip Dupree. "I give this jungle bunny all the black cases and this is what he does to me."

Joanne felt a flush in her face. Alcorn angrily shoved papers on the table. "Sixty-four percent of the crimes committed in Leon County are by blacks against blacks. They come before me guilty as hell and this attorney clogs up my courts with *this*—" he stabbed a pile of briefs with a finger. "One continuance after another."

Alcorn glared at Joanne. "He's applied for retrial of the Swain case."

"Yes, sir."

"You knew that."

"Yes, judge."

"I presume you're responsible."

"I don't intend to discourage Mr. Nathan."

"*Mister* Nathan," Alcorn snapped, "is going to find me a tough jurist, I can promise you. I don't appreciate wasting taxpayers' money and court calendar time with guilty men whose sentences should be automatic."

A tap on the door and Alcorn called, "Come in!"

"Judge Alcorn," John Nathan put his briefcase on a chair, "I apologize for being late. I had an emergency at the office."

"Forty minutes late, Nathan."

"Yes, sir. I had an emergency. I'm sorry."

"Get on with it, Dupree," Alcorn ordered.

The District Attorney stood, formally. "The third of May," he began, "one Farris Dietrich was found outside a motel on North Monroe Street. He had been viciously assaulted. He had been beaten with a chain. There were cigarette burns on his feet, legs and genitalia. He was suffering a concussion from blows to the head, a cervical vertebra was chipped. He identified his assailant, who was subsequently arrested. The two men knew one another."

"Black or white?" Alcorn demanded.

"Sir?"

"These men," Alcorn said, "black or white?"

Dupree consulted his notes. "White, judge." He glanced at Joanne and continued, "The crime was violent and without mercy. The victim was left for dead, apparently. We are seeking a charge of assault with intent to murder at the very least."

Alcorn glared at John Nathan, and the public defender stood as Dupree sat. "Judge, with your permission, I'd like Dr. Fleming to make a statement which is the basis for our defense."

Now Joanne arose. "Judge Alcorn, this case is much more complex than the evidence suggests. We see that assault took place, which the defendant does not deny."

"He's confessed," Dupree interjected.

"To which the defendant confessed," Joanne amended. "The assailant has been identified by the victim, Mr. Dietrich, who knew him well. We also concede that the assault was savage."

"So why are we wasting time?" Dupree mused.

143

John Nathan spoke. "We hope to present information which will temper the facts with wiser judgment, Mr. District Attorney."

"Therefore," Joanne continued, "it is not the assault or the guilt of the defendant which is in question."

"Then what is?" Alcorn rasped.

"It is," Joanne said, "that the assault was invited."

"Meaning, Mr. Dietrich provoked it?"

"Meaning," Joanne countered, "Mr. Dietrich *invited* it. He asked the defendant to do all that was done and specified the acts he desired as the assault proceeded. Mr. Dietrich pleaded for more, indicating he wished to be bound, burned, beaten. It was at his request that he was hurt."

"For God's *sake*—" Alcorn shoved Joanne's report away. "Are you suggesting the defendant is innocent?"

"We're suggesting that this presents mitigating circumstances," Nathan replied.

"I'm speaking to Dr. Fleming," Alcorn said, sharply.

"Jo," Dupree reasoned, "this man nearly killed Dietrich."

"He did," Joanne said, "but at the victim's request."

"That makes it no less attempted murder."

"That's true, legally," Joanne said. "But justice in this case extends beyond the legal aspects."

"In what way?"

"The case should never go to trial."

The District Attorney stood, angrily. "Judge, I'm weary of hearing sob sisters try to free confessed felons for one philosophical reason or another."

"This case *will* come to trial," Alcorn mandated.

"Judge," Nathan began, "with all due respect—"

"Nathan," Alcorn railed, "I suggest you get your act together. I'm tired of handing you business which you use to clog up my court. Seven appeals, four continuances, three requests for delay."

"To give the best defense possible, judge, these cases require investigation. I have no staff and—"

"You're going to find yourself sitting in shantytown with a worn shingle and no business, understand, Nathan? Get your act together and expedite these matters!"

"Yes, sir."

"Judge," Joanne persisted, "the District Attorney is acting on reports of investigators who are not psychologists."

"I'm acting on an interview with Mr. Dietrich who has

144

suffered grievous assault! He said he was assaulted. He said the accused did it. The accused admits it. How much more do you want?"

"The truth," Joanne replied.

"Who do you claim is lying?" Alcorn questioned.

"Neither man, as far as it goes. But as I said, there are mitigating circumstances. May I continue?"

John Nathan sat back, brown fingers laced across his vest.

"Jo," Dupree argued, gently, "the victim has expressed a desire to press charges. He has a clear-cut case. What possible fantasy could you weave that will alter the facts?"

"Mr. Dietrich invited all that happened," Joanne said. "He did so because he is a psychotic masochist. He derives sexual pleasure from that which would be painful to anyone else."

"He didn't feel the pain?"

"He felt it," Joanne said. "But the pain gives him pleasure, and that's the point."

"Judge, Mr. Dietrich denies this allegation."

"Of course he denies it," Joanne retorted. "What else can he say? Cowboy Rogers pushed for a trial and Mr. Dietrich faces a day when a jury and the community will hear his testimony. He told Sheriff Rogers he didn't want to press charges and Cowboy insisted. Now you insist! Left to his own wishes, Mr. Dietrich would recuperate and forget the entire matter."

"Nevertheless," Dupree warned, "this is not a civil matter. Whether Dietrich presses charges or not, the county will."

"And that's the point of contention," Joanne declared. "What we have here is a victim who needs medical and psychiatric care. His assailant, guilty by commission and confession, may be the true victim in this case. Mr. Dietrich is not going to take a stand in a courtroom and admit he's a masochist. Thereby, injustice is done."

"Of all the harebrained defenses," Alcorn grunted, "this is it, Jo. If we let this one go by, nobody will be safe in Leon County. All they have to do is get the victim to say he enjoyed it—and that doesn't make the assault any less a crime."

"I agree."

"Then what are you saying?"

"I'm saying, this case should not go before a jury. The

District Attorney should allow the victim to decide on the charges, which means they'll be dropped. Mr. Dietrich should be placed under psychiatric care, the assailant should be put on strict probation. No publicity. None."

"I will not agree to that, Jo," Alcorn said.

"Nor I," Dupree affirmed.

"Then," Joanne turned to John Nathan, "the defense has no choice."

Nathan spoke without standing. "It will be necessary to present evidence by Dr. Fleming and other authorities which will ultimately destroy the reputation of Mr. Dietrich —and a jury will probably recommend mercy or turn the defendant loose, anyway."

Nathan withdrew a pocket watch, looked at it. "The cost to the taxpayer will be about thirty thousand dollars, with all the wrong people hurt for all the wrong reasons. Mr. Dietrich has a wife and children. He will be shown for what he is—a sick man—and his career and marriage may be ruined. All in the quest for justice. Tell me where the justice is, judge?"

"Now, for heaven's sake," Joanne implored more softly, "this is a case where reason must override the letter of the law. In these chambers, justice can be done. In a courtroom, nothing good will come of this tragic situation."

"Your recommendation is what?" Alcorn demanded.

"First," Nathan said, "the County should drop the charges on grounds of insufficient evidence, which lets both Mr. Dietrich and his assailant off the hook, publicly. Second, the victim should drop all charges subject to his agreement with the court that he will undergo psychiatric treatment. Third, the assailant will be fined court costs, sentenced for simple assault, and the sentence set aside, probation required."

"You don't think the assailant should see a psychiatrist?" Alcorn scoffed.

"He's not psychotic," Joanne replied. "He's just stupid."

Alcorn tapped the table with a finger. "Phillip?"

Dupree lifted the palms of his pink hands.

"Nathan," Alcorn said, "would the defendant agree to these terms?"

"I'm sure he will, your honor."

"Phillip, you agree to all this?"

"Subject to approval by Mr. Dietrich. Yes."

"All right." Judge Alcorn made a note on the bottom of

146

a brief. "This court is already overloaded. In the interest of expediency I will accept the recommendations of counsel."

"Thank you, Judge." Nathan closed his briefcase.

"Nathan," Alcorn spoke, head down, "I think you're a good boy. But I can't have you clogging up my court with trivia. Understand me?"

"Yes, sir, judge."

In the hallway, alone with Nathan, Joanne said, "I want to apologize for that pompous ass."

"That's not possible."

"Then on behalf of all thinking, intelligent—"

"Hey," Nathan's brown eyes darted, "people like you make up for those like Alcorn. One of these days he'll get his comeuppance."

"Jo!" Phillip Dupree hollered from the judge's door, "Can you come back? Telephone—important."

"Dr. Fleming," Nathan said, "I want to thank you for enlisting the assistance of your former husband on the Swain case. He's been very helpful."

"Ralph's a good man, Mr. Nathan."

Dupree held the office door, waiting. "Sheriff's office, Jo. They found two bodies; mother and daughter. Rogers says they're going to treat it as a sex crime."

In the judge's office, Joanne answered the telephone and Rogers repeated the same information. "We haven't moved the bodies," the sheriff stated. "I want you to be there before anything is touched. Can I send a car for you?"

"Yes, please. What condition are the bodies?"

"Dead only a few hours."

"I'll be waiting in front of the Lewis State Bank building."

"Oh, and Jo, do you know where Ken Blackburn went on vacation?"

"Yes."

"Can you reach him? We're short-handed. I need all the men I can get on this."

"I'll try, sheriff."

When Joanne hung up, Dupree had a gleam in his eye. "God looks after drunks, children, and sheriffs up for re-election," he said. "Cowboy has himself a sex murder. What more could he want? That's good for headlines from now until election day."

"We don't know that, yet," Joanne cautioned.

"Didn't he tell you?" Dupree asked. "The bodies are

147

nude, mutilated, bludgeoned about the head, strangled. With Cowboy's luck, they'll catch a guy who'll confess to fifty crimes and it'll make national news."

"Hate to put you through this, Jo." County Coroner Dudley Witherspoon wiped foggy glasses, face streaming perspiration. "I wouldn't let them touch a thing—not even to cover them."

Patrol cars were parked at odd angles, blue lights revolving, the area cordoned off to hold back barefoot youngsters and curious adults. Joanne followed the graying coroner's diminutive figure, picking their way through blackberry briars and waist-high grasses.

A hum of flies announced their destination.

"Doesn't take long to get bad," Witherspoon observed. "In the hot sunshine I can't be positive, but I tested for mortis and I think they've only been dead a few hours, Jo."

She swallowed against surging stomach acid. Insects dabbed at brown flecks, swarmed around the faces of a woman and girl.

"Mother-daughter," Witherspoon commented, reading his notes. "Purse nearby had been emptied, but we found identification in it. Went to their home which is about a mile away, and a second daughter was found bludgeoned, but alive. The hospital says she'll live."

Joanne groaned. The mother's breasts were ripped. Bite marks on the abdomen, thighs. She felt Witherspoon's hand, steadying her. An object protruded—

"Easy, Jo," Witherspoon soothed. "Want to back off?"

"No."

She knelt, voice contorted. "Dudley, we need photos with a ruler beside each bite, to give perspective. We need an odontologist—" She swallowed bile. "We need a serologist. Keep all body fluids for testing."

"Right, Jo."

"Is Richard Jerzy available?"

"I'll see."

"He's the best pathologist," Joanne said. "Get him."

"I'll try."

She bent, examining the daughter more closely. For the sake of Witherspoon, she said, "It's sexual assault."

"Yes."

She pressed behind the skull. "Battered."

148

"Dr. Witherspoon?" A deputy calling. "We found an iron bar—piece of a plow, one of these farmers says."

"Don't touch it."

Alone with the bodies, Joanne swallowed repeatedly. There was no grace in death, but this was obscene. She looked, carefully, from toes to head—a couple of hairs adhered to flesh by blood. Joanne waved a hand and Witherspoon returned. "They think they found the murder weapon, Jo."

"Good. Dudley—see these hairs? Be sure they don't get lost."

The coroner removed them with tweezers, placed them in a plastic envelope and labeled it.

"Tell Jerzy—" she fell silent. Finally, "He'll know, but tell him to do acid phosphatase."

"He will, Jo."

She leaned across the younger body, looking at the rib cage and armpit. "Another hair," she said. Witherspoon got it.

"Need dental records," Joanne said.

"We know who they are."

"Some attorney may try to prove they bit one another."

She lifted the young girl's chin. Around the neck were welts, bruises indicating strangulation. Witherspoon was scraping flesh, putting particles into a bag, his eyeglasses clouded by perspiration.

"We'll need an A-B-O antigens test."

"Jerzy will see to all that, Jo."

She pulled back.

"Jo, you're white as a sheet. Let's get out of the sun. You're through, aren't you?"

Joanne gagged. "Look the area over with a keen eye," she instructed. Another retching threat and she swallowed noisily. "Bottles, rocks; look for flies and if they're on it, bag it up."

"We will. Get out of here, Jo." Witherspoon took her arm, helping her.

Joanne drew deep gulps of air, getting into the front seat of the patrol car which had brought her.

"Where to, Dr. Fleming?"

She gave her address. The deputy turned on his flashing blue lights needlessly, gathering speed.

"How's Ken?"

"All right, I think. He's on vacation."

"Lucky bum," he said. "Ken leaves and we get a murder."

The house was sweltering, air conditioning off. Inside, leaning against the door after closing it, Joanne fought nausea. *Must not retain those images . . . must not . . . think other things . . .*

Inhale. Exhale.

Eyes closed, she insisted, angrily, *think other things.*

"Call Ken," she said aloud. She went to the kitchen sink and scrubbed her hands and arms until the flesh was raw. She splashed her face with cold water.

They had stayed at a small hotel in Rabun Gap once, two years ago. Joanne called information, gave the name of the establishment, and sat on a high stool at the counter, waiting.

"I'm sorry," the voice said, "Mr. Blackburn isn't here."

"Could I leave a message?"

"He isn't registered, ma'am."

"When did he depart?"

"He was a no-show, ma'am. He didn't arrive."

"He'd paid in advance, hadn't he?"

"Yes ma'am. But he didn't arrive."

She hung up. *Went on to Virginia.* Which motel? There must be dozens of them in Front Royal, situated as it was at the beginning of the scenic mountain drive known as Blue Ridge Parkway.

Joanne dialed the operator. "This is an emergency," she said. "The man I'm seeking is at some motel in Front Royal, Virginia. Can you help me, operator?"

But he wasn't there. Not in Front Royal. Not in nearby towns suggested over the telephone by those who answered.

Exasperated, Joanne sat with a hand on the phone. Of course, Ken was under no obligation to tell her of a change in plans. He had left angry . . . he could be anyplace.

Frustration and trauma blended, making her stomach ache, hands cold, shivering.

"Fine. Go into shock, idiot," she chastised herself aloud. "Take a bath. Think other things."

Walking the long hall, the telephone rang. Ken? She returned to the kitchen at a run.

"Dr. Fleming? Sheriff Rogers calling, hold the phone, please."

She waited. Waited. Impatience mounting, she waited.

"Dr. Fleming?"

"Yes, sheriff."

Royce Rogers chuckled gleefully. "We caught the killer, Jo. Thought maybe you'd like to see what a mass murderer looks like."

"Where is he?"

"My office. Bud Diehl wants you to interview him—Diehl says you know the circumstances of the various missing women he's been investigating."

"Bud isn't coming over?"

"He will." Rogers turned aside from the phone, hollering at somebody—laughter. "But he wants you to test this man. I can tell you now, though, he's guilty."

"What evidence?"

"Blood on his clothes, his and the women. He's scratched up, bruised knuckles, and the first thing he blurted when they caught him was—I ain't done nothing!"

"Those were his exact words?"

"Ver-batim."

"I left my car at the Lewis State Bank building, sheriff. Could you send one of yours?"

"Look out your window, honey. He's in your driveway waiting."

Joanne washed her hands again, scrubbed herself hard with a nail brush. She poured hydrogen peroxide over both arms. She stopped to drink a small glass of milk, hoping to settle the queasiness.

Before she walked out the door, the phone rang. "Dr. Fleming, hold the line for Sheriff Rogers, please."

Waited. Waited. *Damn him.* Waited.

"Jo, did you reach Ken Blackburn?"

"No."

"You don't know where he is, then?"

"No."

"See you when you get here," Rogers said, and hung up.

Joanne joined the waiting deputy and gazed out the patrol car window as they drove slowly through five o'clock traffic. *Got the man. Thank God.* Blood tests would confirm. The hair on their bodies could be his. They'll have telexed NCIC by now for outstanding warrants. *I ain't done nothing . . .*

The shortwave radio crackled, blurted, and the deputy held a microphone close to his lips, identifying himself to the dispatcher.

"Dr. Fleming with you?"

"Affirmative. She's listening."

"No need her coming down, the sheriff said."

The deputy looked at Joanne.

"Ask why."

"She wants to know why."

"The suspect killed himself."

Joanne's breath seeped free.

"You said," the deputy confirmed, "he's dead?"

"Dead."

"How?" Joanne questioned.

". . . hanged himself in the toilet . . ."

In her belly, like worms wiggling . . . Joanne swallowed, swallowed. "Take me home."

"Yes ma'am."

Writhing, lashing, crawling, niggling doubts—

. . . *ain't done nothing* . . .

Chapter Eighteen

MARCIE sat in a front booth of The Oaks restaurant, watching tourists come and go. Fishermen with trailered boats, men in Bermuda shorts, weekenders arriving to purchase last-minute items—the convenience-store-service-station-bait-shop next door was doing a thriving business.

She formed interlocking rings of moisture, moving her iced tea glass on the Formica table top. Across from her, untouched, Don's tea grew lukewarm. He'd gone to the rest room fifteen minutes ago. He did that several times a day, long absences in a public toilet. Maybe he had intestinal problems. Maybe he was composing graffiti.

She'd seen a lot of him these past days. He was always there, trying to get her to take a drive, offering to be chauffeur and companion. His attentiveness had engendered feminine wariness; yet, with him, laughter came easily. He made no untoward move. He gave no indication he was thinking about "it." A girl could tell. Like Charlie telling crude jokes as a prelude to sexual advances. As if he thought that kind of humor would wax the way to seduction.

There'd been none of that with Don. He never used diminutives like "little" lady, or "cutie pie." He never employed sexist language such as "gal" or "broad." Which was one of the most irritating things Charlie did.

Don wasn't a homosexual. Or, at least, she didn't think so. Charlie said some of them stayed "in the closet" and it took an expert to tell. Marcie had tested Don, casually repeating comments mom had made on the subject. Thus far, his responses had been unemotional and with thoughtful insights based on things he'd read, people he'd known.

So, she asked herself, why was she sitting here still so leery? Why this vague distress at something as mundane as going to the toilet for such long periods and so often? Maybe she should ask about his kidneys. But there was more than that.

His age, of course. If mom (or daddy) (or Ken) knew she had been keeping company with a man twice her age, she'd be grounded in cement until she turned twenty-five.

Yet it was his age and maturity which were most attractive. She hungered for adult conversation with a male who didn't look at her as a sex object. She longed for the "prince" Darlene Sands claimed to have had at age sixteen.

Don was courtly, almost old-worldly, holding doors, standing every time she stood, seating her at the table—but he lacked the continental flair of a true bon vivant. That's what daddy called actors playing certain roles in movies, "bon vivants."

One thing she'd learned from mom: when you have a hunch, there's a reason. It was this nebulous, worrisome hunch that made her keep her distance. Not once had she allowed him to give her a ride to The Oaks, although she'd walked to meet him here several times. She invented excuses to avoid putting herself in compromising situations.

After their initial meeting, when he'd come to the cottage, she'd manufacture lies to keep him outside, calling through a locked door, "See you at The Oaks," or wherever. Nonetheless, she'd not seen fit to drive him away completely.

She remembered a conversation she once overheard between her mother and Ken. "Examine the evidence and

153

come to your own conclusions, Jo. Don't draw on emotion, empathy, or intuition. If you can't give me evidence, you can't win any debate."

Mom, on the other hand, never discounted intuition. It was, she said, "An opaque glimpse into the mysterious subconscious, which forms conclusions not always with evidence so much as experience from past events."

Marcie had concluded, the truth fell somewhere between Ken the practical, and mom the pedantic.

So she sat here, worrying.

There were the tiny lies. Unimportant, but lies. Don said he was a student at FSU. Criminology. But he didn't know mom's specialty. All right, maybe mom had been teaching mostly graduate students this semester. But how could any student not know Dr. Kreijewski, dean of the department?

Where did he live? "On campus," he'd said. Pressed for where, he'd admitted, "Off campus." When she persisted, he'd said, "That's a secret."

Was he married? She didn't need that problem.

He'd said he was twenty-three. But later, in another conversation, he'd said he had a brother, two years younger, age twenty-three. Stupid blunder? Or an effort to get the record straight?

Sitting with Don in this public place had not precluded some very personal conversations. She spoke of daddy's girl friends. Don had alluded to the "circumstances" of his birth, with no further explanation. It was his tormented expression which suggested these "circumstances" were offensive, disturbing, and a sore subject.

When she talked of mom, he listened with unblinking, almost piercing blue eyes, letting her say anything and everything on her mind. He didn't pry. He made no effort to intrude on her home life—but his expression became odd, almost no expression at all—just a . . . listening.

Why should that bother her? He asked the usual questions, nothing out of the way. But pinned by his unswerving eyes, she had the strangest sort of hesitation . . . like a mouse must feel backed into a corner by a cat.

She—and she admitted this—had no hesitation about asking him *anything*. He was from California. The mountain, Whitney, was named for his great-grandfather. (Another lie, the mountain was named for the surveyor who

154

first measured it. Don had claimed *his* grandfather had no education, eked a living as a hunter and trapper.)

Perhaps he was secretly teasing her. She was, after all, only a child in his eyes, surely. The idea piqued a petulant desire to retaliate.

"Back again." Don came up, catching her unaware. He sat, smiled, hands in his lap.

"You have bad kidneys?" Marcie questioned.

"Yes."

"How come?"

"Tried to kill myself with an overdose of sulfa when I was a child. It scarred both kidneys very badly."

"Kill yourself?"

"Yes."

"How old were you?"

"Nine or ten. I had no idea what it was, except it was medicine. So I took it all."

"Why?"

He replied, impassively, "I heard my stepfather use the word 'bastard' and later my mother told me I was the son of a sailor she'd met during World War Two."

"Then you can't be twenty-three," Marcie blurted.

"Twenty-nine."

"Why do you lie?"

"I can't help it." He smiled, sipped tea. "I'm a psychopathic liar. I lie about everything. Weather, time of day. Everything."

"Why?"

"I don't know. Want something to eat?"

"No." But he summoned a waitress and ordered two hamburgers. He asked for one as she liked it, no onions, no mustard.

"You lie to everybody, just to me, or only to certain people?"

"Everybody."

"To yourself?"

"Most of all."

"How can you build a relationship on lies?" Marcie asked. "Without trust, no meaningful interchange can ever take place."

"You sound like a psychologist."

"My mom's influence." She peered out the window.

"I wish I could find one person with whom I could be completely honest," he said. "That'd be a first."

155

"You could be honest with me."

"You might not like me."

"I live with a mother who is obsessed with sex crimes," Marcie responded. "I hear all kinds of quirky things. Believe me, it wouldn't make me dislike you if—"

"I were a sex deviate?" he grinned.

"Not even then. So long as you didn't foist it on me."

"Never will," he said. "I promise."

"So you can be honest with me," Marcie insisted.

"Fair offer," he said. "You do the same with me?"

"Yes, I will. In fact, I'd like that."

"All right. The truth, from now on. Except—"

An alien expression crossed his face, vanished.

"Except what?"

"See," he said, softly, "I really can't help it. The words come out and a lie is told before I think. I hear myself talking and zap—I lied about something."

"We need a way to erase it later," Marcie reasoned. "Maybe you could make a sign somehow and I'd sit and listen, but then I'd know it was your mouth, not your mind talking."

He laughed. He had a nice, musical laugh. "That's great. Let's see, I once saw a movie about an old man and a little girl who had an arrangement like that. When they were fibbing, they'd tug an ear like this." He massaged his lobe between thumb and forefinger.

"Perfect!"

When the hamburgers arrived, Marcie said, gratefully, "I'm glad you ordered, now I'm starving."

But before she could take a bite, a familiar, pale blue automobile drew up to the gas pumps and Marcie paused, watching. *Ken?* Oh dear. She leaned closer to the glass, trying to identify the vehicle for certain.

"What is it?" Don questioned.

"I think it's my mom's boyfriend."

"Oh, yeah?" He turned to look.

"This is awful."

"Why?"

"If he catches me with a man your age, I'll be sent to a convent until I'm past menopause."

Again, the strange, alien expression, his facial muscles seeming to set, as though to disguise thoughts he had.

"I could leave," he said. Marcie wasn't sure whether it was an offer or a decision.

156

Still watching, Marcie saw Ken round the car and open the passenger door. "Oh, oh," she wheezed, "mom must be with him."

Only, it wasn't mom. Stunned, Marcie saw a brunette, tanned, much younger than mom. Instantly, her chest ached. The woman stood on tiptoes, kissed Ken on a cheek, then ran for the rest rooms in the bait store.

So, she was not caught. She had caught *him*. Eyes searing, Marcie was shocked at a mixture of emotions that rose, eclipsed one another and subsided into the dull, aching throb of her chest. Disappontment, jealousy, hurt for mom, hurt for herself—

"What's he do for a living?" Don asked.

"Deputy sheriff."

"Interesting," he said, flatly.

Returning, the woman hung a forearm on Ken's shoulder, leaning against him. Ken did not resist. Darn him. Darn him! Had a fight with mom? Darn her. Mom certainly did nothing to hold him, made no effort to be more attractive, more available.

"Are you all right, Marcie?" Don asked, but without looking away from Ken Blackburn paying an attendant for gas.

Her distress was so acute, Marcie had to marvel at herself. Ken was a man, wasn't he? Could any man ever be trusted to repulse his biological urges? Were not men victims of their glandular secretions? Marcie blinked rapidly, an overwhelming urge to cry descending on her. It wasn't her boyfriend, was it? It wasn't her father.

"You all right, Marcie?" he asked again, without looking at her.

"I've got to go home, Don."

"I'll drive you to the cottage."

"No, I mean home to Tallahassee."

Still he watched Ken.

"Excuse me," Marcie said. "I'll go call dad."

Not even now did he take his eyes from Ken's car slowly pulling away from the pumps. "I'll drive you to Tallahassee, Marcie." His voice was a monotone, information without emotion, the mechanical voice of a computer answering typed queries audibly.

Marcie went to a phone booth in the rear of the restaurant, hurting physically, mentally, the burning knowledge of Ken's infidelity, she told herself, both ludicrous and unrealistic. They weren't married, for heaven's sake. Mom went to see daddy often enough. She had even attended a few dinner meetings with other escorts. But, somehow, with Ken, Marcie had hoped, dreamed—she sobbed, put a coin in the phone and dialed the operator.

"Long distance," Marcie said. She called her father.

"Anything wrong, Marcie?" alarm in his voice. No, no . . . nothing wrong . . . coming home . . . tired of the beach. "Darling, if you wait, I'll come down earlier tonight. I can bring you back to Tallahassee when I come in tomorrow."

"I have a ride with a friend, daddy."

"Wait a minute, honey, I don't know about that."

"He's a student, daddy. One of mom's students. He's over twenty-one and he's on his way up there."

"Marcie, I have to come down anyway and close up the house."

"I'll do it, daddy. I'll be all right. I'm going to mom's."

"All right. Be careful."

"I will. Bye."

But now, the call completed, she had second thoughts. Had Don been sincere or polite? Did he understand she meant *now?* Dared she ride with him? She needed insurance—witnesses.

When she returned to the table, he was smiling. "I'll take you up on your offer for a lift to Tallahassee," Marcie said. "If you really meant it."

"I did mean it. Who were you calling?"

"My daddy. I told him you were giving me a ride."

A flicker in his blue eyes. He smiled. "What did he have to say about that?"

"He wanted your description, the make and model of your Volkswagen and your Utah license plate number."

The flicker died. "You're very observant."

"Mom's influence," Marcie said, too harshly. *True. Poor mom.*

"Well." Don slipped out of the booth. "I'd better go fill up with gas. You ready to go?"

"Yes."

At the cash register, Marcie told the owner, pointedly, "I'm going to ride to Tallahassee with him. He's taking me home in that Volkswagen with the Utah license plates."

Perplexed, the owner nodded.

She got into the Volkswagen and the passenger seat

158

slipped on its runners. "How do you lock this thing in place?" she said.

"Broken," he said. He drove to the gas pumps and pulled the front hood latch. Outside now, he placed a gas nozzle into the filler cap. In the crack between lifted hood and vehicle frame, Marcie saw brown fabric. Looked like panty hose. Knotted. She leaned forward to see better. Something chrome, shining, under a crocus sack, it looked like—

"Excuse me." Don reached in the passenger window and opened the glove compartment. He fumbled inside and got a credit card. He slammed the pocket door, but it fell open. He slammed it again and still it fell open. He walked toward the bait shop to pay for gas.

Credit cards. Lots of them. Marcie moved them around, looking. Her finger touched something solid and she withdrew it. A necklace. Turquoise, silver, a beautiful—

"Here we go!" Don closed the hood and Marcie jumped in her seat guiltily, dropping the necklace into her pocket. He got in, tossed his credit card in with the others and slammed the glove compartment. It fell open. Then, deliberately, firmly, he pressed the cover shut and it latched.

He drove her by the cotttage, obeyed her command to wait in the car while she gathered her clothing and toilet articles. She locked the doors and windows, returned with her bags.

They rode toward Tallahassee without conversation. Marcie stared out her window, fighting a desire to cry, pained for mom, for herself, for Ken. Don drove with both hands on the wheel, eyes riveted to the road. Any change in momentum made the seat slide forward or backward.

"You ought to get this fixed," Marcie said.

"Yes, I should. Buckle your seat belt, Marcie."

"No, it makes me nervous."

"Buckle it," he said.

She did.

When they reached the southern limits of Tallahassee, he turned on Capitol Circle, skirting the downtown area. Then, without notice, he followed Tennessee Street and went to a restaurant. "We'll eat," he said.

"I should go on home, Don."

"Nope. My price for delivering you to Tallahassee is a

159

meal. I hate eating alone. So come on, pay up, and join me."

As she got out, Marcie questioned, "Should I lock the car door?"

"No need. Nothing of value is in there."

"What about the credit cards?"

"No worry. Anything in there, anybody is welcome to it."

"Why do you have all the credit cards?"

"I collect them. Friends give them to me." He got out a handful, holding them below the window. "See, some belong to women. I couldn't use those."

As they passed a vending machine, he bought the *Democrat*. Marcie waited as he stood reading.

"They caught some guy who's been killing women," Don said. "Is that anything that would interest your mother?"

"She's probably right in the middle of it."

"He's dead," Don said.

"Who?"

"The man who killed the women."

"Police shot him?"

"Hung himself."

Marcie waited. Don read the entire news item before giving her his attention again.

Inside, their meal ordered, Don read it all anew. "Why does your mother get involved in things like this?" he asked.

"It's her job."

"Who pays her?"

"She works for the university. But she gets fees when she works on a particular case. Police departments call on her all the time to study sex crimes."

"What does she do when she studies such a crime?"

Marcie winced. "That isn't such good dinner conversation."

"She works with detectives, what?"

"Pathologists, the crime labs, detectives. Coroners, people like that."

"Is she good at it?"

"Ken says she is. One of the best. She wrote a book—"

"I read it."

"You did? When?"

"Couple of years ago."

Marcie studied his face. "Rub your ear," she ordered. He grinned and did so.

"While we're confessing," Marcie said, "I didn't tell my father about you."

"Rub your ear," he said.

Their meal completed, Don had coffee. "You're quite a woman," he observed.

She'd learned from Darlene: meet remarks like that with no response but a smile.

"I'll let you out at the block where you live," Don offered. "But I won't go to the house."

"All right."

"Does my age keep us from seeing one another again?"

"No. As long as my parents don't know."

Smiling, nodding, he whispered, "Very, very good."

"What is?"

"Somebody with whom I can be totally honest. I've never had that before."

"Neither have I," Marcie said. "I've thought I could trust certain people, but it turned out I couldn't. I hope we can trust one another."

"We can."

"I don't want to have to worry about the sex thing," Marcie declared.

The odd expression, intense, "What do you mean?"

"I don't want to have to worry about you trying to seduce me."

Finally, he smiled. "No need to worry," he intoned. "I'm no rapist."

Chapter Nineteen

MARCIE had been less than her effusive self since her arrival last night. She had been hovering—there was no other word for it—bestowing favors unasked, solicitous and quiet. At first, Joanne thought the girl had fought with her father, but when she telephoned Ralph, he insisted all was right between them.

"Help you make your bed, mom?" Marcie took one side, Joanne the other. Joanne stumbled, mumbling.

"Everything all right, mom?"

"I'm not awake."

"Other than that. Everything okay?"

"Please, no emergencies, Marcie."

"Oh no," Marcie said, "I'm fine."

Finally awake, and to reciprocate, Joanne was helping Marcie make her bed.

"Haven't seen Ken lately," Marcie noted.

"You've been gone."

"Since I came home, I mean."

"You've been home one night."

"All right." Sullen.

"Marcie? What's on your mind, darling?"

Marcie scratched the tip of her tanned nose. "Ken okay, mom?"

"I think so. Why do you ask?"

Marcie fluffed pillows, arranged her old dolls along a wall.

"What's going on in that pretty head, Marcie?"

"You didn't have a fight, did you, mom?"

"With Ken? No."

Marcie nodded, dusting her dresser. She pushed aside a necklace.

"Where did you get that?" Joanne inquired.

"Found it. On the beach at Bald Point."

Joanne lifted the pendant. "Looks like silver."

162

"It's imitation." Marcie flicked a dust cloth.

"There's a silversmith's mark on the back—they don't do that with cheap jewelry." Joanne pushed back a curtain for natural light. "This is turquoise. I think it's valuable, Marcie."

"Really?" Her blonde eyebrows lifted and Marcie took the necklace.

"Did you try to find the owner?"

"How?" Marcie seemed distressed. "There's no newspaper in Panacea. Tourists come through all the time. You must be wrong, mom. I'm sure it isn't expensive."

"Maybe I am. Come on, let's cook breakfast."

But as Joanne left the room, Marcie stood at the window, minutely examining metal and stones.

"Yoo-hoo!" Ken's voice, a falsetto, as he banged on the rear door.

Joanne threw it open and went into his arms. "Missed you," she said.

"Yeah?" Ken kissed her.

When they closed the door, Marcie was there, chin down, unsmiling.

"Hi, beautiful!"

She allowed him to embrace her, but without response. Ken put his chin against his chest, teasing, "Are you pouting today, little girl?"

Marcie shrugged him off. "Any orange juice, mom?"

"I'll make some. Sit down, you two."

"Had some excitement while I was gone," Ken commented.

"You mean the mother-daughter murders?" Joanne asked.

"No, I meant traffic violations, the higher percentage of jaywalking."

"He hung himself," Marcie interjected.

Ken laughed. "Cowboy is raw and bleeding from it, too. In his office toilet! They're saying Cowboy wept when he saw that lovely publicity hanging there."

"Did you eat at the hotel in Rabun Gap where we had such good biscuits and sausage?" Joanne questioned.

"No, I didn't."

"The best biscuits in the South and you didn't get any?" Joanne placed a skillet on the stove.

"No, sure didn't. How've you been, Marcie? Nice tan."

"How many eggs, Ken?"

"None for me. I'm on my way to work."

"You can take time for breakfast."

"No, I told the sheriff I'd come on in."

Joanne studied his face a moment, returned to the stove. "How was your vacation?"

"Good as could be. Missed you."

"Missed you, too," Joanne said. "Was the Skyline Drive as beautiful in summer as it is in the fall?"

"To tell the truth, I didn't notice. I have to go, Jo. See you tonight, all right?"

"How was the weather?" Joanne queried.

"Okay."

Joanne spoke, her back to him. "According to the news, it was unseasonably cold, with torrential rains."

Ken laughed abruptly, kissed her on the neck. "Got to go, Jo. I'll see you this evening. Bye, Marcie."

As he closed the door, Marcie said, "Smooth as snot."

"Marcie! What a horrible expression."

"In your third degree," Marcie challenged, "who did you think he was with?"

Taken aback, Joanne said, "I didn't think he was with anybody. That wasn't the point of my inquiry. I spent two days searching for him at the request of Sheriff Rogers."

"It never occurred to you that he was with someone else?"

"No."

"That may be part of your problem, mom." Marcie's voice was acid. "You seem to believe you have everybody in the palm of your hand!"

Dumbfounded, Joanne watched the girl run to her room. The door slammed. The lock clicked.

As Joanne walked into her office, Beatrice Malbis swallowed a mouthful of cookie, waving messages. "Youse got calls!"

Joanne took them, leafing through . . . pathologist, coroner, Bud Diehl, Thaddeus Kreijewski, *damn* . . . serologist, odontologist, sheriff's office in Albany, Georgia, the Center for Disease Control in Atlanta, a computer company in Los Angeles that did testing work.

"Oh!" she heard Bea holler. "Plus Ken, plus Marcie, plus Mr. Fleming."

Her day was off to a bad start. Joanne sank into her desk chair feeling defeated at the outset.

164

"It's Bud Diehl," Bea shouted.

"Use the intercom," Joanne barked, "and stop yelling at me."

The intercom clicked and Bea's voice was smooth as— what had Marcie said?—"Dr. Fleming, Detective Bud Diehl on line one."

"Morning, Bud."

"Just calling to tell you I'll send back your materials, if you want them, Jo."

"What materials?"

"On the sixteen or so missing women."

"Why send it back?"

"Don't need it. Cowboy's corpse seems to have been our man."

"We don't know that," Joanne said.

Bud chuckled, voice low. "Cowboy said you'd say that."

"But, we don't."

"Looks like he's the man, Jo. Profile or not, he seems to be it. According to the lab, their blood was on his clothes. But if that doesn't convince you, the surviving daughter identified him from photos."

"He may have murdered the mother and daughter but—"

"He was in Orlando picking oranges," Bud continued. "His employer has records that put the man in town at the time the two Rollins College girls disappeared. They now assume those girls are dead, incidentally."

"There are some disturbing discrepancies, Bud."

"And," Bud persevered, "he was here in Jacksonville, stayed at a Salvation Army mission, left town, returned twice more, and the dates are close enough to put him in the area when the Hightower woman was kidnapped."

"Where'd he get a vehicle?" Joanne asked. "He was found hitchhiking by Cowboy's men."

"Could've stolen one," Bud said. "And he had a napkin in his hip pocket from a bar in Albany, Georgia. They're doing a trace on him now to affirm a date that would tie him to the missing girls in the southwest Georgia area."

"Bud, when he was caught, he said, 'I ain't done nothing.' "

"What'd you expect him to say?"

"It isn't what he said, it's his grammar. It suggests he was an uneducated man."

"I remember what your profile said, Jo. But killers can

be dumb, too. However—" Bud took a long pause. "If all that fails to convince you, he was in Panama City, at the Breaker Bar, the night the girl disappeared from the motel."

"He was?"

"Identified positively," Bud said, "by Judith Sizemore, one of the Chi Omega sorority sisters."

"No, no, no," Joanne said. "That girl's testimony won't stand in court."

"No problem," Bud concluded. "The suspect is dead. We're only trying to clear our files now."

"Bud, I know this is jumping the gun, but I don't think this is the man who killed the other women."

"Um." Bud emitted a high-pitched sigh. "Now, I tell you, Jo, I'm not going to get between you and Cowboy Rogers."

"What prompts that statement?"

"Cowboy said you'd fight him. He said you were a bleeding heart do-gooder who thought criminals should be slapped on the wrist and turned loose."

"Absurd—"

"He warned me that you'd protest on general principles to cover any errors made in your profile."

"Bud, you know better than that."

"Listen, Jo, I'm not an arbitrator. Don't want to be. You want those files back, or not?"

"Yes."

"Coming to you then," Bud advised. "See you, Jo."

No sooner had she hung up than the telephone was ringing. "Jo, this is Ralph."

"Yes, Ralph."

"We're taking our case to the grand jury day after tomorrow. One little thing I stumbled on is bothering me."

"Yes?"

"Did you—I have to ask this, honey—did you ever give Judge Alcorn any kind of kickback on fees the court paid you?"

"Ralph! What do you think?"

"You'll have to answer to the grand jury, Jo."

"Of course not!"

"But we have checks from you, endorsed by him."

"Wait a minute," Joanne clapped a hand to her forehead. "I did do that."

"Why?"

"I ask for a retainer before every case. You know how

166

attorneys are about firing you, if your findings don't jibe with what they want you to tell them—"

"Oh me, Jo."

"Whenever I refused a case, or thought I could add nothing new, I sent back the money."

"Jo, Jo, Jo."

"Will you stop simpering, Ralph."

"Why are the checks only a part of your fee?"

"Because that's the way it's paid. I accept a retainer, and only when I take the case do I receive the balance."

"This clouds the issue," Ralph said. "I may have to stand down from this because of these checks."

"Ralph, nobody but you would think to make such a connection."

"No," he said. "No, I didn't make this connection. It was brought to our attention by an aide in Judge Alcorn's office."

"Surely you see what he's doing?"

"I suppose. All right. Bye."

Another call: "Dr. Fleming, this is Tony Eldridge at the *Democrat*. May I see you?"

"Tony, I'm too busy."

"You really ought to take the time," he said.

"Why?"

"Sheriff Rogers is quoted in an interview, and he says you are striving to have convicted criminals set free. He gives several examples."

Joanne put the receiver in her lap, eyes closed. She lifted it to her ear again, ". . . that one particularly vicious assault was nol-prossed on your recommendation, after the victim had identified his assailant, and the assailant had confessed—"

"Come over," Joanne said, brusquely.

"Now?"

"Yes, now."

Bea was at the door, face drawn. "There's a process server here, Dr. Fleming."

The man presented her with a subpoena to appear before the grand jury. He mumbled an apology as Joanne tossed the paper into her desk drawer, nodding.

County Coroner Dudley Witherspoon was on the phone now. "Jo, Cowboy wants me to send these lab reports to you. Want them today?"

"I guess so. Should I send for them?"

"No problem, I'll get them dropped off."

"Was the dead suspect really guilty of the murders, Dudley?"

"Not much doubt about it, Jo. Matching head and pubic hairs on the bodies of the victims. Their blood on his clothes. Cowboy says the survivor—"

"Identified him," Jo completed.

"That's right. So it was him."

She hung up. "Bea! Coffeeee!"

Marcie waited impatiently for her mother to return her call. When an hour had passed, she dialed the criminology office again. Busy. Three lines, busy? She cradled the telephone, looked at her note pad and called the number Don had left.

"Hello there," he answered cheerfully. "This is not a recording. This is the live machine. I do not take messages. I compute and reply instantly. May I help you?"

"You're so silly," Marcie said.

"Now?" he asked.

"Come on."

"Be there in three minutes."

When he arrived, Don was driving a new Chevrolet van.

"Where'd you get this?" she asked.

"Test driving it."

"Thinking about buying it?"

"Oh, no. Just test driving. They provide about a gallon of gas, hold my wee VW until I return, and I find a reason why Ford or GMC is a better deal and leave." He grinned at her. "Pretty smart, huh?"

"Not very honest."

His smile vanished. "Look," he said, "you want me to be truthful—no lies—right?"

"That's right."

"Then you should accept the truth without passing judgment. That discourages veracity."

"Yes. I guess that's the way it has to be," Marcie replied, getting in.

"That's the way."

Cordially, he turned to light-hearted banter, joking about this or that, bringing laughter despite her mood, which was worry-depression.

"Where're we going?" she questioned.

168

"Neat little out of the way place."

"I have to be home in half an hour."

"Half an hour?" he snapped. "So why bother to come?"

"Maybe an hour," she conceded.

"I hope so. Nobody can eat in half an hour."

They turned into a small cafe set back from the highway, parked under trees on a rutted, unpaved lot.

"Lock the van?" she asked as they got out.

"Nope. It isn't mine."

"You forgot the keys, Don!"

"Like I say, it isn't mine. Come on."

They sat in unpadded wooden booths. "Catfish is their thing," Don announced. "You like catfish?"

"Sure."

He ordered, voice brisk, businesslike. Then, his eyes drifted around the room to the few other patrons, wandered over walls, and settled on her.

"You been robbed, Marcie?"

"No."

"Ever been the victim of a crime?"

"No."

"Why are you obsessed with locking doors?"

"Mom's influence."

He stared, his face pleasant. "You were right, though."

"About what?"

"Locking the goddamned doors. What're we talking about?"

"I'm sorry. I wasn't sure."

"Somebody stole a necklace from the pocket of my car."

She had the eerie feeling he was alert for any reaction. "Was it valuable?" Marcie questioned.

"No."

"But you're upset about it?"

"No. Just a trinket. May the thief wear it in good health."

He sipped water, watching her.

"Did they steal your credit cards?"

"No."

Marcie gripped her water glass with both hands to still any quiver which may have been there. She met his gaze, held it evenly, as unblinking as he was.

"So!" He sat back, grinned. "Glad to be home?"

Chapter Twenty

"TONY, do you mind if Dr. Kreijewski sits in on this?" Joanne said. The reporter looked nonplussed, but nodded.

"Jo," Thaddeus Kreijewski suggested, "let's have Beatrice make notes of this interview, shall we?"

Bea sat, steno pad in hand. "Verbatim?" she asked.

"Yes," Thad said. "If that's all right with Mr. Eldridge." Tony Eldridge shrugged.

"Now," Thad said, "how may we help you, young man?"

"I have quotes here from Sheriff Rogers," Tony said. "I wanted to give you the opportunity to reply before I write the article."

"Fine," Thad smiled. "Let's hear it."

Tony addressed Joanne. "Sheriff Rogers makes the statement that you—" he read his notes, "are a bleeding heart do-gooder with an obsession to free convicted felons."

Joanne blinked.

"Well?" Tony queried.

"You want a response to that, is that it?"

Irritated, "Yes, if you have one."

Thaddeus Kreijewski cleared his throat. "Do you mind if I respond, Dr. Fleming?"

"Please do."

"The Department of Criminology is often misunderstood," Thad stated, pleasantly. "Our task is not to arrest the felon, nor even to investigate a crime. We are called upon by law enforcement agencies to assist in explaining the psychology of a criminal, or to put crime in perspective historically, even legally, but unofficially. Thus, it is not surprising that the strict law-and-order branch of criminology is sometimes at odds with the philosophical branch, which we are often perceived to be."

Tony stared at Kreijewski. Then, to Joanne, "Sheriff

Rogers cites two recent examples. One, the convicted rapist, George Swain, a man who—"

"I'm sorry," Joanne interrupted, "but I can't discuss that case since I am currently employed as a witness for the defense."

"Then," Tony said, "there is the case of an alleged assailant who viciously assaulted his victim and—"

"That matter has been dropped by the prosecution, the victim, and the accused. To discuss it now, in print, could invite charges of libel."

The reporter pushed up thick glasses, peering at his pad. When he lifted his gaze, he was clearly angry. "Dr. Fleming, I'm not here as your enemy."

"I didn't suppose you were."

"I find that difficult to believe," the reporter said. "You have a witness and a stenographer to ensure that you will not be misquoted. Are you covering something?"

"What could there be to cover?" Thad smiled, but he seemed pained.

"I don't want to hurt you or the department." Tony spoke to Joanne. "I don't understand the undercurrent here. But I can tell you, if we continue in this vein, you and the department are going to look awful." He closed his notebook.

"Perhaps it would help," Tony said, "if I explain exactly what motivates me. I'm twenty-nine, almost thirty years old. My wife is pregnant and she needs some very expensive dental work."

Joanne laughed, nervously.

"I completed four years of college, went for a master's degree, and I'm starving," he said. "I've been offered a job with the Department of Natural Resources at more than twice the salary I'm currently earning. I would be writing articles for the wildlife magazine. Snappy little pieces about walking catfish and overpopulation of alligators near residential areas. I could take that job, pay for my wife's dental work, support my family, and be miserable. But what I really enjoy is investigative reporting. That's why I'm here. If I do a superb job, I break out of society news, get away from the ladies' club luncheons, and move up to a decent income level. Frankly, this is a crucial story for me. I have a sixth sense that this is my chance. But so far, what do I have?"

He flipped pages with disgust. "The sheriff is out to impugn your position, and he's going at it tooth and nail. I see that to print this would be unfair. But when I ask you for a denial, you skirt the issue. I can't invent quotes for you. If Sheriff Rogers is covering up something, I fail to see it. Yet, you are taking great care to protect yourself."

"What is it you think you're investigating?" Joanne asked.

"I'm not sure, yet. An investigative reporter has to dig out facts. Okay. The fact is this: a man murdered a woman and her daughter, and from the evidence I've seen, the suspect was guilty. He hung himself. Except for some loose ends, that seems to be that. But if so, why is Rogers going to such lengths to discredit you? And why are you letting such statements pass without rebuttal?"

Joanne looked at Thad.

Tony said, "I want to be fair and just. But so far, with what I have, you and the criminology department are going to be left out on a limb, and Sheriff Rogers will be assumed to be right. *Is* he right?"

"No."

"Jo," Thad warned, "you can't attack Rogers personally."

"I agree."

"Nor professionally," Thad asserted. "His job is law and order and it isn't our place to insinuate—"

"I know, Thad."

The reporter waited.

"There are undercurrents," Joanne said.

"What and why?" Tony demanded.

"This attack from Cowboy Rogers is designed to preclude any response from me. He's trying to prove his suspect was guilty."

"Wasn't he?"

"Guilty of murdering the mother and daughter."

"Then I don't understand."

"Now that the suspect is dead," Joanne continued, "Rogers must put the best face on a bad situation. To do this, he is trying to claim his prisoner was in fact a mass murderer guilty of killing many women. Therefore, how could Sheriff Rogers be blamed for the suicide of a man so obviously insane? I heard him say on the evening news last night, 'The suspect killed eighteen or nineteen women—who wouldn't commit suicide after all that?' "

"I must be dense. I still don't comprehend the conflict."

172

"It is this," Joanne stated. "The suspect did not kill those other women."

"You have proof?"

"No."

"Then how can you assert such a thing?" Tony questioned. "Cowboy has established that this man was in the area where other women were kidnapped or murdered."

"That seems to be true."

"What makes you think he was not guilty of the crimes?"

"I have very limited knowledge of the suspect, but what I have indicates the man was not the kind of personality who commits such crimes."

"But he did."

"He killed the mother-daughter."

"If he did it once—"

"No, no," Joanne waved a finger. "That doesn't mean he might do it again. Much less again *and* again."

She opened a drawer and took out a folder. "This is the statement made by the detective who interviewed the surviving daughter. Let me quote it:

" 'When we come home,' the girl said, 'he was in the house searching the dresser drawers. He got real upset and he stood there with a iron bar in his hand. He told us he just wanted to get out of there and didn't want to hurt nobody. He started to leave and my sister said, I know you! You been working down to the mill. He just about cried, saying, "That's so dumb of you to say that. Don't you see what I've got to do now?" and he commenced hitting mama and sister and me with the bar. I crawled under a bed. I saw him tote off mama and he come back and toted off sister. I knowed he was coming again, so I run out to the woodshed and hid.' "

Joanne put aside the report. "That tells us several important things," she said. "The crime began as burglary, accelerated into assault, degenerated into a sex offense. But sex was not the man's reason for the attacks. He was trying to eliminate the witnesses."

"But he did rape and maim them," Tony said.

"Yes he did."

"The rape-bludgeon-strangulation follows the pattern of the other crimes, specifically the Hightower woman in Jacksonville. Perhaps those were initially robberies, too?"

"No."

"How can you be so sure?" Tony insisted.

173

"To kill in passion and do it once is a form of temporary insanity," Joanne said. "To do it repeatedly, one must either be psychotic or without remorse. The chances are, this suspect, had he gotten away, would have suffered agonies over it. Nightmares. Eventually, he might have confessed when arrested for some minor offense, years later. He was an uneducated man, judging from the dialogue between the suspect and arresting officers. He was probably a farm laborer wandering from crop to crop, seeking work. But a sex criminal—I don't think so. Certainly not the cold-blooded and conscienceless man who tortures, rapes and murders. To withstand the assault to one's senses, one must be free of remorse. Such a man would not hang himself, or exhibit regret for his crimes. He'd be distressed about being caught, but it would be animosity he felt, not pangs of conscience."

Tony peered with enlarged pupils. "You think the killer is still out there?"

"Yes."

"All we have to do is wait and he will kill again?"

"It isn't likely he'll kill around here," Joanne said. "He's smart, probably educated. In the glare of Cowboy's publicity, the real killer will leave. Why not? The wrong man will take the blame for at least this many murders if he simply goes elsewhere."

"And you think Cowboy knows that?" Tony asked.

"He ought to."

"May I quote you?"

"That part, yes."

"Very good." Tony closed his notebook. "This explains Roger's vitriol and puts his statements in proper perspective."

When Joanne and Thaddeus Kreijewski were alone, the bearded professor wiped his spectacles. "Pray that reporter is fair, Jo. We're getting a very bad image as unrealistic idealists at odds with the enforcement branch of the legal system."

"I see that."

"I defend you," Thad replaced his glasses, "because you are fundamentally right. Because you are probably correct in your suppositions. I give you that. But the main reason I defend you is because you represent the department at large, criminology as a whole—"

"Thank you, Thad."

"But let me say this." Thad stood, shoved his hands into his pockets. "I don't like it, Jo. I don't like it one bit."

"I know, Thad."

"In the privacy of this office, as your friend as well as your colleague, I feel free to criticize you."

"Of course."

"I do so, knowing that. Now some sage advice from a battle-scarred veteran. The only way you can defeat Cowboy Rogers is by proving yourself right. The killer is gone, you can bank on that. There'll be no more murders with this M.O. So, in your counterattack, your best weapon is truth without speculation. Your only defense is to prove Cowboy wrong. Otherwise, shut up, take your licks, and let it fade.

At the door he turned. "In any event, I am your ally, your friend and staunch supporter. Is that understood?"

"Always," Joanne said.

"Good. Give him hell."

"He's using me for political purposes," Joanne related, over dinner.

"Can he hurt you, mom?" Marcie asked.

"He hopes to," Joanne said, angrily. She passed mashed potatoes to Ken and watched him put huge dollops on the plate.

"It's so unnecessary," she said.

"But predictable," Ken noted.

"Well, I'm not going to idly sit by and take it," Joanne warned. Ken ate, listening without visible indication of support.

"I mean it," Joanne fumed. "I won't allow Cowboy to hurl accusations without substantiation."

"Mom?"

"What?"

"What's a psychopathic liar?"

"Cowboy Rogers."

"Really?"

"No," Joanne admitted. "He isn't."

"What is it, then?"

Obviously, Marcie was as weary of the subject as Ken was. Joanne helped herself to food. "A psychopathic liar is someone who tells a lie without consciously planning to do so, and without any need to lie. In extreme cases he reinforces the lie with elaborate fantasies designed to compound the original tale."

"Is it something a psychiatrist can cure?" Marcie asked.

"Yes. Usually. Pass the salt, please."

"Got lumps in it," Ken observed, taking more potatoes.

"Mom? Is it a serious thing, being a psychopathic liar?"

"It isn't necessarily bad," Joanne said, without interest. "Most actors and writers go through a period in adolescence, telling lies. Eventually, as adults, they channel fantasy into their work. An actor plays a role with great conviction, becoming someone other than himself temporarily, which is a physical form of lying. A writer does something similar, turns the lie into fiction. In childhood such lying is often a sign of creative originality."

"But if it doesn't stop?" Marcie questioned.

"It's then a matter of self-image," Joanne said. "The person feels inadequate, he perceives his existence as dull and uninteresting. It's a self-conceptualization thing, Marcie. Someone who wishes he were someone he isn't. With the actor and writer, that works to their advantage."

Joanne looked at her plate and pushed it away. Ken reached over and patted her hand.

Marcie sat close, an arm linked in his, and Don's eyes were afire with Roman candles, star bursts, and skyrockets. *Like a child. A little boy.* Marcie laughed, watching him, not the fireworks.

"It's wonderful, isn't it?" he said, gleefully.

"Sure is."

"Wow! That one was magnificent."

His face illuminated by pyrotechnics, she felt him quivering, watching the explosion of man-made stars. Every boom reverberated from hills and lake, echoed away, and he reacted with shrill laughter, looking down to see if her pleasure matched his.

"When I was a little boy," he said, "I saved my money to buy firecrackers. I made bombs with them."

"How old were you?"

"I don't know. Seven, eight."

"Where were you living?"

"Seattle."

She felt him tense. "That's a small town in California. I don't think it's incorporated."

"Near Mt. Whitney?"

The muscular tonicity of his arm suggested something other than his casual response; "I was a child. I don't remember, really."

They ate hot dogs, sat on a blanket in damp grass, enjoying the Fourth of July celebration. Their pleasure was contagious. Don swapped jokes with people around them. Sandwiches and beer were exchanged, and in his company his age elevated her own. Marcie found herself talking to a woman who matter-of-factly discussed her pregnancy as if Marcie were an equal.

The festivities over, walking with him, holding his arm in the dark, they strolled amid departing cars, blaring horns, headlights stabbing the night.

"I had fun," he said, quietly.

"So did I."

"I won't be seeing you for a few days, Marcie."

"Why?"

"I have to go out of town."

"Where're you going?"

"Business."

"What kind of business?"

"Dull stuff. Got-to-make-a-living stuff."

"Have you ever thought about being an actor?"

He laughed, put a hand over her hand in the crook of his arm. "You think I'd make a good actor?"

"I think you'd make a great actor."

"Funny," he said, softly, "I thought about it when I was a child. I think I'd have been a good actor, too."

"Or a writer," Marcie offered.

"Yeah! I'd love to be a writer."

"What would you write about?"

He stopped. "I'd write murder mysteries. I think I could write about a murderer like nobody ever has. Insights, you know. People think they know what a person feels, or thinks, and why he does things—but they don't."

"Have you ever tried writing?"

"Poems in college. Things like that."

"I'd like to read some."

"That's all gone." He began walking. "All gone."

"You could write something new."

"All over," he said, voice strange. "I wish—"

"What?"

"I wish I could start life over again. Be somebody totally different. I once tried it. I ran away, made up a name and

177

a whole background. But when I tried to get a job with a construction company, I had to have a driver's license and didn't have one. So that won't work. The only way to change identity these days—is by becoming someone else who really exists. You have to have credit cards and buy license tags and belong to a union. They want to know why you weren't in the army, and if you were, what outfit, and so on."

"When will I see you again?" Marcie asked.

"Few days."

"Where are you going?"

"I don't know."

"You're going off and don't know where?"

"Sometimes I get in my wee VW and drive hundreds of miles in a night. It makes me feel like somebody else, different and far away and unknown."

"But, you said business—"

"Yep."

"What kind of business?"

"I sell a line of surgical supplies. Mostly to physicians, surgeons, usually. It's a good line. Stainless steel with a heavy nickel content which makes it antimagnetic."

He opened the car door, helped her in. When he entered, she was staring at him. "Rub your ear," she commanded. He laughed and did so. "Now," Marcie said, "what *is* your business?"

"That's a secret."

When he stopped, where he always did, Marcie got out fully a block from the house. "Don, please be careful," she urged.

"No worry," he said, soberly. "I'm in no jeopardy."

Chapter Twenty-one

HE left his Volkswagen in Macon, Georgia, where he stole a late-model Buick. The Buick was abandoned in Richmond, Virginia, in exchange for a less noticeable Toyota. He later switched license plates, putting a stolen tag on the stolen compact. His only baggage, carefully transferred, was a crocus sack containing his clothes, panty hose, handcuffs and a tire iron.

He arrived at Walter Reed Army Hospital as planned, shortly after nine A.M.

"Chuck!"

He turned, unalarmed. "Hello, Dr. Thigpen!"

The doctor shook his hand, warmly. "How've you been, Chuck?"

"Couldn't be better." They walked toward the main entrance together.

"How are your studies coming?"

"Really good. I'm a junior this year at Georgia Baptist Hospital in Atlanta."

"I thought that was girls only."

"Oh no," he laughed. "I almost had to go to court to get in, you know. It was reverse discrimination, actually, but they finally allowed me to enroll. Not bad, either— the only male nurse there."

The doctor stopped at the front desk, checking in. "We miss you," he said, signing a roster. "We haven't had a therapist as good since you left."

"That's a great compliment."

"True," the doctor affirmed. "In Atlanta, you say?"

"Right."

"Michael Hoke was an Atlanta man." Dr. Thigpen walked slowly. "Have you studied about him?"

"Oh yes. He contributed substantially to the correction of foot deformities and the stabilization of joints."

The doctor grinned, "That-a-boy. Stay on top of it,

Chuck. Still going to specialize in reconstructive orthopedics?"

"Plan to."

The doctor paused at a ward door. "What brings you back to Washington?"

"Visiting a friend."

"Well." The doctor closed both eyes, nodding, "Come see us, Chuck."

"Will do. So long, Dr. Thigpen."

Alone, he looked both ways down a cool, green hallway. He'd timed his arrival precisely. He walked unhurriedly to a door identified as THERAPY and entered. He greeted a working intern, carried himself as if he belonged here, and continued through to a general admittance waiting room. Public telephone booths lined a wall. He stepped inside and closed the door.

He shoved tissue into both cheeks, wads which distorted features and, more importantly, made his voice hollow. He dropped a coin in the telephone and dialed the operator.

"Collect call," he breathed heavily into the receiver. "This is Dennis Alday. Calling Mr. Seymour Schwartz, Fort Myers, Florida." He gave a number and warned, "Be sure to tell him the call is from Walter Reed Hospital in Washington, operator, or he may not accept."

Over his exhalations, the operator followed instructions to the letter. ". . . From Walter Reed Hospital, Washington, D.C. . . . collect call . . . to Mr. Seymour Schwartz . . . will you accept?"

"Dennis! How are you?"

He raled into the phone, "Doing well, Mr. Schwartz. I'm sorry to call collect."

"Don't worry about that, Dennis. Glad to accept. Are they treating you all right up there?"

"Yessir, fine."

"Got you taken care of, did they?"

"Yessir. Fine."

"Good, good."

"Thought I ought to call you, Mr. Schwartz, and let you know I'll be there the day after Labor Day like I'm supposed to be."

"I wasn't worried, Dennis. But thank you."

"The summer man told me he had to leave a day or two before. Should I come on down earlier?"

180

"No, the place will be all right for those few days. The key will be where it always is, Dennis."

"I wouldn't want to lose my job, Mr. Schwartz."

The man's laughter sounded genuine. "There's no need to worry about that, Dennis. We're happy with your performance. I admit, I had reservations, but you certainly dispelled any concern I may have had. They say you painted all the trim on the main house."

"Yessir."

"Don't fall and hurt yourself."

"I'm real careful, Mr. Schwartz."

"I know you are. Oh, we have a surprise for you, this season."

"You do?"

"We put in cable TV."

"You did!"

"I know how lonely it must get out there by yourself, Dennis. I told the boss it was the least we could do."

"Oh, say, Mr. Schwartz, that's nice. That's really nice."

"Thought you'd like that. Something on every channel, now."

"That's just nice, Mr. Schwartz."

"You'll be there the entire season, right?"

"From the day after Labor Day to April fifteenth, like last year."

"Good, good. Well, I know the place will be in good hands. I won't worry about it."

"You leave it to me, Mr. Schwartz. I appreciate the job."

A note of pity in the man's voice now, "We're happy to have you, Dennis. Call if you need anything."

After disconnecting, he removed the wads of tissue, dropped them to the floor. He straightened his tie and stepped out. Back through THERAPY, down a long hall, and out to the stolen car. Before approaching, he scanned the lot warily. Only then did he get inside, reach under the dashboard and jump start the motor.

He left the Toyota within a block of where it had been stolen, removed the tag and threw it into a drainage ditch. He strolled along a high bank of the James River until he came to a shopping center. Then it was only a matter of finding an automobile with keys in the ignition.

Now, under cover of dusk, he took back roads southward. When he crossed the state line into North Carolina, he began looking . . .

"The handcuffs are hurting my arms," she said. "Could you please loosen them?"

He drove, eyes forward.

"Could you loosen them a little, please?"

Trees rose in the headlights, loomed, and flew past. The center line of the blacktop formed semaphore dashes as they passed beneath the car. He heard her sob, "Oh, God, please—"

He swerved to avoid a cow ambling from high grass onto the right-of-way and she made a short, frightened cry.

"Sir?" she said. "Sir, may I talk to you?"

"Don't get up."

"No sir, I'm not. But may I talk to you?"

He kept his eyes on the highway, the speedometer needle was steady at fifty-five.

"Sir, my parents will start looking for me. They expected me home by eleven. That's the truth."

Like a soaring bird, tethered to the flashing white line of the highway, up an incline, rising, then down again—swooping through North Carolina hill country.

"I don't know you, do I?" she questioned.

"Keep your head down." He struck at her.

"I will," she said. "I'm not trying to get up. But my wrists—could you please loosen the handcuffs?"

It was as if nothing existed except that which was here. All matter formed only at the perimeter of headlights, surged into existence for an instant, zoomed past side windows to evaporate again. He glanced at the speed indicator—must not invite attention.

"My wrists are really hurting."

"You keep your head down."

"If we can talk—"

"Keep your head down."

"See, the thing is . . . sir? The thing is, my parents expect me home at eleven. It's after eleven, isn't it?"

Up a hill, rounding a curve, headlights slashing night, foliage a blur on either side, the car diving down a far slope, the motor humming. She retched.

"I have to get *out*," she cried. "I'm going to vomit, sir."

He made no reply.

"My arms——" she twisted suddenly, pain overcoming fear and he reached down to seize her collar and hold it.

"My arms," she screamed.

He banged her head on the floorboard and she screamed, "My arms. My arms! Help me, somebody! Help me!"

The windows were up. There was no other traffic, no houses—no ears but his to hear.

"God, please," she wailed. "Please, God—help me, somebody!"

Like a bird. An eagle or hawk. A predator with wind whispering through primary feathers of outstreached wings—riding air currents, skimming the surface of the highway, seeing but unseen, alone but alert, coming as if from nowhere and in a second, striking with deadly talons—only to rise again, prey quivering in clutching claws, blood from—

"Sir, please, please, please. My arms are aching, my wrists—please loosen the handcuffs a little, you've got to—"

The speedometer needle quavered, headlights rigid, the woodlands fluid in passing; shadows formed, evanesced and reformed, as the lone automobile drove deeper into the mountainous terrain which ringed a nearby reservoir. He knew it well. He'd been here before.

"God, please . . ." retching again.

"Talk . . . please . . . talk to me . . ."

He smelled bile and his nostrils flared.

"Arms hurt . . . please . . . talk . . ."

He put a hand on her shoulder, patted.

"Sir, could you please let me sit up? My face is in . . . please, I'm lying in a mess."

Her supplications went unheard, her pleas to a deity, unheeded. He had a place in mind, a timber road kept open as a firebreak in the forest. He slowed, watching for it—there'd be reflectors, a chain slung from one creosoted post to another, and a small sign warning, "NO TRESPASSING: GOVT PROPERTY."

She had wept herself weak, cried herself hoarse, the whimpers were now those of an infant blindly seeking the succor of its mother. He pulled off the highway, set the emergency brake and got out, leaving the car door opened as he went to unhook the chain. He let the barrier drop and returned to the front seat. He drove over the chain, halted anew, returned to hang it.

"Arms . . . hurt . . . arms . . ."

In a low gear, easing over jutting roots and stones, the vehicle lurched through underbrush which squealed against the sides of the car. Up a wending lane he knew.

". . . God . . ."

He stopped, sat a moment with the motor running, then turned the car around so it faced the direction from which it had come. He cut off the motor. He extinguished the lights.

". . . please if . . . God . . . my arms . . ."

He opened a package of cigarettes, tapped out one and lit it. The smoke was acrid, searing throat and lungs unaccustomed to it.

"Please . . . please . . ."

He saw his own face illuminated in the rearview mirror as he drew on the cigarette. He rolled down a window. Fresh air. Smelled good. Evergreens. He took a deep breath.

She was whispering, mumbling.

He could stop, this moment. There was no compulsion to continue. If he chose, he could reach down and release her. On the floor, shackled, face and breast smeared with stomach fluids, she begged—and he was her final hope. Her only hope. She was not loath to speak to him now, no indeed. She would do anything, simply to loosen a cuff.

"Sir, may I talk to you? Can't we talk, please?"

He sucked smoke, exhaled, lips pursed.

He had tested himself. He had gone so far and no further. If he were out of control, by now the deed would be done, and she would grow cold in a forest glen. But he had not done her harm. He could stop. Or not stop. This was his choice alone.

"Sir, if I could please sit up. I'll do anything—"

Anything. He couldn't help smiling. Values changed, priorities altered, not so aloof anymore.

"—if I could sit up, please? My arms are numb. If I could sit up for awhile? I'll be quiet. I promise."

He stabbed his cigarette against the exterior of the car, sparks falling, until the butt was dead.

"May I please sit up a few minutes, sir?"

He felt for the seat-adjustment lever, and it slid all the way back. He'd been driving the stolen Dodge with his knees cramped under the steering wheel, the seat confining her to a space so limited she could neither kick nor turn.

Her voice trembling, she struggled to make her tone rational, reasoning. "Could I please sit up now, sir?"

He pulled her onto the seat and she sat, gasping, eyes closed, face palely lit by moonlight filtering through the trees, reflecting on the cream-colored hood.

"If you shout," he said softly, "I'll have to hurt you. You don't want me to hurt you."

"No."

"There's nobody to hear you. But I would hurt you, if you shouted."

He wrapped the panty hose around her neck, knotted them loosely. He hooked one hand in the nylon loop. With his other hand, he unbuttoned her blouse. She sat, eyes tightly shut, chin quivering.

He put a palm on her breast and she tensed, head back against the seat, but made not a sound. He felt with his tongue. She drew a breath, held it, exhaled. Another breath held, exhaled.

He mouthed, kissed. Then, her throat in one hand, he bit with slowly increasing pressure.

Her groan rose to a wail and she kicked frantically and he twisted the nylon but she jerked free, screaming!

He was astraddle her now, her arms pinned by cuffs, his hands in the noose, choking, choking, her tongue protruding—she grew limp.

He let up. Waited. Waited. Waited. She gasped.

He dragged her outside and hauled her away from the vehicle. He spread his crocus sack beside her, put the tire iron where he could reach it. On her back, she stared with eyes glazed, at silhouetted fronds against a cobalt sky and crescent moon.

Now the skirt.

Hands trembling, ritualistically, he removed the outer garment. Stunned, he sat back. A safety pin.

Carefully, he reviewed the entire evening since he had found her. Like all the rest, chin lifted, a toss of the head, every move holier-than-thou—but these? The pin—the panties?

These were not the sheer nylons of a beauty queen. The elastic frayed and broken, held by a pin. There was no silky fabric, no lace on this coarse cotton. This was the deepest secret a girl might harbor, praying nobody ever saw, ever knew; hiding in a closed toilet, her blouse tucked to cover the tiny pin.

But her walk! Her imperious demeanor!

Yet, it was a mistake. This girl suffered, even as he suffered.

He leaned forward, his face above hers. She stared in shock.

He brushed debris from a cheek, wiped mucus from her nostrils. He sat back, looking at the underwear. A mistake. But it was too late.

Gently, tenderly, he turned her over, soothing, "It's over. It's all over now."

He unlocked the handcuffs. "All over," he intoned.

Her arms lay as he left them, wrists in the small of her back. He got the tire iron and knelt at her shoulder.

Careful. Careful. She deserved his best.

He lifted the iron high, a hand on her back, and brought it down with all his might.

Marcie came up, screaming.

Joanne bounded from bed, stumbling, falling, groping for the door.

"Mom! Mom! Help me, mom!"

Into the girl's bedroom, Joanne thrashed at a wall plate, turned on an overhead light and seized Marcie by the shoulders. "Marcie? Marcie, wake up, honey."

Green eyes staring, pupils large, Marcie reached with trembling hands for her mother's embrace.

"You're dreaming, Marcie. A bad dream, that's all. Everything is all right. It's over now. All over."

"Nearly got me."

Joanne rocked her to and fro, whispering, "*Sh-sh-sh*, it's all right."

"Going to—"

"Going to what?"

"Kill—"

"No, no." Joanne stroked her back, massaging.

"Blood—"

"Just a dream, darling. A bad dream."

With a shuddered exhalation, Marcie lay back and turned onto her stomach. Joanne heard a nerve jangling crunch of molars as Marcie ground teeth in her half-sleep.

Tomorrow morning, enthralled as all children were about this elusive alter ego, Marcie would demand an elaborate report. Enchanted by the mystery of her "other" self, she'd ask, "What did I say?" then shrill with laughter, eyes slight-

186

ly frightened, trying to imagine what horror her subconscious had displayed.

But for now, the demons were real. Joanne sat on the side of the girl's bed, patting her behind as once she'd patted when Marcie was an infant in a crib. She felt muscles twitch, involuntary spasms of a body responding to erratic electrical signals in a drowsing brain.

Joanne turned off the light and readjusted the sheets over the contours of Marcie's body. Even, smooth breathing. She bent, kissed the girl on a bare shoulder and Marcie mumbled, sighed, smacked her lips.

Maternal responsibility discharged, Joanne returned to her own bedroom, shivering as if cold. She got into bed but lay with eyes open in the dark. She thought of calling Ken, asking him to come over.

She sat up, thrashed her pillow with balled fists, then fell back wide awake.

In the next room she heard Marcie whimper and Joanne lay waiting, to see if she should return.

Alert, she heard the tick of the kitchen clock, remarkably loud at this distance. A floor creaked, contracting. The air conditioner hummed.

"Please—" Marcie's childlike voice made Joanne rise on her elbows.

"Please—"

"Marcie?"

But Marcie slept.

For Joanne, the night had just begun.

Chapter Twenty-two

RINGING . . .
    Joanne put a pillow over her head.

Bells, bells—*ringing*. She came up with a start, clawing for the telephone.

"Jo? How about breakfast?"

"Ken, what time is it?"

"Six."

Joanne fell back, moaning. Then, "Come on."

She met Marcie in the hallway and without a word they went to the kitchen together. Joanne assembled a percolator; Marcie took milk from the refrigerator, bumped the door closed with a hip.

When Ken entered, he looked from one robed figure to the other. "Mama zombie, baby zombie." He got a mug from the cupboard, placed it on a folded newspaper on the table.

"Up all night," Joanne explained.

"Were you ill?"

"No. Marcie."

"Me!" Marcie said.

"Nightmares."

Marcie poured milk over cereal. "What about?"

"I don't know."

"Did I talk?"

"Murder, mayhem."

"What'd I say?"

"I don't remember, Marcie." Joanne reached for the morning paper and Ken pinned it.

He shook his head, "Not yet."

"Let me see it," Joanne demanded.

The headline: FSU CRIMINOLOGIST ACCUSED BY ROGERS. She blinked her eyes trying to dispel a veil of sleep. As she read, Ken spoke to Marcie. "Better stand clear, she may splatter."

Marcie leaned forward on her elbows, scanned the headline and sat back, disgusted. "No wonder I have nightmares," she said. "What did I say last night, mom?"

"Not now, Marcie."

"How can I analyze my dreams if I can't remember them?"

"Nightmares are not indicative . . ." Joanne trailed off, reading. "Rogers is a creep," she fumed.

"There's no telling what I'll end up," Marcie complained. "I'm up to my derrière in deviates. My mind has been subjected to scenes of rape, sodomy—"

"Hush, Marcie."

"That article isn't why I came by, Jo," Ken stated.

"My psyche has got to be contorted," Marcie said. "Most kids hear fairy tales. I hear about abused fairies—"

"Marcie, hush, please."

Ken sipped coffee. "Cowboy is on my back, Jo. When you're awake enough to discuss it, we need to."

"He's growing more personal in his attacks," Joanne noted.

"He is," Ken said. "And it promises to get worse if you don't let this thing die down."

"Probably end up frigid," Marcie grumped. "Or a nymphomaniac."

"Actually, that isn't a contradiction, psychologically."

"What'd I say last night, mom?"

"I don't recall. Ken, Rogers is getting downright insulting. Listen to this: 'Conclusions drawn on female intuition and wishful thinking.' "

"I read it, Jo."

"Any calls, mom?" Marcie washed her bowl in the sink. Joanne reread the article. "Mom, any calls?"

"Marcie," Joanne exploded, "we arose at the same instant! Have you heard the phone ring?"

"That's what woke me."

"And here sits the caller," Joanne indicated Ken.

"Cowboy met me at the end of my shift this morning," Ken related. "He said something that's been worrying me."

"What?" Joanne pushed away the newspaper.

"He said the district attorney told him you were 'as guilty as anyone' where Judge Alcorn is concerned. What's he talking about?"

"Rogers said that?"

"Guilty of what?"

"Sheriff Rogers said that?"

"I just said he said it," Ken replied, sharply. "Now, will you please explain?"

"I can't."

"I'm going out." Marcie left for her room.

Ken put a heavy hand on Joanne's forearm. "Jo, what is going on? Guilty of what?"

"The case is going to a grand jury," she said, voice low. "Until indictments are rendered or quashed, I can't discuss it."

"Then why would Rogers say anything?"

"Because he's trying to slander me, apparently. He *told* you that Phillip Dupree said—"

Marcie entered, halting conversation. "Go right ahead," she stated. "I'm going out."

"Out where?"

189

"Out, out, damn spot," Marcie waved a hand. "Out!"

"Marcie, I'm in no mood for juvenile theatrics."

"I'm going to the red-light district, mom. I'm going to watch the prostitutes pay off their pimps."

"Hey, hey," Ken chided, "easy, you two." He reached for Marcie and she veered, wheeled.

"You," Marcie sneered, "have no right to say anything to me. Or to mom."

Stung, he withdrew an outstretched hand.

Marcie slammed the rear door.

Ken peered into his coffee, the mug held between the tips of thick fingers as he turned it a quarter-circle this way, then that.

"What brought that on?" Joanne queried.

"I'm not sure."

"You two been feuding, Ken?"

"Not me."

To vanquish hurt feelings, Joanne tugged him nearer, kissed him. "You know what a battleground this can be before I've had coffee in the mornings."

"Jo—listen to me—this thing with Cowboy is getting ugly. He suspects me of being a courier of office gossip, arming you with inside information."

"Nonsense."

"My job may be on the line. Not that I mind all that much. But I may be asked to resign."

"Rogers is playing a two-faced card, Ken. On the one side he is trying to bolster his public image, making it appear he caught a mass murderer. On the other side is all this wonderful controversy which overshadows the fact that he blundered and let his prisoner commit suicide."

"That doesn't alter the fact that he suspects me of a certain disloyalty."

"Then get the hell out," Joanne said. "Tell him you and I broke off. Why ask *me* to stop defending myself for his sake?"

"That's the second arrow to my ego this morning."

"I'm sorry." She poured coffee with shaking hands. "But Ken, I cannot allow this country bumpkin sheriff to—"

"Hold it!" Ken stood. "Let's be honest if nothing else. This 'country bumpkin' sheriff holds a master's degree in criminology. He's on his way to a doctorate. He's an elected official with all the attendant failings thereof—but that isn't his fault, that's the fault of the system. He has to counter criticism from his opponents, defend his tactics to civil rights groups, and somehow amid it all, gain convictions of felons better armed to evade justice than we are to bring them into court. If you take an unbiased look at Cowboy, you'll see that because of him—directly because of him—we now have a shortwave radio that will actually transmit to the far end of our territory. We have walkie-talkies, flashlights with a beam that will illuminate a suspect at fifteen hundred feet. That doesn't sound like much, but it gives an officer in a dark alley a sense of security to know he might see his assailant before the assault."

He strode to the cabinets, back again. "I'll tell you something, Jo. Cowboy does a lot of things I don't like. But so did my mama. Overall, on a scale of one-to-ten, Rogers rates about eight with me. He's pretty good at what he does and he treats his men fairly. He doesn't pistol-whip suspects. He follows the book. Then when you and your more idealistic colleagues step in to spring a guy like Swain, we begin to wonder what the hell we're doing out there."

"A difference in philosophical approach does not necessarily imply a breach between theory and practice, Ken."

"That!" He jabbed a finger at her. "That's the kind of nonsense that drives Rogers to pull out his hair. You sit in an air conditioned office mulling philosophy and we go out to get our guts splashed on a wall by double-ought buckshot from some turkey you turned loose on a technicality."

"I didn't know you were so opposed to my views."

"You're welcome to your views. Until they're patently prejudiced, I listen politely. But to call Rogers a country bumpkin—that is false."

"Then I withdraw that characterization."

"Now, I want to know, Jo—what is this about Alcorn and you?"

"I said—"

He slammed the table, "To hell with that! The world doesn't run on watchworks, goddamn it! Dirty guys do dirty things. Whatever judicial secrecy is threatened, so be it. Rogers mentioned it, said that Dupree told him and now I'm standing here asking *you*—what the hell is going on?"

Joanne poured the last of the coffee. "Alcorn is under investigation on allegations of taking bribes and kickbacks. I don't know the charges, specifically. A grand jury may not bring in a true bill. Ralph is preparing the case. Apparently, if Ralph is correct, the implications are politically explosive."

"Alcorn, the man up for Supreme Court Justice?"

"Yes. Anyway, an aide in Alcorn's office sent Ralph copies of some checks I'd written to Alcorn. The checks are payments I returned from advances required before I take a case. The explanation is that simple. But by sending the information to Ralph, they are implying that Ralph's former wife is involved in giving Alcorn kickbacks."

Ken sat again.

"I'll have no great difficulty proving to the grand jury that I'm innocent," Joanne said. "It's merely a clumsy attempt to blackmail Ralph into easing up."

"It's brilliant, actually. Don't you see what Alcorn is doing?"

"Blackmail."

"No, not blackmail. Alcorn knows Ralph doesn't dare leave such an allegation untouched. Ralph will be forced to call you before the grand jury almost as if to defend *himself*. But Alcorn knows you will prove the checks are what they are."

"So?"

"Ralph played into Alcorn's hands," Ken said. "You will prove the transactions with Alcorn were legitimate, despite the way it appears. Alcorn will lift his hands and say, 'A simple misunderstanding. That's how it is with all these charges.' The grand jury will then have doubts; Ralph's real evidence will be skeptically reviewed and his case will be weakened."

"Ohh—"

"Better tell Ralph."

"Ohh," Joanne groaned. "You're right."

"But," Ken murmured, "that does tell me one thing."

"What's that?"

"Sheriff Rogers and Dupree are up to their eyeballs in Alcorn's mess. Otherwise they wouldn't have known to discuss it, nor would they have attempted to draw you into it."

"We can't accuse them of that."

"No." Ken rubbed his unshaven chin with the heel of a hand, his whiskers making bristling sounds.

Joanne went to the telephone and dialed Ralph's office.

"Jo," Ken asked, absently, "what's the deadline for filing intentions on running for sheriff?"

"Next month, I think. Why?"

"Thinking, that's all."

Marcie walked down Tennessee Street, past the university campus, the sun warm against her bare legs. Without purpose or destination, she debated where to seek out any of her high school friends. They'd be at the beach. Or camp. Anywhere but here.

"Hello, there."

"Hi, Don!" Marcie looked both ways, ran across four lanes to the far side.

"Hop in," he offered. "Where were you going?"

"Nowhere. I thought you would be away several days."

"Nah." He pulled into traffic. "Changed my mind."

"You aren't going?"

"Nope. How about something to eat? I'm starving."

She leaned closer. "Are you growing a mustache?"

"Sure am. Like it?"

"Not especially."

He laughed, "Don't worry, I'll shave it off right after Easter next year."

"Why Easter?"

"It's a religious thing." He stroked an ear.

He seemed so vibrant, so filled with energy. "Your mom's in the newspaper this morning," he said. "How's it feel to be the daughter of a celebrity?" He was bobbing his head, as if in time to music.

"She's not too happy about all that."

He snapped his fingers, one leg jiggling, the heel lifted.

"You must feel good," Marcie said.

"Never felt better. I feel—fantastic."

Marcie turned away, glumly.

He poked at her ribs, playfully. "How come you're so sour?"

"I don't know. It's hot. I just had a fight with my mom and her Neanderthal boyfriend."

"Oh-ho, insults! Goody. Let's rip them up, verbally." He went through a caution light, accelerating, then watched his rearview mirror for possible legal interception. "What's happening between your mother and the sheriff?"

"I think it's a battle of philosophies."

He laughed uproariously.

"Mom's been studying some sex crimes for months," Marcie explained. "So when Sheriff Rogers caught a man who didn't fit her profile, it hurt her image, I guess."

Don laughed again, laughed so exuberantly, Marcie studied his cerulean eyes to see if the pupils were dilated.

"So now," he finally croaked, "they're slugging it out in the newspapers, right?"

"That's about it."

He laughed. Laughed and laughed. Laughed until tears flowed down his cheeks. He would look away, then once more erupt mirthfully.

"You been drinking, Don?"

"*Nein, fräulein.* 'Tis the nectar of life upon which I imbibe. Pray thee, drink deeply the sweet breath. Look, yon bird winging ever nestward—"

"I think you have."

"Nay, have not," he insisted, eyes glittering. "I am alive, aware, absorbing this that is existence. My heart beats, my world it is the old world yet, I am I and my life is yet—"

"Housman," Marcie said, "poorly paraphrased."

"Precisely, and good for you." Another amber light and Marcie heard a screech of brakes.

"Don't get us killed, Don. I would never be able to explain it to my mother."

"That's true." He gunned the motor, weaving through slower traffic. "So! Your mother has been having this battle with the county gendarmes."

"Yeah." His mood was catching. "She was boiling this morning over some things the sheriff said."

"Ah, yes, but which orator speaks the truth?"

"Mom, I suspect. She's a stickler for details, so she doesn't mess up very often."

"But she has. She did. The culprit lays in the morgue tried, true and executed. What more is there to say?"

"He isn't the man."

"What?"

"He didn't kill all the other women. Just the mother and her daughter, out the Quincy highway."

"The sheriff does not agree, apparently."

"Apparently. Where're we going?"

"A tiny oasis where susurrant palms wave in tropical breezes. Where the scent of dates perfume the air. Where—"

"Watch it!" Marcie braced herself as they swerved around a car making an improper turn.

"—where the food is palatable and the liquids potable—"

"To the hospital, if you don't slow down."

But he was wild with himself, quoting e.e. cummings and plunging unexpectedly into all seven stanzas of Franklin Waldheim's "Help Wanted," a poem about a law firm advertising for a clerk.

"Hey," Marcie acknowledged, "that was pretty good."

"Every young law student hears that, at least once."

"You studied law?"

"I told you, criminology at FSU." He turned into a restaurant where they'd never been. He leaped from the car, came around and opened her door with a deep bow at the waist. "Fair lady, behold, the caterer awaits. Let us favor them with your presence." He kissed the back of her hand and stood ramrod straight, offering an elbow, to escort her.

"Boy, are you high," Marcie said, amiably.

"No truer words were ever spoken."

"On what?"

"Life, love. Life!"

His mood was euphoric. He seemed to peer at everything with childish glee, barely able to contain himself, bouncing physically.

"Now let's talk about your wee mommie," he said, grinning, reaching across to pat Marcie's hand.

"What's there to talk about?"

"The fray! The conflict! Is this not the stuff of life?"

"What's the matter with you?" Marcie laughed.

"Have you never seen joy, dear Marcie? Have you never seen *félicité?*"

Caught in his joviality, Marcie sat watching him, grinning. "What have you been taking?" she asked.

"Not animal, vegetable or mineral," he replied. "What you see is mental, emotional, a case of serendipity gone amok."

"Wish it would rub off on me, then."

"Let it! Touch me. Feel those vibrations?" He quivered for her benefit.

"Now," he leaned across the table conspiratorially, "I want to know a secret."

"What?"

"What good witch makes you so lovely to behold? What rare herb is in your tea?"

"Don, you nut! Let me see your veins, you've been taking something."

He exposed his arms. "You know why race car drivers drive race cars?"

Before she could respond he put his fingertips to her lips. "Do you know why men dive from airplanes with their very lives depending on the stitch of a seamstress and sixty yards of silk? Or why we go to the moon?"

She kissed his fingers and pushed them away, gently.

"Because," he whispered, "only then do they know life. Only when death is imminent, when luck and chance blend with skill and art—then they are exhilarated, and only then. No drug can duplicate it. No accomplishment can come within a million hectometers."

"You're trying to be ostentatious," Marcie accused.

"Ten hectometers is a kilometer," he said. "Until you have tasted death, you cannot savor life. Only when you have watched a fibrillating heart quiver and halt, *only* then can you appreciate the mysterious universe that is the human body. Have you ever seen a chest laid open, the heart beating those final few faltering pulses?"

"God, no."

"Then," he sat back, smiling, "you live in elements you will never fully comprehend. All about you is life, and like a fish in the sea, you accept it. But if ever, once, you faced the true threat of death, suffocating, the air would then smell sweeter than any blossom. And that's the truth."

"Heaven forbid."

"Not heaven," he glowered in exaggerated reproof. "It is not God that has the final say."

"You don't believe in God?"

He waved an arm at a waitress, shouting, "Come hither, woman! We're starving!"

His order: a dozen eggs scrambled softly, half a pound of bacon, six pieces of toast and a pot of coffee. He yielded to Marcie with a flourish, "Plus whatever the lady would like to have."

"I just ate."

"Eat again."

"I'm not hungry."

He dismissed the waitress and said to Marcie, "See, that's what I mean. You've probably never been hungry."

"I've been hungry."

"Not ravishingly hungry," he said. "I mean real hunger.

Where your abdomen is so empty the entrails are drying and stomach acid begins to feed on the flesh of the belly itself."

"Must we be so gory?"

"An ache that is so intense," he continued, "that anything is acceptable—roaches, rats, reptiles—"

"Will you shut your mouth?" Marcie squealed. "I get bloody talks at home, and now with you!"

"You do?" He cocked his head quizzically.

"Blood and guts and gore," Marcie snapped. "I'm sick of sick things. I'd like to talk about nice things for a while."

"What bloody things?" he asked, his mouth drawn in a lopsided grin.

"Rape and sodomy and such."

"With whom are these things discussed? Your wee mommie?"

"Yes."

"Interesting."

"Not after all these years."

"Psychopathic sexualis," he said.

"Don!" Marcie moved to rise and he grabbed her arm.

"No more," he conceded. "Forgive me. Sit down, relax."

He glanced around the room, furtively, leaned across the table. Inches from her face, he laughed. "So where were we?"

"When?"

"Ah, yes," he whispered. "Your wee mommie."

Chapter Twenty-three

THADDEUS Kreijewski stroked his Vandyke, huffed, stroked, huffed. Behind his spectacles, dark eyes darted like wrens against a window. "This isn't going to go away, Jo. It'll continue until either you or Sheriff Rogers stands down."

"You think it should be me?" Joanne demanded.

"I haven't the right to make that decision."

"Forget political protocol, Thad. Do *you* think I should back down?"

Unable to restrain himself, the dean stood, paced a step, returned and sat at his desk. "You've been reading the letters to the editors? The editorials?"

"I saw some of them."

"The hue and cry is for law and order. The man on the street wants criminals put away. Who do you think they blame now for mitigating circumstances and early probation? They think recidivism is primarily the fault of people like us, anyway. Crooks turned loose too soon, that's what they think."

"They, meaning the public."

"Yes, the public! This is not a battle between opposing attorneys, this mess with Rogers. This has degenerated into a public relations fight and nothing else. In this corner, Florida State University Department of Criminology; in that corner the sheriff of Leon County. The people don't know about law. They do know the value of regular police patrol and adequate protection against crime and violence."

"You're saying I should shut up."

"If you do, all this will die down. But that's a decision you must make."

"My father pioneered in psychological profiles, Thad. Did you know that?"

"I read his book."

"During World War II," Joanne said, "a German psychologist was responsible for studying General George Patton. He knew Patton was obsessed with military history. He knew about Patton's belief in reincarnation. Patton believed he'd fought on those same bloody fields before. He believed his life was predestined. The German psychologist predicted Patton would attack Sicily, right down to the route the battle would follow. The high command wouldn't listen and many German soldiers died as a result."

Joanne lowered her voice. "My father said, 'Be sure, then be adamant, if lives depend on it.' "

"But can you be so sure?"

"I'm so sure that I cannot, I must not yield."

"You're in jeopardy, Jo."

"*If* I'm wrong. But you know what I've begun to think? I'm really beginning to think this fellow was in areas where he saw news reports of missing girls. Later, he heard about bodies mutilated and maybe read Tony Eldridge's articles in the *Democrat*. He must've thought, 'If I have to kill these women, I'll hang it on the unknown sex criminal—' "

"What manner of scientific deduction is that?" Thad growled. "Conjecture of the worst sort, Jo. Putting imaginary thoughts into the head of a dead suspect."

"Why else would he have had intercourse with the murdered mother and daughter, Thad?"

"I don't deal in conjecture! I don't know why. But neither do you, Jo. It's this kind of guessing that hurts us."

He paced, she silently watching.

"You aren't going to win this fight on a public relations level, Jo. Not by debating law and order with Cowboy Rogers. If you continue, if you must continue, you have to get evidence to support your claims. Cowboy's got you. He knows, I know and you should know, this murderer isn't going to strike anywhere in this three-state area again. Unless the killer comes forward and confesses, you will never prove the dead suspect wasn't their man."

"That's true."

"In which case," Thad said, "you'd better start calling on the police departments involved, interviewing those people firsthand. Pray that you uncover something that substantiates your theories."

"I've read all their reports—"

He waved a hand, fishtail fashion, "Forget that. Go see the investigating officers, the pathologists, the coroner in Jacksonville. That's the only body you have to work from anyway, except the mother-daughter, and if they aren't connected, you have *only* the Jacksonville body to work with. What an investigator thinks—the tiny doubts, the suspicions and impressions and guesses—that's what you need. It may be totally irrelevant in terms of legal clues, but it may have some psychological significance to you. You won't see conjecture in a coroner's report. If he can't prove his thoughts, he doesn't write them up. Well. Go for what is not in the reports. I don't see any other way. I'd begin with Bud Diehl because he's a friend of yours—and where else could you begin?"

He gazed at a wall filled with bookcases. "I'd like to investigate one lousy murder in the polar region," he said. "I'd like to have one perfectly preserved specimen with which to work. Damn the South, anyway. A body left in a warm, humid swamp starts to deteriorate instantly. Inside a week, opossums, raccoons, foxes, bear, bobcats and buzzards have strewn the corpse far and wide. What they don't get, the beetles and ants devour. Fabric bleaches, shoes rot, metal corrodes. If a month goes by, we're working with a bone or two and the murderer has peace of mind knowing all the clues are probably destroyed."

Joanne stood to leave.

"How'd it go with the grand jury, Jo?"

She told him what Alcorn had tried to do with the checks she'd returned, then laughed. "Ralph handled it brilliantly, I thought. He said, "Ladies and gentlemen, now I want to call my former wife, who has had a perfectly proper business transaction with Judge Alcorn. But the judge handled these transactions in such a way as to cast doubt on himself, and Dr. Fleming. We will walk you through this, not because of any wrongdoing on Judge Alcorn's part, or on the part of Joanne Fleming. Rather, to show you the care we took in sifting evidence where improper office procedures give an impression that something illegal had transpired. Later, we will see transactions between Alcorn and other people which were also improper procedure—but criminal.' It was something to see, Thad. Ralph turned the ploy and used it on Judge Alcorn."

Thaddeus Kreijewski nodded grimly.

"Does that upset you, Thad?"

"Yes, Jo, it does."

"I'm sorry."

"Don't be. Sit another minute, will you?" He removed his glasses, cleaned them with a tissue. "I have no children."

Uncertain, Joanne said, "I know."

"When I first came to Tallahassee and FSU," Thad replaced his spectacles, "one of the first people to welcome me was Albert Alcorn. He was a rising jurist. Ambitious. I was a New York Pole in the Deep South, out of my element, preaching scientific criminology which went over like a pregnant elephant. But Judge Alcorn got me into the country club, idiot ideas and all. His children—they're grown now—became our children. We celebrated holidays with them, sent birthday, graduation gifts."

"I'm sorry, Thad."

"No, don't be. But as so often occurs in life, the real tragedy is something other than it seems, Jo. Obviously, Ralph has a case or the grand jury wouldn't have handed down indictments against a man so respected and powerful as Albert Alcorn."

"That's right," Joanne said.

"And Albert may be guilty. I'll presume his innocence until proven otherwise, merely to be archaically democratic. But common sense suggests the worst, doesn't it?"

"Yes."

"I remember in the 'sixties," he mused, "Judge Alcorn was the first Florida judge to rule strongly against racial segregation. It took guts. It isolated him and his family from the community for a long time. Bricks through the windows, that sort of thing—"

"I've been under the impression he's a very prejudiced man."

"A truly great jurist never lets personal opinions or personalities enter into his deliberations, Jo."

"I must confess, I'm surprised."

"He's a surprising man. When his wife, Peggy, was dying of cancer, Albert did his best to enact a law legalizing medical euthanasia. It was defeated by the Baptist element, but he tried. In the end, he had to kill her himself."

"Kill her?"

"There's no proof of that," Thad said. "Only, the last night, when she was suffering so, my wife and I were there and she said good-bye in a certain way."

"Thad—"

"The tragedy is," he said, "not that Albert has done wrong. But he is a troglodyte of the old order, the Old South, who should have died in his cave, long, long ago."

Joanne looked at her hands.

"When I was a federal probation officer," Thad shifted moods, "one of the more interesting people I met was a pornographer. Very successful one, too. We nailed him on use-of-mail charges. At any rate, he calls occasionally to tell me that if he had been publishing now, he'd never have been incarcerated. The law, community mores, moral standards, everything has changed. Compared to what's on public TV these nights, his magazines were fairly tame. It's just the other way around with Albert. What he has done was once accepted. Ignored. Known, but never contested. He's lived too long. Too bad, too."

As she rose again, Thad motioned her down. "A few more observations about your killer," he said, gruffly. "You're dealing with paraphilia and, as with most sex deviates, once the pattern is set and classified, it tends to hold. But you should remember that the murderer you

201

chase may not be the same man today that he was yesterday, a week ago, or a month ago."

"What do you mean?"

"You are proceeding on the assumption that his rape-murders are *à la soutenu,* is that right? That is to say, he will not vary his modus operandi. Correct?"

"That's correct."

"As of the murder of the Jacksonville woman—what was her name?"

"Hightower."

"As of the murder of Mrs. Hightower, you felt you were profiling a classic sadist-murderer with all six conditions thereof: periodicity, mutilation, return to the scene, sexual arousal concomitantly, normal behavior between attacks, and most importantly, he's sane. Right?"

"Right."

"I offer this observation as a personal theory, not necessarily scientific, Jo. But I think you must be aware that he may change."

"How?"

"If he ever has a single shred of remorse, the tiniest misgiving even fleetingly, he may change psychologically. He may become a different animal from the prey you think you're seeking now. He may stop killing, as did Jack the Ripper. He may go into a psychological remission; years may pass before he strikes again—at which time his modus operandi would be so alien to these cases you wouldn't recognize the murderer as the same man. Which could even be the case with the suspect who hung himself, you know."

"That thought haunts me."

"It should. Cowboy could be right, bless his tin star."

"Silver," Joanne amended. "He wouldn't be caught in anything less than sterling."

"That's another thing," Thad snapped, "get this fight off a personal level."

"All right. I agree."

"Go away," Thad ordered. "You've given me an executive headache."

"Anybody here?" Joanne called, needlessly—Ken's car and another vehicle were parked in the driveway.

"In the kitchen, Jo."

She entered, halted abruptly. "Well, hello, Mr. Nathan."

The black attorney smiled. "Good evening, Dr. Fleming."

202

The telephone rang and Joanne excused herself, leaving the two men as they resumed a discussion.

"Jo, this is Ralph!" He fairly shouted into the telephone.

"You sound happy."

"I am. Alcorn's trial date has been set, and I may run for district attorney or judge before this is over."

"Somehow, I can't imagine you in politics, Ralph."

"Why not?" He sounded hurt.

"What about your law practice?"

"Nothing helps a law firm like having a sitting judge as a senior partner. I'm returning your call, Jo."

"I didn't call you, Ralph."

"You didn't? This note has your telephone number and it says 'Re: Swain.'"

"That must be John Nathan. He's in the kitchen. Hold on."

Nathan answered on the extension. "Mr. Fleming, we can apply for retrial of Swain in good faith now. One of the women he raped conceded she had agreed on a prior date to have intercourse with Swain. She didn't want to admit that because she was married. Now she's divorced and her conscience has been hurting her. I think that will overturn the conviction, don't you?"

Nathan scrawled a note on a pad, listening. "Yes, I will. Thanks for your help, Mr. Fleming."

When he hung up, Joanne said, "Congratulations. And good work."

"Yes." Nathan sat at the table with Ken again.

"Ralph says he's thinking about running for district attorney or a judgeship," Joanne reported to Ken, amused.

"Tell him to run for judge," Ken advised, "not D.A."

"Why?"

"John Nathan is running for district attorney."

Flustered, Joanne said, "Well. How about that."

"A drop of chocolate on snow white vanilla, right?" Nathan offered.

"In all honesty, John," Joanne said, "do you think you have a chance?"

"I think so, with what Ken has outlined."

"Ken!"

"We're sort of running together," Ken said. "I'm running for sheriff."

"Ken, are you crazy? Cowboy is a shoo-in. His only

opponent is Republican, and they don't do well in Leon County elections."

"I'm running and I plan to win. Our campaign slogan is going to be 'Bring law, as well as order, to Leon County.' "

"The two of you together?"

"That's right."

"It should be interesting, if nothing else," she said. "I'll provide sutures and gauze for wounded egos."

"Actually," Ken said, soberly, "Dupree has no opponent in the race for D.A. Except now, John Nathan."

"That's because nobody can beat Dupree," Joanne stated.

"*Today*," Ken said. "Tomorrow, John will win."

"You seem confident," Joanne laughed, a bit too forced.

"When the trial of Alcorn breaks," Ken surmised, "Cowboy and Dupree will be in the thick of it. Not even Ralph knows that, maybe. But I think I'm right. When the public finds out and the candidates are tainted, underdogs in the race will become top contenders. In the case of district attorney, it'll be too late for anyone else to qualify and John Nathan will win, even if by default. I'll become sheriff, too. Same plan."

"There's an outside chance that may work," Joanne agreed cautiously. "But suppose the trial is delayed, as surely it will be. You can't make accusations of impropriety without evidence."

"We'll gamble on the trial," Ken said. "We'll run hard, cast aspersions by innuendo, and when the facts emerge, John Nathan and Ken Blackburn will ride a crest of public indignation."

"May I reveal this grandiose plot to Ralph?" Joanne asked. "Or is this a state secret?"

"I'll tell him," Nathan said, rising. "I have to go by his office anyway. If he's serious about running for judge, we may have a triumvirate here."

When he reached the door, Nathan turned, his voice syrupy with a southern drawl. 'Y'all can burn yo' Confederate money now. The Old South ain't going to rise again."

"Which may be for the better," Joanne conceded. "I hope so."

"That was delicious," Marcie sat back, "and I ate too much."

"Me too." Don reached into his pocket, paused, then

204

patted his other hip. "Marcie, what're your plans for Labor Day weekend?"

"Going to my dad's cottage at Panacea. Mom and me. Dad got the cottage as part of their divorce settlement, but now that the ice has been broken by mom spending a day there, his conscience is hurting him. So dad offered the cottage to us and mom accepted just to set a precedent."

Don pulled out several credit cards and shuffled through them.

"Everything that comes to me is a result of somebody's guilty conscience." Marcie saw female names, men's names on the cards. Don put them back into his pocket.

"I don't think mom really wants to go down there," Marcie said. "But it's one of those adult psychological things and we're all caught in it."

"I wanted to spend Labor Day with you," he said. "Could you get out of going with your mother?"

"I don't think so."

He wiped his new mustache with a napkin. "I'm leaving town the day after Labor Day."

"For how long?"

"Long time. Several months."

"Oh."

"So could you spend the holiday with me?"

"I don't think so. I'd have to have an excuse. Mom catches me in every tiny fib—I'll try, though."

"Wish you could." He was frowning. "Listen, Marcie, meet me in the car, will you? I want to wash my hands and pay the bill."

She went out to his Volkswagen, an inner alarm quietly pinging. Through the restaurant window, she saw him go to the rear of the dining area and disappear. A few moments later, he came out, walked past the cash register and joined her.

"I'll have to come back tomorrow and pay the bill," he said. "I don't have any money with me."

"Why didn't you use a credit card?"

"I don't like to use a credit card here in town." He backed out, quickly, pulled away.

"Don," Marcie twisted to face him. "The cards are stolen, aren't they?"

"No, no, no," he grinned. "I collect them. That's why I didn't use a card—I didn't have my own with me."

"Don," Marcie said, earnestly, "I wish you wouldn't do

things like that. I really do. It isn't because it's immoral or even because it's illegal. It's just that—I'm so sick of wrong things. I'm sick of crime and violence and bloody gore. I have a friend named Charlie who is so square I call him a cube. But I'll tell you, he's looking better and better to me because he *is* so square. I'm just sick of pettiness, thievery, immorality—do you understand?"

He drove, face red. Marcie put a hand on his arm. "I had money. I would've paid."

"If you'll feel better," he offered, "I'll go home, get some cash and go back right now."

"No. Later is fine."

"Marcie?"

"What?"

"Have I told you what you've meant to me this summer?" His expression surprised her. "I have felt more free, more at ease with you—" He stopped, looked away. "I've felt you were a friend. I know you—if anybody ever will —you understand me."

"I hope so."

"I thank you for that."

She moved nearer, the seat slipping on its runners. "Let me tell you something I have appreciated," Marcie said. "I appreciate you never making a pass at me."

His chin dimpled, quivering—"That doesn't mean I didn't want to."

"Why didn't you?"

"I've been testing myself."

Chapter Twenty-four

DON'T shut the door." Bud Diehl mopped his forehead with a handkerchief. "They haven't repaired my air conditioner. Sit down, Jo."

A fan too large for the small cubicle blew Joanne's hair. Bud had weights on everything to prevent papers from flying.

"What can I do for you, Jo?"

"I'm here regarding the Hightower murder."

"The case is closed."

"It shouldn't be."

"Jo," yellow flecks intensified in his eyes, "I told you I wasn't going to get between you and Cowboy, and I meant it."

"That's not altogether why I'm here."

"Nonsense, Jo. You and Cowboy are punching at one another through the Tallahassee *Democrat*. I read the papers."

"He's wrong, you're wrong," Joanne said bluntly.

"Now you want some ammunition to shoot at the sheriff."

"I want the truth, nothing more."

"Look at this," he gestured at his desk, "see all this? I'm working sixteen-hour days, Jo. I come into the office every morning and get a little sick knowing clues are growing cold, witnesses are evaporating—and there aren't enough hours in a day to get it all done. Now, you want me to take some of my precious minutes to salve your professional ego."

"What if the killer is still out there?" Joanne demanded. "What if you're wrong?"

"He may be. But I've gone as far as I can go on that one. I have a new case every week or two. There are two violent deaths a week in this city, and they have to be investigated."

"Then allow me to pursue the Hightower case, whether you're still interested or not."

He kicked his chair backward, walked to a wall of files. He snatched out a thick folder and slammed it on the desk. Photographs spilled forth and Joanne grabbed for them. "What is this?" she asked.

"Those pictures? All the same girl," he said. "One of the bodies we identified."

"Doesn't look like the same girl—"

He slammed down a second folder. Then another. "Now this," he said over his shoulder, "is what I've accumulated since we dropped the cases. On my own time. *After* the department quit considering the cases active, Jo." Wham. Another file folder, as thick as the others.

"You university people are a real pain, Jo. You sit and study sanitized crime reports and feed your computers and draw your conclusions—crime is a statistic to you. It's photos of bodies, pathology reports—when a crime is settled, you adjust the digits on your fact sheet and it's all over. I go out and interview agonized parents, grieving husbands, distraught friends. The image of that girl's mother is etched in my brain forever. I've been at this thankless task most of my adult life and I still think about the first unsolved case from sixteen years ago. God damn you. Crime to me is the morgue smell of oil of wintergreen preservative, the scream of a father as he identifies remnants of a figure so bloated he doesn't recognize anything but a ring he gave his child! I can live without your insulting remarks."

"I apologize."

"When you're through with those files, bring them back to my office. You can use a booth in the interrogation room, if you want."

Joanne pushed around dozens of photographs. "Why so many?"

"Because she's a girl," Bud said, brusquely. "Because identifying runway girls is next to impossible. They change their hairdo, use tints, rinses, comb it differently, cut it. They change the shape of their eyeglasses, or don't wear them anymore. They use rouge, mascara, lipstick and false eyelashes. They gain and lose weight—and even if not on a diet, they get puffy during menstruation. Their clothing styles change in a given week, adding accessories from jeans to evening gowns. Their height is altered by high heels or sandals. Hats, scarves, barrettes, jewelry. All that is normal for women. If she's trying to fool you, she can wear a wig, sunglasses, maybe buy tinted contacted lenses which change the color of her eyes. Then if she's trying to elude detection, *really* serious about it, she can go to a plastic surgeon and bob her nose, or get a face lift. A woman—a girl— changes her appearance in the course of a week without consciously trying to disguise herself."

"And the pictures are to get the scope of all that?"

"Yes." He lit a cigarette; smoke swirled by the fan.

Joanne studied the smiling image of a youthful brunette —something here—she turned the photo and on the back was stamped, "Estes Park."

"Bud, what is this?" She held it up.

"One of those photos they take at a tourist attraction and sell to you for a couple of dollars."

"Something about this—"

Joanne stared—*something*. The necklace!

"You look as if you've seen a ghost, Jo. What is it?"

"I want to talk to this girl's parents, Bud."

"Oh, no you don't. It would be excruciating for you. The parents would suffer. You would suffer. You don't want to—"

"Call them please."

"Jo—"

"Bud! Call them, please."

He reached for the phone, muttering oaths.

Mr. and Mrs. Ramirez sat on a dark, stained couch. Beside them, their daughter, Carlotta, wearing freshly laundered and pressed slacks and a bright blue blouse.

"There was hope," Mrs. Ramirez said, "but dread and fear. Wondering if Juanita was suffering."

"When they found her body," the father added, "it was almost a relief. At last, after so many months—it was over."

"Such a horrible thing is—" Mrs. Ramirez paused, facial muscles quivering. Her husband patted her hand. "Afterward, people do not know what to say, how to act," she concluded. "They are uncomfortable. If I speak of the good memories, all talk stops until the subject changes. They make it for me as if Juanita had never existed. I cannot talk to them, even my best friends, because they quickly change the subject. That is the worst part."

Joanne sat on the edge of a straight back chair they had brought in for her.

"Juanita was a good girl," the mother said, looking now at her husband who returned her pained smile, nodding assent. "She was all girl! She had the problems of a girl growing up, of course—"

"She quit school," Carlotta offered.

"She read all the time," Mrs. Ramirez said.

"She wouldn't do her chores," Carlotta amended.

"She read everything." Mr. Ramirez reinforced his wife's statement. "Comics, paperbacks, good books too. *Don Quixote*—" he paused, searching his memory. Carlotta peered at a far wall.

"She saved her money," Mrs. Ramirez noted, softly. "When none of us had money, Juanita had a few pennies."

209

Carlotta's mouth twisted and she stared at a crucifix hanging on the wall.

"Mrs. Ramirez," Joanne brought out the photograph and extended it, "tell me about this picture."

"Her hair was darker than that," Mrs. Ramirez said. "She was standing in a bright light."

"Where did the photo come from, Mrs. Ramirez?"

She turned it, reading, "Estes Park—Colorado."

"Juanita was visiting there?"

"She had quit school," Carlotta said, flatly.

"So," Mrs. Ramirez added, "she wanted to go to Colorado for a summer job."

"A job," Joanne said. "What kind of work and where?"

"She didn't write all summer," Carlotta reported.

"Something with a state park," Mr. Ramirez suggested.

"But when Juanita came home!" Mrs. Ramirez beamed now. "Her mind was different. She planned to go to night school and—"

"Her boyfriend broke off with her," Carlotta commented. "My sister was very jealous and possessive. She came home because of that."

"Night school," Mrs. Ramirez said, "and studying decorating, I think. She was good with home decorating, wasn't she?" The question was aimed at Mr. Ramirez. He nodded, smiling.

Joanne touched the photo in the mother's hand. "That's a lovely necklace."

"Her boyfriend in Colorado made it."

"It looks like silver."

"Real silver, and turquoise, Juanita said."

Chest constricting, Joanne asked, "Could I see the necklace?"

"We don't have it."

"Where is it?"

Mrs. Ramirez spoke, lips taut, thin. "She wore it the night she went—"

"To meet her boyfriend from Colorado," Carlotta completed the thought.

Joanne's heart jumped. "The boy who made the necklace?"

"Yes." Carlotta smoothed her slacks with slender fingers. "Juanita saw him by accident. He told Juanita he had only then arrived and he had planned to call her when he found a hurt woman. He was taking her to a hospital. Juanita told me this as she dressed to go meet him."

Now the parents were weeping, holding hands.

"I told Juanita he was lying," Carlotta related. "He lied all the time, she told me so. But she said the woman was truly hurt, there was blood."

In silence, they sat, each looking at something other than one another. Joanne took back the photograph and examined the necklace. She couldn't be sure. "Carlotta, what was the boyfriend's name?"

"Larry," Carlotta said. "Larry Etna."

Her own voice sounded afar, "What kind of car did he drive?" Joanne questioned.

"I don't know."

"Do you have a photograph of him?"

"No."

"Can you describe him?"

"We never saw him."

"Would you recognize the necklace if you saw it again?"

"Juanita wouldn't let us near it."

"It seems so distinctive. Expensive."

"Not really," Carlotta said. "Cheap, really."

Legs trembling, Joanne stood, thanked them, made her way to her automobile. She reexamined the photo of Juanita Ramirez. The necklace was one of those things artisans produce by the hundreds. Yet—yet—oh, God—

"Do you know about the boyfriend?" Joanne demanded.

"Of course I do," Bud said.

"Then he's your best suspect, Bud."

"Jo, give me some credit, will you? I got this case months after the disappearance was reported. I got it when it became a bona fide murder. However, I ran down every hospital and clinic in the county, checking records. There were twenty-six women admitted for treatment of injuries, and I contacted every one of them that I could find—nothing. I ran a story in the *Times-Union* Sunday edition: Police looking for information regarding the man who drove an injured woman to a doctor for treatment. Nothing, not one call. I did what I could."

"Did you go to Colorado?"

"Are you kidding? I won't even be able to take off for the Labor Day holidays. I can't get enough money from the city to repair this lousy air conditioner. But I did call the

Colorado Highway Patrol and they went to Estes Park. The boyfriend wasn't there and nobody knows where he went. Dead end."

Joanne sat looking at the photograph.

"The injured woman may have been a tourist passing through, Jo. The girl, Juanita, may have been lying. She was giving her parents a lot of trouble. Or, she may never have made the meeting with her boyfriend and he left town unaware. They'd recently broken up, according to Juanita's sister."

"Maybe."

Bud smoothed his mustache, flicked his tongue over parched lips. "I'm busy as hell, Jo."

"Bud," she put the photo in her purse, "let me draw a scene and see how it strikes you."

He checked his watch, sighed.

"Suppose this Colorado boyfriend is the sadist-murderer? He had a victim in his automobile and by sheer bad luck ran into Juanita. He couldn't allow Juanita to live if he'd harmed his victim and planned to kill her. So he invented a story about finding a hurt woman, taking her to a hospital, and told Juanita to meet him a little while later. Did you ever identify that second female found with Juanita's remains?"

"No."

"All right," Joanne continued, "the killer takes his first victim out and dumps her. He comes back, meets Juanita and kills her, dumping the body with the first body."

"Returning to the site because it is a good place to dump a second body is not what makes a sadist-murderer return to the scene, Jo. It appears he used the same place because it was expeditious, not because he was drawn to the locale by some psychotic fascination. There was no appreciable time lapse between the murders—so that weakens your 'returning to the scene' theory."

"No, it doesn't. He later dumped the Hightower woman there and that's why you found the bones of Juanita and the other body."

"That's true."

"Were there any other missing women in the Jacksonville area who are still unaccounted for?"

Bud got a clipboard, reading off dates back to the time of Juanita's disappearance. "Nope. Except—" he studied the board. "There's one girl who was reported missing, but she isn't really listed as missing."

"What?"

"She had accepted a job with a local TV station," Bud explained. "She was staying in a motel and they found her baggage, clothes and such, but not her. Her employer reported she didn't show up for work. Anyway, no member of the family came forward to file a missing person report, so it was never investigated any further. I know all about that because I was keeping an eye on missing girls at your request."

"In a motel," Joanne said. "Which means she was probably from somewhere else. Wherever her family lives. They'd file a missing person report there—not here—right?"

Bud dialed an interdepartmental number. "Diehl, homicide," he said. "Listen, do you people have an out-of-town inquiry on a——" he read his clipboard, "Sharon Murtree?"

He tweaked his mustache, gazing at Joanne, waiting.

"Nashville, Tennessee?" Bud sat up, made a note. "Better get with me," Bud said. "I think we may have something."

He hung up, eyes twinkling yellow darts. "You don't suppose?"

"I do suppose."

"Damnation, Jo."

"May I keep the photo of the Ramirez girl?"

"Send it back when you're through. Jo——" he was keeping pace, both walking fast toward the elevators, "keep me informed now. Okay? I want to know what you find out in Colorado, okay?"

She pushed the elevator button and turned, frowning, "I'm not sure I'm going, Bud. But, if I do, I'll let you know."

His mustache crawled over a wide grin. "Wish I could go with you."

The elevator doors closed with a swish.

Ken sat on a far side of the kitchen table, legs extended, stocking feet in Joanne's lap. She held the photograph of Juanita Ramirez under a magnifying glass and the necklace from Marcie's drawer in her other hand.

"Marcie may have stolen it," Ken said, quietly.

"I realize that's true," Joanne responded. "Or some friend may have given it to her and Marcie knew it was too expensive to keep, so she fibbed on that account."

"Or," Ken noted, "she may have found it on the beach,

213

like she said. It's a little far-fetched to assume it's the same necklace."

"It may not be the same necklace," Joanne conceded. "The Ramirez family didn't think they could identify it, even if they saw it again."

Ken withdrew his feet, sat forward, peering at the photo between them.

"I questioned Marcie again," Joanne said, "and she insisted she found it. I don't dare accuse her of being untruthful unless I'm positive. She thinks I'm accusatory enough as it is."

"I agree." Ken took the magnifying glass and picture. "Never ask someone a question that you believe will make them lie. For surely, they will lie."

"Such as with whom you spent your vacation?"

"That's a good example," he said, without looking up. "I was hurt, lonely, angry and have no commitment from you, so therefore no ties—is that about the size of it?"

"I suppose so."

He shoved the photo and magnifying glass toward her. "You're going to have to go to Colorado, Jo. Common sense says this is not the same necklace, but that's about all you can do."

"When I was a child," Joanne mused, "my papa was a brigadier general, much decorated for various battles although he had never seen a gun fired in anger."

"Oh?" Ken opened a loaf of rye bread, took out a slice and bit into it.

"His job during World War II," Joanne said, "was to do psychological profiles on all German generals. Rommel, Jodl, the whole batch. Papa used to say, if he knew how a man acted in the privacy of his bedroom, he knew the man well enough to predict how he'd draw battle plans."

"Could he?"

"Quite accurately. That's why he was decorated for the battles. He contributed to Allied victories while sitting behind a desk in some remote intelligence outpost."

Ken chewed, eyes shadowed by the overhead swag lamp.

"Papa always said," Joanne continued, "if you thought about someone long enough, hard enough, worried about him diligently—you formed a mysterious mental link with that other person."

"Mind reading," Ken grunted.

"He called it a 'universal wave,' " Joanne laughed. She blinked moist eyes. "Papa was such a tyrant."

"How?"

"Socks folded in precise military order, everything had to be shipshape. He drove us to distraction, sometimes, checking the tops of doors for hidden dust we'd missed. My brother, who died in Korea, hated papa for all that. Yet my brother decided to make the military a career. Which was diametrically opposed to all he'd ever professed."

"You too, of course."

"What?"

"You took after your father. Picky-picky, isn't that what Ralph said?"

"Ouch."

"A place for everything and everything in its place."

"Ouch again."

Ken tore off another piece of bread, munched it, watching her stave off tears of reminiscence. "Did you have a happy childhood, Jo?"

"As good as anyone." Joanne put the necklace and photo in her briefcase.

"Strict father," Ken said. "How about your mother?"

"Perfect for papa. If a general can have a commanding officer, mama was it."

Ken swallowed, tore off more bread.

"Do I detect psychoanalysis in progress?" Joanne queried.

"You're the psychologist, Jo. You don't need me to analyze."

"Yes. I know."

A moment later, she added, "And knowing, I am helpless to alter that which I find unpleasant about myself."

"What you need," Ken lifted craggy brows, "is a strong man. Somebody who will share, but not dominate; yield, but isn't wishy-washy. Somebody who loves you deeply, doesn't want to change you. You need a man who worships your daughter, can abide your continuing relationship with Ralph, and this man should be somebody with the ambition, drive and talent to make something of himself."

Hands in her lap, Joanne sat waiting.

"Bread is dry," Ken said. "Is there any milk in the refrigerator?"

"Anybody you know who'd want the task?" she asked.

"For what?"

"Don't play games, Ken."

He reached under a lip with a finger, raking at his gum. "Me, maybe, if I become sheriff."

"That's a terrible, terrible insult to me," Joanne countered. "I didn't give a job description for marriage. You did."

"Would you marry me, Jo?"

"Is that rhetorical or personal?"

"Where's the dictionary?"

"Ken!" Joanne burst into tears. "Stop playing with me!"

"God," he came to her, hugged her to him, "I hate a crybaby. Oh, all right—*will* you marry me?"

"Yes!"

Marcie's high-pitched squeal preceded her and she came from the dark hallway to bound into Ken's arms.

Chapter Twenty-five

"THAT'S my chair, John." Ralph maneuvered the attorney around Joanne's kitchen table. But before he could sit, Ken reached for the seat. "That's my chair, Ken," Ralph said. "That's where I always sit."

Ken shot a glance at Joanne and sat across from John Nathan.

"Republic Airlines?" Joanne leaned on the kitchen counter. "I'm calling about my connections for the flight to Denver."

"First of all," Ralph told Ken and John, "I've been assured by the State Attorney General that the trial will take place immediately. Judge Alcorn wants that, too, because of the upcoming elections."

"Stand-by?" Joanne said. "But, I was assured I'd have reservations confirmed this afternoon. Could you check your computer? You did?"

"Trouble, mom?" Marcie kept herself near enough to eavesdrop on the men, far enough not to be noticed.

"My flight—" Joanne listened. "Yes? Good. This afternoon, three o'clock. Good, I'll be there to get my ticket."

"Wish I could go with you," Marcie said.

"Darling, I wish you could—"

"It's all right," Marcie grinned. "Labor Day weekend is when all my friends come back from their summer activities."

"You can stay with your father," Joanne advised.

Ralph halted, mid-sentence. "What was that, Jo?"

"I'm going to Colorado on a case, Ralph. Marcie can stay with you, can't she?"

"Uh—well, uh—" Ralph sniffed. "I'm having guests this weekend, Jo. Uh—" he sniffed, wiped his nose. "Sure."

"No, no, daddy," Marcie said. "I'm old enough to stay here alone."

"No," Joanne responded.

"Mom, I don't need a baby-sitter."

"No."

"Jo, I can stay over here," Ken offered.

"You're busy with your politicking, Ken. Marcie, it would be best if—"

"Mom, really! I'm almost seventeen!"

"Five months from seventeen."

"Jo—" Ken lifted his eyebrows.

"All right," Joanne conceded. "Ken will check on you."

"I'll be out until eleven tonight, Ken," Marcie announced.

"Marcie, I'm working the late shift tonight, so I'll be gone when you get here," Ken said.

"And I'll be gone when you come in tomorrow," Marcie said, watching for Joanne's reaction.

"I'm not going to worry about that," Joanne snapped. "I have enough on my mind. Marcie, I expect you to be responsible for yourself. Is that clear?"

"All right, John," Ralph continued, "let's hear your background so we can get our publicity coordinated."

"Attended Harvard on full scholarship," John Nathan recounted, dryly. "Graduated magna cum laude. My wife has a master's degree in political science—"

"Why in the world did you come here to practice?" Ralph asked.

"My great-grandmother was a slave on the Millbrook Plantation," John said. "Over a hundred of my relatives

217

are buried out there. My pappy was a gardener at Mill-brook until he died two years ago. I'm one of thirteen children, and of eleven surviving, eight have college degrees which my parents struggled to provide. This is my home. My family has been here since 1815."

"With those qualifications," Ralph said, "you could've gone anywhere."

"This is home, Ralph," Nathan insisted. "I'm not running for district attorney because I want to be a powerful black man. I'm running because I'll be a better district attorney. Dupree's family, and Judge Alcorn's, have ruled this area almost by fiat for over a century. Dupree serves a very narrow constituency. I intend to serve not only blacks, but whites. I'll draw on the newcomers who've moved here, as well as the so-called racial block of voters."

"All right," Ralph made notes, "that sounds good. Jo, how about a pot of coffee?"

"Ralph, I'm trying to get on a plane!"

"You realize," Ralph said to Ken, "the one most likely to be elected is John. When that case spills over on Phillip Dupree and Sheriff Rogers, Dupree will be the first to get burned."

"I see that."

"If Cowboy Rogers isn't pulled into it rapidly," John Nathan warned, "Ken doesn't stand much of a chance."

"I'll mention that to the state attorney," Ralph said, concerned. "Maybe he'll hurry it along."

"I'm unemployed after Labor Day," Ken noted. "My two weeks notice will be up."

"We'll all be unemployed if this fails," Ralph cautioned. "Politically, we'll be anathema around this city."

Joanne had her briefcase and overnight bag. "Ken, Marcie is driving me to the airport. I'll call you sometime this evening, if I can."

"Won't be here," Ken said. "I'm giving a speech to the Woodland Baptist men's group."

"Tomorrow then." She kissed him. As she rounded the table, Ralph lifted his head, expectantly. Joanne patted his cheek in passing. "Be good boys," she said at large.

"Dupree prepares his cases poorly." Nathan addressed Ralph. "The Swain case is a good example of that."

Joanne closed the door, slightly hurt that Ken had not

chosen to walk her out. Marcie was behind the steering wheel waiting, the car radio blaring.

They sat in the airline terminal waiting room. "How do I look?" Joanne inquired.

"You look fine, mom."

Joanne put her tickets in her handbag and clutched the purse with both hands.

"You scared of flying, mom?"

"No."

"You look scared."

"It's my purpose in going that has me tense, Marcie."

"Why are you going?"

"Some work for Bud Diehl in Jacksonville, Florida."

Marcie sucked a part of her lower lip. "Well," she said, "lots of luck. They're announcing your flight."

As Joanne reached the metal detecting machine, and presented her parcel for examination, Marcie hugged her long and hard. "I love you, mom."

"I love you. Please don't give Ken cause for worry."

"I won't."

A moment later, Marcie was walking away into the crowd.

Liar. She was terrified of flying.

After her mother's airplane rose and tucked its wheels, Marcie ran to a pay telephone and called the number Don had given her weeks ago. *This is not a recording,* he had said, anticipating her voice.

Now, anxious to relate the good news that she was free, and Labor Day weekend was theirs, Marcie listened to the ringing sound.

"Hello?" A small voice, tentative.

"Is Don there?"

"Don who?"

"Don Whitney," Marcie said.

"This here's a coin phone at Jerry's Restaurant," the voice replied. "There ain't nobody standing here but me."

"Oh. Thank you."

He hadn't said it was his home phone, had he? Marcie glanced at a clock in the terminal area—four hours until Don was supposed to meet her at their regular rendezvous. She hated to waste four hours of their last weekend before he left town. Impulsively, she dialed her mother's office.

"Hiya, Bea, this is Marcie."

"Hey, Marsha!" Only Bea ever called her by her given name. "Your mom isn't here, sugar."

"I know, I just put her on a plane to Colorado."

"What's cooking?"

"Bea, can you give me the address of Don Whitney?"

"I don't know him, Marsha."

"He's a student in the criminology department," Marcie said.

"I'll check the student directory," Bea offered. "Hold the phone a sec."

Marcie heard a flutter of pages riffling. "Who is this guy?"

"A friend."

Bea giggled. "What's he look like?"

"He's okay."

"Handsome?"

"Have you got it, Bea?"

"Don't see it," Bea related. "Youse said Whitney."

"He's not mom's student."

"That was wise," Bea said. "But this has all the criminology students. Wait and I'll check the full college directory."

A moment later, "Nothing here, sugar. Sorry."

"Okay. Thanks. Bea, would the general admissions office have it?"

"They're closed, Marsha. Labor Day. This is semester break, too. He might not have been registered in time for last semester's listing. Or he may be a special student. Or taking courses without credits, which would put him on the blue ledger, not white."

"Have you got that?"

"No, I don't." Bea's voice lilted. "Why don't youse describe this guy and I'll see if I recognize him."

"Pointy ears, beady eyes, bowed legs, buck teeth," Marcie intoned.

Bea laughed. "Hope youse find him, sugar. With your mom out of town, now's a good time. Going to Sherrod's tonight?"

"No. Bye, Bea."

Three hours fifty-four minutes until time to meet Don.

Marcie sighed, left the booth and walked out to the parking lot. . . .

She dawdled away an hour but still arrived early at the restaurant on North Monroe where she'd told Don she'd see him before leaving town with mom to go to Panacea for the weekend. Maybe . . . maybe he'd made other plans himself and their final four days would be lost.

She ordered a "suicide"—a fountain concoction made with Coke and cherry syrup, Seven-Up, lime, strawberry extract and carbonated water. It was delivered by a middle-aged waitress whose opinion was clearly written in her expression as she watched Marcie take the first sip.

"Awful," Marcie advised, smiling. "I love it."

Left alone, she stared out the restaurant window. He'd never be early. Or late. Punctuality was one attribute he'd proven repeatedly.

She chewed her drinking straw, fretting over the necklace. At some point in the past few days, mom had taken it, which Marcie didn't dare acknowledge. Mom couldn't let it go. She wasn't constituted to leave it alone. She would worry and agonize and investigate until she found the owner. Years from now, she'd be showing the thing to Panacea tourists, saying, "Did you lose this?"

Resentfully, Marcie had decided she must not admit she had inadvertently stolen it. If she did, she'd have to say where and from whom. Mom and Ken would descend on Don, and when they learned Marcie had been keeping company with a man twenty-nine years old, that would be *that*. She'd had to wrest every ounce of freedom she now enjoyed, as it was. If they found out she had a boyfriend that much older, she'd be sent to a blacksmith and fitted for a chastity belt. That *would* be that.

Having disavowed the necklace, she couldn't dispose of it. She couldn't return it which would invite ten thousand questions as mom demanded to know all about that, too.

But Don was leaving in four days. Maybe forever. There'd be no way to trace the necklace to him then.

It was titillating to have these clandestine meetings. More so because Don clearly had psychological problems of his own. Which, if Marcie could say so, she'd handled with the same aplomb as might mom, confronted with such a personality. But truly, and actually, all that didn't matter. Don accepted her as an adult. Everybody had problems—mom, dad—everybody. It became, therefore, a matter of

221

which quirks one found most interesting. Unless you were marrying the person. Then it all became serious.

Well, she wasn't marrying Don. Soon enough he'd be gone.

Mom took the necklace probably to make photos and run ads. That's the kind of thing mom would do.

Marcie sipped her drink slowly, paying the lowest possible "rent" for occupying the booth as she waited.

She should've called the FSU law department, not criminology. He was probably a law student, despite what he'd said. He knew Waldheim's poem, "Help Wanted," which was about lawyers. Or, perhaps he was a creative writing student, an English or drama major.

Whatever—she wasn't going to spoil their final few days.

Still, she worried.

"Another horrible drink?" The waitress prepared Marcie's bill.

"Yes," Marcie said. "This time make it a double."

Suppose mom did find out about Don? Would she believe Marcie's relationship had been intellectual, platonic? That seemed difficult for adults. Maybe all adults put out, and anything to the contrary seemed unbelievable.

"If you get ill," the waitress delivered Marcie's drink, "rest rooms are in the rear."

"Cast-iron stomach," Marcie assured her. But somehow, the double beverage looked awesome.

She realized, now that Don was about to leave, she knew little about him. His fibs, his evasions, all information imparted was subject to challenge. Yet, they'd had fun, hadn't they? He'd never once gotten out of hand. "Which doesn't mean I didn't want to," he'd said. That might have been just an effort to bolster her ego.

She pondered the possibility of surrendering her virginity to Don, as opposed to Clumsy Charlie. She really didn't want to, not really. Too much time was spent on sex. Movies, novels, advertisements, everywhere she looked, sex, sex, sex. She hoped Don would remain what he'd been all along—courteous, thoughtful, charming.

But, if he insisted—what then?

She blew air in her drink and watched cross-eyed as ice cubes danced on ascending bubbles.

If she must, she must, that's all. It had to happen sooner or later. This certainly wasn't any worse than an affair with an Italian prince in Milan. Better, maybe, because at least she and Don knew the same language. Or maybe worse, for the same reason. In Italian, the prince may have been saying filthy words to Darlene Sands. Even vulgarities would sound delightful in Italy.

She sipped, worried.

Before Don left, she wished he'd be candid. Tell her about himself, his parents, his childhood. What was his major in college? Was he married, was that his secret? Or a pansy? He'd said he was "testing" himself. Wanted to see if being with a girl made him nauseated, maybe. She wished she knew more about homosexuality. She'd thought about asking mom, but recent questions about Peeping Toms and psychopathic lying had made mom too inquisitive as it was. With her, you had to sneak in your serious questions. *Don't* ask if a nipple-tip condom is better than contoured. Make the question quantitative, "How much sperm is ejaculated?" Mom could handle things like that. Nipples made her fidget.

Marcie felt bloated. Another hour fifteen minutes. She could go sit in the car, of course. Or take a walk through a nearby shopping mall. Or sit here and add ten ounces more on top of the twelve already imbibed.

She had decided to take the walk when she saw a familiar Volkswagen swing across four lanes of traffic to a chorus of blaring horns. Don was grinning as he wheeled into a parking space and halted. Such a little boy. Even if he *was* twenty-nine.

When he saw her, Don threw up his hands and came toward Marcie with long strides. "You're early! Good gracious, what is that you're drinking?"

"Suicide Coke," Marcie groaned. "Want some?"

"No," he said, dubiously, "I'm particular what I put in my tummy. Well! I'm glad you're early."

"I can spend Labor Day weekend with you."

"Ah, Marcie—I'm so pleased. That's nice. Really nice. Have you eaten?"

"No, but I'm full of drink. I'll never have another suicide Coke as long as I live."

He laughed, motioning for a waitress. "Menus, please."

Then, hands clasped, blue eyes sparkling, he grinned broadly.

"You still want to spend the weekend with me, don't you?" Marcie asked.

"Certainly do."

"Good."

He took the menus, put his hands atop both, smiling at her. "What happened to plans of wee mommie?"

"She had to go out of town on business."

"During the holidays?" He withdrew a menu to look at it.

"Probably some kind of meeting," Marcie noted, "she's always going to meetings."

"Where'd she go?"

"Out west."

"Think I'll have a steak, Marcie. How about you?"

"I'm not hungry yet."

"Then," he put aside the menu, "I shall await your pleasure." Still smiling, he said, "Out west. Have you ever been out west?"

"No."

"Beautiful. Things don't look real. The buttes, the mesas sheared off perfectly flat, peaks with snowcaps. You'd love it. I hope your mom gets to see some of the sights while she's there. California, you say?"

"No, Colorado."

His smile altered slightly. "On second thought," he said, "I'm hungry, Marcie. Do you mind if I go ahead and eat?"

"Not at all."

He ordered a sixteen ounce sirloin medium rare. As the waitress started to walk away, he snapped his fingers and whistled softly. "I think I'll have a Scotch and water, too. All right, Marcie?"

"Sure."

"The girl has to show proof of age," the waitress warned.

"The drink is for me," Don responded. "You want my proof?"

"No sir."

Suddenly surly, he glared after the woman. "Bitch," he whispered.

Marcie gazed out the window.

"Hey, Marcie, I'm sorry—"

"I've heard the word before."

"The apology still stands." He reached across the table and playfully slapped her hand. "Colorado, you say."

"Yes."

"Wrong time of year for skiing," he said.

"Have you been there?" Marcie questioned.

"Never have."

"Even when you lived in Utah?"

"Utah? Oh, the license plate. Yes, well, I've passed through a time or two. I meant, I've never been there to stay. Has your wee mommie been there before?"

"I don't think so."

"Whereabouts is she going?"

"I don't know."

"Umm." He stared at the waitress. *Glared* at her, marking the woman's passage from the bar to their table. He accepted his drink, face drawn.

"Hate to drink without you," he commented, then sipped.

"I keep trying various alcoholic drinks," Marcie confessed, "and they never taste as good as movies make them seem."

"That's the way it is with most things, Marcie. Seldom as good as expected. Filled with anticipatory pleasure and constantly disappointed—that's the dreamer."

"Are you a dreamer?"

"Realist." He sipped, staring at her, expression odd. He sighed heavily, sipped his drink, sighed again.

"Is something wrong?" Marcie asked.

"Nothing."

When the steak came, he cut into it and recalled the waitress. "I said 'medium rare' and medium *rare* means hot pink center in most establishments," he said, sharply. "Feed this one to your cook."

"I'll get another, sir."

"Forget it!" He gulped Scotch, standing. "Come on, Marcie. Let's find a decent place to dine."

He snatched their bill from the waitress and presented it to the manager, saying loudly, "I'm not paying for the steak. I didn't get good service and I didn't get what I wanted."

"I'm sorry, sir. There's no charge—"

"Fair enough." He grabbed Marcie's arm and almost shoved her through the door.

Driving north to the interstate highway, he huffed, glared, sighed repeatedly, and turned eastward to a connecting highway south. The sun was sinking, a shimmering bloody orb beyond spikes of conifers when he shoved back the driver's seat as far as it would go. "Too bad," he said. "Really too bad."

"What?"

Another inhalation of air, as if oxygen were rare. He

225

swung around slower traffic, driving toward Capps, Florida.

"What is it, Don?"

"You took the necklace, Marcie."

"I didn't mean to. I was going to return it. When you mentioned it, I couldn't. You'd have known I took it."

"I should've thrown it away long ago."

"I'll get it back for you."

"You don't have it."

"But I do!"

"Wee mommie has it."

She wedged the sliding seat with a foot, twisting to face him. "Don, you said it was worthless. Is it?"

"In the hands of anyone else, it is of questionable value," he said. "But, Marcie—" he swerved, horn squalling, passing another car.

"—in the hands of wee mommie, it is a matter of life and death . . ."

Chapter Twenty-six

ESTES Park was breathtaking in two ways: the beauty of a level valley surrounded by mountains—and the 7,500-foot elevation. Located sixty-four miles northwest of Denver, the town had a population of less than 3,000. Joanne drove a rented automobile up Highway 36 through towering peaks, along plunging gorges, over cascading rivers. When she arrived in "the village" she was surprised to find traffic jams and many pedestrians. Following the directions of a secretary she'd telephoned, Joanne located the police station, "One block off Elkhorn Avenue, one-seventy MacGregor."

"I thought this would be a tiny town," Joanne commented to Chief Lorimar.

"Population twenty-three hundred," he said. "But during the summer we swell to a hundred thousand."

"How large is your staff?" Joanne questioned.

226

"Twelve officers including me. We add four more during the summer. We have five dispatchers and a secretary."

"Your territory?"

"City limits. Couple of miles by a couple of miles. What can I do for you, Dr. Fleming?"

"I'm investigating a possible suspect wanted for questioning in the murder of this girl." Joanne presented the photograph of Juanita Ramirez. "Do you recognize her?"

"No."

Joanne quickly explained the situation. "The suspect made the necklace she's wearing," she summarized. "His name is Larry Etna."

"Do you have a picture?"

"No, I don't. Nor a description."

"Don't know the name."

Joanne brought out the necklace and placed it on his desk. "This may or may not be the necklace," she said. "There's a silversmith's mark on the back."

He examined it, pushed it to her. "Dr. Fleming, what police department do you represent?"

"I'm here under the auspices of the Jacksonville, Florida, Police Department, Detective Bud Diehl."

"May I see some identification?"

She gave him her university faculty card, driver's license, and an identification card issued by the Federal Corrections Center.

"Why have you not made inquiries through normal channels?" he queried.

"We did, through the Colorado Highway Patrol. But we know how it is, most departments are understaffed and overworked. We thought it best if I came out, personally."

Chief Lorimar sat back, chair squeaking. "Our season here is from Memorial Day to Labor Day," he said. "But we're having fine weather and we've still got a crowd. There are a hundred and eighty motels in this immediate vicinity and they're filled. I can't turn anyone loose, I'm afraid."

"That won't be necessary."

"I don't know where to tell you to begin," he said. "That necklace looks like a thousand others sold to tourists around here every summer. You might call on some of the curio shops."

"Thank you, Chief Lorimar."

227.

"Would you like me to check our files for this fellow, Etna?"

"If you would, yes."

It took only a few minutes. Nothing. Joanne departed feeling giddy and slightly queasy from the rarefied air. She began at one end of town, working her way up Elkhorn Avenue. In each establishment, she presented the photograph of Juanita Ramirez, and the necklace.

In the Rocky Mountain Gemologist Mart, Joanne put the photo before a jeweler and his dark-skinned, petite wife.

"We don't know her," the wife said to her husband.

"Looks familiar, Estelle."

"No she doesn't, Hubert."

"Something about her."

"Hubert, you walk up to strangers on every trip we take and say, 'Don't I know you?' Everybody looks like somebody and this girl looks like all the other Chicanos who come here summers."

He returned the photo, saying, "I guess we don't know her."

Joanne placed the necklace on the glass counter. "How about this?" she asked. "Or the silversmith's mark on the back?"

He turned it. "Good quality. Excellent turquoise. From New Mexico, probably. That particular color—" He peered through bifocals at the silversmith's mark.

"Etna," he said.

"Who?"

"That's the imprint," the jeweler stated. "Mt. Etna, the volcano. I remember the craftsman's name was Larry Etna."

"You can't be sure, Hubert."

"Can about this, Estelle," he countered. "This boy has talent."

"Could be anybody," the wife cautioned, studying the mark.

Heart skipping, Joanne asked, "Do you know where he lives?"

"You remember that handsome young fellow, Estelle," the jeweler argued. "Eyes somewhere between syenite and sapphire?"

"More like indanthrone," she amended.

"Didn't he work up at Micky's Lodge?"

"Fawn Valley," the wife corrected.

"He's been gone, let's see—" the jeweler gazed past Joanne, considering.

"Couple of seasons," the wife ended.

"About that."

"Where is Fawn Valley?" Joanne questioned.

"Maybe two miles up the Highway Thirty-four by-pass," he said.

"More like three," Estelle suggested.

"How do I get there?"

"Remember seeing Lake Estes when you drove in?" the wife said.

"Yes."

"That was Highway Thirty-four. Go west three miles and the chalet is on your left—looks Swiss."

"French Alpine," the husband offered.

"Chalet," the wife labored, "is a Swiss house, not French."

"I think the word's French, Estelle."

"That's because, in Switzerland they speak French, Hubert."

"Thought they spoke—"

"Thank you," Joanne smiled. "You've been very helpful."

Fawn Valley Lodge bordered a rushing stream. High up barren mountainsides, huge boulders seemed precariously perched. Placed there by glacial action millennia ago, the massive stones appeared to threaten all below.

"Murdered, you say." The lodge manager was in his seventies, shaggy white hair jutting on either side of a bald spot.

"Yes, she was," Joanne affirmed. "She'd gone home to her parents in Jacksonville, Florida. It's this photograph which brings me here. We're trying to locate her boyfriend."

"Larry."

"You know him."

"Oh, yeah. Spent two winters up here, Larry did. When the season closes, they need somebody to caretake the place. Larry did that."

"Is he here?"

"No, he's gone. You said your name is Fleming?"

"Yes."

"Drink coffee, Mrs. Fleming?"

"Yes."

"Go sit on the veranda and I'll join you."

She went out back, the view magnificent, and waited. When the old man arrived, it was with a tray, coffee pot and cups. Sugar was in a dented pewter container, cream in another.

"You think Larry killed her," he announced.

"I didn't say that."

"Didn't have to. Came sidling up sideways with questions and I could see your neck veins pulse when I recognized Juanita."

"The Jacksonville police would like to question him," Joanne conceded.

"I'll bet they would."

"I don't understand."

"Ah." He poured her coffee, spilling some. "Larry was a strange sort. Moody as a brooding hen. He could go from high to low so quick it left you wondering if he was all there."

"You mean a swing in moods?"

"From schoolboy silly to the dark holes of hell," the old man related. "Me and him did some hunting. This is a great place for game. Rocky Mountain bighorn sheep, mule deer, mountain lion which some folks hereabouts call cougar or puma; American wapiti which the same folk call elk. But Larry told me he didn't like guns. Didn't like killing animals, either. After that, we confined ourselves to trout fishing. He'd go along whistling and happy and casting those flies—he had a Royal Coachman he did right well with—then all of a sudden he'd go silent. Brooding. Deep dark brooding."

"Can you describe Larry, Mr. . . ."

"Bill," he said. "Just plain Bill, I tell folks. Bill Grant's the whole moniker. You call me Bill. Yeah. Curly brown hair, very blue eyes, real courteous and mannerly type. Women loved him."

Joanne made notes.

"Like I say, though," Bill continued, "he was a strange sort. Perfect for a job of caretaking. A loner. He'd go off hiking for days. Once told me he'd walked the whole Trail Ridge road which traverses the park. Eleven miles of it is above the timber line—that's eleven thousand feet. You been over that, yet?"

"No, I haven't."

"Nice ride, if your car's tuned for it."

"He was caretaker here two winters?"

"Sure was. How's your coffee?"

She sipped. "Good."

"The water," he said. "Best in the world."

She sipped again, smiled. But her heart was hammering.

"Rocky Mountain National Park is four hundred and ten square miles," Bill stated. "Established in nineteen-and-fifteen."

"I see."

"I was born down at Estes in ought-five."

"Been here all your life, then."

"And didn't know the park as well as Larry did."

"He was a great hiker, I take it."

"And skier, and foolhardy. He'd take off through the mountains on snowshoes and skis in the dead of winter, sub-zero temperatures, and be gone for days! Snow slides can get you times like that. One snap of a twig and down comes an avalanche. But he must've been careful. Never got hurt, so far as I know."

"How big a man is Larry?"

"Six feet plus," Bill said. "Close to two hundred pounds. I told you he was strange."

"Yes?"

"Always washing his car, even the inside, using a hose. His room was neat, nary a speck of dust anywhere."

"Washing his car?"

"Beat up bug, Larry called it. He said he liked it because it'd go so far on a tank of gas."

"Volkswagen—"

"Smart boy, though," Bill chuckled. "Always doing crossed-word puzzles and little gram things, he called it."

"Do you know where he is now, Bill?"

"I suspicion, but I don't *know*."

"What do you suspect?"

"Florida."

"Florida—where?"

"Don't know. Never told me, you understand. But we had a fat cat come here one season, owned a island resort place off the Florida coast. The man offered me a job. I told Larry. Not that I mind, I guess. But I suspicion he went."

"Do you know where?"

"Florida's all I know."

"East coast or west?"

"I don't know. I could be wrong." He jabbed a finger at her cup. "Going to be cold, lady."

She drank the coffee and he poured more. Her stomach was churning and she was swallowing bile, the altitude making her head hurt.

"More than seven hundred species of plants out there." Bill waved a hand in a broad arc, indicating the national park. "More than two hundred named peaks, over ten-thousand feet elevation."

"Beautiful," Joanne said.

"He knew them all. He told me he once climbed Longs Peak which is over fourteen thousand feet. By himself."

"Is that possible?"

"He said so."

"I was told," Joanne said, cautiously, "that Larry had a way of lying."

Bill smiled, leathery face creasing, "I wasn't going to *say* that."

"You agree then, that he lied?"

"He had one of those educated names for it."

"Psychopathic liar?"

"Sounds about right. Lied about anything, everything, and for no cause. Mention this or that and he'd hold forth like a real authority. He was a botanist, he'd say. Or a biologist, or a mammalogist—which I thought had something to do with cow tits until he said no, it was mammals. Did you know that?"

"Yes."

"You went to college too, I guess."

"Yes."

"So'd Larry, to hear him tell it. Law, philosophy, all those -*ologies*."

"*Was* he smart?" Joanne queried.

"Funny thing was, he was smart! He didn't need to do things like he did, but he did it anyway. Always scaring that little Spanish girl half to death—"

"What?"

"He'd lay in wait for that child," Bill said. "Hide in bushes and jump out at her. She'd stand there screaming, stiff as a starched collar, and he'd hold her arms pinned to her sides, laughing until she knew it was him. She told me he would come up to her window and stand there looking through the screen until she happened to notice him.

Her getting hysterical seemed to give him pleasure. I told him he was going to give that girl heart failure some night, and he just laughed and laughed."

Joanne pulled out the necklace and gave it to him. "Do you recognize that, Bill?"

"One of Larry's."

"How can you be sure?"

"This mark on the back. It's a volcano named Etna. That was his name, so he used that triangle with a wisp of smoke rising out of it. Catchy way to make folks remember, I thought."

"Juanita Ramirez had a necklace made by Etna." Joanne showed him the photo again. "You can see, she's wearing it in the picture."

He nodded.

"Could it be the same necklace?"

"I wouldn't know. He spent all winter making jewelry to sell to tourists in the summer."

"Hey, Bill!" somebody inside yelled. "Telephone for a guest named Fleming. We have a Fleming here?"

Bill looked at Joanne.

"Nobody knows I'm here," she said.

"Let me go see what it is, then." Bill arose and walked inside. A moment later he called, "Are you a doctor?"

"Yes."

"It *is* for you."

But who—a hundred and eighty motels, Chief Lorimar had said. *Nobody*—

Joanne hurried to the telephone, imagining the worst, Ken, Marcie, Ralph—"Hello?"

"Person-to-person call for Dr. Joanne Fleming," the operator said.

"Yes, this is she."

Joanne heard the operator speak to the calling party, "Go ahead, please."

"Boo, wee mommie."

"Boo yourself," Joanne laughed, nervously. "Who is this?"

"Go home, wee mommie," the voice advised. "There's a surprise for you."

Click.

Joanne staggered, head swirling, temples throbbing. Who? Nobody—she held the receiver, shaking, ". . . a surprise for you . . ."

233

Who would know—Ken, Ralph—psychopathic liar, Peeping Tom—*Marcie!*

"This is the operator, your party has disconnected."

"Operator," Joanne quavered, "please—where did that call come from?"

"I have no way of knowing that, ma'am."

"Operator, this is Dr. Joanne Fleming of the Department of Criminology at Florida State University. This may be a matter of great urgency. Please, I must know where the call came from."

"Dr. Fleming, I have no way of knowing."

"What state?"

"Florida."

"Can you tell me what area code, what exchange?"

"The area code is nine-oh-four," the operator said, warily. "There is no way to know the exchange, the call came from a pay telephone, the call went through our computer."

"Which is where?"

"I'm in Lake City, ma'am. But the call could have come from dozens of cities in the Bell system."

"Let me speak to your supervisor. Hurry, please."

She waited, trembling, and a more mature voice spoke. "May I help you?"

"This is Dr. Fleming, Florida State University Department of Criminology," Joanne began. "I received a call from someone in the nine-oh-four area code. It may be an emergency situation, operator. I need to know the calling number."

"We have no way of knowing, Dr. Fleming."

"Is this the Bell system?"

"Yes, it is."

"Your operator would know which exchange, wouldn't she?"

"I'm sorry, Dr. Fleming, regulations require—"

Joanne hung up, shivering. She sagged against the counter, called collect for her own number at home. Twice last night she'd tried to call Marcie and got no answer. The child slept like the dead, or may have had her bedroom door closed—"Hello?" a sleepy grumble.

"Ken! This is Joanne. Is Marcie there?"

"Don't know, Jo. Something wrong?"

"Hurry, Ken. See if she's there."

234

Bill Grant turned, saw Joanne, "Lady, you're suffering altitude sickness, I think. You're gray!"

"Jo—she isn't here."

"Is there a note on the bulletin board in the kitchen?"

"No."

"Ken," her voice was tremulous, "where is she?"

"I don't know, Jo. I haven't seen her since you left. Is something wrong?"

"Oh, God, Ken—"

"Jo! What is it? Have you had an accident?"

"He's got her, Ken."

"Who?"

"The killer."

"Nonsense, Jo—"

"Damn it," Joanne screamed, "he's got her! He called me here at Fawn Valley Lodge, in Estes Park. How else would anyone know to call here? Not even I knew I'd be here until an hour ago."

"Let me see if the car is out front, Jo."

"Lady, sit down." Bill put a chair behind her, but Joanne stood, leaning against the front counter.

"No car, Jo."

"He told me to go home. He said there'd be a 'surprise' for me. I'm coming home."

"Hold it," Ken commanded. "I need more than this to start looking. Where did the call come from?"

She told him what she knew. "I'll see what I can do through the sheriff's department, Jo."

"The necklace," she croaked, "that's what did it. He must know I have it, guessed I'd be here, called to see—"

"You know Marcie, Jo. She could be out with Charlie right this minute."

"Put out a bulletin on my car, Ken."

"I will."

"I'm returning immediately. Find the car. And look for a caucasian male, brown curly hair, blue eyes, about six feet tall. Read my profile—that's the man."

"Beat-up bug," Bill offered.

"May drive a VW," Joanne said to Ken.

"Right."

She hung up and sank into the chair, shaking.

"Lady, we have no rooms, but I can set up a day bed for you."

"I have to drive to Denver."

The old man glanced at a young clerk, then Joanne. "I'll drive you to Denver."

"No, the car's rented."

"If you were my woman, I wouldn't let you go like this."

The telephone rang and the clerk turned, eyes wide. "For Dr. Fleming."

She lifted the receiver, quivering. "Hello?"

"Boo, wee mommie. I told you—go home. There's a surprise for you."

Click.

Chapter Twenty-seven

AS Ken pulled into the driveway, Joanne asked, "Is that Ralph's car?"

"He's here. The house is full of people, Jo."

She glanced up and down the street. "Where're they parked?"

"We didn't want to appear obvious. This guy could be next door for all we know."

Despite Ken's warning, Joanne was surprised that a dozen men were waiting. Cowboy Rogers, Ralph, the city police chief—the telephone was ringing. Nobody made a move to answer.

"Ringing every ten minutes for about an hour," someone said. "Dr. Fleming, wait until I point at you, then answer. If it's him, keep him talking."

They started a tape recorder. Ralph, Ken, and the man with the recorder put on headsets and then, Joanne lifted the receiver. "Hello?"

"Where've you been, wee mommie?"

"I just got in."

"The plane landed fifty minutes ago. Where've you been?"

"The flight was delayed."

"Stand by, mommie."

"Hi, mom."

Joanne's heart leaped. "Marcie? Are you all right?"

"I'm fine, mom." Suddenly, "Don Whitneytwenty-nine-pro—" the phone went dead.

"Marcie? *Marcie*—"

"They hung up, Dr. Fleming."

Ralph motioned for a tape rewind.

"Did they have time to trace the call?" Joanne asked.

"A long distance call can't be traced, Jo. It moves by microwave, no telephone lines—listen."

The men listened intently. "Don-something."

"Whitbee?" Ken queried. "Whitley? Whitney?"

"Twenty-nine—is that an address?"

"His age, maybe."

"Okay, right. Prof? Proof? Sounded like she said 'pro.' "

"Profile," Joanne said.

"What does that mean?"

"My profile of the sadist-murderer," Joanne stated. "This man, named Larry Etna in Estes Park, Colorado, was described as having curly brown hair, blue eyes—a guess I'd made doing the profile. I suspect Marcie was trying to say I was correct and—"

The phone, ringing again. The headsets went on, the man pointed. Joanne's palms were slick with sweat. "Hello?"

"A chip off the old blockette, eh, mommie?"

"She isn't stupid, and neither am I, Mr. Etna."

"Oh-ho," he chuckled softly. "Smart mommie. Knows so much. You stupid wench—if it weren't for you, Marcie wouldn't be in this mess. You had to poke your nose into other people's lives. Okay, mommie. I'll kill Marcie in a second, understand? With no remorse. Do you believe that?"

"Yes."

"You'd better believe it." He was breathing heavily. "If anything happens to that girl, it's your fault, understand? I'm the most heartless sonofabitch you'll ever meet."

"All right, Mr. Etna."

"You think you're so smart." He heaved air into the phone. "Well, mommie, you are about to get an object lesson in criminality, psychology, and intelligence. You *will* do precisely what I tell you. Is that clear?"

"Yes, it is."

Heavy exhalations. Joanne strained for other sounds, a bell, a passing car—anything.

"I ought to kill her anyway," he said.

"I don't think that is necessary."

"Maybe, maybe not," he said. "We'll see. But I can promise you one thing: if you don't follow my directions to the absolute letter, do exactly what I say—she's dead. You'll find a piece here and a piece there. Once she *is* dead, you can go to your grave suffering for your smart mouth and moronic misconceptions. It'd serve you right, too. But Marcie doesn't deserve that from you, or it'd be over right now."

"What are your instructions, Mr. Etna?"

He laughed. "I love the way you psychologists try to gain the upper hand. Assert dominance even in the face of total failure." He mimicked her voice. "What are your instructions, Mr. Etna?"

Joanne waited, swallowing. She heard him suck a lung of air, exhale. "You have something that belongs to me."

"The necklace."

"That's right, mommie, the necklace. If things go well, I'll have it and you'll have Marcie. If things go badly, you'll have nothing."

"What do you want me to do?"

"Go to Venice, Florida." He turned aside, coughed. "Stay at the Seascape Motel north of the Highway Seven-Seventy-five junction."

"Seascape Motel, Highway Seven-Seventy-five junction," Joanne repeated.

"I'll telephone you there. If anyone answers but you, forget it. If you aren't there, forget it. If the phone is out of order, forget it. The onus of this falls on you. You got Marcie into this, so it's your doing. It would be easier for me to kill the girl and get it over."

"We know who you are, Mr. Etna."

"You know," he growled, "you're going to be a special pleasure to me. I'm anticipating meeting you. Part of your trouble all along has been the assumption that I am stupid."

"Mr. Etna, that's the one thing I do not assume."

"Run, wee mommie. Be at the Seascape when I call. Don't have a flat tire, don't run out of gas. Don't bring the army with you."

"I'm too tired to drive alone."

"Bring that dumb cop boyfriend, then. Nobody else. And I mean *nobody*."

"Very well."

"Run, wee mommie." The phone went dead.

Driving through the night, headlights illuminating a monotonous expanse of highway, Joanne stared ahead, thinking. "Try to get some sleep, Jo," Ken urged.

"Did they find my car?"

"It was at a restaurant on North Monroe."

"Marcie has known this man for some time, Ken. She's been seeing him regularly."

"That's right, Jo. How did you know?"

"He's formed a bond with Marcie. She with him."

"Strong enough to protect her?"

"I doubt it."

"Evidently," Ken reported, "Marcie had been meeting him often, Jo. The manager and a waitress said he created a scene and refused to pay for food he'd ordered. They said he and Marcie had been coming in several times weekly."

"Brown hair, blue eyes."

"With a mustache. Driving a Volkswagen."

Joanne put a hand on her aching chest.

"I'm afraid that's not all, Jo. Marcie was probably seeing him in Panacea, too. At the Oaks, they remember the two of them sitting together when Marcie was down at Ralph's cottage."

"Oh, Ken—that child." Joanne drew a shuddering breath. "She asked me about Peeping Toms and psychopathic liars! I know I tend to be too suspicious, and this time—I must've blanked it out. Busy. Oh, dear Lord—"

"Recriminations aren't going to help this, Jo."

After a long silence, Joanne said, "I must think as objectively as possible. Try to anticipate what he'll do, how he'll do it. I don't think it's Marcie he wants to hurt."

"Meaning, it's you?"

"Yes. But failing that—Marcie; which *would* hurt me. He may kill her even if he gets the necklace." She began to cry and Ken patted her leg, his face grim in the green glow from the dashboard light.

"We have to do precisely what he says, Ken."

"Yes."

"No fancy police tactics, no chances—precisely what he says."

239

"That's right, Jo."

"Do you promise?"

"To the best of my ability, yes. But now we have a great many people involved in this thing, Jo. They're going to be thinking first of you, second of Marcie. That's the only sensible thing to do."

"Because they think she's already—"

"Because," he said, sternly, "never deliver a second hostage into the hands of a man holding one hostage already. That's the reasoning, and it's sound."

"God," Joanne prayed fervently, "please don't allow this man to hurt my baby. Please guide and direct us."

"Jo," Ken said, "we aren't alone in this. You need to know that. They have police departments in Fort Myers, Tampa, and various cities in between—the sheriff's departments, state patrol, a special terrorist team from Miami, the marine patrol, and the coast guard—all poised, waiting. Whatever else happens, this maniac isn't going to get away."

"If he sees them!"

"He won't. Do you? They won't make a move until you are wherever the necklace is to be exchanged for Marcie. Then they'll have him so tightly bottled, he can't get away. In the face of certain capture, few men dare commit murder."

"This man will."

"You said he's sane."

"I think he is."

"Then he won't kill." Ken turned into a motel driveway. "If he thinks he's sure to be captured, and he's sane, then he won't kill."

Fog swirled around them as the car halted. The motel sign was off. Pale yellow night lights gave the imitation brick exterior a ghostly luminance.

"Let me see if I can wake somebody," Ken grunted. "Let's hope there are no bedbugs."

While he stood in the shadows trying to rouse someone, Joanne forced herself to make a realistic appraisal of the situation. Marcie, alive to testify as to where she got the necklace, would be a witness—the only witness—who could positively tie him to a dead girl; he made it, the Ramirez girl was wearing it, and he had possession again following her murder. With the necklace, Marcie could prove that to a jury. Without the necklace, everything was circumstantial, even if they caught him. Would he take it back and risk letting Marcie go free?

Of one thing Joanne was positive—if he did *not* get the necklace, Marcie was sure to die. Joanne dared not gamble with that. Give him the necklace. Even then—

"The jerk wants twenty dollars for a night," Ken reported, getting in. "Pay in advance, he says. No credit cards. You all right, Jo?"

"Yes."

He turned on an interior light, examined her face. "Honey, how do you feel?"

"Mad, Ken. Mad as in insane; mad as in anger."

He pulled in to an allocated parking space and got out. Joanne waited, watching Ken examine a room with the manager.

Mr. Etna had a price to pay, too. And she would see to it. But, even thinking it, her heart hammered furiously, fearfully.

"What a ripoff," Ken complained, returning for their luggage. "Twenty dollars for a sagging bed and roaches. Come on, Jo. I hate to do this to you, but this is the place."

"Is there a telephone?"

"Yes. I had him check to be sure it worked. Come on, Jo."

She got out, feeling faint, shaking with a sick rage. Inside, she turned full circle, dismayed at the worn chenille bedspread, the soiled shag carpet, and rusted shower stall.

Nevertheless, when she sat down to rest, she fell asleep.

The shrill ring of a telephone brought Joanne up, confused, floundering for the instrument. Even after she lifted the receiver, it burred in her ear.

"Hello?"

"This is the manager," a voice said. "You people plan to stay another night?"

"I don't know."

"Check-out time's eleven," he said.

"What time is it?"

"Noon."

"Then," Joanne said, meeting Ken's gaze, "we'll pay for another night. Have there been any calls?"

"No calls."

Groggy, stumbling, she went to the sink to wash her face. She felt gritty, sweaty.

"This place ought to be reported to the Better Business Bureau," Ken griped. "That bed must've belonged to a contortionist."

"Ken, will you go find coffee somewhere, please?"

Hair still rumpled, Ken went out and midday heat flowed in. Joanne looked for an air conditioner. There was none.

The telephone rang and she grabbed it.

"I'll call later," the voice stated, "stay there."

"Hello, listen to me," Joanne began. But the line hummed. "Damn you!" she shrieked, and slammed the receiver into its cradle.

When Ken returned, he had four paper cups. "Today is Labor Day, Jo. I bought this horrible concoction at a convenience store. It was the best I could do."

The coffee was old, burnt, caustic. Joanne drank in sips that drew her abdomen taut with each swallow. Ken tried the ancient television set and got a crackling sound, broken reception. He swore, complained about the creaking bed, tried to stomp the roaches that skittered when anything was moved. Relentlessly, the heat of day rose, humidity making everything sticky to touch.

When the manager's wife arrived to do maid service, Ken angrily demanded a TV which worked, another set of sheets, and washcloths. He got washcloths.

"This is what Etna wants," Ken fumed. "He wants us miserable."

"Knowing that," Joanne replied, mildly, "stop complaining."

Shirtless, sweat streaming, Ken sat in the open door watching a kitten pounce at grasshoppers on the motel lawn. Day became evening, finally night. Twice Ken went out for food, more awful coffee, and Joanne sat by the telephone, waiting.

"If I were going to kill somebody," Ken observed, "I'd want to knock off guys who charge twenty dollars for a dump like this."

He walked around the room, nude, trying to kill mosquitos with loud claps of his hands, banging the floor with a shoe in his quest for roaches. The room was beginning to smell like a gymnasium.

The telephone rang and Joanne answered, "Hello?"

"Are you there, wee mommie?"

"I am."

242

He laughed. "Stay by the phone."

Joanne kept her voice unemotional. "I will."

Ken looked up over the foot of the bed. "Him?"

"Yes." Joanne laid back, closed her eyes.

"Sonofabitch," Ken growled.

She pressed her temples with her fingertips. She had a splitting headache.

Joanne had been up since daybreak, sitting by the telephone, Ken lying on his back naked, snoring. The call came at eight o'clock.

"Yes?"

"Are you up, mommie?"

"Yes."

"Dressed and ready to trot?"

Joanne shook Ken's leg, "I'm ready, Mr. Etna."

"Listen carefully," he said. "Take Highway Seven-Seventy-five south to the dead end before the toll bridge. The name of the place is Placida."

"Spell it."

He did so. "There's a small store there," he said. "Sells bait, serves as post office, you can't miss it. Right at the dock. Inside, on the wall, is the only public telephone in that town. Wait by the phone, mommie. I'm going to call there in exactly forty-five minutes."

Ken drove at seventy, and they arrived at 8:25. Joanne ran inside, found the telephone and stood next to it. When a woman entered and approached, Ken blocked her way. "We're expecting an important call in a few minutes, do you mind waiting?" The woman withdrew, glaring with animosity.

"Here comes the mailman!" the proprietor hollered. "Set your watches, folks, he leaves promptly at eight forty-five."

Through windows covered by burglar bars, Joanne noticed two fishermen working with their trailered boat. A sedan drove up and parked, the occupants gazing across the water. Police. Even she could see that.

It was 8:40. The telephone rang.

"Hello?"

"Mommie, have you had your coffee this morning?"

"No."

"Too bad. No breakfast?"

"No."

"Sorry to hear that," he said, amiably. "Too late now. Do you see the fellow about to get in his power launch?"

"Where?"

"At the dock."

"I think so."

"Go catch him. Get in and go with him. Do not—let me repeat, mommie—do *not* bring your dumb cop boyfriend. Only you and the launch operator. Understand?"

"Yes."

"Bring the necklace, mommie."

Ken grabbed the receiver. "Listen to me, pal," Ken snapped, "if I don't get a telephone call from Joanne in one hour, I'm coming after you."

Joanne heard the caller yelling so loudly, Ken had to hold the telephone away from his ear. "Keep your nose out of this, you dumb—"

Joanne took the phone. "I'm sorry, Mr. Etna, he took it away from me." She heard the rale of heavy breathing.

"I told you," he screamed, "nobody but you! Come alone, nobody else!"

"I must give him a time when I can telephone, or he won't allow me to come."

"Forget it."

Click! Phone dead. Joanne started for the boat and Ken restrained her. "Wait. I'll hold him. You stay by the phone." He ran out, caught the launch operator and stalled him. The telephone rang.

"Hello," Joanne said.

"You can call when you get where you're going."

"How long?"

"That depends on the launch."

"Approximately how long?"

"Four to five hours. Warn that dumb brute, Marcie isn't there. Understand? She will not be where you're going."

"Where am I going?"

"Do as I told you, damn you!"

"Stay calm, Mr. Etna. I'm sure you can understand our reticence, delivering a second hostage into the hands of a man already holding one."

He exhaled into the phone, gasped air, exhaled again.

"Mr. Etna," Joanne modulated her voice, "Do I have your word that Marcie is still all right?"

"My word?" He laughed abruptly. "Yeah. You have my word."

244

"May I speak to her?"

"She isn't here."

"I must go catch the boat, Mr. Etna. May I bring you anything?"

"You're a cool bitch," he said. "I'll give you that. Cool and restrained. Tough, right?"

"No, very frightened in fact."

"Mommie," he wheezed, "you ain't seen nothing yet."

The telephone popped as he disconnected.

"Take this." Ken opened her purse and put in his service revolver.

"I don't know how to shoot a pistol."

"Point the barrel at him," Ken said. "Hold the handle with both hands, pull the trigger. If he's close enough, it'll knock him down. If you miss, it'll scare him. Take it."

"He said I could call in four or five hours, depending on the speed of the boat," Joanne related.

"Where to, lady?" the launch operator inquired.

"I'm not sure."

Ken threw in Joanne's overnight bag, helped her aboard. "He delivers mail and supplies to small islands along a sixty-mile route." Ken held the craft close to dockside. "I paid him fifteen dollars."

"Cast off," the man commanded, and Ken let go.

"Jo!"

His voice was lost in the roaring motor. She tried to read his lips—Ken cupped his hands—but as the boat shuddered beneath her, Joanne heard only the rumbling engine, the slap of water.

She felt as if she were being lowered into a dark pit with a rabid animal . . .

Chapter Twenty-eight

HIS name was Smitty and he maneuvered his boat standing behind a wheel. Spray torn from choppy water was thrown up to spatter Joanne, leaving salt flecks on her parched flesh. In a corner, greasy cans of extra fuel; canvas bags marked U.S. MAIL. Below and forward in a narrow, low compartment, cigarettes, foodstuff, and other items were boxed for delivery.

"He was a one-eyed, red-headed, evil tempered man," Smitty shouted. "Narvaez landed near Cape Haze north of here in fifteen-twenty-eight. He came to claim Florida for Spain. That was the *first* land bust. These islands are some of the others."

He pointed off to the right. "Boca Grande," he said. "Lots all staked out, paved roads, one or two houses, a fortune invested. I delivered there until they put in a toll bridge at Placida."

The boat had two sickening motions: a pitching, bumpy lunge, and a side-to-side yaw when current or wind caught the beam. Her stomach was trying to twist inside out.

Smitty spoke of Indian mounds, early white settlers, pirates, and fates which befell them. Finally, clearing open water, coming leeward of several islands, he eased the throttle and the motor subsided to a grumble. "Smoother going now," he said. The hull sliced still water and Joanne fought on against nausea.

Leaning overboard, in case something came from her empty belly, Joanne saw horseshoe crab, mullet. Around them, like a scene from a jungle film, mangrove thickets posed on spider leg roots. Egrets, spoonbills, blue cranes, and pelicans watched stoically as Smitty passed through.

A mailbox rose incongruously from the end of a low dock. Smitty brought his boat alongside, placed mail in the box and gunned the motor, pulling away.

"Who could live out here?" Joanne asked.

"Old-timers, mostly. The fellow I delivered to there is pushing a hundred. He claims his wife is older than him."

"Must be lonely."

"They like to be left alone," Smitty said. "Here's another one." They approached a dock and an elderly man was waiting.

"Hey, Smitty!"

"Hold the line, partner." Smitty tossed a rope. "I'll get your booze." Two bottles of bourbon, two vodka. Cash changed hands and the inhabitant shoved them free as Smitty backed expertly into the open again.

"How do they make a living?" Joanne asked.

"Fishing, hunting, selling driftwood. It doesn't take much to live like this. Of course, there are places like Useppa, too."

"What is that?"

"Back in the early nineteen-hundreds, sportsmen built a hotel there. Not but eighty acres to the whole island. It was a favorite place for tarpon fishing. I once ran a barge twice weekly, delivering diesel fuel to run their generators. They have electricity now—so do most of these islands."

The conversation ceased as they drew up to another secluded dock and Smitty bantered with a dark-skinned resident, accepted payment, and shoved off again.

"On Useppa," Smitty continued, "there's a nine-hole golf course, good water, telephones—all the comforts of home. Famous people live there. All of them rich."

Another stop, this time Joanne was left in the boat as Smitty disappeared up a sandy trail to make a delivery. When he returned, he had a jug of amber liquid. "Iced tea." He poured her a cup. "Hope you like it sweet. I've got some saltines and sardines, if you'd care for it."

"No." Joanne quelled a surge in her abdomen.

"Eat some crackers," Smitty advised. "It helps motion sickness. I can tell by your green freckles you don't have sea legs."

She ate as they cruised, unhurried.

"Most of these islands are uninhabitable," Smitty recounted. "No drinking water. Susceptible to flooding and hurricanes."

As they made a slow turn, the boat lurched, briefly aground. "This is Cabbage Key," Smitty announced. "Mary

Roberts Rinehart once lived here. She gave me autographed copies of her books."

Through palm fronds and palmetto, Joanne saw a dwelling. She waited in the boat as Smitty stepped ashore, keenly aware of places where somebody could be hiding, watching, waiting.

Smitty's laughter came from afar and then, the laughter of another man. She heard a female voice.

"Stay for lunch," somebody offered.

"Got a passenger." Smitty appeared on the pier with two companions.

"Where away?" the man queried.

"Don't know," Smitty said. They looked at Joanne and smiled, nodded.

"Good sailing, Smitty."

And they were off again, Smitty talking incessantly. "That was one of the typical land deals . . ." He spoke of Cabbage Key. "Promoters came here at the turn of the century dreaming of island resorts and millions of dollars. But the swamps breed mosquitos, water moccasins, and the lagoon bottom is mud, hip deep. That's the case with the next island. The tide sets pretty good through here when the moon and sun are at tropical perigee. It creates a venturi effect and water rips at ten knots or more. Small boats couldn't buck the tide; large boats with enough power found it too shallow to reach dock. So the place failed."

As he spoke, the boat rose as if something below had lifted the hull. "You can feel the current," Smitty observed, giving the motor more fuel. "Can't many boats get in here. Every time they dredged a channel it shoaled over. Now, they have cottages where nobody stays, cabanas nobody uses, and a lodge with no guests. Owned by some outfit in Fort Myers."

He blew a horn and the sound brought birds from hidden roosts, rising like feathered rainbows, squawking. Smitty blew the horn again.

"This is as close as I can get," he said. "He has to come out for his stuff."

"I don't see anybody."

"He's there. He called in his order yesterday."

Smitty was getting boxes from below. "It takes a while," he said. "He lost a leg in Vietnam. Sometimes he answers

248

the horn, sometimes he doesn't. Poor fellow runs on a warped keel."

Sixty yards distant, Joanne saw a figure hobble out and lower himself into a skiff.

"Gave his manhood to Uncle Sam and his leg to the Viet Cong," Smitty nodded, softly. "Ahoy there, sergeant!"

"Got my beer?"

"Two cases."

"Budweiser?"

"Bud it is."

Joanne heard oars dipping, the man rowing toward them. He wore a red bandana headband, a straw hat, baggy army fatigues. Once, he paused, removed his hat from a bald pate, and wiped it with a handkerchief. Then, tediously, he began to row again. The boats clunked as their hulls scraped and Smitty looped a rope over the man's oarlock, making it fast.

Joanne gazed down at a misshapen grin which twisted the features oddly lumped around a sunburned nose. "You Joanne Fleming?" he asked.

She couldn't breathe. Nodded.

"Larry Etna called and said you'd be along."

"Smitty—are you coming ashore?"

"No, lady, I have a long way to go yet. Easy with the beer, sergeant, or you'll be diving for it."

A hollow guffaw and the disabled veteran clumsily stacked goods in the middle of his skiff.

"When will you reach a telephone, Smitty?" Joanne asked.

"There's a phone here at the lodge," the sergeant said.

"You're getting off here?" Smitty questioned.

"Apparently." Joanne was shivering as she accepted the extended hand of the man in the boat. The skiff lurched as she stepped aboard and Smitty had to hold the gunwale to keep it from swamping.

"Enjoyed the company, lady," Smitty said. "Should I pick you up on my way back Thursday?"

She looked at the oarsman, but he was busy counting boxes, checking contents. "I don't know," she said.

Joanne asked, emphatically, "Will you telephone the Placida general store for me, Smitty? Tell them where I am."

"It won't be until tonight, lady."

"Will you do it?"

"There's a telephone ashore," her companion stated again. He squinted at her with brilliantly blue eyes.

"What's the name of this place?" Joanne asked. Smitty handed over her bag and purse.

"Carlos Key, lady," Smitty said. "Named for a famous Indian chief."

"Smitty." Joanne grabbed his arm. "Don't forget to call the Placida store."

He studied her face. "Are you all right?"

"Please," she urged, "promise to call."

"I will."

Then, even when she released his arm, Smitty did not untie from the oarlock. "You're sure you want to get off here, lady?"

"Yes."

The sergeant used a paddle to push away from Smitty's craft. He turned, pulling the oars, and Joanne heard Smitty's motor rumble to life. *Oh God—please help—*

His cheek was a knot, one eye barely open, a glint of blue catching the light. He rowed, staring, and belatedly, Joanne realized he was looking up her dress. She shifted her position, knees together. Slowly, his gaze lifted to her face and he made short sucking sounds, as if his breath passed through liquid. Drool fell in a silvery dribble from a corner of his mouth.

"You Larry's girl friend?" he asked, voice guttural.

"No."

"He said you'd be here tonight."

"Has he been here today?"

"No."

He rowed, staring, spittle trickling. He wiped his chin with a sleeve, returned to rowing.

"Going fishing?" he asked.

"No. What—what is your name?"

His reply was unintelligible. "I'm sorry," Joanne said, "what is it?"

He moved his mouth as if preparing muscles to follow mental command—"Dennis," he said.

"First or last name?"

"First."

"May I call you Dennis?"

"Can I call you Joanne?"

"Yes. That's fine. Joanne. And Dennis."

"Grab the dock," he ordered. Joanne did so and the

250

boat jerked, bumping. He threw a rope over a post. "Get up there and I'll hand you the boxes," he said. She had to climb on one knee, then rise to her feet, his eyes following every move.

She took the delivery, box by box, and followed his instructions, tying off the skiff. Then, he bounded up onto the dock, on one hip, twisted, and arose to hop several feet to his crutches. His leg, ending at the knee, was huge in the thigh. His arms flailed as he jumped from one place to another. "Come on," he said. "I'll come back for the supplies."

He followed her along a boardwalk built above a low marsh wending through a bog to higher ground. A fresh breeze brushed her face.

"Pretty," he said. Joanne tried to smile. She was aware of every whisper, every movement in the dense undergrowth on either side of the walkway. His crutches thumping, breathing heavily from exertion, he stopped at a bifurcation built into the walk. A shaggy palm grew up between the walkways. "Up ahead," he directed. "I'll get the supplies."

"I need to make a telephone call, Dennis."

"Up there." He pointed at steep steps.

"Please. Go with me, until I have made my call."

Slowly, wincing, he negotiated the stairs one at a time, Joanne just ahead of him. She caught a whiff of liquor on his breath.

The lodge had shuttered windows, broad cypress porches. Here, the walkways were fenced with close-mesh wire.

"To keep out snakes," he said, as if reading Joanne's mind. "Doesn't stop the rats." He held his hands about eighteen inches apart. "That big," he said. "Wharf rats. Killed my cats."

As they reached the entrance, he added, "Snakes climb over, hide in limbs. Be careful going under limbs."

"Yes," she said. "I will be. Where's the telephone, Dennis?"

"At the desk."

Joanne glanced down a long dark corridor, into an adjoining dining room with chairs stacked on tables, legs jutting toward a ceiling of stained acoustical tile.

She lifted the receiver as he stood by. "Operator, I want to call the general store at Placida."

When the phone stopped ringing, it was Ken's husky voice Joanne heard.

"I'm here," she said.

"Where?"

"A place called Carlos Key."

"Is he there?"

"No. The man here says Larry Etna called and will be coming later."

"Describe this man."

"I can't very well—"

"He's listening?"

"Yes."

"Hair," Ken said; "black? Brown? Red—"

"None."

"Bald."

"Right."

"Clean shaven?"

"More or less."

"His name?" Ken asked.

"Dennis, what is your last name?"

He leaned over and hollered into the phone, "Alday!"

"We'll check him out, Jo. Are you all right?"

"Yes."

Something down the hallway banged and Joanne cried aloud. The sergeant chuckled. "Shutters," he said.

"What is it, Jo?"

"Nerves."

"Jo, the officials here say it will be impossible to cordon off that island. We're trying to locate airboats that skim over shallow water. I want you to call me every hour. Every hour, understand?"

"Dennis," she said, "I have to call out every hour, is that all right?"

"Local call?"

"I'll pay all charges, Dennis."

"I can't take credit cards," he warned.

"Cash."

"Okay."

"I'll call every hour, Ken. Don't make a move that will scare him."

"No, we won't. There are dozens of fishermen in the area. We'll stay away until we know he's there."

"I love you, Ken."

"I love you, Jo. Keep that pistol where you can reach it."

Breathless, Joanne said, "I will."

"What's the phone number there, Jo?"

She told him, asked Dennis if that was correct, and he nodded, the lopsided grin drooling saliva.

"One other thing, Ken. Just one."

Long pause. "One what?"

"Only that."

"Eye?"

"No."

"Arm?"

"No."

"Leg?"

"Correct."

"We'll check him out, Jo. Know that we're close by, darling."

When she hung up, the sergeant was bobbing on his crutches, shirt front soaked with spit, face contorted.

"Dennis, could you show me to a room, please?"

The hall smelled musty, as if mildew were lurking in the shadows. The doors were not solid, but slatted to allow a flow of air even when closed. He shoved open a door and Joanne looked in at a zebra-like pattern of stripes caused by the shuttered windows and the afternoon sun.

"Is there a telephone in this room, Dennis?"

He shook his head, grimacing.

"Hot water?"

He nodded.

"Good," she said, "I think I'll take a quick shower."

That odd sucking sound, liquid inhalation, exhalation. He thumped away down the hall.

Inside, quaking, Joanne shut the louvered entrance and stood with her back to it. She turned to secure it—no lock! She peeped out, down the hall. Silence. She crossed the corridor, tried a door—no lock there, either. Then, another.

As she pushed open the portal, a sibilant murmur rose from the dark and she threw herself back against a wall.

The tone of the sound shifted. Shutters. Wind in the shutters. None of the doors had locks. All louvered. She closed them, returning to her room. Then in semi-light, she crossed to the window and opened jalousies. A web of strangler figs and vines sheltered her from exterior view. Nobody could come through that thicket quietly. But, there was no lock here, either. Nor screens. She glanced around the room for a light switch. None. Damn him! Her eyes adjusting to the dark, she saw a kerosene lantern and a package of matches.

The toilet reeked as of rotten eggs. Sulphur water. Anything was better than this sticky, itchy layer of salt spray and perspiration. She removed her clothing and stepped into a weakly running shower. The odor of sulphur made her hold her breath, scrubbing quickly, the soap lathering easily but difficult to rinse away.

She had gathered courage to wash her hair when she heard something in the bedroom. Joanne leaned out of the shower, listening. On the commode, her purse with the pistol. A shadow crossed the louvered door and she froze —unable to force herself to action.

"Huhhh!"

"Who is it?" Joanne bounded for the commode, grabbed her purse and dropped it. "Who is it?" she yelled.

"Huhhhh—" the door knob turned slowly. She fumbled for the gun, clutching it in slippery wet hands, shaking so violently she couldn't bring it to point steadily.

"Who is it?"

The door creaked, opening slowly, and Joanne pulled back the hammer, pistol extended.

A hand appeared. Towels.

She snatched them to her, stood with gun wavering as the door closed again.

Almost shot him. Nearly killed him!

Every breath a shiver in her throat, she slowly let the hammer down again. She placed the wet pistol on the back of the commode, shaking uncontrollably.

Another instant—she would have shot him.

Crying, sobs muffled in the towels, Joanne sank to the commode and sat staring at the door.

When she emerged, the bed had been turned down, its freshly laundered sheets and pillowcase white and unwrinkled. She dressed, slapped at a mosquito feasting on her upper arm, and put the gun in her purse. In the gathering gloom of evening, she returned to the lobby. Dennis was there, in a wheelchair.

"Dennis, please do not come into my room without knocking."

"I did."

254

"If there's no answer," Joanne reprimanded, "don't come in, please."

"I had to check—"

"For what?"

He pointed at a large ashtray.

Joanne bent, peering, and swallowed. The unmistakable tangle of plated legs lay entwined with the curled tails of black scorpions. She sank to a chair, purse in hand. He was drinking beer and already three empty cans lay on the floor. Following her eyes, he lifted a can, offering.

"No, thank you."

"Hungry?"

"Yes."

He wheeled his chair toward swinging doors and disappeared. Joanne telephoned Ken.

"Jo, we're less than two miles from you now. We've moved to the Pine Island National Wildlife Refuge office." He gave her the telephone number. "It's a local call from here," he said. "We have about two hundred men."

"Don't let him see you."

"No, no, we're keeping out of sight. We're not stopping anybody, and this is an area closed to the public."

"He's going to play games with me, Ken."

"We figured he might."

"Did you check on the man here?"

"He's a veteran of Vietnam, twice decorated for bravery, Jo. He lost his right leg and suffered facial damage in combat."

"All right."

"He may be a victim of shell shock, too."

"That," she said, "I am trained to handle."

"Good girl."

The swinging doors bumped open and Dennis came with a tray across the arms of his chair, sandwiches cut into quarters.

"His employer in Fort Myers," Ken said, "assures us this fellow Alday is intelligent, capable and trustworthy. We've requested his Army records, but that'll take time."

"No move without warning, Ken."

"You have my word—so long as you telephone every hour."

Dennis was close now, his wheelchair touching Joanne's leg. He sat grinning, blue eyes sparkling, waiting.

Joanne hung up. "Where is Larry Etna, Dennis?"

"Coming tonight, he said." He extended the tray of food. "Eat. Good."

"Yes." Joanne said, gratefully.

"I'm not dumb," he gurgled.

"I didn't think you were."

He gazed at her a long moment. "Yes, you did."

Chapter Twenty-nine

JOANNE held the telephone to her ear, opened purse in her lap, the pistol where she could reach it. In the darkening lobby, alone, she could hear Dennis somewhere in the kitchen, clattering pans. From here, she could see the front entrance, down a long corridor toward her room. Through the dining room, the sun was backlighting cypress trees as it settled beyond nearby Cayo Costa.

"There are a lot of small islands around you," Ken said. "The marine patrol office says a man can hide in a hummock and watch a boat go by thirty feet away. It would take a thousand men to close off the area completely."

After a pause, Joanne said, "All right, Ken."

"It means," Ken advised, "we don't dare move into position until we're certain he's there. He could be one of the fishermen boating in backwaters, or he might be wading with a light as if gigging flounder. We can't approach those people for fear we'll frighten him away."

"I know."

"The burden is on you, darling," Ken said. "When you think he's there, call. We have several men with walkie-talkies in fishing boats nearby. But they say anybody could slip past unnoticed. There are canals, lagoons, rivers, and the open sea if he chooses that route."

Joanne wept quietly, "Ken—Marcie—"

"Don't think about Marcie right now, Jo. That's what this man is counting on. Think about what *you* must do."

"I nearly shot Dennis," Joanne sobbed.

"Don't do that."

"He came to my bathroom with towels. I almost shot him through the door."

"Jo, don't shoot anything you can't see. The closer he is, the better chance you have of hitting him. Wait. Be certain."

"I'll try, Ken."

"Listen to me," he insisted, "stay by the telephone. Make him come to you. He wants the necklace. Assuming he comes at all."

"What?"

"This may all be a ploy to create suffering on your part, nothing more."

"Oh, Ken—"

"But then again," Ken said quickly, "he may. He's the kind of man who would—am I right?"

"If he thinks he can get away, yes."

"The more we study the terrain," Ken confessed, "the less certain we are of catching him. When he goes to land again, we'll block off highways and bottle him up. But until then—"

She blew her nose, moved the telephone to her other ear. "I dread hanging up, Ken. But I have to. He might call."

"I agree."

"Ken—he probably has already—I mean, common sense tells me Marcie is—"

"Think of what you must do," Ken said, sharply. "Nothing else!"

"I'll try."

"The caretaker there," Ken said, "could he help you?"

"He's drinking."

"Feel him out, Jo. Tell him what's going down."

She heard Dennis swearing. Joanne hung up and stood in the dimness of the lobby, pistol in hand. To reach the kitchen, she had to pass through the darkened dining room. Senses keen, she walked slowly toward the swinging double doors and the sounds of Dennis at work.

Through small windows in the doors she saw him wheeling his chair, face shadowed by the straw hat, tossing pots and pans from one deep sink to another. He'd been drinking since she arrived; his breath suggested *before* she arrived. He wiped his chin with a swipe of a long sleeve soaked to the elbows by dishwater. He swore lustily, snatched out a pan and flung it to another sink.

Her back to a wall, Joanne circled the dining room, checking corners, the pistol pointing. Outside, the wide porch encircled the dwelling in shadows. A hum of insects droned, beetles bumping both sides of the few screened windows.

Dennis wheeled through the double doors with a bang, hurtling his chair toward the lobby. He passed her unaware, and Joanne watched him lift his weight as if to rise, peering into unlighted areas.

"Joanne!" he yelled.

"I'm here."

He seemed to freeze, then slowly turned the chair as he pushed one wheel, pulled the other, rotating in a tight circle. He saw the gun.

"What are you doing with that?" he asked.

"I'm watching for Larry Etna."

"Is he here?"

"I don't know."

"You're going to shoot him?"

"He may try to hurt me."

"I won't let him hurt you."

"He may."

"He doesn't like guns. He won't have a gun."

"How do you know that?"

"I've been hunting with him. He comes here to fish."

"How well do you know him?"

"Well enough to know he won't have a gun. He seems like a nice man."

"He might not be as nice with other people, Dennis."

"No," Dennis responded, "he won't hurt you. Larry!"

The unexpected yell made Joanne jolt, back into shadows. Dennis bellowed down the halls, "Larry! Come out here, Larry."

"Dennis, no more. Hush."

His eyes were sky blue specks in an unshaven face. "Why are you afraid of him?"

"He kidnapped my daughter, Marcie."

"Kidnapped?"

"He's holding her, Dennis. I have a piece of evidence which ties Larry to a murder he committed. He may try to kill me to get it."

"I won't allow that to happen."

"You might not be able to stop it, Dennis."

"Because I'm crippled."

"Because he's a cold-blooded killer. He'll strike without warning, maybe."

"I don't think you should walk around with a gun," he said, voice hollow.

"I don't want to hurt him," Joanne argued gently. "I simply do not want him to harm me."

"Do you have the necklace?"

Warily, she side-stepped. "How do you know about the necklace?"

"Larry said you stole it from him."

"I didn't steal it."

"He said you did. Now you have a gun."

She heard the floor creak, the wheelchair inching toward her.

"I didn't steal it."

"Who, then?"

"My daughter had it."

She held the pistol with both hands, aiming at a point somewhere between them.

"Marcie stole it," he said.

"I don't know that to be a fact."

"Do you know where Marcie is?"

"No."

"Then you dare not shoot Larry until you know."

"I don't want to shoot him!"

"But you're shaking, pointing the gun at me."

"No, I'm not. I'm holding it—"

"Give me the gun, Joanne."

"No."

"I know how to use a gun. Do you?"

"No."

"Then, if somebody has to shoot it, I'll do it."

"No."

"You'll be shooting at everything, Joanne. You're afraid. I can hear your voice trembling."

"I have to make my telephone call, Dennis."

He blocked her way.

"Dennis, I have to make a call."

"Give me the gun," he said, evenly.

"I can't do that, Dennis."

"Give it to me," he said, "then make your call."

"No."

"It's better for me to protect you, than for you to try and shoot him yourself, Joanne. I wouldn't miss. You would."

She edged around a sofa, putting it between them.

"I've been in combat with men who were as frightened as you," Dennis intoned. "They shoot at everything. Shoot their own men. Give me the gun and I'll protect you."

"I'll need it."

"No," he said, "I'll protect you."

"We need light in here, Dennis."

"Give me the gun, Joanne." He sat, hand out, barely illuminated.

"Dennis, turn on the lights."

"Then Larry could see us from outside. You give me the gun. He won't be expecting a threat from me. It's you he's after."

"I'll make my call," Joanne bartered. "If my friend says give you the gun, I'll do it."

"Either give me the gun, or you must leave."

"I'll ask him, Dennis."

"Let me talk to him." She heard the floor groan beneath wheels, the chair backing away. Joanne walked far around him, reached the telephone and placed her call.

"Ken?"

"Yes, Jo?"

"Dennis wants my gun. He says I have to give it to him, or leave."

"Did you tell him the situation?"

"Yes."

"Let me speak to him."

Joanne placed the receiver on a table, stepped back. "Talk to him, Dennis."

She listened as the men introduced themselves. Dennis spoke in hollow, guttural tones. "Second battalion. Right. Da Nang. That's right." A few moments passed, Dennis listening, answering tersely. "She has to give me the weapon or leave here, mister. I've seen men in that mental condition before. They get you killed."

A long pause, Ken reasoning, probing. Dennis sat, head hung, listening. "Hey mister," he said brusquely, "she leaves, or I keep the gun. If Etna is a threat, I'll be more likely to stop him with a pistol than she will. I won't kill him, but I'll drop him, if necessary. Which is it going to be?"

In the dark, the exchange continued and Joanne kept her back to a wall. Finally, Dennis said, "He wants to speak to you."

"Hello, Ken."

"You're going to have to give him the revolver, Jo."

"Ken—"

"It's his territory, Jo. He has a right to ask you to leave. He has offered to guard you and I'm not sure that isn't a preferable alternative."

"Drinking," Joanne blurted. From the dark came a low snicker.

"Nevertheless," Ken said, "you must divest yourself of the weapon, or pull out. Personally, I think we should pull you out of there."

"No. I have to stay."

"In which case, you must give him your gun."

"All right."

"His employer says the man is reliable and steady."

"To the best of his ability, perhaps," Joanne said, acidly.

"Don't underestimate those combat vets, Jo. He knows more ways to kill a man than you can dream of. I could come over there and try to stay out of sight."

"Too risky."

"Then," Ken concluded, "give the man your gun."

She hung up. To the night, she said, "Turn on some lights, Dennis."

Immediately, the room was illuminated.

"Why is there no electricity in my bedroom?" Joanne demanded.

"They wired this room, the kitchen, the caretaker quarters," he said. "Nobody comes here. It wasn't worth the investment."

"Larry Etna is holding my daughter," Joanne said, angrily. "He's responsible for the brutal slaying of many women."

"He's crazy?"

"Unbalanced, of course."

Dennis laughed softly.

"The question is," Joanne snapped, "would you shoot him, if you had to?"

"If I had to."

"If I give you this gun, will you stay with me, every minute?"

"If that's what you want."

"I must try and get my daughter free."

"How?"

"He wants this." Joanne withdrew the necklace from her

261

purse. "When he gets it, I'm hoping, praying, oh, God! I'm praying he hasn't harmed her."

He took the necklace, examined it. He turned it, held it up to the light and squinted at the silversmith's mark. "Give me your pistol," he said, casually.

Hesitantly, Joanne placed the revolver on the table. "No more drinking," she mandated.

"Nice necklace." He was smiling.

She sat in a wicker chair watching him turn the necklace, scrutinizing it. He wheeled to the table and got her gun. "Is this the only weapon you have?"

"Yes."

"Do you think you could've shot him?" Dennis seemed amused.

"Yes."

"Umm." He pointed at the telephone. "Your boyfriend is somewhere nearby with many police officers?"

"Yes. But it would take time to get in here."

"Indeed it would, and there are a thousand ways to get out of here by water. Do they have helicopters?"

"They're trying to get some."

"Roadblocks?"

"I don't think so. They're waiting to be sure he's here. They think he may not come at all."

"He'd be stupid if he did," Dennis noted. He wiped saliva and examined the pistol, turning it to see the cartridges. The necklace was in his lap.

He jumped, suddenly. "What was that?"

Joanne stood, shivering, listening.

"Sounded like a boat down at the dock," Dennis whispered.

"Turn off the lights," Joanne ordered.

He did so and in the dark, eyes wide, Joanne stood listening to the shrill of cicadas, peeping tree frogs, a night fowl calling in whimpering coos.

"Did you hear it?" he whispered.

Heart pounding, Joanne heard only her pulse.

"Sit down," he commanded. "He can see you standing."

Gripping the arms of the wicker chair, Joanne heard Dennis breathing . . . gurgling inhalations, almost asthmatic sucking of air. Her eyes adjusting to the dark, she saw him wheeling from window to window, latching shutters. That left only the corridor to the rooms, the dining area, and entrance for entry.

"I've known Larry a long time," Dennis said. "He's always been nice to me."

Joanne subdued a cry.

"He said Marcie stole the necklace," Dennis reported.

"I don't know that to be a fact."

"She wouldn't admit it."

"You've seen Marcie?"

"This morning."

"You didn't tell me that!"

"I didn't know she'd been kidnapped until you told me. I still don't know Larry's side of this."

"Dennis—for God's sake—"

"Larry said he'd be here tonight," Dennis said. "He's a man of his word. He'll be here."

"Was—was Marcie all right when you saw her?"

"Hurt."

"Hurt?"

"Bleeding."

"Oh, God."

"She wouldn't talk." The floor crackled as he rolled through the dark, his face dappled by faint light from the kitchen and from a full rising moon. "Larry said, 'Tell Dennis you stole the necklace, Marcie. Tell him.' But Marcie wouldn't talk."

"Oh—God—"

"So he hurt her."

"Is he—where did they go, Dennis?"

"Somewhere on the island."

"I have to make a phone call, right now."

But as she reached for the phone, he pushed away her hand, whispering, "Listen—"

"They need to know he's here, Dennis. They'll come!"

He knocked her hand away with the barrel of the pistol. "Shhhh—listen!"

He wheeled to the front door, closed it. She heard a bolt slide into place.

"It takes a particular kind of person to kill someone," Dennis said, his voice at a more conversational level. "People think they can kill—but at the last instant, they can't. You believe you could have shot him."

"I wouldn't want to." Joanne was quaking.

"Maybe you could," Dennis agreed. Joanne heard a clink of metal and saw him rise from the chair. Adjusting his belt. To hold the gun, maybe.

"All you really want is Marcie, isn't that right, wee mommie?"

Her heart stopped.

He turned on the lights, spit wads of cotton on the floor and faced her. He removed the straw hat, the bandana, his head white—as if recently shaved.

Petrified, she watched him unbuckle his trousers, shove them down—the leg unfolded and he massaged it with both hands.

He grinned. "Boo, wee mommie—"

Joanne bolted and he leaped at her. She tore free, slinging him off, throwing a chair in his way. She heard him stumble as she clawed at a window trying to open shutters.

His laughter made her wheel, teeth bared, prepared to fight for her life. He held the gun, legs spraddled, his underwear stark against tanned flesh.

"Where is Marcie?" she shrieked.

"Dead."

"You bastard!" She ran at him and he knocked her aside.

"In a thousand tiny pieces, she's spread over acres," he taunted. "Do you want to know what I did to her before she begged to breathe her last?"

"Ken!" Joanne screamed. "Ken! Help!"

He advanced, limping on the numbed leg, and she clambered for cover beyond a couch, gaining distance.

"Would you like the details in vivid lexicon, mommie? Or would medical terminology be more to your taste?"

She fought for calm, for a steady voice. He was what he was and she should be able to handle—"Mr. Etna, let's—"

He advanced and Joanne dashed for the corridor, throwing the doors wide, seeking escape.

"Remember the snakes, mommie," he called. "Remember the scorpions and rats. There's quicksand out there. Be careful where you step."

Her mind blocked by shock, she fought panic and panic came anyway. She reached her room, hauled the bed in front of the door and held it. She turned to see the window; jalousies were opened, but beyond the portal stood undergrowth so dense nobody could run through.

"I'm coming with the gun, wee mommie. Coming to get you."

The slats of the door shattered, splinters struck her face. Shrieking, she backed into the bathroom. She tried to wrest towel racks from walls, for a weapon. She grabbed the heavy commode lid and it fell, breaking.

"I've anticipated this, wee mommie. I've told myself what a joy you were going to be."

Joanne vomited, completely unexpected, the gush of fluids spattering door, floor, herself. She backed into the shower, her own voice a piercing, unending screech. He was throwing furniture in the dark.

"Oh-ho," he said softly. "Mommie had an accident. Puked on the nice man's floor."

Her fingernails scratched the shower stall walls like a child rasping a blackboard. She couldn't stop the unceasing, deafening, reverberating scream.

He seized her and snatched her into the bedroom. He shook her roughly and Joanne tasted blood as her teeth snapped. Like a dumb beast being torn from under by wolves, she submitted in shock, unresisting except to hide her face in her arms. He slammed her to the floor—pinning her so tightly her lungs collapsed in a rush.

"Listen to me, wee mommie." His breath was fetid, his face close. "Listen to me, wee mommie," he said again.

She couldn't breathe, his weight on her chest.

"You did this," he railed. "You stuck your nose into something you know nothing about. What did it get you, mommie? A daughter who may be dead and dismembered—"

May be?

She felt the heat of his exhalation. "If she dies, it is your fault, not mine. You did this, not me. You are so smart, aren't you, Dr. Fleming?"

She gasped, weeping, "I'm sorry—"

"Too late," he said. "Now that we're here. Shut up! Listen to me."

He slapped her and face stinging, Joanne lay sobbing without sound.

"Are you a realist, mommie? I've got the necklace now. That leaves you with circumstantial evidence and a few confused witnesses. They could never prove anything 'beyond a shadow of a doubt.' And there'd be absolutely nothing to even link me to the necklace if Marcie is dead. Isn't that right?"

"In Tallahassee," Joanne cried. "At the restaurant! People saw you together. Saw you leave—"

"Then you aren't a realist," he said. "Any lawyer could beat them down, cast doubts. Possible kidnapping? Marcie left of her own free will, by herself in fact, if you'd care to know. We parted company. I haven't seen her since. Assuming they ever find a body—and they won't—but assuming they did, you have a weak case. I can beat that, mommie. Isn't that the realistic view?"

The courts—the reality of how it is—she nodded.

He demanded, "Isn't that right, mommie?"

"Yes."

"So not killing Marcie would be stupid of me."

"She's just a child."

"She's my death sentence, mommie. Because of you."

"I'm sorry."

"Yes, I know you are. Like all fancy psychiatrists who claim to know the mind—you don't know anything. I shouldn't be here, if I'm smart, or sane."

For a long moment, he loomed over her, Joanne incoherent with terror. Then, he loosened his grip slightly, the hair of his inner thighs abrasive against her flesh as he eased back.

"Now hear me," he said. "Marcie is somewhere far, far away, mommie. She's been there since Sunday night. Two days and three nights without water or food. She'll be suffering from insects, exposure, but she's alive."

"Oh, God—"

He shook her shoulders, banging her head against the floor. "There is no God. Hear me? Nobody will help you but me."

"I'm sorry . . . I'm—"

He shook her again, and Joanne's ears rang, her skull hitting the floor.

"If she lives, it will be because you are a criminal, mommie. If she doesn't—you can be proud of your principles."

Joanne tried to reach her face to wipe away vomit, but he shoved her arm down again.

"Aiding and abetting," he said. "Here I am, within your grasp. Your duty is to law and order, mommie. All right. So be it, then. If I am captured on the way out of here, there will be no necklace. They will never find Marcie. She'll eventually starve to death. I don't have to tell you, mommie; you know what happens when a body is left in the elements."

"Please—" Joanne begged. "I'll do anything—"

"They always say that," he mused. "They will do anything."

"What do you want me to do?"

"I'm going to dress and leave here by boat, mommie. Me and my necklace. Within a few minutes, the necklace will be gone forever. If I escape—I'll call and tell you where she is. If I don't—all you have is circumstantial evidence which suggests a kidnapping may have taken place. No body. Only suspicions. Isn't that so?"

"Yes."

"So my escape is fully your responsibility, mommie. If I make it, I'll call and tell you where to go for Marcie. If I don't—your fault or not—Marcie dies."

He got up, holding her wrists, lifting her. Joanne smelled the putrid fumes of her own egestion.

"Tell them I'm here and that you've seen me with Marcie," he dictated. "Tell them Marcie is all right. You will do this one hour after I leave, so they can close in on this island. Is that understood?"

"Yes."

He led her down the hall, holding her arm in a vise grip. "If you are a good enough criminal, mommie, you may break even. If you make a mistake—if you spook those cops—you can blame only yourself."

He released her. From a sideboard, he took out trousers, a fresh shirt, tennis shoes from another drawer, and discarded the one heavy boot he had worn. He dressed before her, smiling. "Isn't it time for a call?" he asked.

Chapter Thirty

SOMEWHERE in the night, a low horn moaned; the building snapped as wood contracted and creaked. Joanne sat by the telephone, the stench of her blouse rancid. She lifted the receiver, demanding of herself the last ounce of control.

"Ken?"

"Yes, darling. Are you all right?"

"Dennis has—he's gone out searching for Larry Etna. He thinks Marcie is on the island."

A long hesitation. "Do you believe that, Jo?"

"He said he saw her earlier in the day."

"Jo! Do you believe that?"

"I have to believe it."

"If Etna's there—" Ken turned aside, spoke to someone and Joanne had to hold the telephone with both hands to steady it.

"Why would Alday leave you alone, Jo?" Ken asked.

"To go hunt for Larry Etna, I told you."

"Something wrong here, Jo. Does he have the pistol?"

"Yes."

"How long has he been gone?"

"A few minutes."

"Jo—we're coming in."

"Stay away, damn you! You stay away and stay out of sight until I tell you to come."

"This isn't my jurisdiction, Jo. There are men here who have advocated assault all along. Now—I have to agree."

"I think Marcie is alive, Ken."

"How long did you say Alday has been gone?"

"He wouldn't have risked coming here," Joanne said, "if he hadn't been positive of escape. It would've been easier to kill Marcie and never to have come at all. She must've gotten close to him—a bond—it happens between captor and hostage—"

"You don't know he's there yet, Jo. It could be a trick. Alday may be a friend of his."

"No," Joanne quavered. "I don't think so. Dennis said he spoke to Marcie this morning."

"Why didn't the sonofabitch say that earlier?"

"He had no reason to trust me—" Joanne sobbed. "He didn't know Marcie was my daughter, that she'd been kidnapped."

"Jo, are there extensions to that telephone?"

"I don't know."

"Someone could be listening."

"I don't think so."

"Listen, Jo," Ken whispered, "a team of specially trained men from Miami are almost there. They've taken a long land route, the direction least expected, sweeping the island as they come. The owner of the island is here and he's drawn a map of all the cottages, the access routes and possible ways to escape."

Joanne bit her lips, the warm, salty—"I told you no fancy tactics, Ken! You promised, no tricks!"

"It won't be long, darling. They're coming in now. We have no way to warn them that Alday is out wandering around with a gun. If you see him—"

A sound in the rear of the building made Joanne cry, "Ken, someone is out there!"

"Jo, darling—"

A shutter crashed and Joanne screamed, a figure dressed in black jumped through, shouting, "Hit the floor! Hit the floor!" He knocked her down, fell on her. Others now, through doors, windows, from down the hall, feet thudding as they ran through.

"You're all right," the man soothed, but Joanne could not halt her own hysteria. "You're all right. Everything is all right."

"My baby!" She clawed at him. "Marcie!" He grabbed her arms, murmuring assurances. Somewhere a whump-whump-whump of helicopter blades, the roar of other motors. "Oh, God," Joanne cried. "Did they catch him?"

They guided her to a chair, wrapped her in a blanket.

"Did they catch him?" Joanne screamed.

"No," a man stated. "Not yet."

Ken helped her into a fresh blouse. Every muscle was stiff, even her joints ached.

"Wash your face with this pan of water, Jo." Ken placed it next to a kerosene lantern. "Kitchen water comes from a different well. No sulphur."

She laved liquid against flesh that felt starched, seared as if raw. A doctor had tried to give her an injection but Joanne had adamantly refused. She recognized shock, knew the signs, but she feared sleep more.

Would he call? Why should he? But he came here, outsmarted them all, rubbed her nose in it—that would be important to him. Maybe enough—

"Here's a towel, Jo. Stiff, but clean." Ken turned the lamp wick for better light. She smelled oily smoke; yellow patterns danced against jagged furniture, Ken's face.

"The place is crawling with scorpions," Ken said. "When you're ready, we'll get out of here."

"Mr. Blackburn?" a voice at the door.

Joanne listened to whispers. Ken returned and stood by her chair, a hand on her shoulder.

"Did they catch him?" she asked.

"They'll search again by day, Jo. But they don't think anyone is here."

Joanne stared.

"Jo, you're suffering shock. We need to get you to a warm bed, a doctor's care."

"No."

He tried to lift her. "Come on, let's go. There's no reason to stay here."

"No!"

A tap at the door and Ken said, "Come in."

"Dr. Fleming," the figure introduced himself, "I'm Detective Warren. We need a description of the caretaker."

"Bald. Tall. Distorted features. One leg."

He made notes, glanced at Ken.

"We can't find either one of them, Jo."

She stared.

"Jo, honey, the man has aroused suspicion."

"Bald," Joanne said, flatly, "tall. Misshapen face. One leg."

The detective arose, mumbled apologies. Ken knelt beside her, deeply set eyes pools of shadow, face grim.

"What is it, Jo?"

"I can't leave."

"Why?"

"He'll call."

"Jo—you helped him."

"I had to."

He patted her arm and started to rise. "Ken," Joanne said, levelly, "if he escapes, he said he'll call and tell us where to find her. He said she's alive."

"She's not alive, Jo."

"But he came. He wouldn't have come if she were dead."

"He lied. Hurting you. Punishing you. He's a psychopath."

She held his arm. "Wait," she pleaded. "One full day without telling them—please wait."

A very long moment passed and Ken sighed. "I wouldn't know which description to offer, anyway," he said. "We'll wait."

Somebody cooked breakfast in the lodge kitchen, the owner nervously assuring everyone there was "no charge." He apologized to Joanne repeatedly, pudgy face strained, offering the resort for "an unlimited vacation, another time."

Drinking coffee, hot food sparingly taken, Joanne saw dawn become day, noon passed, and daylight waned. By now, without being told, these men had guessed the truth and they sat by, smoking, silent, waiting with Ken and Joanne.

The telephone rang.

Joanne looked at Ken and he nodded.

"Hello?"

"Listen to me," the voice said. "It's all over, wee mommie—"

Friday night, driving southward, Don had seethed with anger, huffing and puffing, berating Marcie for "ruining something wonderful" he claimed they had shared. She had attempted to assure him, anything he had done she could forgive—she'd help him. But as midnight passed, still driving, taking a zigzag course over empty back roads, he obviously would not debate her freedom.

They arrived at the deserted fire tower Saturday at dawn. The rusting metal structure rose from scrub pines planted in symmetrical rows, situated far from a narrow, paved highway which traversed a sandy, swampy area.

Through Saturday, she'd tried to reassure him, reasoning,

271

offering friendship, using the word "love" in a tentative, but genuine way. He fell into long silences, blue eyes distant, the two of them perched high above the flat lands, the metal roof crackling under the hot summer sunshine.

She was not chained tightly, Saturday. The cuff was a loose bracelet allowing her to stand, or sit at will. But when he returned after a long absence Sunday morning, he heard her shouting for help, mistaking his vehicle for another. When he threw open the trap door, his face was livid. He slapped her, dragged her to a low pipe welded to brace the floor and wall, and there he handcuffed one arm so she could not stand, could only reach as far as her hand and legs would extend. Her apologies went unheeded and his glowering mood darkened as day ticked slowly away.

Repeatedly, he left her. When he returned, he came as quietly as possible—as if testing. Obediently, Marcie lay still, even when she felt his footsteps coming up from seventy-five feet below.

Sunday evening, he hauled her down, roughly, ignoring her cries, her fear of height. He shoved her into the Volkswagen and drove to an isolated telephone booth at a crossroad with no identifying marker. There, he placed his call to mom, holding Marcie's chained hands, his finger on the disconnecting hook. When Marcie attempted to blurt out information, he cut her off, slung her to the ground, and slapped her until she wailed in pain. He dragged her to the car, hooked handcuffs to the steering wheel, and returned to call again. Marcie heard him say, "A chip off the old blockette—"

When he left Sunday night, Marcie lay in the tower, her back and shoulders aching, parcels of cookies and dry foods close but unappetizing. The imitation orange drink he'd purchased went sour. She took it sparingly, or not at all.

Somehow, though frightened, she did not surrender to panic. Not until shortly before dawn of the second day alone. By then, her sense of chronology warped by sleepless nights and napping afternoons, she had shouted herself hoarse. Laryngitis set in, and every effort to holler came as a muted whisper with less volume than a breeze in the pines below. A crow came, perched in a broken window frame and sat looking at Marcie until she moved suddenly.

272

She waited as long as possible before relieving herself. Then she awoke to find herself sleeping in it, rolling in it, her wrist now so numb she could not feel her fingers touching one another.

It was some time later that she decided she might be dying. The thought came in an abstract way, as if recognizing imminent failure to achieve some goal. *Oh, oh, I'm not going to make it.*

Mosquito bites had festered and become sores. Her tongue adhered to the roof of her mouth. Lips cracked and eyelids burned. The stench was overpowering. Her scalp itched and she scratched so furiously that her fingernails were stained rusty brown by a bloody sediment.

Then she decided she might die.

She knew well enough the condition of bodies found long abandoned. Mom's research had not been totally lost on her, even if one did not wish to hear it. Bugs, beetles, ants, vultures—in a matter of days she'd bloat and turn black, then the flesh would split and even the innards would become accessible. Blow flies.

The image of her deterioration was not as unpleasant as she might have assumed. In her near delirium, it held a macabre fascination.

Restrained as she was by one wrist, she soon learned the precise distance she could reach with her other hand. Or a foot. In a crack between heavy plank flooring, an ascending breeze would slice past her cheek, and she lay with her nose close, to overcome the outhouse smell which seemed to remain undisturbed by what little wind came through the broken windows on all four sides of the hut.

She tried to think of the good things. Like Pollyanna. There were no ants at this height. Nor ticks, fleas, sandflies, or snakes. Yet. Mosquitos came to assault her in the deep of night, but almost always they had been borne on capricious land breezes rising to some higher elevation. Once fought off, the mosquitos didn't come again for several hours, affording her that much time undisturbed.

She worried about mom and Ken. And daddy. They'd all suffer deep regrets because that was natural, telling themselves they should've given her more freedom, should've agreed to put her on the pill so she and Charlie could fornicate and she wouldn't have to go to her grave a virgin. She thought about what her friends would say.

How many people would attend her funeral. *Was* there a funeral, without a body? Did they wait to make certain, clinging to hopeless hope? She abhorred memorials. It was like a picnic with no food—nobody really felt the decedent was present, as they did at funerals with a casket right there under a blanket of roses. Well. A wreath. Roses had gotten so expensive.

She thought about flowers.

Mostly, she wept until her tear ducts were dry. Mostly, she spent her time fighting an ascending sense of futility. It was not the specter of death which frightened her so much as the quality of it. She'd hate to be found here in soiled clothes, her agony more acute in mom's imagination than in reality. Although, the agony was real enough.

Yet, even thinking she might die—somehow she wasn't completely convinced. Reasoning about her predicament, recognizing her quandary, she nonetheless did not *truly* think she'd die. It was, indeed, an abstraction.

She hurt from wrist to ankle, head to toe. The effort required to move was monumental and took all her will. She'd drunk the stale orange drink, eaten what she could of the cookies. Now, her throat was taut, breathing painful. She realized Don had no intention of returning. She damned him. Damned his parents. Damned herself.

When found, there would be scraps of cloth, perhaps. A few bones, maybe. Children might discover her and take the fleshless skull as a memento. Or toss evidence to the wind, unaware of the consequences of their action.

She couldn't close her mouth. Her lips felt huge, so large she could see them by looking down her nose. Her gums hurt. The roots of her teeth hurt.

By now, she knew every square centimeter of her reachable area. Every niche, every fleck of paint. The bolts in the corrugated metal roof—there were 288 of them—and the ingredients listed on a package of crackers.

Within her reach, as if someone had minutely examined it before, there was not a single splinter which could be pulled free from the floor. Not one sliver of wood or metal gave way.

Except for the nail.

It was loose in its hole. As if the wood had expanded, or the metal contracted and the hole was now only for keeping the nail until needed. When her finger touched it, the

274

nail moved and she lifted it out. It was surprisingly clean, not corroded. She put it back. Later, she took it out. Put it back.

Now, she held it again, looking at it. Her head was hurting, rapid, streaking pain shooting between the temples and down a stiff neck.

If she were to leave her name, the name of her slayer—would that not be better than to die anonymously, perhaps never to be identified?

But where?

She crawled toward her anchored wrist, looking. Suppose Don returned and read her message? He'd obliterate it, of course. He mustn't see it.

Marcie twisted beneath a heavy ledge that ran around the interior walls. Under here, only somebody down low in this position could see it. But, ah! If they found a body, surely her mother would make them search the area with great care and her message would be discovered. Don would pay for this, then. She'd come from the grave to haunt him, her accusation scratched in the wood or metal of this, her bier.

Her fingers shook as she tried to grip the nail as she would a pencil. She hadn't the strength anymore. She grasped it like a dagger, clawing against metal, but her hand veered and the effort was an unintelligible slash.

Wait.

A motor. Marcie listened. Passing? On the paved road? It stopped. How far? Don, maybe. She'd have something to say to him!

As she listened, her eyes wandered over the underside of the ledge and horrified, she read deeply etched words of another occupant—

KIDNAPPED.

Marcie touched the message with her fingertips. KIDNAPPED ROLLINS COLLEGE APRIL 3 DAY KILL ME UTAH VW   BLUE EYE   BROWN HAIR

Not the first.

Survival was not proof she would survive his return.

Listen.

Marcie squirmed to the crack, peering down. She felt the tower tremble. Footsteps.

Help! a squeak.

275

Help me! a whisper.

Help me!

She thrashed, snatching the manacled hand, blood running at the wrist as she yanked with all her might, panic and adrenaline giving her the anesthetic desperation of a trapped animal. She flung herself, would have torn the hand from her arm if possible, peculiar little sounds coming from her esophagus.

The footsteps quickened and Marcie searched frantically for a weapon. Plastic bottles empty, cracker boxes—the nail. Highpitched squeaks came in peeping sounds, though she screamed with all her strength.

She heard a bump, the tower shivered—climbing around missing steps below.

Help! no sound.

Ascending more rapidly now, the footsteps coming. Marcie grabbed a paper carton and hurled it as the trap door began to lift.

Help! Help!

She threw a plastic bottle and crawled backward, her arm oddly bent, the snap of a bone unnoticed. Help!

Strong hands brushed hair from her face. Below, pounding footfalls . . . a man's voice . . .

"Poor baby." The trooper held Marcie's head. "Poor baby," he said. "It's over now. All over."

A week later they were home with Marcie. Her cast, which spanned her wrist from forearm to fingertips, was covered with signatures of well-wishers.

"If he hadn't given us instructions to the fire tower," Ken noted, softly, "we'd probably never have found Marcie."

"I know that." Joanne drew a deep breath, exhaled. On leave of absence, she was recuperating more slowly than the girl, Marcie's ebullience back in force. Except now and then, an uncharacteristic pause in the middle of pandemonium, a lapse in the teen-age frenzy.

"He had more colors than a chameleon, Jo," Ken was saying. "All false, of course. He was Larry Etna in Colorado; a physical therapist at Walter Reed Army Hospital in Washington, D.C. While he was there, he apparently got the medical records of the *real* Dennis Alday who lost a leg in Vietnam, suffered facial damage, and was twice decorated for bravery under enemy fire. The real Dennis Alday lives in Canada and he hasn't been to a veteran's hospital in several years. As a therapist, the killer picked up the identity and background which he used to get his seasonal job at the deserted island resort. The owner says they hired him over the telephone, checked his credentials by mail. They never saw the phony Alday but once, briefly, when he was first employed. They needed somebody for a tedious, lonely job and he seemed perfect. The boat postman saw him rarely, a few minutes at the time—he never questioned the identity—why should he? The bastard knows human nature. People don't look at someone who is unfortunate, and they don't linger in the presence of an unsociable drooling man and—well, you see what he accomplished."

Ken continued, speaking softly. "Here in Tallahassee he was Bob Brantley; to Marcie he was Don Whitney. We have a dozen descriptions, all different. Mustache, bald, brown hair, GI-close-cropped. About the only way the witnesses agree is his eyes—blue."

"Very blue." Joanne sipped coffee. The kitchen counter was littered with political posters, pamphlets, news articles generated by a hotly contested race for the offices sought by Ken, Ralph, and John Nathan.

"They have fingerprints, if they ever catch him," Ken continued. "From the rooming house here in town, from the lodge at Carlos Key. But the FBI has nothing on him. He's never been in the armed services. He never had a driver's license requiring a thumb print."

"If they catch him," Joanne said, "a conviction would be very difficult to get."

"I'm afraid that's true."

A tapping sound caused Joanne to jerk, spilling coffee. She peered at the night beyond closed windows.

"Only a limb, Jo."

She was shivering. Ken put a hand on her arm.

"You want to hear the rest of it, Jo?"

She nodded.

"They found the girls from Rollins College. Near the fire tower. Marcie's report on the message was the tip-off."

"Bless them," Joanne whispered.

The clock sounded loud, seconds ticking away. Joanne sipped coffee. "How's your campaign coming?" she asked.

His reply was lost. ". . . will win . . ."

Another tap at a window and Joanne grew rigid under Ken's touch. "Want me to go cut off the twig?" he questioned.

"No."

"It's over, Jo."

She nodded.

"It *is* over," he said.

Marcie was away for the night, visiting a friend. The house was hushed, but Joanne's ears rang. A doctor told her it was a common occurrence following trauma.

She sighed and Ken shook her arm, gently. "Jo, you want me to stay here tonight?"

"I'm all right."

"You could go with me and hear my speech."

"No, thank you, Ken. I need to take a hot bath, get some rest."

"I agree with that." He stood, kissed her forehead. "I'm going on, then."

When he stopped at the back door, checking the tumbler, Joanne called, "Good politicking!"

"I love you, Jo."

And she was alone. Instantly the rising tide of fear surged and she had to force herself to be calm. She went to the sink, rinsed her cup, poured more coffee.

The telephone rang. Startled, Joanne threw coffee on the table. She stared at the phone, waited. Waited.

It rang again.

"Hello?"

"Is Marcie there?"

"Who's calling?"

"This is Charlie, Dr. Fleming."

"Hello, Charlie. Marcie is visiting a girl friend."

He spoke in glissando tones, from adolescent tenor to approaching baritone. Joanne stared out the kitchen window, politely responding as he told her of his summer adventures.

She'd get over this. Her education, her background, she could master this. Something rasped an exterior wall and Joanne must've made a noise. Charlie asked, "Are you all right, Dr. Fleming?"

"Yes, Charlie."

"I could call back another time," he suggested.

"No, no. I have plenty of time. Please go ahead."

He needed no more urging than that, relating the joys and trials of youth to his captive audience.

Captive.

She stared at the dark beyond the window. *He was gone.* Like a horrible dream. Gone.

But—she knew—somewhere, a carnivore seeking prey—he was still out there . . .